THE QUEEN'S JUSTICE

A novel of Estia

MARK EVERETT STONE
& BRANDIE M. STONE

coffeetownpress

KENMORE, WA

coffeetownpress

A Coffeetown Press book published by Epicenter Press

Epicenter Press
6524 NE 181st St.
Suite 2
Kenmore, WA 98028

For more information go to:
www.Camelpress.com
www.Coffeetownpress.com
www.Epicenterpress.com
www.Markeverettstone1.com

This is a work of fiction. Names, characters, places, brands, media, and incidents are either the product of the author's imagination or are used fictitiously.

Cover design by Scott Book
Design by Melissa Vail Coffman

The Queen's Justice
Copyright © 2024 by Mark Everett Stone & Brandie M. Stone

Library of Congress Control Number: 2023952025

ISBN: 978-1-68492-195-9 (Trade Paper)
ISBN: 978-1-68492-196-6 (eBook)

This book is dedicated to my friends who encouraged me to keep writing. Thank you all. Also to our dog, Sammy. You are gross, dude.

ACKNOWLEDGMENTS

We would like to thank those friends that keep us grounded and sane during this process. You know who you are, even you Dave.

PART ONE

Now and Then

ONE

NOW

DEAD THINGS CREEP THROUGH THE STREETS of the rotting city under the red moon and I am one of them. A cat, fur falling off in patches, stares at me with sagging, milky eyes and opens its jaws in a silent hiss before quietly slinking into the darkness of a collapsed tenement.

For six months I hunted the necropolis of Ramashur, braving those more ambulatory dead who mistake my more or less pristine flesh for living, but once they draw close they come to realize I inhabit the same state of being and leave me alone. Most of the dead are content to remain where they stand or lay, dangerous only to foolish treasure hunters who comprise the bulk of their food.

The dead eat the living, which offers a temporary regenerative effect, bringing them closer to what they were, but not close enough to a real sense of self, and in that consumption infect the newly feasted upon with their condition. The dead have forgotten what it is like to live, although they strive to do so every day and this is what passes for torment for them.

Not for me. My torment is that I remember everything despite my status of not quite being alive. In all my travels, I find myself unique in this.

I enter a building not completely collapsed, passing a naked child with gray skin, hollow cheeks and gums so receded that her teeth look too large for her mouth. She deigns not to notice me. The foyer and the room beyond are preserved without even the presence of rat dung, so perhaps the girl has stood guard over the place all this time. Perhaps this is her home, where she died. The dead do not remember, but some seem to have an affinity for the places they visited or lived when their hearts once beat.

After a few minutes of examination and a quick spell, I conclude that the residence is not that of the one I seek, the wizard Hengeth Isobold.

Ramashur was once the shining jewel of the Kingdom of Gylleth, a center for trade and culture for centuries from the icy waters of Beryl Bay to the north to the warm climes of the Shorebridge Peninsula to the south along the Long Road. Then along came Isobold, a wizard and a necromancer of some skill. As history tells, Isobold cast a necromantic spell during a Melosian Shift, the sudden changing paradigms of the laws of nature altering and empowering the spell to the effect that both caster and city perished.

Malosian Shifts have dried rivers, broken mountains to dust and even reduced entire civilizations to barbarism. In this case, it tossed the city onto the ash heap of history.

This event came after my death and is second and third-hand information gleaned by accounts of Hengeths's contemporaries. Treasure hunters, some successful, most not, added to the sad tale of Ramashur and though riches do not interest me, Isobold does.

I need his bones. One will do.

Three years since I woke to find myself among the living, six months of them searching for the wizard, for his remains so I may use my limited skills in necromancy to glean what answers I may. I need information. I need justice. On to the next building.

The necropolis is so big that in all my searching I have only managed to effectively examine one-fifth of the royal and merchant quarters of the city, the two areas where a wizard of Isobold's caliber would rest his head. Unfortunately, many of the buildings are in ruins, which hinders my search and I am not good with divination spells at a distance. I should have studied more, perhaps. Perhaps not since such magic is beyond most spell crafters.

A man, clothes long since rotted away, slowly shambles by, the sad flap of his sex dangling uselessly between his legs. I can tell that in life he must have been big, perhaps part of the military or a gladiator, but now he is stick-thin, skin hanging like bunting from his bones. He looks at me in interest for a moment, white eyes gleaming, but they slide off my body as some instinct inside tells him I, too, am dead. He looks somewhat familiar but I cannot place his slack face, death and time have leeched his features of humanity

Although I have no vital humors to amplify my emotions, whispers of melancholy pass through me as I walk shattered streets and old growth vegetation that did not exist when I drew breath. Ramashur once shone with mighty ivory walls and the veins of its streets flowed with the blood if its vigorous citizenry, but all that remains are dust and rubble, even rats fear the hungry dead. Not for the first time I wish I could cry, to let vent some physical response to the gloom that shrouds me.

Next house. This one mostly intact except for the windows which are absent glass. My boots crunch over debris as I enter. The foyer is also intact save for the dusty remains of tapestries and splinters of furniture gone to insects, rot and the slow, inevitable march of time. Deeper in I find a marble faced staircase withstanding the centuries, its red veined magnificence tarnished by dust and shards of glass. A chandelier lies in front of the staircase, a heap of twisted metal bent and riven of beauty.

From a pouch I produce a handful of bone dust and tiny sprig of dried rosemary wetted slightly with virgin's tears. Dust and rosemary go into a bronze cup and I muddle the mixture with a thick glass rod. I take a pinch and inhale, then blow a bit to the cardinal directions and say words that have no origins in human language. I wait.

To the south, east and west the mixture settles to the floor, but to the north the cloud of dust and powdered rosemary hang in the air as if waiting for instruction. If my heart could beat it would skip one in shock, so I settle for an indrawn breath that I don't feel.

North . . . where the stairs climb.

I ascend carefully, testing each step. While marble lasts, wood does not. It takes all that is within me to keep from bounding up like an excited rabbit. At the top a hallway branches to the left and right so I perform the bone dust ritual again. The dust tells me to turn left and I walk down the hall over carpets that crumble as I step on them. I want to run, but I don't want to take a chance on injuring my body should the floor collapse. There is no one to save me should that happen.

There are three doors, one to the left, right and at the end. Three more rituals tell me that my destination is to the right. My hands clench.

The door dissolves at a touch, the iron hinges and doorknob clattering to the floor amid a shower of wood dust. When knob and hinges hit the marble floor, it is surprisingly loud in the tomblike atmosphere of the house. Inside is a large room, each wall a bookcase filled with the crumbly remains of volumes that would fetch a king's ransom were they whole, but my eyes are drawn to the pile of bones in the center of the floor, a pile topped with a ochre skull with yellowed teeth. I blow more dust and incant the throat-tearing words and the dust refuses to fall, instead it hangs over the skull like a banner constructed of motes.

"Oh my," I breathe in wonder. Six months of searching and finally the answers I seek are within my grasp. My hands shake as I remove from my pack four beeswax candles infused with basil and thyme and set them at the four cardinal points around the pile of bones, but before I continue, I gently take the finger bones from the heap, tucking them away for later. The bones of a necromancer are powerful components for spells relating to the deceased.

My fingers caress the small bejeweled rod at the bottom of my pack. Nine inches long, the gems alone are a small fortune, but the rod itself is an artefact that I suspect is beyond price. It is what woke me from the long sleep into this twilight world of the undead among the remains of my comrades known and unknown. At one end there is a setting for jewel, but it remains empty and has been that way since my awakening. For a moment I stare at the near flawless gems: three rubies, two emeralds and three sapphires, each as large as a pinky nail, and wonder for the umpteenth time what happened to that last gemstone.

I want to rush, to hurry the spell, but the slightest mistake means failure and I have come too far to fail, so I slow myself, placing the dust from a warrior slain in righteous combat in small piles near each candle before lighting them. The words of the incantation come to my lips, a foreign tongue not related to those I usually use for spells because this is a form of necromancy, a different kind of magic from the witchcraft I normally use. Learning this spell cost me a small fortune in illicit manuscripts and three years of searching for the correct components. I will not fail. I cannot.

The bones of my friend Hengeth almost seems to admonish me for my apparent drive to use them as mere components, base objects to carry out my will and I remember the days in the Hidden Academy, the once-shy girl I had been and the slender reed of a boy who earned my trust and friendship. Those days are long gone, melted away like snowflakes in the sun, but their memories live on sweetly. I offer a prayer to Father Sun and Mother Moon in thanks and to Tilla in memory of a dear friend whose necromantic efforts destroyed a city. I know in my heart it had not been a purposeful thing, his spell perverted by the Shift and I hope he felt some measure of peace in Tilla's Hold.

Gently, I take the skull in my hands, still chanting, and stare into dark sockets, feeling the texture of brittle bone. It begins warm in my palms and I know the spell is working. If I had a pulse, it would be pounding.

Slowly, the small piles of dust at the base of the candles begin to stir as if invisible fingers caress them, then they begin to rise, the motes swirling and dancing on currents of air that do not exist. This dusty dance gently swirls around the skull in my hands until I hold a ball of airy specks that start to form a face and I nearly forget to keep breathing, to keep chanting the alien words that dribble from my cold lips. When the particles cease their motion, they settle into an aspect I know better than my own and I know the spell has succeeded. Eyes with pronounced epicanthic folds stare into the world of the living and my throat closes, but I force words out anyway.

"Beloved? Mirallelle?"

The lips move. "Niendra?" The words don't disturb the air, instead they echo inside my head, the tone heartbreakingly familiar. Eyes of dust focus on me.

"Yes, beloved," I reply, pushing the words out, forcing them past a closes throat and through numb lips. "It's me." For the first time since my death I feel something besides anger and despair.

I feel love. Warm and glowing. Here is the visage of my dear wife and I yearn to kiss her lips, to hold her to my chest and feel her warmth. That is a dream I dare not indulge because I think I would go mad with longing.

"My love, why do you drag me from my contentment?" The words carry a slight bit of petulance, as if I have woken her from a deep slumber.

"It has been over five-hundred years, beloved, since we died."

Mirallelle gave me a dusty frown. "So long? How are you alive?"

"I'm not."

"Ah. My poor love."

By Tilla's sorrow and Mother Moon, I want to cry. "It's all right, dear. I will find my rest soon."

"You have summoned me, but you are no necromancer. Have you given up your witchcraft?"

I shake my head. "No, beloved, some aspects of the craft mirror necromancy and it was easy for me to learn what was needed to summon you from Tilla Hold so we may talk. Once I possessed the required materials."

A small, sad smile formed of particles creased Mirallelle's face. "I know you, dear. You want revenge."

"Justice!" I hiss. Not just a word, but once upon a time a vocation. The dead rarely feel extremes of emotion, but at that moment hate and rage suffused me. "Justice *and* revenge!"

"Oh, my love, come with me back to Tilla's Hold, those two are so different despite being siblings. My killer and yours are long dead and there is no more use for hate and vengeance in the afterlife."

"I am a Queen's Justice, I cannot let this pass."

"When you were alive, you were a Justice, but now the queen you once served inhabits Tilla's Hold like I. Your responsibilities are done, over with, no longer part of the Queen's Justices. Lay your head down and come with me."

For an instant I am tempted. My wife is in the grasp of the Tilla, Mistress of Grief, Funerals and the Dead. There is always room in her Hold for more and the thought of reuniting with my wife in peace brings a pang, but my slow simmering rage and my hate hold me back. They are forces I have little control over.

I could not let my murderer escape my wrath, even if they are dead and I need to know *why*, I have to know. There are ways and dread magics that will let me have my revenge and I will find out who murdered me. The desire for that knowledge is a burning torch in my breast and the emotions that plague me makes me feel almost alive.

Although I admit justice and a reckoning motivates me, there is that niggling little bit of my soul that cannot let go, that stubborn mote, that refuses to relinquish the search. My ravening curiosity. It steered my mind toward my profession as a wizard, made me hunger for knowledge for its own sake it and its iron talons grips my mind with implacable ferocity. I must have answers, I must *know*. Obsession is too kind a word to describe the feeling.

"I cannot," I reply. "For some reason I have been brought back and I like to think it is so I may, one last time, dispense justice upon the wicked." When I awoke in the Catacombs south of Ramashur, confused and alone (aside from the slumbering dead), Mirallelle was my first thought and the memories of us sustain my desire for justice.

"The grave has hold of you, love," Mirallelle murmurs. "I can see its barbed grasp upon skin. All you have to do is follow me to the Hold and we can be together like before."

Like before? I have been awake in the living world for a few years now and have no memory of Tilla's Hold and being with my beloved, no memory of anything after I died. Perhaps the Goddess of Death removed all recollection of the afterlife from me when I was brought back into the world. I say this to her.

"It is of no matter. Come with me."

I cannot.

Her lips turn down in grief and she lets loose a soft cry like that of a morning dove. It tears at me with hooks of grief.

"Beloved. I need to know who killed me. I provided justice for your death, but there was something about mine, some thread that will not pull loose. There is more to the circumstance than I could see at the time, some mystery and I will have it out." I have to know.

"What matter?" she asks. "Those involved are long dead and inhabit a part of the Hold I dare not visit. Come back to me."

"Do you know?" Did it really come to this? I could follow my wife back to the eternal rest that waits all of us, but the part of me that abhors injustice, that cannot abide the thought of not facing those that killed us rears its stern head and forces me to an action I loathe. Reluctantly, I let loose a thread of magic to coax the answer from Mirallelle. The pain of doing so, forcing her with magic, nearly unmakes my resolve.

But I have to know.

"Yes."

I lean forward until my nose near touches hers. "Who?"

It takes a while, but she answers. I cry out in anger and betrayal, accidently dropping the skull in my surprise. The dust disperses as the skull is rendered into flinders. The spell breaks with the sound of crystal shattering against stone and I sit there, angry and fuming at the result as I stare the chipped and broken teeth that once belonged to a man I called friend.

For six months I searched the corpse of Ramashur for the wizard Hengeth Isobold's bones and now that I have found them I am not sure it is worth the effort.

Feeling gut punched, I exit the manor, walk silently past the big man with his loose, flappy skin and make my way out of the city toward the boundary of the curse to cross over to the living world. Passing through the curse wall is difficult for me because it is meant to contain the dead to the city and its surrounds, but my un-life is not part of Isobold's magic and I struggle through, feeling as if the air pushes against my entire body. After a few moments my feet emerge and the boundary suddenly lets go and I stumble forward.

Looking back I see again the soot-stained, time-crumbled walls of the city I once called home juxtaposed with the vision of their former glory and again grief assails but finds no purchase, rebuffed by the bastion of my resolve.

My dapple gray gelding, Artoch, waits patiently where I have staked him, cropping at the long grass with his rubbery lips near bushes with thorns as long as my little finger. No destrier, Artoch is an elderly beast who is absent of all fear, but staking him inside the curse wall would bring the dead as if ringing a dinner bell. This way the only things he need fear are wolves and treasure hunters willing to settle for rustling. I saddle up and begin my ride to Orthengar, my unbeating heart broken.

Two

THEN

"**F**OR THE LAST TIME, JINNIA, I DON'T DO LOVE PHILTRES." Hand on hips, I gave the woman a good glare that should have melted iron, but she stood there glaring back fully unmelted.

Jinnia, one of my regular customers, kept right on with her own stare, thrusting her chin out stubbornly. She was a whole lot of woman, busty and big with auburn curls down her back. "Niendra Goisien, you have a good love all your own while some of us do without. It's hard to make my way by myself. Why can't I have some of what you've got?"

I wanted to say it's because she possessed a face might have been comely had her personality not ruined it all. Rumor had it she'd been a kindly soul before her husband Viskio died of the skin rot, but now I considered that he was just hiding.

"It steals the free will from a person, as you very well know, Jinnia," I replied through lips thin with anger. My temper was starting to fray mightily and bad things happened when it snapped. "It's illegal and I don't traffic in illegalities. Besides, I got mine without potion or artifice, so I reckon you can put yourself to task and find someone willing enough."

The widow gave with a mighty 'harumph' and stormed out of my shop, slamming the door hard enough that the stuffed alligator over the counter shook, releasing dust that caused my nose to itch. I rubbed my face, knowing that she'd be back in a few days contrite and with bountiful apologies

and excuses on how loneliness ate at her temper, but the routine was starting to wear as thin as hand-me-down clothing.

My wife finally showed her face from the back room. "She gone?"

I snorted. "You always know when she's about. Maybe you're the witch
and I'm just a shopkeeper. Next time you deal with her."

Mirallelle laughed, a sound like tiny bells, and snuggled in close for a
kiss, our bodies fitting together fine like puzzle pieces. "I'm just waiting for
the time when you turn her into a newt."

Our lips met and I felt the old familiar tingle between my breasts. Even
after all these years her touch sent my blood rushing. "As a Justice, I'd have
to arrest myself." I leaned into her arms, appreciating once again the beauty
of her bronzed Coadian skin and her almond eyes that always seemed to
stare into my soul. My eyes wandered down to where her plum-colored
bodice was cut just low enough to show some of her charms and I grinned
mischievously.

"We can't do this here." She grinned, knowing exactly what was on my
mind. "Not at work. Our customers will talk."

My own laughter, harsh and braying compared to her silky tones, buf-
feted us both. "All right," I said when I finally caught my breath. "Can
you imagine the look on Parsian Mead's face if he were to catch us naked
behind the counter?" More braying laughter.

Mirallelle smiled wide, the small crow's feet at the corners of her eyes
deepening. "He gossips worse than anyone. The whole city would know
within the hour and it would feed his ego something terrible."

Old Parsian with his knuckles the size of walnuts did love to talk and
came in every two days as steady as the workings of a water clock to purchase his arthritis medicine. Customers like Parsian were what helped us
afford our house on Merchant's Lane and kept us in a comfortable lifestyle.
Almost as if the thoughts of the dear old man were a spell, we heard heavy
bootsteps approach.

"Speaking of which . . ."

But it wasn't Parsian Mead's seamed face that hit my eyes when the
door opened, but that of Her Majesty's own lapdog, Baronet Devanis Tol-
Walcifer himself. Tall enough that he had to duck through the door, the
young baronet possessed a handsome enough face with boyish good looks
and a ready smile that hid the cold and calculating mind of a serpent. Eyes

as blue as the winter sky and shiny as oiled marbles stared at me over a smile that gave no warmth to his face.

"Justice Niendra Goisien," he began before the door shut. "You are summoned by Her Majesty. A carriage awaits."

I had a sense he didn't care for me (which mirrored my own feelings for him), but he was always, *always*, unfailingly polite to the point of excruciation, which made being near him a giant pain in the behind.

"Of course, Baronet," I replied with the same level of politeness. "I shall attend. Allow me to gather what's necessary."

Normally it would be the Master of Justice who summoned, but for Queen Bet to send her own puppy for a Justice meant that the situation must be either dire or politically sensitive. Quite possibly both.

Devanis gave a short bow, just enough to convey respect, but not much, and exited quickly. He never bothered to stay in my presence one second longer than absolutely necessary. Perhaps mages and crafters bothered him. His reluctance didn't hurt my feelings.

As ever, I became all twitterpated. It's not every day the queen summoned and my heart began to race at the implied possibilities. "How's my hair? All my braids look fine?" I asked my wife. Unnecessarily, of course, because she'd checked earlier after we woke. Fifty-six shoulder length small braids. Fifty-six was the sacred number for Mother Moon, one of the two patron deities I'd chosen for my craft (commonly referred to as witchcraft), the other being Father Sun and my devotion to him was displayed by a gold sun tattoo on each eyelid. Without my two patrons, my crafting would be a feeble thing and my use as a Justice severely curtailed. Many assume that crafters would look to Wom, Goddess of the Earth, Fertility and Storms, but she proves too fickle and fickle doesn't work with the exacting practice of the craft.

"Bat!" I snapped my fingers.

A large slice of darkness detached itself from the ceiling in one corner of the shop and my familiar fluttered toward me, but not before flapping by Mirallelle's head, his four-foot wing span threatening to knock over glass jars of herbs and rare elements, to circle back and brush against her hand as she held it up for a flyby rub for luck. Through our link, my familiar felt the love I held for my wife and that affection filled him like water filling a skin. As big as a small dog, Bat *cheeped* excitedly, ready to go somewhere different.

At a little over two pounds, Bat was a goodly sized specimen for a fruit bat. Many crafters chose ravens or cats and they do come with certain benefits, but I chose Bat because of his versatility. When I first brought him home Mirallelle objected mightily, but after a while became used to, and showed affection for, the little fox-faced mammal.

I held up a covered bird cage and Bat obligingly entered through a large slit in the black cloth, happy to find comfort in the darkness within. He *cheeped* twice and I tossed a peach inside for him to eat.

Most people don't understand the bond between a crafter and their familiars, finding it kind of creepy that we used animals for many of our rituals. They couldn't know that the bond allowed a crafter to see through a familiar's eyes, hear through their ears and sense what they sense, which allowed a deeper connection to the natural world that enabled more coherent, stable spells to be cast. I tried several times to tell my wife, but words were useless when describing the link. Good thing Mirallelle was a patient woman willing to put up with many of my peccadillos.

Leather satchel filled with items definitely not for sale to the general public in one hand and the bird cage in the other, I exited our little shop dressed in my customary leather trousers and blue cotton tunic, stepping into the intense summer sunlight and climbed awkwardly into carriage.

"Palace?" I ask as the baronet sat opposite and stared through the curtain.

He picked at some imaginary lint on his burgundy hose. A real fashion plate was the baronet. "The Summer House."

I almost smiled. Castle Gylleth was a dreary affair and even the seven Pearl Towers couldn't lighten the harsh, dark stone of the main building, which originally served as a fort after the last Malosian Shift eight hundred years ago. Since then it grew like a cancer, additions sprouting from the ugly main mass and tall towers spiraling up like spines on a hedgehog. From damp little fort to a giant, sprawling damp mass of stone and wood squatting in the most beautiful city in the kingdom like a carbuncle on the bum of a courtesan. The Summer House, on the other hand, was light and airy and as beautiful as birdsong.

Despite Castle Gylleth squatting like a bloated toad in the middle of the city, there was no other place I'd rather be. From the poorest to the highest, each citizen knew they belonged to the richest, most culturally advanced of the six kingdoms. Gylleth and Ramashur was where things *happened*.

Ramashur passed outside the window as Devanis and I studiously ignored each other. Someday I should make peace with the man, but his grasping for status unbalanced my humors to the point I couldn't bring myself to be the bigger person.

We passed the west gate in silence and clattered along enduring every hump and bump in the road with the air thick between us until he suddenly broke our almost companionable tension. "Best prepare, Her Majesty is filled with ill humors that sours her mood." He never took his eyes from the window.

"Why tell me this?" I asked.

"My sole purpose is to see to Her Majesty's well-being and the well-being of Gylleth," he replied, lips barely moving. It must have hurt to reveal to me such candid thoughts. "When you join in audience with the Queen as her Justice, you must be aware of her mood so you may perform your duties with greater efficacy."

I regarded the baronet, nonplussed, reaching into the birdcage for the solace of Bat's silky fur. For him to confide in me was akin to a snake sparing a mouse. In my four years of service to Queen Bet, he never spared me a kind word or look and this set me aback more than a little bit. I thanked him with utmost courtesy and decided to refrain from further conversation that might bring about more uncomfortable revelations.

Every minute of the half-hour ride felt like five thanks to the excruciating silence between us, so I had to content myself with playing with Bat, letting him lick my fingertips, his tongue tickling skin. Most people didn't care for bats, but Bat could fly and he could get about on the ground well enough, which made him an excellent snoop. Both helped me in my pursuit as Queen Betelial Til-Amre's Justice, a job with its fair share of hazards.

I hadn't looked to become a Justice, an enforcer of the Queen's Law, not the sort of thing that someone versed in the craft aspires to, but when the queen of the kingdom in which you live insists there's very little choice in the matter. Especially when the crown foots the bill for the tuition at the Hidden Academy.

Located to the far west and south of Gylleth, the Hidden Academy was an autonomous city state deep within the Valhurst Desert where most of Six Kingdoms sent their mageborn to learn what magics they could. In exchange for a steep tuition, the kingdoms received a trained magic user in return. My affinity was for crafting, so Gylleth grew one witch richer.

Truth be told, though, I grew well into the role and learned to cherish the notion of helping Gylleth to maintain it status as a paragon of civilization.

The carriage pulled into the long road up the to the Summer house where we fell under the shade of the Forever Tree. A gift from the sylvans to Queen Bet's many times great grandfather, it was a symbol of the trust between the two peoples and legend had it if it thrived, so would the Til-Amre line. The smooth-barked, beech-white tree stood well over one-hundred fifty feet tall with a trunk as thick as a house and branches wider than the carriage in which I rode and it dominated the mansion that was the Summer House that stood far enough away so that if a branch fell, it wouldn't flatten the building.

Guards in plate-and-chain patrolled the grounds just inside the ten-foot wall in pairs carrying crossbows with hand-and-a-half swords sheathed at their hips. These men and women were the best warriors to come from the army and the gladiatorial arena and had proven their efficacy several times over the past decades by thwarting no less than half-a-dozen assassination attempts. They offered the carriage hard-eyed stares even though the driver wore the livery of the royal house of Til-Amre and gave escort all the way to the grand doors of the Summer House.

If the guards patrolling the grounds seemed impressive, the two that waited by the stout oaken doors banded in iron failed to do so spectacularly only because of their stature. Both wielded the customary double-bitted axes their race favored and covered themselves in sturdy looking, no-nonsense chain that looked heavy enough to stop a spear cold. Sporting identical white beards and moustaches, they stood only as tall as my shoulder, yet were nearly twice as wide. From Gaor to the far north, the two snow dwarves (as they called themselves) broke into smiles and vied for the honor of offering a hand to help me step down from the carriage.

"Skakhir, Haddeg," I said, ignoring both hands and settling for giving each a hug when I descended. "You two look wonderful."

"By my clenched butt cheeks, not as wunnerful as yer," said Skakhir Shadowmail with a wink in his thick Khulasch accent. "Been a beet o' tyme since weeve laid eyes on yer."

"Aye," chimed in Haddeg Whitgut. "Yer and Mirallelle donna come aroon much annymir, dooya?"

"Only when my job as Justice demands it." I saw Devanis frown. Understanding dwarves was an ability not many could master. Fortunately, I had an ear for such things. The two were actually great, big softies and the kindest people a body could meet, but for some reason the baronet didn't care for them or for those who weren't native Gyllethians. Myself included, obviously, considering my Irramerian ancestry.

After untangling more pleasantries, the two dwarves opened the massive wooden doors and ushered us inside, saving some cool looks for the baronet.

Queen Bet might call the mansion the Summer House, but it was large enough to room half of Ramashur and their horses. A bit much for my taste, but then again I wasn't the ruler of the richest kingdom on Estia and the second largest next to Suurmae to the southwest

I followed Denavis across the floor of polished pink granite through too many halls to count until we came to small room outside of the queen's offices where the hairs on the back of neck began to prickle as I sensed someone behind me.

"Ah, Niendra Goisien. Heartbreaker."

That voice! I turned to see the owner. "Hengeth Isobold! Madman!"

In an instant I found myself engulfed by brawny arms attached to a barrel chest while lips surrounded by a neatly trimmed brown beard bussed my cheeks. I returned the affection enthusiastically.

"My darling," enthused the tall wizard as he held me at arm's length. "You have not aged a day in a decade."

"Sweet of you to say," I replied, setting Bat's cage and my satchel on an ornate side table that was worth more than my shop. "You're probably right."

A tall, skinny kid in his academy years, Hengeth still retained his size, but added considerably more muscle and his large hands were thick with callouses that mages did not accumulate, ones that came from sword work and I said so.

"Ah, I learned a few things while in Nerrinnia working for Rikard."

I goggled, scarcely believing my ears. "*You* worked for the Wizard King himself? What, were you feeling suicidal."

"Oh, he's not so bad once you get to know him."

"So, he mellowed after he killed his two brothers and sister for the throne, then? What, he's now giving silver crowns to the poor and showing unbridled love for peoples everywhere?" Rikard had the reputation of the hardest, meanest ruler in all the Six Kingdoms, a self-made wizard who did not scruple to destroy anyone that stood in his path. Although he ruled Nerrinnia well and it prospered, he did so with an iron fist and an utter disregard for mercy. I took a closer look at Hengeth and noted the green hose, cobalt doublet with mother-of-pearl buttons and the frilly lace spilling like foam from his cuffs and collar. He exuded wealth and taste, completely at odds with his academy days when he stood a half-step from poverty. "Is Rikard the source of your new found wealth?" I fingered his fine doublet.

A small smile quirked his lips, but his eyes traveled to a point past my right shoulder. "Baronet Tol-Walcifer, I did not notice you before," he commented drily. "Please inform Her Majesty that Justice Goisien and I await her pleasure."

The baronet's face became oak and I swore I could hear teeth grinding as the big muscles at the corners of his jaws clenched. The one thing Davanis hated more than dealing with people he considered his social and racial inferiors was condescension from those a rung or more above him in station. Forcing a smile that looked as tight as a noblewoman's corset, he nodded slightly and exited the room through the far door.

"You have just made an enemy, Hengeth."

"He's a pain in a part of my body best left unsaid," the mage grunted, the smile finally reaching his eyes.

"But favored by the queen for his keen mind and facility at politics. At least for now." I headed back to the issue at hand. "What were you doing for the Wizard King? The man is more dangerous than a house full of vipers and what in Mother Moon's name are you doing here of all places? I thought you'd be teaching at the academy, raising a new crop of mages and womanizing up a treat. At the very least working for Ehtalia of Emment as her court wizard."

Hengeth took my hands, suddenly as excited as a little boy who's just been told he can have a pony. "I no longer am beholden to Emment for my tuition, having paid it back in full and with interest, so Ehtalia has no hold over me. As for Rikard, did you know he has one of the most extensive libraries in all the Six Kingdoms? Books that rival Queen Bet's personal collection, texts you cannot find anywhere else. It was there I found writings concerning the Malosian Shifts, some original works, a folio of sorts, by the wizard Malos himself that are at least three-thousand years old!"

"The wizard the shifts are named after?"

"That very one!"

"There's a reason why they called him 'the Mad', you know that, right?" Malos the Mad Wizard tried to research the world-changing shifts and disappeared, his unknown fate a cautionary tale for those who tried to grasp power of which they had no concept. Even the arch-mages of the Hidden Academy weathered the Malosian Shifts instead of trying to yoke them. Better off grasping a tornado by the tail.

My friend gave a long sigh, but the smile never left his face. "Of course, but I have always wanted to understand the shifts, why they happen, why sometimes a shift seems to change the nature of magic or causes a river to dry up or a volcano to erupt. Each shift makes a physiological reaction to the world or a paradigm change to the fundamental rules governing nature itself in some manner. If I can learn how to predict a shift and what the effects will be, then I can lessen the damage, perhaps even stop a shift altogether. Imagine a world where civilizations didn't have to crumble and rise again after every few centuries."

I tried not to roll my eyes, but failed miserably. Wizards had been trying to understand the shifts for as long as there had Six Kingdoms. Hengeth laughed off my apology. "Never mind, Niendra, scoff all you want. I'm fully aware of the new science, the wizards who call themselves Astrologers, are trying to do the same thing, but none of them have what Rikard does." He leaned in close and whispered, "The Wizard King has been collecting artifacts all his life and the Malos writings are merely the beginning. It's rumored that somewhere he has hidden the secret of his power, the reason why he was able to kill his siblings, who were greater mages than he, taught by the Hidden Academy, but never took the vows." He shook his head. "Rumors, but interesting, nonetheless."

"So why would the notorious Wizard King, the only spell slinger to hold a throne, allow another mage to even breathe the same air as what caresses this Malos Folio? He isn't rumored to be the soft and cuddly sort filled with cooperation for his fellow wizards."

"Her Majesty will see you now," interrupted the baronet, who managed to sidle up on our conversation unnoticed. He graced us with a superior smirk that told me saw my barely perceptible start of surprise and, as for Hengeth, he gave the baronet a slightly condescending nod as if he had known of the man's approach all along.

With very little ado we found escorted into the other room where we faced the ruler of Gylleth, the richest of the six human kingdoms of Estia, Her Majesty Betelial Til-Amre, first of her name.

Wizened like a prune with pale, pale, crepe skin and iron gray hair, Queen Bet fussed around a desk that could have been mistaken for an obscenely large banquet table. She examined a scroll while slowly while walking the perimeter of the desk, the train of her heavy purple and white dress slowing her progress somewhat. Rumor had it she did this every working day, walk around and around the desk until lunch when she took a small break followed by more walking around the desk reading dispatches and having her secretary, a young man named LeRoy who sat in the corner, take dictation. According to her staff, she never walked less than ten miles a day, which might be the reason she stubbornly clung to life at the age of ninety-six.

The queen stopped as the baronet announced, "Wizard Hengeth Isobold and Justice Goisien, Your Majesty." He concluded by bowing and exiting, the door closing softly behind.

Settling with the grace of a swan easing onto the still waters of a lake, Queen Bet sat in her large, uncomfortable looking wooden chair which seemed to swallow her whole. Her small, wrinkled face barely cleared the large desk, but somehow she seemed grander, larger than the mahogany monstrosity that sheltered her.

I averted my eyes. It was good policy never to stare down the boss. Normally I reported directly to Lord Petre Ul-Mavre, the queen's spymaster and Master of Justice, a position he served in for over fifty years. Almost as old as the queen herself, Lord Petre was rumored to be the queen's lover, confidant and father to two of her six children.

"Sit," commanded the queen in a high, bird-like voice. After we sat, she continued, turning her beady eyes upon me, "No doubt you are wondering why We summoned you personally."

"Yes, Your Majesty."

A sigh barely moved wrinkled lips the color of liver. "Our Master of Justice has been struck ill and is bound to his chambers. The matter before Us is of sufficient sensitivity that We do not believe Lord Petre's underlings are of a temperament to be privy to such information."

Translation: There is someone in the offices of the Master of Justice with loose lips.

I nodded sagely and kept my own mouth firmly shut.

"You know of the merchant Soro Divver."

"Yes, Your Majesty." Soro Divver, owned several quarries near Orthangar. A construction tycoon, he was one of the richest men in Gylleth and contracted with the government to build various civic improvements, such as the aqueducts that brought fresh water to Orthengar and the roads between Ramashur, Nooce and Port Bucc. "A very important man, Your Majesty. A rich one as well."

"We believe he has been murdered. The alleged crime took place at the Frost Quarry near Orthengar."

"Beg your pardon, Majesty, but isn't that Justice Canlo's jurisdiction?"

Queen Bet gave me a small nod. "Assuredly, but We think, due to the nature of the supposed crime and its ramifications, you would be the best Justice to serve Us in this matter. We have full confidence in Our servant Justice Canlo, but he is warrior, not a mage, and We believe that because there are no witnesses to this supposed crime, a mage is what is called for. You are, Justice Niendra Goisien, Our only mage Justice."

I nodded, sighing inwardly.

THREE

NOW

I REMEMBER WHEN ORTHENGAR, NESTLED IN THE BOSOM of the Frostbacks, barely qualified a notation upon a good map of the kingdom, but now it sprawls out in front of me, a monstrosity that ran from the mountains to half way across the valley. Almost as large as Ramashur, it eschews walls for a series of nine fortified citadels throughout the city named for each of the gods, rallying points for the army and the citizen militia. Any force foolish enough to invest the city would find themselves fighting a sizable force house-to-house, citadel to citadel, made to bleed for every foot taken. A sensible precaution, although the Six Kingdoms have been at peace for the last few shifts and are held together by a web of diplomacy, intermarriage and alliances that guarantees mutually assured destruction called The Great Peace. That and the Mage Treaty, the Hidden Academy's own contribution to the balance of power on Estia so that the continent does not devolve into complete barbarism after each shift.

Five hundred years since my death and three since my return and I still feel a shock at the changes time and industry have wrought. Again, I feel a sense of nostalgia for the Gylleth of the past. This new world puzzles me somewhat, but I prevail because I have no choice.

Artoch and I enter from the east, toward the mountains, along with a river of humanity that call Orthengar home. Guards in garish green tabards patrol the streets, strange, thin swords called rapiers at their sides and a new kind of weapon called a musket at their belts. They are ferociously wicked devices that can throw a ball of lead farther and faster than a heavy crossbow bolt can fly. When fired it makes a godsawful barking noise accompanied by a plume of whitish smoke and the lead ball can pierce the heaviest armor, which is why the guards have only linen tabards to protect them. What use is cumbersome mail against firearms?

Wide-brimmed, plumed hats festoon the guards' skulls and they walk with an arrogant swagger that offends my eyes, but I keep them downcast because these new men and women warriors are quick to take offense at the slightest provocation. Duels have become a favorite pastime, eclipsing the gladiatorial arenas in the eyes of the public. Not a day goes by without blood spilling into the gutters.

Gylleth seems to have become much more cosmopolitan in the centuries since my death, becoming a host to more people of varying ethnicities. I spy many of my dark skinned Irramerian cousins as well as the bronze of Coad islanders, sylvans with their arched eyebrows and pointed ears and even a few boisterous dwarves who seem to have no fear of the rapier-wielding guards that swagger down the streets.

I keep myself to myself, not engaging eye contact and dismounting Artoch as the crowds become thicker and thicker. As I lead my gelding down the street, I remove a small vial of lavender oil from a pouch and dab a few drops behind my ears and on my wrists. While my flesh retains the appearance of living vigor thanks to the agency that drew me from Tilla's Hold, I lack the odor of those whose hearts beat. No secretions of sweat or bad breath, only the slight swampy smell of decay.

After paying three copper crowns to stable Artoch, I shoulder my pack and set my destination to the boarding house where I rent a room from an elderly widower who knows not to ask questions of his tenants if silver crowns cross his palms every week. I enter the house to smell of bacon and biscuits.

"Hello, Mateous," I say as walk through the kitchen where the landlord cooks the afternoon meal for his tenants.

The landlord jumps, hand clutching his chest as if his heart has begun to fail. "M-mistress Niendra," he stammers, clearly shocked at seeing me. "Y-you're b-back."

Something prickles at the nape of my neck and I offer him a hard look. "As I said I would be, Mateous."

"Six months, though, mistress."

"And I paid a year in advance." Something is wrong, the elderly landlord with his crown of wispy white hair is far too agitated at my return than he should be. I take a deep breath and let it out slowly, saying, "What is wrong?"

"What he's trying to say is he rented your room, woman." The voice grates and I look to see a whip-thin man leaning against the doorway to the dining room. The bacon begins to burn, along with my temper.

At least six feet in height, wide shoulders under a long-sleeved white shirt tucked into soft, brushed leather trousers tucked into knee-high boots, the man exudes confidence and restrained lethality. I dislike him immediately.

Giving Mateous a steely glare which causes him to gulp and gabble uselessly. "Fortunate that you happened by in time to add clarity to the subject."

"Lucky me," he answers with a barely repressed sneer. His languid pose and air of contempt insults. "Are you done with the bacon and biscuits yet, old man?"

"Y-yes," comes the stutter. "It'll be served in a moment."

"My money," I growl, letting a small thread of anger coil from my lips. "My room."

"Mine now, bitch." The thin man is all smiles.

I realize he is trying to bait me, force me to say something stupid so he can take umbrage. He takes umbrage, calls me out and we duel so he can keep my room because he knows I have the law on my side and the only way to sidestep is to kill me or make me yield. If I take offence and call him out, he will have the choice of weapons and if my judgement is still sound, I believe him to be one of those swaggering peacock guardsmen.

I do not feel much like yielding. Not at all.

"Your wording is off, young man," I say. "It is 'witch'. And a very good one at that."

For a moment he looks nonplussed, having figured me for a relatively powerless woman despite my height. He blinks twice and a twitch begins at the corner of his mouth. Perhaps he feels fear for the first time. I know

Mateous is now deathly afraid of me if his pallor is any indication. He shakes as if palsied.

The thin man decides I am bluffing, stepping into the kitchen to try to intimidate me with his air of coiled menace. "The room is mine, *bitch*," he spits, gray eyes flashing. "I suggest you leave."

I am tired of this. Keeping my head down to avoid trouble is one thing, but I have been a target for venal men due to the color of my skin and my gender for far too long. Some things cannot be let to stand and I decide to goad him further in the belief that not many choose to insult him. "Little dog, I have the law on my side. The only person who will leave is you."

He follows a predictable pattern, which confirms the reasoning that he is one of those swaggering guards with their rapiers and muskets. All ego and bravado. "My name is Artelious DiChenzi and I take offense at your tone. We shall settle this with a duel, if you aren't a coward."

My nod is near imperceptible. "The first to yield, or first blood."

Artelious nods, his smile reappearing and I know he will try to kill me. "Name your weapon."

This is the crux. Now that he has taken offense, the choice is mine. "Hand to hand."

That sets him back on his heels and for a moment doubt mars his features before it settles into stone. "Done. When? Where?"

"Tonight, in the courtyard. No witnesses except Mateous and our seconds." The house's courtyard is barely big enough to be called such, but it will serve and I want this to be out of sight from the public. At his nod I turn to the landlord. "I will use your basement."

Even more pale, Mateous nods, wattle under his chin waggling. I turn from the enterprising duelist and open the door to the basement. I have work to do.

SANDALWOOD SMOKE AND PINE, SAGE AND THYME. Fifty-six chants to Mother Moon and twelve to Father Sun.

I sit in the basement inside a circle of salt and the powdered carapaces of dung beetles, eyes closed and chanting softly. Fifty-six silver crowns, a small fortune, lies stacked in front of me outside the circle along with twelve crowns of gold, another small fortune. Nine beesewax and bearberry candles add an earthy sweet odor, but I am too lost in the incantation to notice.

For three years since my awakening in the Catacombs of Justice I have studied this new world and the changes wrought upon it by five centuries of absence. I am a time traveler in my own land and, although the Six Kingdoms still prevail, even the language has changed. The world has passed me by and I have worked to learn what I could so I can blend in, escape notice, seek a reckoning for my death.

The Royal Library of Orthengar provides me with much information, the scholars and librarians only too happy to assist a foreigner who spoke an ancient Estian dialect. In all that time I chose not to pursue a familiar, but the time for justice to be served is drawing close and I will need all the help I can get.

The fifty-sixth chant to Mother Moon in old Dendrich, the language of magic, is complete, the last hard consonants falling away from my lips as a firm pressure begins to build behind my navel, proof that the magic is working. Father Sun and Mother Moon are answering my summons to bring me a familiar to aid me on my quest and I cannot help but smile a bit.

Keeping my eyes shut, I count the seconds. *One Ramashur, two Ramashur* . . . fifty-six then twelve. The pressure eases and I relax, opening my eyes. Two of the candles are out, seven gutter with flames the color of old wine, an auspicious result. The coins are gone.

Sighing, I break the circle and clean up the dank little basement with its barrels of preserved meats and cheeses, the chill not bothering me at all. In fact, very little does. My flesh feels as if it is encased in thick wool that removes the finer sense of touch. In fact, I carry a morbid fascination with my dulled sensation often pinching myself because all pain is absent. I can feel pressure, yes, but pain is a sensation that has been put behind me.

Soon the familiar will come to me, sent by Mother Moon and Father Sun. I chose to ask for a bat out of a sense of continuity and nostalgia, but in the end the creature will be decided upon by my patron gods. Normally the crafter's request is often granted, but the gods can be fickle.

Searching Ramashur with a living familiar would have brought the unwanted attention of the dead, who will devour even insects for their vital essences. Now that the second part of my plan is in play, a familiar is just what I need.

Outside the day is starting to fade, but it is early enough to go shopping near one of the ten citadels where marketplaces thrive. The nearest is Phezdes, who is the God of Blessings, Kindness, Artists and Festivals. He is often depicted as a grandfatherly old man with twinkling blue eyes and long, white mustaches that fall past his chin.

The crowds at this time of day are becoming thin because it is close to suppertime, so I have no hindrance walking to the Berry and Branch, a small shop that caters to crafters and midwives. They carry a fine selection of reagents and herbs, almost as fine as my shop of old and as I enter, a familiar pang stabs through me. Nostalgia and sorrow. At least I can still feel something.

"Mistress Niendra," says the man behind the counter, a large Coadian with a protruding belly. A tonsure the size of my palm decorates the top of his head, a sign of his devotion of Himir, the God of Sleep and Knowledge. He raises his arms in welcome. "It's been too long."

There is no fear in me that a citizen of Gylleth will ever connect the dots between the Irramerian crafter and Justice Niendra Goisien of the past with Niendra the Irramerian crafter of today. Five hundred years buys a lot of forgetfulness. I force a smile I do not feel, hoping it looks sincere and begin to shop for the ingredients I think I will need for the next phase of my quest. Many are costly, but Ramashur has many treasures and the dead do not mind if I help myself. It beats having to work for a living. Or un-living, in my case.

The time for the duel with the arrogant Artelious DiChenzi approaches and I as I walk the Phezdes market I silently curse myself for an idiot. What matter my ego when I need to pursue matters of greater import? So what if I give up a room at a nice boardinghouse run by a more-or-less honest widower of modest means, it is not like I plan to stay for much longer. I feel as if my temper might be the final death of me.

The truth hits me with ease because the dead have no turbulent humors to bother them. I hate to be taken advantage of (as do most people, I suppose) and I *really* hate smug, arrogant, condescending asses like DiChenzi with a passion I should have left in the grave. Or, in my case, a nice sarcophagus in the Catacombs of Justice.

A quick flash of pale skin intrudes upon my mind, lean fingers dipping toward me quick as a blink, but I am faster, my hand moving as if it possess its own will, a dark blur and my fingers grasp a sinewy arm.

"Hey!" The voice is high-pitched and carries panic.

A merchant minding a fruit stand filled with lemons points. "Thief! You caught a thief, I saw it all, the kid was trying to rob you!"

Just a boy, perhaps twelve or so, emerald eyes wide in fright, small in stature but broad, with shoulders that indicate that he will grow to be strong man. Should he last that long. His clothes are threadbare and ragged, his skin covered in soot and grime.

"Let me go!" he urges, fear etched across his face. He is strong, but I am far stronger and all his pulling and squirming does not break my grip. I take in breath so I can sigh. The sparse crowd of Phezdes market begins to gather around the pair of us, drawn by the entertaining drama and the possibility of violence. They get their wish as the boy kicks me hard in the shin with the dull sound of a hammer hitting wet wood. I feel very little.

With a twist of my wrist I spin the boy around and lever his arm behind his back, raising it along his spine until he yells in shock and pain.

"Do not kick me again," I say softly with enough menace to cause him to blanch.

"Yah, yah, please stop," he pleads. "Sorry, sorry, so sorry!"

I relent just as a droll voice says, "So, Tennic finally meets his match." My eyes rise to see a wide man in fine scarlet trousers tucked into black leather knee-high boots. A soft blue shirt with puffy sleeves lies under a sable half-cape. He wears a rapier at his side and simple, black, short-brimmed hat over his long hair.

"Esquire?" I ask.

"I am not of the nobility," he answers with a smile. "The honorific is wasted upon me. Besides," he laughs. "I work for a living."

Ah, a man used to physical labor. Perhaps a warrior of some sort. "Then, good man," I say, ignoring the squirming boy, "you know this pup?"

He nods. "I do." Breaking from the crowd, he gestures for me to surrender the boy. I do so and the man places a large hand the lad's shoulder, who has gone from fearful to absolutely terrified.

"This young man, Tennic, has been the scourge of the marketplaces for quite some time now." The man offers a stern glance and the boy withers under the gaze. "He's never been caught. Until now." Hand still firmly in place on the boy's shoulder, he gives me a short bow. "Allow me, good lady. I am Justice Antonius Valerius."

A Justice! One good thing about being dead is that shock rarely meets my face, so I keep my expression blank and nod in return. "Well met, good Justice, I am Niendra."

He is quite handsome and he knows it, giving me full force of a charming smile. "And well met to you, good crafter. Father Sun, if my eyes aren't playing tricks, and by count of your braids, Mother Moon as well."

"Your eyes are as keen as the rapier at your side, Justice. Yes, I am a crafter."

Mages are rare enough that his next question comes as no surprise and is one for which I possess a ready answer. "What brings you to Orthengar?"

"My family in Irrameria, Tilla bless them, paid in full my tuition to the Hidden Academy before they perished. Now I am in search of home. So far, I am not in love with Suurmae or Emment, so I came to Gylleth to see what is what."

Antonius cocks his head to the side as I rattle off my ready response before saying, "Well, allow me to welcome you to Orthengar and to say that if you seek employment, we can always use more Justices at Hall of Law, especially a lovely crafter such as yourself." He approaches and gently takes my hand, kissing the back. I do not feel his lips brush my skin. "Lavender. Delicious."

He flirts with me! And the invitation . . . Mother Moon! The last thing I need is to put my dead self in the middle of a cabal of observant Justices. I force a laugh and gently disengage my hand. "It is a thought I shall consider."

"What about the boy?" cries some wag from the crowd.

That narrows the Justice's focus. "Ah yes." He looks around. "As I have an appointment, I think a guardsman should be summoned to take care of the rascal."

For some reason this sends a pang through me and the sight of Tennic's face screwed up in misery tugs at emotions I thought dead. "Hold a moment," I say loudly, raising a hand before someone from the crowd could scarper off for the guard. "This little rat tried to pick my purse, but failed." Inspiration struck. "Give him to my care. I think I can set his feet on a straighter path."

The crowd mutters, sensing that their entertainment is not heading in their desired direction while the Justice strokes his firm chin in thought. Tennic looks at me in alarm, obviously unsure of my intentions, but staying put under the Justice's heavy hand.

"That is a kindness, crafter Niendra. Why?"

Good question, one I cannot answer, only a gut feeling that the boy is important somehow, some way. I am not big on hunches or flights of fancy, but a feeling this strong can only be influenced by Mother Moon, the Goddess of Secrets and Magic and to ignore it would be stupid and I am pretty sure I do not qualify for stupid. Only time will tell.

"Because I hate to see potential wasted and there is always room for kindness in this hard world where such a thing is a rarity."

That earned me a quirked eyebrow. "You realize he belongs to The Man Behind, right?"

My answer is to raise an eyebrow in return.

The Justice snorts and leans in so the crowd will not overhear. "The Man Behind is a blight that plagues Orthengar." His whisper is fierce, his hate almost palpable. "A crime lord that uses children to steal in the markets, adults to rob houses and extort protection money from shopkeepers. His fingers are long and deep, his methods brutal and . . . final." Antonius lowers his voice even further. "There are city guards on his payroll, he has assassins and enforcers. This man won't take kindly to you poaching one of his earners."

This is nothing I have not heard before. Five hundred years ago when my heart beat as a Justice, Ramashur was infested with a similar criminal element called the Widow. "Why is he called the Man Behind?" I ask after mulling his words over a moment.

"Because you'll never see him in front of you, he comes from behind."

Clever.

I turn to the boy Tennic. "Do you like working for the Man Behind?"

An indifferent shrug is my only answer. The little rat has gone from terrified to nonchalant with a swiftness reserved for the young and the addled.

Reaching into the bag of goods I purchased at the Berry and Branch, I pull out a small vial of coppery powder and pour a dab into my palm, then using a spit wet finger, drew marks on Tennic's forehead, cheeks and chin. "This is our bond, by Mother Moon and Father Sun," I say gravely, magic thrilling through both of us. The boy sweats, smearing the brownish streaks. "Do you see the tattoos on my eyelids?"

He nods, reverting to terrified. I nod back and wipe the marks away. The cinnabar runes are no longer needed, the spell is complete.

"They are my pledge to one of my patrons, Father Sun, who sees all in daylight, the God of Truth and Healing." For an instant I see myself as the boy does, a tall, dark-skinned Irramerian woman with a scalp full of braids and yellow sun marks on her eyelids, face solemn and somehow desperately weary. "You and I are now joined. You cannot hide from me, my eyes will find you, my nose will smell you out. As long as you stay by my side, you will have a full belly and I will fight to keep you safe. This is my oath as a witch, a crafter of the Hidden Academy. Do you understand?" This is not only a magic ritual, I also want him scared enough that he obeys.

Tennic looks like he wants to swoon, but he gathers himself and slowly nods.

"Are you sure?" asks Antonius.

For some reason it feels right and I tell him so. He nods and says, "For what it's worth, I hope your fit of madness here benefits you and the little rat." With that he turns and shoos crowd away. They mutter and curse at the lack of drama but they disperse at the whipcrack authority of his voice.

"What now?" asks Tennic, rubbing his shoulder where the Justice's hand had rested.

"You come with me. I have more shopping to do because you are ripe and in need of a wash and proper clothes." I look at his unshod feet, dirty, with callouses thick enough for riding boots. "And some new shoes."

We spend an hour buying necessaries for the boy, who moves as if in a daze, then a good scrubbing at a bath house, which turns the water such a grimy gray I give the owner a silver crown for his trouble. Before too long we return to my boarding house minus his ratty apparel, plus two pair of trousers, shoes and three new shirts in cyan, green and black. I can also see his skin clearly now that it is absent enough dirt to fill a planter.

"I have something I need to do," I say, handing the boy a copper crown as we enter the kitchen. Mateous looks at the two of us and stays silent, his face closed with fear and regret. "Wait for me here and have a bite. When you are done, pay the nice man."

Tennic nods. "Yes, Lady Witch."

"Niendra. I am no lady."

Another nod. He is so polite and accommodating I am immediately suspicious. "Yes Niendra."

My landlord breaks his silence. "Master Artelious and his second await in the courtyard, Mistress." His voice quavers. I know he fears what violence might do to the reputation of his house, but I find that I do not care one whit.

I give him a cold nod and head out the back door to the small courtyard populated by an old fountain long since gone to ruin and see two men. Artelious smirks at me from his seat on the rim of the fountain, the dirty gray stone cracked and crumbling. He looks like a mountain cat lounging around waiting for a tasty morsel on which to pounce while the other man stares at me in shock. I nod to Artelious' second.

"Justice," I say.

Antonius curses under his breath before saying, "Hello, Niednra."

Four

THEN

"Soo the wee knobblegrott says ta the sylvan, 'yer nae heer fer the huntin', are yer?"

Skakhir finished his joke with roll of his white-crested eyes and a leer while Haddeg laughed so hard he nearly fell out of the saddle.

I shook my head ruefully. "That is the filthiest thing I've ever heard."

This prompted Haddeg to turn beet red and gasp for breath while Skakir said, "Of course, all gud jokes need a bit of salt in 'em or they'd not be gud!"

As Justice I was given the power to name my own escort when on the job and I chose the two snow dwarves knowing they would do their utmost to see me safe should things become . . . hectic. Very few people are willing to face an enraged dwarf, let alone two.

The down side was I had to listen to the pair's raunchy jokes for two days straight. I felt like I needed to bathe.

Fortunately, I was saved from further filthy humor by the smudge of Orthengar appearing on the horizon. "There we go, boys." I urged my horse to a faster pace and our pack mule hastened to keep up.

"Anna gud thin' it is, Niendra," said Haddeg Whitgut. "Yer nut such gud coompany coonsiderin' yer know squat all aboot jokes."

I swear I could hear my eyes roll.

Orthengar, nestled in foothills of the Frostbacks within spitting distance of the Shorebridge Peninsula where it slid out into the South Sea.

The only city of note farther south on the peninsula was Drayport, where trade with Coad and Irrameria was conducted, but considering the port town's reputation of general lawlessness and vice, Orthangar looked like paradise to me. After the last shift, the city all but disappeared, semi-erased by the shift's reality-bending effects and people were still leery about repopulating a town they believed might be haunted. It was Queen Bet's mission to regrow the city due to its proximity to the sylvan nation and the Long Road.

Still, calling it a one-horse town was one horse too many.

At least they installed cobbles since the last time I visited, but the smell of human waste and horse dung still clung to the place like an overcoat. Very few people ever lived to see a dwarf, so my companions drew a crowd, *oohing* and *aahing* over their shiny chain hauberks, their flowing white hair, and the breadth of their muscular shoulders. Truth to tell, they were enough alike that most couldn't tell them apart. Shakir was the handsome one and Haddeg told the better dirty jokes.

A young raven-haired girl in a much- patched frock standing next to her mother held up a little blue flower as we passed and Haddeg leaned over to pluck it from her fingers. "Thank yer, wee missy," he crooned in his best Estian. She giggled and hid her face in her mother's skirts.

Haddeg pounded his countryman's shoulder. "I tole yer wimmen lyke me moore," he bellowed in delight as he twirled his luxurious, snowy mustache.

Skakhir snorted. "Wimmin be too beeg a term for that wee lass. She thinks yer looks lyke a wee stuffed animal, she doo."

Our destination wasn't the headman's house, but three-quarters of a mile beyond, before the Frostbacks grew too tall for men to climb easily and where the trees, such as lodgepole pines, aspens and fir, began to thin. Out there near streams so pure it could crack the heart lay the Divver Frost Quarry, the second largest in the Divver merchant empire.

Most knew that Soro Divver, now formerly one of the richest men in Gylleth, used to call Caenwylln, four days ride to the north and east, home. Divver had been found dead at the bottom of his quarry having fallen from a cliff face, apparently during false dawn with no one to witness the event.

Being rich and important meant that there were conspiracies theories by the score concerning his passing. Some said the Fel Rosso, a rival family for the contract to construct and maintain the burgeoning road system killed him, while others blamed the sylvans, who had summoned Justices a time or three for purported violations of the Boundry Treaty. I disregarded that particular rumor. If the sylvans wanted Divver dead, they wouldn't have left a body to find, they were far too subtle for that, however only Tilla knew the truth and she wasn't talking.

A quarter mile long and half that wide, the quarry was a gray slash against the lush green of its surroundings, a visual assault on the beauty of nature like a gaping wound in the belly of a gorgeous woman. Our little trio stood atop a hill overlooking the quarry below, now so still and peaceful by order of Queen Bet so her Justice could investigate absent disturbance.

"It noo be a beauty, that's fer sure," muttered Skakhir.

"Noot at all, cousin," replied Haddeg. "Noot at all."

Something about the scene struck me as wrong and it took a few moments to understand why. No people, no sound. There should have been workers scurrying around like ants in a nest accompanied by the metallic din of hammers striking wedges and rock, but all that remained here was the occasional chirp of a lonely bird and the light drone of insects.

I pointed. "Let's head over to the overseer's cabin." My heels hit my mount's barrel and she broke into a canter. We rounded a small grove of aspen to see a small, motley collection of rough cabins nestled together a stone's throw from the quarry edge. Nearby stood a much larger, more refined two-story house that stood among the buildings like a queen among peasants. Where they were constructed of wattle-daubed logs, the house was built with planed, well-trimmed and whitewashed boards and had windows of real glass instead of oiled parchment.

Standing in the front of the house with arms crossed was a tall, sylvan woman with hair so dark it ate the light in chunks, giving no sense of detail to the individual strands. She had razor thin eyebrows over gold eyes in a face as severe as a death sentence and as beautiful as a glacier and she regarded us sternly as we crossed what could laughably be called a street in this workers' town. I took note of her no-nonsense canvas trousers and black shirt, both of which had seen better days and a gutful of hard labor. Scuffed and worn boots capped her feet and I realized that this sylvan lady, the overseer Taalis I was told, worked as hard as any of the people she supervised, that this was no dainty lickspittle bureaucrat afraid to get their hands dirty.

"Overseer Taalis?" I asked as we rode up.

She gave a slow nod. "Justice. You came sooner than expected."

"I don't like to dawdle."

That brought a slight quiver to her lips. "Good."

"This wee scrumpeet of a sylvan is the overseer of the quarry?" Haddeg cut in, face agog with disbelief. "How does a sylvan geet to oversee what a dwarf shud?"

"This quarry borders sylvan lands, dwarf," replied Taalis coolly, not looking at him. "And that allows my people first right to any ra-iron ore, should any be found. I also ensure that no boundary offenses occur, forestalling any further disputes between Gylleth and Dorendiriar. I work as overseer to see that all is done proper."

Ra-iron ore, the metal most coveted by the sylvans and used in most of their weapons for its efficacy against knobblegrotts, snot-goblins and trolls alike. The sylvan valued it like the dwarves valued diamonds and gold.

"Be that as I may," I interjected. Last thing we needed was a sylvan/dwarf death match. The two weren't known for cuddly interactions. "Let's get to business."

Nodding, Taalis urged us to dismount and we did so, tethering our horses to a hitching post. With a mental nudge I urged Bat to disengage from beneath my light cloak and sent him flapping away as I pulled a backpack from the mule and shrugged it on. Taalis narrowed her eyes, offering me a thoughtful look and nodded her head toward the quarry.

"Four kinds of stone are produced from this quarry," said Taalis as we squelched through the thick muck of the street. The mud smelled like horse dung and old urine and I wondered If I'd have to throw my boots away after. "Flagstone, marble, granite and argillite." We came to a stout wooden staircase attached to the cliff wall that cut into the side of the hill. "Which makes this a high-demand business, but Coventio Divver, Soro Divver's son, was adamant about preserving the area as is so the Justice assigned could conduct a thorough examination."

"Sounds like a reasonable sort," I remarked we reached the staircase. Built zigzag with large beams thrust into the guts of the hill, it looked well-constructed, but had seen some hard use over the months, the wood faded and splintering from sun and rain. The floor of the quarry lay far below and I could not only see large boulders, but the shattered remains of some as well. Still pools of muddy water dotted the floor of the quarry like sores. I kept my mind on Taalis' words so the thought of falling so far and splattering open when I hit the bottom wouldn't unnerve me. Behind the dwarves kept up a constant low bickering about whose body would look the best after such a fall. I knew it didn't matter, no one looks good after such an impact and I resisted the urge to toss both of them over at once to see who would land first.

"Coventio Divver is his father's son: scrupulous, honorable and shrewd." The words dropped matter-of-factly from the sylvan's mouth, but I could sense real admiration there. Quite of feat to earn the respect of a member of that long-lived race. "He is the one who asked the queen for a Justice."

"Why?"

"Because Soro Divver knew this quarry like he knew his own face and he spent copious time in all his quarries. He was a hands-on businessman and smarter than most humans and the thought that he slipped and fell to his death off this very staircase is ludicrous, an insult to the intelligence of all who knew the man, so before you ask, yes . . . I believe that Soro Divver was murdered."

Now we reached the middle portion of the zigzag staircase with the dwarves in full bicker mode (Haddeg maintained his body would produce best splat while Skakir argued that his would land with more grace) as the sylvan continued. "The theory was that he came out in the early hours of the morning during false dawn to inspect the quarry and slipped on the steps and flipped over the rail, falling to his death. The problem is that Soro Divver was one of the most careful, methodical men I've ever met and would never inspect the quarry without being accompanied by either Grotek or myself."

"Grotek?"

"The foreman. However, he was found alone and Grotek and I were in our respective homes when the incident occurred."

A grayish something, camouflaged by the surrounding stone, shone below. It looked to a rectangular box of some kind. Haddeg mentioned something about a cold, misty smell and I sensed it as well. An odor like a forest in winter with frost on the leaves and snow on the ground. It tickled my nose pleasantly.

At the quarry floor we stood around a grayish rectangular box some three feet wide, eight long and three high, with tiny bits of shattered, whitish stone speckled with red flakes, likely blood, littering the area. The surface of the box glistened like shimmering glass, sparking every color imaginable and it hurt to look at, as if I stared at the sun. I blinked away after images and looked elsewhere, noticing the black dots of dried blood that spread out in a circle around the box. For once the dwarves were silent, eyes round in awe. From that rectangular box came the pleasant, snowy forest smell.

"What is that?" I asked, pointing and definitely not staring.

"Sylvan magic," came Taalis' calm reply. "It is a bubble of solidified time preserving the remains of Soro Divver, placed there by me at the request of his son."

Blood rushed to my face in excitement. This was a magic unheard of! "You can manipulate time?"

Her eyes turned to me, cool and appraising Taalis nodded. "To an extent. Enough to stop time within a certain area. What you see here is not a physical object, but time refracting around Soro's body giving the illusion of a box. Time itself stopped around a physical space. For all intents and purposes, a box made of solidified time."

I tried to wrap my head around the concept and gave it up because there were other things I needed to focus my mental energies on. "Please remove the time box, then."

A slow nod. "As you command, Justice Goisien."

Long, graceful fingers gestured toward the structure of petrified time and it flickered once, twice, three times before disappearing altogether, popping like a soap bubble to reveal the body that lay beneath.

"Did yer have to show us that, did yer?" yelled Haddeg in disgust. "Poor wee human."

I wrinkled my nose at the smell of fresh blood and bowels. "You must've cast the spell quickly."

"Less than an hour after his death," Taalis replied impassively. "It was Grotek who discovered the body after hearing what he thought was a scream. Coventio was also in the main house and when roused, gave the order. He accompanied his father to the quarry for a personal matter."

"What personal matter?"

Cool golden eyes met mine. "Personal matters," she repeated. "That means I don't know."

Well, I stood corrected. She seemed touchy on the subject and I filed that away for alter. "Grotek was awake when it happened?" Was that an arm? I looked closer. No, that was Divver's spine.

"Eating breakfast."

It looked as if Divver landed head first and his skull had burst open like rotten fruit, spewing blood, brains and bone in all directions. It looked like he'd been a big man condensed down to the size of a twelve-year-old. Bones stuck out through great rents in the flesh and what was left didn't look human at all. Behind me the Haddeg and Skakhir muttered in dwarvish, eyes round and solemn as they stared at the mess strewn at my feet.

Closing my eyes, I reached for Bat and saw the quarry through his eyes in a grayish monotone as he flew overhead and with a flick of my mind I had him fly around the stairs a few times. Still looking through his eyes I noted the position of the body and where it lay in relation to the wooden structure.

"Murder all right," I said, abruptly severing the link.

"Hoow kin yer tell?" asked Skakhir.

I pointed to the ground beyond the body toward the staircase. "Stand there, if you would." The dwarf obliged, careful not to step in anything wet.

"You're about what? Five feet from the stairs, right?"

Skakhir nodded.

"How far from the stairs is the body?"

"I'd say aboot fifteen gud feet, mebbe twenty."

"So unless he jumped or was thrown, there's no way he could have landed so far from the stairs. If he flipped over, you'd be stepping in his guts right now. If Grotek heard his scream, then he didn't want to fall, so suicide is out, so he didn't jump. That leaves someone or something tossing him over the rail. Someone strong to throw him so far." Someone *very* strong to hurl a grown man fifteen feet and that stunk to me of magic, but I kept quiet on that issue in case I was mistaken.

Taalis looked up, then looked down at the body. "Call me stupid . . . I didn't even catch on to the distance." She shook her head. "I guess that's why you're a Justice."

"I'm a Justice because I owe the crown enough gold the break a mule's back. If I had my way, I'd be in bed with the wife. That being said, I made a vow to Father Sun and Mother Moon to perform my duties to the utmost of my abilities and no wizard of the Academy would dare go back on a vow made to their deities." What I didn't say was that my tenure as Justice proved to be personally rewarding and, dare I say, enjoyable for the most part. Being a Justice allowed me to indulge my curious nature, which was quite often.

"What is that there?" Skakir practically bellowed, pointing across the quarry at a small opening halfway up the cliff opposite to us.

"Cave we found two days ago when cutting laterally over on the cliff face after a nice chunk of flagstone. Nothing much. I wanted to let it air out as a caution, you never know what kind of a gasses could be in there. Then Master Divver died, the work crews were sent home and I completely forgot about it."

Of course, count on a dwarf to spot a cave. Spelunking was in the blood and there wasn't anything more tempting than an unexplored cave to lure a dwarf from duty. Both my short and stout companions gave me pleading looks, practically vibrating in place in their eagerness to see what lay in the dark, dank hole.

I raised my eyebrows and sighed. "Really?"

"Ah, dooncha want ta see what lyes in the wee hool, Niendra?" pleaded Haddeg wringing his hands. Actually wringing them, with big puppy eyes and everything.

"Aye!" Skakhir cut in. "Cuud be gems and the lyke. Gold, lass, gold and a greet big pyle of treasure!"

"By Mother Moon," I whispered, regret at my choice of companions unbalancing my humors for a moment. "All right, when I'm done here, we can go, but I want you two to keep your lips buttoned shut until then."

Both snow dwarfs nodded in unison, eyes gleaming and I could practically hear the *chink chink chink* of gold crowns tumbling about in their imaginations. Sighing, I slipped my backpack off and began to lay out the instruments of my craft: candles, salt, ink from an albino squid, a sheet of parchment and a single turkey feather.

My companions watched curiously as I lit the candles, poured the salt in a complex pattern, laying the feather and ink in the middle of the swirling design. Sitting criss cross, I began to chant the ancient language of magic that fuels spells, although certain words, specific turns of phrases dictated the discipline of magic used. Shaping the words to the task of crafting, I felt the magic flow through my body, a sweet hot rush that sent shivers up my spine, an almost sexual arousal flushing through me. No ordinary human could understand the feeling of casting a spell, sweeter than any wine, more intoxicating than any drug and it took years of discipline not to succumb to the feeling, to burn one's soul to ash in the heated use of too much magic.

The turkey feather rose into the air, hovering two feet above the salt pattern, and ink slowly flowed out of the bottle to float above the piece of parchment and leisurely descended, the feather beginning to trace dark lines on the delicate, white surface as the ink provided the black. I held the sight of Soro's body to my eyes and let the image flow from my mind to the feather and ink for many long minutes, sweat flowing from my brow as I furiously concentrated. The world all around disappeared, only the body of Soro Divver existed in my mind and the spell quill put image to parchment until I believed I'd captured every nuance and detail before letting the spell lapse. The feather softly fell to the ground.

"Impressive," said Taalis as I stood and wiped off my soft brown suede trousers. "Subtle."

I nodded. "Thank you."

"Wudyer lookit that!" exclaimed Haddeg, staring at the parchment. "It's like yer an artist, lass!"

Skakhir elbowed his cousin to take a look. "And she be one, yer dimwit. Lookit how the drawin' be the spittin' image of the boody. Even the splintered ends o' the boons! Amazin'."

"Thanks, guys." I yawned, feeling sleepy and content. Magic does take a toll on a body, even an easy spell like this one. I stoppered the ink bottle and picked up the paper. The drawing of the murder scene was exquisite, rendered almost perfectly down to last detail, good enough that it would serve as evidence long after the body was interred. I blew gently on the paper to dry the ink. "I will need signed witness statements from all three of you as to the veracity of this drawing." After receiving their assents, I nodded and stretched, working the kinks out of my bones. "Give me a moment to grab a bite to eat and we can check out this cave of yours." I really didn't want to explore, but I promised my companions and a mage never goes back on their word.

Never.

FIVE

NOW

HARD KNUCKLES BRUSH MY JAW AS I LEAN TO THE RIGHT. Artelious overextends, leaving himself open to a blow to the ribs which doubles him up hard and I bring my knee up to crunch into his nose, which cracks. Blood gushes upon my trousers as he falls to the paving stones.

"Yield," I say, standing at the ready.

The guardsman spits blood and snarls something intelligible.

"First blood, cousin," says Antonius solemnly. "Yield."

My surprise at learning the Justice and the arrogant DiChenzi are related did not last long when introductions had been completed, although it is less than Antonius' look of shock at finding out that Tennic was my second. It turns out the boy is not much into doing as he is told not matter my grousing and protestations. Children are adaptable and this one adapts to my being a crafter fast enough, fast enough to offer insolence in the form of disobedience.

Artelious DiChenizi leaps to this feet, graceful as a Suurmaen antelope and swings again and I dodge that blow as well. Years of working as a Justice prepared me for fighting and all that training comes back to me quickly despite it being five hundred years in the past.

I kick and my boot hits the guardsman on the thigh and he falls again. I do not wait for him to rise, instead I swing a fist with all my weight behind it and break his jaw, scattering teeth, then kick him again in the stomach. He makes a *hurking* sound and vomit splashes my boots. From behind I hear Tennic swearing under his breath, words that no young person should know. I really must talk to him about his vocabulary. Quite shocking.

"You are done, cousin." Antonius places a boot on the fallen man's hip and shakes a finger at him. "She has won the day and you will surrender the room."

"I never—" begins DiChenzi as he takes a deep breath.

"Enough!" Antonius is furious, I can see that. The veins in his neck and temples stand out and his face has become pomegranate red. "You shamed yourself by attacking after first blood, so now as a Justice and your second I declare this duel done." The words drop with grim finality. "And now we must wake a mage healer to take care of that mouth of yours, which are crowns spent better used for other purposes."

"Thank you, Justice Valerius," I say while Tennic cheers. The boy's enthusiasm fills the tiny courtyard.

Antonius offers me a rueful look. "You have a penchant for making enemies," he says as he assists his cousin to his feet. The man glares his hate at me through the blood that coats his face. His nose is canted heavily to the left. "First the Man Behind and now my thickheaded cousin."

I perform a short bow. "The room will be available soon. I am leaving the city."

This catches Tennic's attention. "Am I coming with?"

What choice do I have? "Of course. For a while until I can get you sorted out."

"Yay!"

"Thish isn't over," DiChenzi slurs. He spits blood at my feet. "We will meet again."

This time I feel a thread of anger. It takes a lot for me to become angry. "Pray that you do not," I say through gritted teeth.

DiChenzi shuts up, but continues to glare as his cousin the Justice hauls him out of the courtyard and into the house where he assists in clearing out the contested room. A remarkably short time later the two exit the room with full bags, DiChezi with a tense, wooden expression, while Antonius Valerius tosses me a thoughtful look. They disappear into the shadows of evening.

Fortunately, I travel light, having no need for many comforts, so I square myself away in my re-acquired room with a disheveled bed and a thoroughly empty wardrobe. I take a few moments looking around, pack on my shoulder before bringing the lack of my former items to the attention of my landlord and he confesses that my possessions, some clothes and a change of boots, have been sold. The look I give him brings a few crowns to my palm and a promise not to trespass against me again. One does not anger a mage more than once.

"What now?" asks my charge as I close the door and sit on the bed.

"I must wait for my familiar," is my reply.

"What's that?"

Before I can reply, there is a heavy knock at my door. Tennic reaches it before I do and throws it open to reveal a man and a woman of unusual aspect. The boy shrieks and dives under the bed, feet disappearing as if by magic and the two stride in, one with a face long and grim, one filled with a manic madness.

The woman is dressed in black leather pants, jacket and boots, her head shaved down to skin, which gleams with a light bronze Coadian hue, her almond eyes slitted dangerously and for a moment I feel a pang for my lost Mirallelle. She holds a leash, the other end of which is tied around the man's neck as he squats on all fours, white hair disheveled over an albino face containing burning eyes and teeth filed to points. He is dressed in bloodied bits of rags that barely conceal his lean, muscular frame. His fingernails are jagged and black.

Their identities are known to me and while I never heard of the Man Behind before today, these two have made reputations that even the dead know, especially considering the numbers of the living they have converted to the deceased. They are the two most notorious criminal figures in Gylleth, assassins and bone breakers, the best in the business and there is only one person in the city who could afford their rate who is not of the nobility. They have evaded Justices for years, seeming to disappear into the shadows at will and rumor has it that they are mages of serious caliber, ones that use their gifts to line their pockets through mayhem and murder.

"Blood and Vicious," I say, offering a nod. "What brings you to my room this evening?" As if I did not know.

"The Man Behind wants his boy back." The woman, Blood, has a beautiful contralto that shimmers pleasantly across my skin.

Vicious gargles something unintelligible, staring at me with a vacuous intelligence. There is nothing remotely sane in that gaze. Drool drops from his bottom lip.

Casting a spell without knowing what kind of countermeasures your opponents possess invites calamity, so I merely stand passive and ask, "What boy?"

Blood smiles slowly. It is not a pleasant sight. "Funny. Hand him over and the matter will be forgotten." She produces a stiletto from beneath her jacket and twirls it between her fingers. "If not, you will be."

Cute. I take a breath so I can sigh and consider my options, which are dangerously few. One: Hand the boy over. Of course, that will not happen because, for some reason I cannot name, he is important to my mission. Two: Do not and fight two on one and while they cannot kill me, *per se*, they can do tremendous damage to this body which will delay my quest considerably.

Or . . .

"I think I will speak to the Man Behind personally, if you would be so kind."

Vicious blinks and snarls, more drool falling from his lips while Blood cocks her head to the side and rubs her chin in thought. "Escort service is not something we do," she finally says.

"You are a mercenary pair, are you not?"

Her laughter chimes throughout the room. Vicious just barks like hound until she tugs his leash. "Of a sort."

I remove my pack carefully and pull out a fat purse, spilling gold into my palm. "Five gold crowns ought to buy Tennic and I an audience with the Man Behind, don't you think?"

Blood's smile is answer enough.

"So, you're the one wants to take one of my best earners." The voice is casual, almost bored, deep, cultured and oddly youthful.

I nod.

The man behind the screen, a silhouette cast upon white silk, nods in return and says, "Why in the name of Yrusis' sagging breasts would I do that?"

Invoking the Goddess of Peace, Love and Prosperity in such a manner surely is not the way into her good heart, but I do not feel the need to correct him.

True to their word, Blood and Vicious escorted me to the Man Behind, a move I know to be more than a little dangerous, but my ability to give a cuss is severely curtailed by my death. Apparently I left most of my fear back in Tilla's Hold.

The two assassins led me blindfolded through the sewers (being dead did not kill my sense of smell) a long way with many twists and turns until we exited the sewers (and the smell) in favor of a tunnel system that consists of many large rooms or caverns. After what seemed like an hour I found the blindfold removed and myself in a chamber made of well-dressed stone with colorfully pornographic tapestries on the walls and thick rugs on the floor. Coal burned in a stove in the corner, the smoke piped up through the ceiling. A large, wood-framed silk screen stood in one corner with a light behind throwing a shadow of a sitting man upon the white fabric. The Man Behind.

Now Blood stands against one wall looking bored while Vicious squats at her feet and drools, smiling, his pointy teeth wet. I consider the silhouette as beside me Tennic remains still, obviously petrified but holding his ground well enough. The boy does not lack courage.

"Money. I have money and I will pay for the boy's freedom."

"You paid Blood and Vicious handsomely for the pleasure of my company, I'll give you that, but you'd have to be Royalty to afford the boy's freedom. He's my best earner and has the potential to be somebody of note in my organization."

Blah, blah, blah. Too much noise, not enough negotiating. "Gone from one of the best to *the* best so quickly, eh? Name your price."

On the opposite side of the room Blood rubs her bald pate and Vicious says, "Gah, blarg, voggie blah!" and drools some more.

"Five hundred crowns," is the reply. "Gold."

No words are uttered after that pronouncement, the silence a heavy thing in the air and the two assassins smile, waiting for my response, for me to shout or scream or fling up my hands in exasperation.

Five hundred gold crows is enough to purchase half of Orthangar, enough to live off of for the rest of one's life and leave enough for the next four generations. It is a sum so outrageous the Man Behind knows I will fling it back in his face with a curse, he believes this with a moral certainty. I feel this, I know this and it amuses me to no end. People in all their complexities are a wonder, but they also carry inside them a consistent predictability that makes me ponder why the gods created us in the first place. Entertainment perhaps?

My answer to this insane sum is simple enough. "Done."

Both Blood and Vicious become deathly still as the man behind the screen moves his head slightly and suddenly there is violence in the air. My hands clench as the scene hangs in front of me like a delicate painting and I know that one wrong word will bring blood and death.

The assassins stare at me as Blood slowly reaches up and scratches her nose. From behind the screen the crime lord says, "Impossible."

I smile and even Vicious flinches while Tennic does his best imitation of a statue. "Not impossible. I can have the money to you within the hour of my exit from . . . wherever this is."

Vicious drools and scratches his armpit, whining slightly. "All right, done," says the Man Behind. "You will be escorted to where you need to go."

"Not necessary nor is it wanted." I put every inch of steel left in my body into those words. "I do not trust these two. Drop me off at the Dhiione Market and I will meet them at the boarding house soon after. Do not have me followed, I will know." The Dhiione Market is a good fifteen-minute walk from my room and I wanted them to think I have squirreled the crowns away in a secret location. I hoped Dhiione, the God of War and Valor, would look kindly upon my endeavor, but I doubt it. "Oh, the boy comes with me."

"No."

"Yes. I do not trust you, so I will take him with me. Do not tell me you cannot find a lone Irramerian crafter with a boy at her heels, it is insulting."

Again the scene becomes delicately still until Blood blinks rapidly and shakes her head. "Done," says the Man Behind. "But if gold doesn't cross my palms by dawn, you will not see the sun rise fully."

"Understood."

And we are once again blindfolded and led through a maze of tunnels, my hand on Tennic's shoulder. His steps are heavy and I can almost smell his fear over the stench of the sewers as we enter them, so I give his shoulder a gentle squeeze. Shortly we find ourselves outside in the gaslight of the city in an alley that smells of rotten fruit and quite possibly a dead cat. I look out to see the dark granite face of the Dhiione citadel a half block away, the stalls against the walls closed for the night although there are plenty of people taking their ease with a fine stroll on a warm summer's evening under the gas lights.

"Are you dead?"

I stop suddenly, looking down at Tennic who stares up at me guilelessly. "What?"

He repeats himself. "Are you dead?"

"Why do you ask such a thing? Do I look dead?" I raise my arms and waggle my fingers.

A tentative smile lights the boy's face. "You only breathe when you want to speak and you stand so still." He points to a couple across the street who walk hand in hand. "See that? People gesture when they talk, they twitch and blink and make all sorts of motions, but you don't. You're like a statue of Aris that comes to life to talk or do something, but when you're not doing anything, you're still and your skin never changes color. Even Coadians and Irramerians can blush, but you don't. And I figure you must be really, really old because you talk funny. Not that you don't speak right, but the way you say things, using really old words sometimes and such. Rusty Tyllet's nan talks a little like that and she's old, although I'll bet you're older than she is, even though you don't have wrinkles, which is because you're dead, you don't age or nothing." He finished with a deep breath as if telling me all this reasoning took a toll on his body and mind.

It is not within me to lie to him, yet I cannot tell the whole truth as it is hard for me to accept sometimes. "Yes," I say simply.

Tennic's eyes light up and I hold up a hand. "Not now, though. I will tell you the story when I feel the time is appropriate," I promise to his crestfallen face. He nods slowly.

"What does appropriate mean?"

I stare at him, realizing that he lacks a decent education and it up to me fill in his knowledge gaps. "Fitting, proper."

"Ah. Good word."

Taking him by hand, I lead him through streets glowing by greenish gaslight as fog begins to lift off the cobbles. The sight still startles even after a couple of years of acquaintance and I marvel once again at the ingenuity of humans.

In my room I pack a bag of meagre belongings while Tennic stares, holding himself still yet watching my every move as if his life depends on it. When I am done I open a concealed compartment on my backpack and my belt, spilling gold crowns onto the bed.

"Where did you get all that?" the boy breathes, awed. He moves forward to run his fingers over the coins. I let him.

"Ramashur."

He straightens with a gasp. "Ramashur? But it's filled with hungry dead people and folks say they eat the living. How did you survive that?"

"As you said, little man, I am not alive. The dead don't bother me." Five hundred gold crowns, many in twenty-crown increments. Coins used by bankers and merchants who deal in large sums. "If I need money, I simply walk in and take it." Oddly enough, it is just that simple.

Treasure hunters by the score have tried to plunder lost Ramashur, but are immediately attacked by the undead, who can easily sense the living and the freshly killed find themselves joining their ranks. Each bite of living flesh rejuvenates rotting flesh and if the living would only leave the place alone for more than a decade, the undead will be an unpleasant memory, but the greed and desperation of people will never let that happen. Even arch mages are too smart to try to penetrate Ramashur's secrets.

"Like your own personal bank."

I nod. "Yes. But a dangerous one."

Hand in hand, we leave the boarding house and I halt in the middle of the street where we wait. It does not take long.

"Where's our money?" The contralto slides around me and I wish I could feel a flush of something, anything. Desire perhaps.

I know Blood is standing behind me and has a weapon in hand, but there are enough people taking their ease with a leisurely stroll that she will not risk stabbing me and getting caught by the guard or a Justice. Beside me I sense Tennic's trembling as fear courses through him and I place a hand on his shoulder. "Your money is waiting for you. Where is your partner?"

"Around."

"Five hundred gold crowns as I said. It is lying in a heap on my bed."

"It better be."

Unnecessary threat. I know she will try to kill us if I have stiffed her and she knows I know this and she knows my chances against the pair of them ranges from very slim to just go and buy a comfortable coffin.

"We are leaving now. Do not try to follow us, I know will know if you do." I know no such thing, but I want them to think I have some witchy way about me and I turn to see the tall woman a few steps away covered in a hooded cloak. Eyes like brown glass glitter at me. She nods once.

The boy and I walk away and as we pass an alley clothed in shadows I say, "Oh, there you are, Vicious."

From the dark comes, "Blegh, argh," then silence. We leave the assassin to his darkness and gather Artoch from a sleepy stable boy who did not want to be disturbed at the late hour. Soon the city retreats behind us as we head toward the Callic Pass and sylvan nation of Dorendiriar, the past at my back, the future beckoning.

SIX

THEN

AFTER QUIZZING TAALIS OVER ANY CONNCETION between the cave appearing and Divver's death (there appeared to be none, but that didn't mean the timing wasn't suspicious). First the cave entrance appears, then Divver is murdered. Coincidence? Perhaps, but it was excuse enough to investigate the cave the dwarves so wanted to spelunk. Leave no stone unturned, no cave unexplored.

It was Haddeg who entered the hole first, torch in hand and a look of fervent anticipation on his weathered face, like a child waiting for gifts on Phezdes Feast Day. Skakhir stood behind wringing his hands in excitement, goldlust and the thrill of adventure warring in his dwarfy little heart. Me, I expected to find old animal bones and desiccated dung, nothing more, nothing less.

Reaching the cave at the midway point up the cliff hadn't been difficult, the face had been cut in a series of ten-foot terraces that allowed me to jump up, fix a rope, then haul my companions up while Taalis tended to the remains of Soro Divver now that the evidence had been recorded. Besides, she said she had no stomach for underground adventures and I didn't blame her much seeing how I would rather be drinking a jack of ale and considering my next move in the investigation.

"I leave caves to the dwarves and take the forests for myself," she'd said with a grimace. My companions were so enthralled by the mysterious cave that they didn't bother to respond. She shrugged and said that Divver would be transported to Caenwylln to be interred in the family mausoleum. I wished her well.

"What yer seein'?" Skakhir shouted the second Haddeg's booted feet disappeared into the small opening.

I rolled my eyes. Dwarves.

"This is beein' interestin'!" came the reply. "This be noo a natural wee cave, cousin."

That piqued my interest. "What do you mean?" I placed a hand on Skakhir's shoulder to keep him from bulling forward. "Is it an abandoned mine or something?"

"I mean this be noo carved by hand or nature." Haddeg's words sounded odd, almost hollow. "By my clenched butt cheeks, this be noothin' lyke I ever seen, lass."

Knowing that Skakhir would never forgive me if I entered before him, I let go of his shoulder and he bolted through the opening quicker than a greased eel. A moment later an awed 'ooh' and 'ahh' floated out.

"Oh, by Mother Moon," I swore. With a nudge to Bat that sent him to the nearest tree to rest for a I while, I sighed, knelt down and crawled in, following the light of Haddeg's torch.

Just inside the entrance I was able to stand, the ceiling more than a foot above, but that's not what captured my attention. It was the walls and floor . . . they were of some black stone, utterly smooth, polished, and glistening, with crystals imbedded into the rock sucking up the light and spitting it out in warm beams. I rubbed my hand along the wall, marveling at the cool slickness beneath my skin. The smooth surface ran in a semi-circle and I realized we three stood in a tunnel that led slightly downward and arrow straight into darkness.

"This is noo dwarf craftsmanship, nor hooman, lass," Skakhir marveled. "I never saw the lyke, yer know."

"A mage made this," I said, still running my hands over the wall. "What are these crystals?"

"If I'm not mistaken," said Haddeg. "It be a mixture of various types of quartz. Amatrine, agate, and rutilated being the most dominant." For once his voice lacked the heaviness of its dwarven brogue. He sounded like a school teacher giving a lesson. "But all these different kinds of quartz, at least a dozen or so, shouldn't be all jumbled together like this. It doesn't make much sense."

"You're right," affirmed Skakhir, nodding. "Most passing strange. It can only be magic, but what kind?"

I knew it! By Father Sun I just *knew* they'd been bamboozling humans with their thick dwarfy accents and my grin stretched wide as I answered, "Weel, that's the wee question, isn't it just? A geomancer cood doo it, laddies, and make noo mystake aboot it."

Both snow dwarves turned beet red in the yellow torchlight and Haddeg said, "By my clenched butt cheeks, it's a wee bit of spoort yer havin' with us noow, isn't it, lassie?"

"Laying it on thick, aren't you, short stuff?"

Skakhir held up a hand and Haddeg's mouth *snicked* shut. "She's got us fair, cousin. Our marvelin' did us in." He shook his head. "At least Niendra is one of the good ones."

"Why guys? Why the bumpkin dwarf routine?"

The two confirmed in Khulasch for a few minutes with a lot of hand waving and exclamations that rang down the crystalline tunnel. When they were done they both turned and gave me a small bow. "Sorry, lass," said Haddeg, "for fooling you for so long. It was unfair considering our friendship. Call it a force of habit, but if humans think we're rather stone-headed northern dwarves, they let their guards down at cards."

I goggled. "You talk like that so people think you're a pair of idiots, so you can win at *cards*?"

"Aye, that's so," they affirmed with sheepish grins.

"By Mother Moon and Father Sun, you are the both of you morons!" I ran my fingers through my braids. "All this time, for four years?"

"But it's been all in good sport, lass," said Haddeg. "We do win quite a bit at cards, you know."

Mother Moon save my sanity! I rubbed my eyes and began to chuckle, a slow hitching of my lungs that evolved into a solid belly laugh that shook my entire body and by the time tears were rolling down my cheeks both dwarves joined me. I laughed until my lungs began to burn and my throat ached, until I could barely breathe and the blood suffused my face to the extent that my head felt ready to pop like a soap bubble.

After a while, my side hurting and Bat's emotional queries ringing in my mind, we stood there on shaking legs and wiped our faces. I sent a mental hug to my familiar and took a deep breath and picked up the torch where Haddeg dropped it. The light bounced off of the walls in jagged spears providing plenty to see by.

"Okay, boys," I said, still grinning. "Let's see what this mysterious wizard made."

The dwarves nodded in excitement. "This was obviously the end of the tunnel, the quarry workers opened it to the outside world, but didn't bother to explore." Haddeg pointed to the small exit. "Whoever it was may have had plans to dig further but they stopped because the quarry was already here." Not one of us could figure out why this place was built so close to the quarry. I chewed on that but needed more information.

"The quarry hasn't been around that long." I ran my fingers through my braids. "Are you saying this is less than five years old?" Why would a geomancer dig so close to a quarry? Perhaps as a quick egress to obtain necessary supplies?

"Newer," said Skakhir. Hadded nodded in agreement. "Except for the debris from the pick axes, I don't see much dust or insect activity. My guess is less than five, more than two."

Father Sun! That meant that some wizard was casting major geomantic spells within the kingdom most likely without royal approval, a heady crime and one that queen Bet probably wouldn't forgive. I looked at the various examples of quartz the mage drew forth to decorate the tunnel and knew that they must be one of considerable power and talent, not to be taken lightly if they were still in Gylleth. The smart move would be to head back to Ramashur and report to Lord Petre Ul-Mavre, but he was ill and bothering the queen with this without further evidence would be foolhardy. My grin stretched tight as I realized I wanted to have a bit of an adventure myself. I reasoned that Grotek would wait. Nothing wrong with taking a break now and again.

I gave the two a short bow and pointed toward the dark. "Well, let's go explore, shall we?"

With excited grins, Haddeg and Skakhir scurried off down the tunnel like excited kids with me chaperoning their heels, the light reflected from the quartz all around. The air felt cool and dry, not moist like most caves, but this was no natural construct made by time, water and the slow shrug of the earth, this was a crafting by magic and an impressive one at that. We walked for a goodly amount of time, our footfalls echoing oddly off the smooth walls, before we came to a three-way split: left, right and straight ahead.

"Well, lass, where shall our feet take us?" asked Haddeg as he peered down each tunnel.

I raised my eyebrows. "What happened to the intrepid dwarven explorers? You decide."

"Left it is," said Skakhir, urging his cousin in that direction. "I feel kind of lefty."

I raised an eyebrow. "Lefty?"

Skakhir looked down his large, dwarven nose and wrinkled it about. "Never underestimate a dwarf's feelings when it comes to caves, lass. Trust the nose. The nose knows." He turned left and we followed.

It wasn't long before the tunnel ended in a cave that wasn't a cave but a fifteen-by-fifteen room occupied by a cot, a half-filled bookshelf, a stout, banded oaken chest secured with a large, imposing padlock of cold iron. A skeleton covered in desiccated flesh and dressed in moldering clothes lay on the cot as if in repose, arms at its side and wisps of brown hair still attached to the paper-thin flesh that stretched tight across the bones. Salt runes decorated the floor around the cot, runes I'd seen before while studying at the Hidden Academy. The corpse was old enough that the smell of rot had long since dissipated and the only thing I could catch a whiff of was dust and moldering parchment.

"I think we found our geomancer," I said, breaking the silence.

Haddeg looked up. "What makes you say that?"

I pointed to the salt runes. "See that one? That's the rune for Wom, Goddess of the Earth and that one is the symbol for Mother Moon in her aspect as the Goddess of Magic. The rest are a bit more cryptic, but I think they have something to do with binding, moving or transporting, and that one that looks like a fish hook is definitely a rune of shaping. Perhaps this person was in the middle of casting when they died, maybe to enlarge this tunnel system, or to finish it." I considered the body and the runes for another moment. "But I can't be sure. All I have are best guesses."

Skakhir hefted his axe. "Well, then, he won't be needing this chest, will he?"

"NO!" I yelled. Too late.

The dwarf's double bitted axe thudded into the lock with spectacular force, clanging against the cold iron with the sound of rending metal and the result was equally spectacular. A bright bolt of lightning burst from the keyhole to the axe with a loud thunderclap that shook our bones and the room. Skakhir was flung hard against the wall whereupon he slowly slid to the floor, white hair curled and smoking, eyes dazed and unfocused. He slowly slumped to his side and lay there as his hair continued to smolder.

We were at his side in an instant, checking his pulse (fortunately he had one) and slapping his cheeks. Haddeg patted Skakhir's moustache and beard before the flames could devour his face.

"Oooh," breathed Skakhir, blinking rapidly. "That . . . hurt . . . a lot." After a minute he managed sit unaided, although his eyes were still a bit crossed. The smell of burnt hair filled the room.

"Idiot," I breathed, much relieved. "You muck about a wizard's things you're bound to find some protective wards." I pointed to his axe, the blade melted and chewed through by the lightning bolt. "That took the brunt of what would have killed you."

"My axe!" he cried in alarm, snatching up the weapon and cradling it to his chest. "Ah, my poor baby."

"Baby?" I whispered to Haddeg while Skakhir mourned, rocking back and forth.

"He made that axe, it was his rite of passage into manhood," came the reply. "He's had it for over seventy years. This is a grave loss, lass. He's lost a piece of himself."

Oh. This was an interesting bit of information, a new look into the minds of dwarvenkind. I probed further. "Is this true for every dwarf? Are your people so warlike that making a weapon is a sign of maturity?"

"Aye, lass. We are a warlike people because we've had to become one. From humans to sylvan, knobblegrotts to trolls and snot goblins, all made war on us in olden days for our gold and gems. For what we were able to wrench from the ground and create in our forges, wonders that others seem to prize above all else and it has been so for as long as we remember. Then the dragons came for what is ours, taking our hoards and homes, killing us by the thousands and we were on the verge of losing everything, forcing us to leave our northern mountain homes." He licked his lips. "It wasn't until fifty years ago when your queen cemented the Great Alliance between our three nations, Gylleth, Dorindiriar and Gaor, that we realized some stability. Our people thrive now and with the help of human mages, the dragons were sent flying away to lick their wounds and plot revenge and recovery of what they lost."

The country bumpkin was gone, replaced by a sad-eyed person with a great weight on his shoulders, holding the hands of his cousin who lay on the floor recuperating from a shock that would've killed a human. This made Haddeg and Skakhir more . . . relatable somehow, more real to me and I smiled softy at my friends. "Well, you two are still grand idiots for leaping without looking."

"Aye, lass," Skakhir groaned, trying to sit up. Haddeg aided him and soon he was on his feet, a little singed around the edges. He gingerly set his ruined axe down. "A hard lesson. Next time I'll leave magical matters to you."

I nodded. "That is wise. Now, let's see what this mage wanted to protect." I closed my eyes and looked through the Father Sun tattoos that graced my eyelids and concentrated. A world of runes greeted my closed eyes, a multicolored tapestry of Dendrich script that flowed about and through the chest. "Whoever this mage was they were skilled. These wards are intricate, very complex, woven together subtly. Wow, this is some work." The Hidden Academy was protected by wards more complex, skeins of magic so complicated it took my breath away and far more powerful, enough to annihilate any one of the Six Kingdoms in destructive orgy of magical energy. However, these wards were pretty impressive and would take a few hours to unravel . . . one strand at a time and I told the dwarves to relax for a while.

It turned out my companions were right after all. Adventure, mysterious happenings and very possibly some sort of treasure considering the room didn't look like it had been looted. Everything appeared to be neat and tidy, from the tomes on the bookshelf to the body on the cot lying as if in repose, dead for a couple of years if I were to hazard a guess. I sat criss cross and continued to stare through my eyelids, lifting my hands to direct magical unraveling through my fingertips, counterspells to the wards that protected the chest. Not really the bailiwick of a crafter, but I had made it my purpose at the Hidden Academy to study several different disciplines. Most mages do so to increase usefulness.

If time passed I was not aware of it, my full focus was bent on carefully untangling the gossamer strands of magic one by one, ward by ward until holes appeared in the brightly colored skein covering the chest. *There!* A strand that seemed to be part of a ward to tear flesh from bone neatly clipped from the rest, weakening the protection. *There!* A ward of weakness designed to steal all energy from an intruder's muscles.

More wards, more protections, each one insidious and dangerous, a good half of them fatal in some grisly manner or somesuch and I wondered what lay inside this wood and iron surface that needed such protection.

Another thread pulled, clipped and let loose, the ward attached to it faded into mist and revealed another hole in the skein, a flaw that showed me that my unraveling of this tapestry of magic was working.

Strand after strand cut, ward after ward, unraveled and erased from the surface of the chest until, suddenly I found myself back to the real world, sweating and panting heavily. I sat a couple of feet from the chest, my limbs shaking as if I'd run a mile or three and my skin felt like I'd stepped into steam room, all flushed and sensitive.

"Ah, there you be, lass." Haddeg's gravelly voice startled me and I looked to where he sat against the far wall, stuffing what looked like a whole roasted chicken into his mouth.

I blinked. "What?"

"Yer bin gone a wee whyle, ain't yer?"

"Why—why are you talking like that?" What happened? Why did I feel so dizzy? I knew dismantling wards was hard work, but I shouldn't feel like my limbs were about to fall off the trunk of my body.

Haddeg's eyes flicked to a point behind my back before resuming his stare. "Ach, I always talk lyke this, lass. Yer must bee a wee gud tyred seein' how you been oot for a gud whyle starin' at that chest. Don't that bee ryght, lady Taalis?"

Oh. Right. I craned my head around to see Taalis the sylvan overseer staring down at me, a concerned expression on her severe face. "What your dwarven friend is trying to say, Justice Niendra, is that you've been sitting there for the past two days." Skakhir entered the room, eating an apple and tossing me a broad wink.

"Must be why my bottom hurts so bad." Not just hurt, but a profound ache that traveled up through the small of my back to the base of my neck. Two days? I tried for a deep breath but my lungs could only continue their panting rhythm. I was always pretty good with wards, but the protections on this chest amazed me.

"Wee didn't wanna wake you uup, lass," said Skakhir, looking mildly concerned. He seemed ill at ease, holding himself as if he felt naked and I remembered the loss of his beloved axe. "Yer wee bat's been flappin' 'round yer head, snooglin' up to yer, but hee floo ooff a lyttle whyle agoo."

Yes, I could feel Bat chewing on a juicy pear and his joy at my mental petting and I bid him to finish before he returned. I looked back to the chest and the cot beyond and its grisly occupant. "Good thing you didn't. I was untangling the ward and if you had disturbed me it might have activated them."

"Bad, I assume?" asked Taalis.

"They could have destroyed this entire complex."

Haddeg nodded. "Bad then," he mumbled around a greasy mouthful of chicken.

"While you were gone into your trance," Taalis said, "I took the liberty of checking out this little collection of books." She held picked one up and flipped through the pages. "Treatises on magic, theorems and what looks to be a textbook on geomancy, minus the actual spells."

"Those should be in the Hidden Academy!" I blurted, alarmed. In the hands of the uninitiated, those books could cause grave harm. I looked to the skeleton on the cot. "Maybe that's how he or she died . . . they created this place using theories of geomancy rather than having studied it at the Academy. Magical backlash from a misplaced rune or incantation can be devastating."

Taalis nodded while the two dwarves greedily stared at the chest. I knew what was in their stout little hearts and I had to smile a bit.

With Taalis's help I stood, knees knocking and sweat dripping and my bottom feeling numb. It took a couple of minutes before I could finally stand unaided. "Skakhir."

"Aye?"

"Do the honors."

The dwarf didn't have to be told twice. He used a pick from the quarry to break the lock and opened the chest and began to rummage inside. Papers flew from his fists, a couple of blankets and a set of leather armor that had seen better days.

Abruptly, the dwarf became still, staring into the chest. "Oh, *yesss*," he crooned in delight. "Aren't yer a beauty." He reached and picked something up.

It was a hammer, an ordinary war hammer by the shape but not by the material. Silver from handle to the wicked spike behind the blunt head, it gleamed with bitter violence and held a sheen of magic, a subtle aura that only a mage could see, a shine like a slick of lamp oil on the surface of a still pond. Skakhir swung the shining weapon about his head once, twice, three times, a wide grin splitting his beard before he settled it into a loop on his belt. "This'll doo, lass, this'll doo."

"Mother Moon, Skakhir, you ought to be careful," I warned, my heart beating rapidly. There were stories about magic items that could curl a dwarf's beard, cautionary tales not for the faint of heart. "That's a wizard weapon."

"Aye, that I already knoow."

"Wizard weapons are *dangerous*," said Taalis, taking a step back. Haddeg looked uneasy himself, not quite sure what to make of his cousin's new toy. "It could be cursed."

"Is noo cursed." Skakhir folded his massive arms, face setting into stubborn lines. "I'm a dwarf, I knoo these things." He looked to me. "Yer either trust me on thys, lass, or yer don', but I tell yer troo aboot thys."

"He's ryte, lass," said Haddeg, stroking his beard, still eyeing the gleaming weapon. "Dwarves knoo weapons and magic too, just lyke magefolk. Our magic roons deep in our blood and I trust me cousin, I doo. It be magic, true, but if Skakhir senses no mean turn to it, then he be safe."

The hammer didn't bear any runes, no dire sayings to freeze the blood, it merely lay in Skakhir's belt shiny and untarnished, which made me believe it definitely *not* silver. "All right, keep it." I raised a finger. "But be careful with that thing." It wasn't like I could force the thing from his hands, dwarves were notoriously resilient to magecraft.

"Aye, lass."

Taalis shuffled some of the papers Skakhir threw aside with the toe of a boot. "What's this?" she said, picking up a single, age-yellowed page. She scanned it for a moment. "Interesting. It's in ancient Estian, a dialect that hasn't been heard for many shifts."

I leaned in, intrigued. "What does it say?"

The sylvan recited in a somber voice:

One for Phezdes for He is Kind,
One for Dhiione for the Brave,
One for Father Sun to clear the Mind,
One for Aris to voyage from the Grave,
One for Wom to leave clutching Earth,
One for Himir to stave off Sleep,
One for Yrusis for a Rebirth,
One for Mother Moon for magic Steep,
One for Tilla to leave her Keep.

"Verse," spat Haddeg in disgust. "Always verse wyth the mage folk. Why can't they speek plain?"

SEVEN

NOW

THE FIRE CRACKLES WARMLY BETWEEN US as we relax on our bed rolls, the jagged walls of the pass leer down upon us in the dark and Tennic belches contentedly, patting his full stomach. Rabbit bones lie in a nice tidy pile on the tin plate at his feet. The kid does not know the first thing about preparing food, but he is handy with a rock and managed to bag a brace of coneys.

"You can cook," he remarks happily.

"That is nothing. My wife is," I pause from where I sit criss cross on the opposite side of the fire, "*was* the chef in the family." Melancholy grips me but does not reach my face, yet the boy senses it anyway.

"Sorry," he says, shifting a little closer for warmth. In the mountains the nights are colder than the valleys, but it is of no matter to me. I could stand in the middle of the burning wood, humming a happy tune while my flesh cooks and I would not feel a thing.

I hear Artoch's gentle breathing as he sleeps soundly nearby, a sleep aided by a minor cantrip so he will not be spooked if trouble occurs, as I suspect it might. "No need. It was a long time ago." A long time ago, but the need for justice is still an ember within my breast. Soon I will begin the next phase of my quest. A slow, bubbling sense of satisfaction comforts me.

"If you don't mind, Niendra, how did you die?"

It is the first time anyone has asked me that, which is not surprising because only Tennic knows of my state. My hand brushes the yellow scarf around my neck and I am hesitant to answer, but I realize that I have established a connection to the boy, he is dear somehow and it is time I invest in some trust. My fingers unwind the small knot at the base of my neck and I remove the scarf.

Tennic gasps. Not surprising considering the jagged catgut stitches along my flesh keeping the hole in my neck shut. The lips of the wound are still visible, clean and straight, the wound deep. "Someone cut the large vein here and I bled to death. This is the only wound that will not heal."

The boy looked a little ill. Ill and fascinated. "Did—did it hurt?"

I hide the stitching once more with the yellow scarf, knotting it firmly. My own handiwork, done in a mirror. "Not really. The knife was very sharp. My death was quick."

He ponders that for a moment. "How did you come back then?"

An easy question. I smile and reach into my pack and pull out the bejeweled rod. "This was inside my sarcophagus in the Catacombs of Justice, its magic brought me back from Tilla's Hold." The rod glints in the firelight, blue, red and green light shining through the beautiful baubles. I do not know why I reveal the source of my return here under the stars in the middle of a pass, halfway to sylvan territory, it is more trust than I intend, but it seems right. I have learned to trust my instincts for they are rarely wrong. I return the rod to a hidden compartment I had sewn into the bottom the pack.

I can feel the shock that runs through Tennic's body. He says, "You were a Justice?"

"You have no reason to fear me, boy," I reply.

He shakes his head. "I don't, but I didn't know there were any witch Justices, I thought they were big warriors and the like."

A smile actually breaks through to my face and it feels good. "In my time, Justices were picked not just from warriors. Why, Justice Orliss was an elderly man in his seventieth year. It was his mind the queen valued; his wits so sharp you could shave the hair off the back of your arm. Justices were chosen from all walks of life, many unusual. I guess you can say I am rather unusual, yes?"

"Yeah." He grins and I return the expression, surprised at my capability to do so.

It comes to me that in our short association that the boy and I are like puzzle pieces fitting together snugly and the look in his eye tells me he feels this strange bond as well. Not once in our journey to the pass did he try to bolt, instead staying with me the entire ride, giving me the burden of his youthful, near boundless trust. The trust of a child. I could no more betray him than I could stick my elbow into my ear.

We sit for a while in comfortable silence, staring at the fire for a long while before a sudden tingle itches the back of my mind.

One thing about the Hidden Academy, one learns many different wards and the ones surrounding our little campsite at a hundred feet work perfectly. I am very glad I paid attention in class. I close my eyes and turn my head.

"Duck, boy," I urge. He does not hesitate, slamming into the ground as a crossbow bolt pierces the air where his head had been a second before. It hits me above my right breast, knocking me on my back.

"Dammit!" The voice, deep, male and angry, slices through the darkness.

Two figures enter the light. One a familiar Coadian hue in a long cloak, the other a tall, slender man with head of dark hair slicked back from his forehead and clothes like pitch, his leonine features marred by the snarl twisting his lips. I watch them advance, my eyes in slits.

"You hit the woman," snarls the man, handsome face tarnished by dark emotions.

"I didn't mean to," replies Blood, lifting her heavy crossbow. At their feet Tennic whimpers. "That bolt was meant for you, rat, but now that this woman is dead, maybe you can help us."

Tennic begins to wail. "You killed Niendra!"

"That much is obvious." The man shrugs and casually kicks Tennic hard enough to drive the breath from his lungs. As he squirms, gasping and spitting, the man places one booted foot on his hip. "Those coins were old, rat. Centuries old and were minted in Ramashur. How did this woman get coins from the city of the dead? Tell us her secret and we'll let you live."

Mother Moon! How stupid could I be? We would have been better off if I melted the coins into bars.

After a minute, the boy catches his breath and I can almost feel the pain in his stomach from where the man kicked him. "Ask her yourself," he snarls, showing some real spine.

Blood laughs. "Oh ho! The little rat bites."

"Harder than you can *imagine*!" The feral snarl on Tennic's face surprises her, but not as much as the slim little misericord he produces from a hidden sheath at his ankle and suddenly thrusts into the man's calf. He pulls the blade free along with a spurt of blood and thrusts again.

Tennic is a dead shot with a rock, but he is better with a knife as he demonstrated when skinning the coneys. The man howls, falling hard on the ground and Blood pulls her own blade.

That is my cue. I vault to my feet, my cloak billowing as I leap forward. Blood does not see me, she is too intent on killing Tennic and the man is writhing, so my boot catches her unawares, her knee snapping, folding in a manner not natural. It is her turn to howl. I prepare to finish her off with a quick thrust of a knife.

I do not see the blow coming, only the change of perspective from standing to lying on the ground with the cold stars overhead. The man comes into view and places a boot on my throat. I can feel the blood from his calf trickle down my jaw line. "Don't move." His voice is thick with pain and anger barely held in check. To Blood he says, "Are you all right, sweetie?" His eyes never leave mine.

Sweetie?

Blood responds, "She is faster than she looks. She's trained." A grunt. "I'll be fine once you spell my leg, love."

The man nods once and says, "You know who we are, correct?"

I grunt and the pressure on my throat eases so I can draw breath. "It is only obvious. You are Vicious. Nice change of character."

Vicious shrugs, drawing a musket from within his cloak and pointing it off to the left. "It allows me to walk about during the day without being recognized. Surprising what a wig and false teeth can do, yes?" He slowly kneels and yanks the bolt free, perhaps in an attempt to torture me but I feel nothing. Fortunately, the head is not barbed, although I know this particular wound will heal slowly over time. "Turn onto your belly. Misbehave and the boy dies."

I comply.

Strong hands bind mine and then my feet as well. Before too long I am trussed up like a turkey at Midharvest Feast and Tennic is as well. The two assassins sit next to the fire and compare injuries.

"Not bad," says Vicious of the stab wound to his calf as the blood flow slows to a trickle. He bandages it neatly. "It's yours I worry about."

Blood grimaces and snarls, her Coadian features haunted by agony. "I think she broke my godsloving knee."

Sighing, Vicious tenderly takes his partner's knee in his large hands and probes it with his fingers, muttering under his breath as she hisses in pain. I feel the magic of a small casting, confirming that at least one of the pair is a mage of some sort. "Yes," he murmurs finally. "There's damage to the ligaments, muscles and tendons, but nothing I can't handle, dear."

"Thank you, love," she responds, caressing his cheek. Vicious leans into her hand like a dog seeking affection.

"Hold still," he says and begins to chant while his hands pass over the injured leg. I feel the magic in the air like prickle one's skin receives before lightning strikes and the smell of ozone permeates the air. A faint, reddish glow emanates from Vicious's hands. The entire spell lasts for less than a minute and when he stops, Blood stands slowly, testing her knee.

"Perfect as always, love."

His smile sickens me.

"Sorcerer," I grate. "Body mage, healer."

"At your service," he grunts, standing. He tips me a nod. "I prefer the term Holistic Sorcerer, if you will. It's more precise." Sweat covers his face. "And apropos."

"A follower of Phezdes or Father Sun has no business being an assassin," I state flatly, hiding the sudden anger that suffuses me. "It's insincere".

"Who said I follow Father Sun or Phezdes?" He smiles at me as if I am a dimwitted child. "I know you must have some difficulty understanding all this, but not everyone worships the gods. They don't demand our love and devotion; they merely request it."

"You studied at the Academy." Not a question.

"Of course, but I left before unlocking my full potential at the Pillar of Sholtoth."

"But why?" Not unlocking your true powers at the Pillar condemns the mage to wait possibly decades for their power to grow to their full potential. How does one live with that, know that such might is but one ritual away?

Viscous laughed . . . well, viciously. "And be beholden to a gaggle of mages hiding in the desert? Going to where they tell me to go? Sitting around trying to unlock the magics of the ancients? Doing what they tell me to do? No thank you very much, young lady. I work for myself." He gestured toward Blood. "And my lovely wife. As it is, my power has grown quite well. Perhaps in the next decade I will be in full bloom of my talent."

It was not uncommon, in the time when my heart beat, for the Academy to expel a student who proved to be recidivists. They did not benefit for the burgeoning of their powers by the Pillar, but were released back to their respective kingdoms. Most of them found death while practicing their wizardry, some gave it up altogether, while a few, very few indeed, managed to accumulate enough wealth to acquire what grimoires not belonging to the Academy and furthering their education. Apparently Vicious has been circumspect enough to be successful in his wizardly career.

Blood stares down at me, face impassive. There is no hate there, no anger that I injured her, just a sort of distant calculation you would see in an eagle staring at a plump rabbit. "She's not bleeding, love. There should be blood everywhere. In fact, she should be dead."

This has not escaped Vicious' s attention at all. He nods and kneels at my side, probing the wound. "I think," he whispers, "she's already dead."

"Lich!" The word lands between us with an almost audible thump.

"No, Blood dearest, liches are mages who seek undeath to stave off true death. This one is different, I think she's a revenant, one who wronged so foully that even death cannot stop them from seeking revenge. It's very rare, but it happens."

"And that's better?"

A shrug and a smile from the man. It does not reach his eyes. "It could be worse. And it explains a lot. Everything, in fact."

"Then, dearest, would you mind explaining it to me?"

"Of course, Sweetie. You see, our captive here is already dead, or I should say undead and this is why she has so many Ramashurian gold crowns. She can enter that city and the dead don't bother her, allowing her to loot to her heart's content." He pokes me. "Isn't that right, Niendra?"

I do not bother answering. He continues his cold grin.

Blood taps her chin the a long finger. "She won't loot the city for us, though, and we can't follow her in."

"We don't need to. We have the boy."

My jaw tightens and I am tempted to cast a spell, one of the few wizard cantrips I know, that will temporarily blind him, but I know the cost will be steep, so I hold my mouth shut and glare my distain at the man.

"I don't know what brought you to this state," he purrs, pulling close enough that I can tell he drank fortified wine a short time ago. "I don't care. All I care about is getting enough money to buy a duchy." The musket barrel grows large in my sight while I continue to glare. "And I will let the boy live. Don't help us, then I start to take him apart piece by piece. Your choice."

Tennic is still unconscious, the fire highlighting the bruise that is forming over his right eye. It will be a shiner and I am sure he will be half-blind by the morning. For some reason I cannot fathom why this hurts me and I want to take the boy in my arms and provide comfort.

"Heal his face, treat him well and let me cast a binding upon you that if I do as you say in regards to Ramashur, you will let him live and be free." A Binding Oath is a terrible spell that forces the oath taker to comply. It was developed hundreds of years ago by Queen Bet's resident caster to bind a Justice to duty, the bedrock of the entire system at the time. This *geas* can only be cast upon the willing and it ensures that the oath taker will not break their promise, effectively stealing the will of the recipient in regards to the promise. It is a simple, yet insidious spell and I should know. I created it as my graduation project at the Hidden Academy. No one leaves the school until they create something new in the world of magefolk.

Vicious certainly knows of the spell if the widening of his eyes is any indication (as I imagine any mage living in Gylleth would), but he merely laughs wryly. "Simple enough," he says. "Agreed, but after we arrive at Ramashur."

Moments later I am minding Tennic, watching as Vicious tends to the boy's hurts. The spellcasting lasts for a remarkably short time and the boy is healed, the puffy purpling bruise around his eye gone and any scrapes or scratches accrued healed. He does not wake, slipping from unconsciousness to a deep, healing slumber with a flick of the assassin's will.

"Not bad work for the Man behind," I remark as Vicious drinks wine out of a tin flask.

He coughs and sputters while Blood curses in her beautiful contralto. Any stirring of attraction I might have felt for her is now ashes. There is nothing in that pretty, bald head but snakes and worms and I know I will kill her if the opportunity arises.

"How did you figure it out?" Vicious's voice is low and . . . well, vicious.

"During my negotiations with your . . . ah, cutout character behind the screen, I saw Blood use the thief's Gabble, an old sign language developed in the time before the last Malosian Shift. Actually, I am surprised you know it at all and that it has survived all this time."

Blood figures it out first. "How old are you?" she blurts, coppery skin pale.

"Perhaps I read a lot. Perhaps I am old, or perhaps I knew a lot of thieves when my heart once beat, who knows?" I smile. I want them to be unsettled. This might make them more cautious, but I want them to be afraid to cross me in any way. Time is on my side.

"We might have grabbed a dwarf by the beard, Sweetie."

Dark eyes narrow. "We aren't without resources ourselves." She stands and begins to walk out into the dark, her enchanting voice floating back to us. "Let's rest then break camp, love. We have a treasure to gather."

EIGHT

THEN

MISSING TWO DAYS OF INVESTIGATION while enmeshed in the unraveling of the geomancer's wards was frustrating and the need to find Soro Divver's killer tugged at me, but the adventure before me was a little more immediate considering Divver couldn't get any deader. I felt that finding out what a rogue geomancer was doing in Gylleth was a bit of pertinent information to the safety of the realm. Deep down I knew the queen would forgive the delay.

After searching the chamber for more clues as to the identity of the dead geomancer (there were none) I let the dwarves lead the way to the next phase of the search with Taalis in tow. The sylvan remained emotionally detached, but I could tell that the thought of an unknown geomancer so close to Dorendiriar bothered her somewhat.

Mages are a valuable commodity in the Six Kingdoms and made more so by their scarcity. The thought that there might be such powerful mages outside of the Hidden Academy who were *not* under the control of the six sovereigns was cause for worry.

From the mage's bedroom we headed straight instead of turning left, which was the continuation of the original tunnel. Torch held out in front, we followed this branch for a short while before it sloped steeply downward, so much so that we were forced to brace ourselves with one hand against the wall as we walked. Fifteen minutes of careful travel terminated into a dark pool of water that blocked the tunnel.

"Looks like a dead end," said Taalis with a frown.

Both dwarves grinned and rolled their eyes. "Troost a sylvan ta gyve oop soo soon," said Haddeg, thickening his brogue so much that even I could barely understand him.

"Aye, coosin," chimed in Skakhir, not to be outdone in the ridiculous accent department. "Issa cryin' shame tha' oothers doo noo have a gud oopreciation oof speeloonkin."

Mother Moon but my ears were about to bleed. "Stop it you two."

"Sorry, lass," replied Haddeg somewhat sheepishly, slyly glancing at Taalis. "But we think this myte be a water trap."

Taalis cocked her head. "What?"

"Water seeps in, yer know." Haddeg toed the pool and watched the ripples in the torchlight. "So it collects here, wych be what I think the mage intended. Soomewhere beelow the floor ryses rapidly and the water be trapped in the curvature. Noo torches, nothing. Yer haveta swim in darkness, yer doo. Mayhap there be bars or such blockin' the way."

"So this adventure is done," replied the sylvan in resignation.

Both dwarves laughed. "Yer might be a mage oof tyme, but Niendra can make lyte for uus and noo bars oof metal can stop a dwarf."

"Wait a minute," I cut in. "You two want to continue?"

"Aye, lass. There be treasure." Skakhir tapped his bulbous nose. "I can smell it."

I chewed on my lower lip for a moment before dipping a hand into my belt pouch and pulling forth a tourmaline the size of a pea and holding it up to the torch. Concentrating, I chanted a few words in Dendrich and held the gem close enough to the fire that my fingers started to sting, but a moment later the fire bent toward the gem and a tendril of flame touched it. Within a few seconds the fire was sucked into the gem, leaving the torch dark and smoking while the gem shone with a deep green light. I gave the gem to Skakhir and placed my fingers into the water to cool them down. The only problem with that particular spell is that the caster has a good chance of badly burning their fingers. In my case they merely stung. A lot.

"Nice, lass," said Skakir and before we could stop him, he jumped into the pool, taking the green light into the depths.

"Fool dwarf," I swore. "By Father Sun I should strangle him." The darkness swallowed my words the as the green glow faded into the depths. "Not only did he take our light but he's going to sink like a stone in that armor."

"Do not worry, Niendra," said Taalis. "I can see just fine in the dark."

"A grand talent that be," muttered Haddeg. "But by me clenched butt cheeks, yer don't haveta worry none, lass, dwarves be strong swimmers. We kin swim in armor for gud amount of tyme."

The dark never bothered me much considering my Father Sun tattoos, but using them required concentration I didn't want to spare at the moment. Standing in the depths of the earth on a floor slanting into chill, black waters while waiting for an aquatic dwarf to reemerge set my nerves on edge. I couldn't even see my hand when I waved it in front of my face, but it's a good thing the Hidden Academy taught several classes on centering the mind to avoid the kind of stress that can cause spellcasting to go awry, usually with fatal results to the spell caster. I slowly counted to and back from one-hundred until I could feel the anxiety evaporate like sweat from my skin.

"What's taking him so long?" muttered Taalis and I realized that even the normally reserved sylvan who could see in the dark was feeling a bit tetchy. This comforted me a little.

A short time later the green glow returned to the depths and Skakhir surfaced, skin slightly blue and shivering mightily.

"A-ah, l-lass!" he stammered. "There's soomthin' over there for yer too see."

Haddeg shook his cousin. "What is it, yer great buffoon!"

"It's a-a-a room, yer idiot," came the reply. Shakhir surrendered the glowing tourmaline and tried to rub some feeling back into his hands. "B-by my clenched b-butt ch-cheeks, that w-water wyll wake yer up!"

"Or drown you," I growled, prepping a cantrip. After a few passes with my hands, Skakhir's body began to steam, the water quickly turning to vapor and his skin pinked up nicely. Heat radiated from his body and his clothes dried in a matter of moments. His teeth shone whitely through his beard. It was a simple spell, one I could cast all day without great effort.

"Ah, lass, yer bein' a wytch be such a lifesaver."

"Never mind my crafting capabilities," I said, fixing him with stern look. "Tell us."

"There be a greet beeg room oon the other syde there and in the center a small chest on a pedestal, but noo one can geet too it because there be wryst-thyck bars between. Noo way to get past."

Treasure indeed. Taalis and I shared a look that communicated everything. Whatever was in that little chest was something worth creating a secret underground lair and hiding it away from the world. But was it worth risking our lives for?

I knew if I turned tail and rode back to the queen to make my report, Taalis would leave immediately for Dorendiriar and return with a small cadre of sylvan wizards to claim the prize for their nation, settling the diplomatic kerfluffle later. That wouldn't do. The treasure resided in Gylleth and belonged to Gylleth. Besides, the dwarves would never let me live it down if I forced them to leave now and might just well disobey.

"Oh . . . Mother Moon," I grumped in resignation. "Let's go."

"Wait, lass," said Skakhir. "Can yoo doo that wee spell again when wee get too the oother syde? I don't fancy stayin' cold."

"No worries there."

After that, we were swimming.

The water bit into my skin with teeth of ice and would have had me shrieking the air out of my lungs if I hadn't been worried about breathing. As it was it felt like my flesh wanted to contract away from my bones and even my eyes ached from the frigid water as I watched my surroundings in the rich green light given off by the gem. Beside me Skakhir swam with brisk, powerful strokes looking for all the world like an aquatic brick. A brick with a beard. The other two swam behind.

Fresh air came soon enough and the gemlight shone greenly upon the large room as we surfaced next to a wall, the exit wider than it was long. To my eyes the room looked flawlessly cubical, a twenty by twenty by twenty-foot area fashioned with the kind of geometric perfection I could only dream of achieving. When a mage creates an object from reality, even a room, the totality of the thing must be precise in their mind down to the tiniest detail. Their imagination must be up to the demands of the craft or what they create won't come to pass, so the discipline required to hold the image steady in their thoughts is incredible, even some of the arch-mages teaching at the Hidden Academy have a difficult time with creation spells.

All this came to me as I stared all around at the dark rock thick with millions of fragments of quartz reflecting the light back at us as we hauled ourselves out of the pool. It took several tries, but I managed to stammer my way through a few cantrips and return our bodies to their correct temperatures. Even the stoic Taalis looked frazzled by the frigid water. As our bodies steamed with warmth, I looked around.

Dividing the room neatly in half were the vertical, wrist-thick bars Skakhir mentioned, except he left out the fact that they shone like mirrors in the green light and that the center bar, at a height of five feet, bore a six-inch plaque. That plaque was also mirrorlike and had three small runes on its face clustered in the center. Five feet beyond the plaque stood a small stone pedestal on top of which was plain wooden box about eighteen inches long and nine high. I stared through the sun tattoos on my eyelids and saw the thick weave of magic that encased the entire construct.

"Mother Moon," I breathed, staring around through the Father Sun tattoos. "I haven't seen such magic before."

Taalis raised an eyebrow. "Really? You just saw me manipulate time and magical bars excite you?"

Despite the overweening pride that filled the question, I answered, "Yeah, the time spell was impressive, but this . . ." I waved a hand, "this is *amazing*. The bars aren't just set into the stone, they plunge all the way through and encapsulate the entire back half of the room like a cage! Not only that, but there are glyphs hidden in the stone that renders it much harder than steel, so digging through it is well-nigh impossible." I took a deep breath and opened my eyes, allowing normal sight to intrude. "And the bars aren't steel, they're magic given solid form, a near indestructible substance . . . the only way to go through is to somehow negate magic in the entire area, but if you do that, the room collapses. This is a *masterpiece*."

Yes, that finally impressed the sylvan, who looked around with new eyes at what the geomancer wrought. She pointed to the plaque. "And that?"

"That's a little bit more mundane. It's a Portal Lock, it allows passage only if the person has the key, which could be anything from an object, word or phrase. If we have the key, we can get the box, which, I might add, is not warded as far as I can tell."

Skakhir removed the shiny war hammer from his belt and before I could stop him placed the head against the center of the plaque. I winced.

Nothing happened. He tapped the plaque again, making sure the head came in contact with the runes, but still there was a heaping pile of nothing. *Tink, tink, tink.*

"By Father Sun, don't *do* that!" I snapped. "What, you have a death wish?"

He shrugged. "Ah, it seemed a gud plan, lass."

Dwarves.

I snorted, urging him back and he returned reluctantly, placing the hammer back in his belt loop. "Obviously Skakhir's new toy is not the key, so we have to put our heads together and figure it out if we want to see what the geomancer hid inside that box."

"Ahem."

We looked to Haddeg whose face was set into an expression so smug I had to resist the urge to slap it off and by Taalis's mien, she did as well. The stout dwarf sauntered over to the plaque and said,

One for Phezdes for He is Kind,
One for Dhiione for the Brave,
One for Father Sun to clear the Mind,
One for Aris to voyage from the Grave,
One for Wom to leave clutching Earth,
One for Himir to stave off Sleep,
One for Yrusis for a Rebirth,
One for Mother Moon for magic Steep,
One for Tilla to leave her Keep.

The shining bars shimmered for a moment before fading into a mist which in turn dissipated quickly. Haddeg turned to us and said to our stunned faces, "I have a grand memory, yer know."

Taalis and I picked our jaws up off the floor and slowly walked toward the pedestal as I again stared through the Father Sun tattoos to see if there were any wards. Once more I could see nothing to worry about, which worried me even more. It seemed that all magic stopped past the now nonexistent bars leaving us with a mundane wooden box of simple design and several, perfectly round holes in the floor and ceiling.

"What do you think, Taalis?" I asked.

"A trap, definitely." She stroked her chin. "Poison needle, perhaps?"

"Perhaps. Or a gas of some sort."

"Yer wee lassies should stand back," cautioned Haddeg."

"Why?"

Before he could answer, Skakhir struck the box on the lid with his silver hammer, shattering wood and sending what was no doubt a complex locking mechanism (now so much scrap) flying. Despite the force of the blow, the box didn't move. Perhaps it had been glued there?

"Yer talking too much," he said, sliding the hammer back into his belt loop.

Dwarves.

For a moment I thought Taalis would lose her icy calm because in that split second of time I saw something deep and savage lurking beneath that exterior and it frightened me. Sylvans live a long, long time, perhaps forever barring violence or accident and I wondered what kind of magic and mayhem that ancient a creature could produce. All I knew is that I didn't want to find out.

I gave a hard glare to my two stout companions. "Next time a little warning, you two."

"Aye, lass," they chorused innocently.

Now the box. Front end smashed in, the rear hinges intact and no sign of physical traps or wires. Something glinted from within, a hint of color and luster that quickened my pulse and for a moment I wished Mirallelle was here to share the moment.

"None of that," I whispered.

"What?"

I glanced sidelong at Taalis. "Nothing."

Taking I deep breath, I flipped open the lid with the tip of a knife, leaning back just in case of . . . something. Nothing except what lay before our wondering eyes.

"Mother Moon," I whispered.

The other three drew in deep breaths as we saw a nine-inch wooden rod lying on a blue velvet cushion, eight large gems were inset at regular intervals along its length: three emeralds, two rubies, three sapphires and on the tip, larger than the rest sat the ninth, a diamond.

"Nine gems," said Taalis in wonder. "Nine for the nine gods."

"That's why the other chest was warded so heavily, the key phrase was inside, and if someone had tried to steal it, it would have been destroyed." My mouth felt dry and my pulse thundered through my ears. I closed my eyes and marveled at the intensity of magic that emanated from the artifact, a citirine glow so powerful my eyes watered even though they were closed. "This this is magical like the ocean is a bit wet." But I felt no danger from the rod, no sense of wrongness, but I murmured a simple Find Curse cantrip just to be sure. Nothing.

I saw Taalis try to snatch the rod, but I was faster, my action instinctive. The rod rightfully belonged to Queen Betelial Til-Amre, first of her name and ally to the sylvan people. Taalis looked as if she would object, but a hard glare from me and the sudden tensing of both dwarves had her swallowing any protest. As the rod left velvet, I felt a peculiar thrumming through my bones and I mentally prepared for the worst. Somehow, I missed a ward and I tripped it.

Taalis felt it and the room seemed to shimmer a bit as if we stood within an illusion and the dwarves grumbled in their beards. We all looked around, but when the thrumming passed and the room returned to solidity, nothing happened.

"We are so lucky," I breathed.

Taalis nodded.

"What happened?" asked Haddeg.

"Ward," I replied. "But nothing happened. At least to us that I can tell." A look through my Father Sun tattoos showed a brace of dwarves and an elf, all in good repair.

"Why aren't we dead?" Skakhir held his silvery hammer so tight his knuckles turned white.

"I don't know." My guts felt watery and I was sure my humors were quite unbalanced. "Perhaps a test of some sort?" There existed wards that could sense intent. Perhaps that was what I triggered. Either way I cursed myself for an idiot. I had justice to mete out and here I was playing in a lair of an unknown wizard with two over enthusiastic dwarves and a truculent sylvan.

Time to get back to work. I lifted the bejeweled rod. It felt cool and dry in my hand, nothing special to indicate any magic potential, but when I looked at it through my eyelids it shone bright enough to hurt.

"I lyke me wee hammer better," said Skakhir. "It doosn't haave strange wards, lass."

"If you could see what I see, you wouldn't be saying that." My voice barely rose above a whisper, but it carried well, nonetheless.

"What does it do, though?" asked Haddeg.

Taalis and I shared a glance. "That's the real question now, isn't it?"

NINE

NOW

FOR A PAIR OF MURDERERS-FOR-HIRE, they know how to travel in style. Lush velvet cushions surrounded by mahogany stained oak with cedar interior trim surrounds me. Tennic sits next in the carriage while wearing enough chains to weigh down a galleon and a hangdog expression that makes me want to comfort him. Someone so young should not carry such harsh concerns. As for me, I spent my time silently cursing the fact that we rode *away* from my intended mission, the delay causing me much irritation.

It has been two days since our capture and we draw ever nearer to Ramashur while staying away from any population center larger than a village, so we bypassed Northbrom, Heddenshire and Wylclow. All three smaller than Orthengar, but plenty large enough to house sizable garrisons.

Our captors sleep in the open, usually in a small glade or hilltop while Tennic and I make do inside the carriage. Blood and Vicious seem comfortable in the sturdiness of our bonds and the fact that this is the only carriage where the doors lock from the outside, which begs the question: what did they use it for? It shows enough wear that we are not its first occupants and I am flattered that they think so much of us, while their confidence is exhibited by the leisurely pace they set. Perhaps they treat this as a vacation.

Stars wink down on us as the summer clouds decide they do not wish to be present and I stare though the barred windows of the carriage as Tennic slowly falls asleep on the opposite bench, comfortable despite the manacles that bind. The adaptability of youth. He bears some fresh contusions upon his stout little body, courtesy of our Coadian captor. While Vicious plays the animal for the masses, it is Blood who possesses the fiery temper, often lashing out physically and since I do not react to pain, she vents her fury upon the boy. My warnings to stop go unheeded and each bruise adds to the tally of my anger.

There will be a reckoning. The Justice in me needs to balance the scales.

Viscous cooks a quail on a spit over a small campfire, focusing entirely on the task at hand, but I know this is deceptive . . . he is quite aware of his surroundings and the fact that I am peering out the window. As if to prove my point, he slides the fowl off the spit onto a tin plate and opens the carriage door.

"I don't suppose you eat?" he says softly so as not to wake the boy.

"No."

"Come out then, enjoy the night."

Nodding, I take him up on the offer, sitting criss cross in front of the fire and adjusting my manacles. We are in a modest clearing, fireflies dancing thick among the trees a few dozen feet away, the air heavy with moisture and the smell of roast quail.

Daintily and with great precision, he begins to debone the bird with knife and fork, piling the succulent, steaming meat onto another plate for Blood. He smiles and it is the first expression I have seen on that face that I feel is genuine. This man wears a variety of masks like an actress performing a morality play, a false face for every occasion.

"Tell me about yourself," he says.

"I would rather not."

Half the bird is deprived of bone and he continues handiwork, the knife and fork flashing in the firelight. "I'll tell you if you tell me."

Intriguing. A trade. I pretend to ponder the idea for a minute. "All right," I say finally. "But you begin."

Vicious's smile widens. He expected this. "Agreed." A pause. "As you may have guessed, Blood and I are married."

I nod.

"We have two children."

This surprises me and I say so.

"They are grown, one is far away, one is a cleric, a worshipper of Yrusis, and is very devout."

Yrusis, the Goddess of Peace, Love, Childbirth and Prosperity. A goddess worshipped by midwives and merchants alike. Most of her clergy are priestesses, as she is a deity whose aspect encapsulates all that is feminine, so I guess this child of Vicious's is a woman. The lopsided grin he gives tells me he knows my thoughts and confirms my unuttered supposition.

"Go on," I say.

"It's your turn, Niendra the witch."

"I was married once, long ago, but my wife is dead, obviously." My mind edits each word that spills from my mouth so I do not impart too much information. "As you surmise, I am a crafter, a former apothecary who is caught between realms through an agency I do not understand." I skirt the edge of the truth, trusting that Father Sun will forgive any sins of omission and misdirection considering the situation in which I find myself. Thankfully, Blood and Vicious have not found the bejeweled rod secreted away in my backpack because if they had, I might consider drastic action, no matter the cost to Tennic and myself. "That is all the personal information I feel comfortable to tell you."

"How old are you?"

"It is not polite to ask that of a woman."

Vicious is not deterred and his eyes are keen, drinking in what little expression I might show. "Why do you talk like that?"

"Like what?"

"So formal, as if you are addressing people of quality. Were you a person of quality? I have doubts about your apothecary story. I've never known an adventurous apothecary, or one who commands magic enough to come back from Tilla's Hold."

Astute observations, this man is far cleverer than I realize. I take my time before answering. "I think the absence of vital humors that plague the living frees my mind for pure thought, which explains my speech. I do not suffer from an abundance of emotion or physical distraction."

Vicious becomes still, eyes narrowing and I realize I have let slip far too much, yet I do not know what.

"Vital humors," he says slowly. "Vital humors. Now *there's* a term that hasn't been used in long, *long* time. In my study of medicine, I know that hundreds of years ago there was the theory of the vital humors: blood, phlegm, black bile and yellow bile, were the fluids that ruled the human body. Such theories have been tossed in to the waste bin of history as we know many compounds exist in a body that govern its major functions. Use of this term, vital humors, tells me you are old . . . old enough, perhaps, that you walked Ramashur before it fell." His grin contains nothing related to good will. "Interesting."

Mother Moon! This man is far too intelligent and I curse myself for a fool. Instead of filling the space between us with words I let silence reign.

Time passes slowly and when the quail is reduced to two plates of meat and bones, Blood decides make her appearance, folding out of the night like a specter haunting a manse. She assesses me coolly before saying to Vicious, "Why let her out?"

He shrugs. "Information, which she has graciously provided."

A skeptical look is her reply, but she nods and sits, producing a tin plate and fork, scooping up still steaming slices of roast quail until half is taken. She begins to shovel the meat into her mouth with no sense of decorum and I look away, still embarrassed by my mistake.

"What did you learn?" asked Blood as she finished the last shreds from her plate and licked it clean. "Was it worth it?"

"I believe so, my sweet. You see, our guest here is old, old enough to have walked the streets of Ramashur when the living once inhabited that fair city. Interesting, yes?"

Blood smiles, only one half of her mouth in on the effort and it gives her face a roguish cast. "Yes indeed, my love. Yes, indeed."

Mother Moon, I am an idiot. In the trees darkness rules and my eyes look anywhere but at Vicious's smug face and, vital humors or no, I feel, the urge to plant my fist in the middle of his smarmy smile.

Darkness among the trees? *Wait.*

My mind races, accessing risk and information at frightening speeds. Straight ahead darkness rules while to the left and right fireflies dance in the scant breeze between the trees. Casually I adjust my seating so I can glance behind me and see even more fireflies on the edge of the glade.

Blood and Vicious go quiet, very attentive until I settle down once again and calmly stare at them both.

All this time I consider my options. Do I say something or do I remain quiet and let events unfold without interference? I run through possible scenarios in a flash before finally deciding to hold my tongue for the time being. Things are about to get very interesting.

"Hello, father. Mother."

Both my captors whirl, startled at the voice emerging from darkness. "Seth?" blurts Blood in a brittle voice.

A figure slid from the shadows like oil from a pan, a tall man with wavy auburn hair and a thin face filled with a mixture of good humor and petulance. I would consider him handsome if it were not for his condescending air and the cruel twist to his otherwise full lips. "Yes, mother. Aren't you happy to see your only son?" He gives a mocking bow, his black canvas coat flapping loosely about his lean body.

"I told you to stay in Drayport, Seth." Vicious's voice whipcracks through the night. His normally calm visage is given over to one of great fury. Blood also looks as if a blood vessel on her temple feels ready to burst.

"You should be running our concerns down south, son," says Blood through gritted teeth.

"Yeah, about that. I don't think so. I'm after something more than just taking your handouts, like, say . . . oh, I don't know . . . a woman who can enter Ramashur at will without fear of being eaten, perhaps?" At the look of surprise on his parents' faces, he laughs. "Oh, come on! You had to figure I'd put one of mine in your organization, didn't you?" He removes his canvas coat to reveal black boots, black leather trousers and a shirt so dark gray it might as well be black. Oddly enough, it compliments his light bronze skin and cap of wavy hair. As if by magic, a pistol appears in his off hand, not quite pointed at his mother. "What do you think of my surprise?"

Her answer leaves even me shocked. Seth laughs, bellowing his mirth to the stars.

He should keep his eyes on his mother. I almost smile.

Blood whips her legs around and torques her body so she flips to her feet, a snarl on her face as she kicks Seth square between the legs. He gasps and folds nearly double, dropping the sword. Vicious reacts with such speed that I almost do not see what happens.

While Seth begins to gasp in shock, holding his pride and joys in his hands, and dropping the pistol, Vicious spins in the air, delivering a kick that sends the young man flying back in the dark to land in a moaning heap.

"Don't make me really hurt you, son," says Vicious, face set in paternal worry. I almost feel for him.

Almost.

Before he can take more than three steps, he's confronted by a pair of figures in black cloaks, pistols in hand. "Don't move," says the one on the right, voice muffled by a dark scarf.

He should not have bothered speaking. Before the last syllable hits the air Vicious swipes with a rapier that he draws so quickly a snake would have been surprised. One pistol flies through the air, the man on the right falling back in shock, buttocks hitting cold earth.

As for the man on the left, he is less surprised and knows that even at close range hitting a man like Vicious is improbable at best. With a speed that matches his opponent, the remaining man in black also whips forth a rapier and the two engage.

I am in awe. The man in black is a virtuoso with a blade, the rapier a shining net of steel that even the impossibly quick Vicious cannot pierce, no matter his expertise. He drops to one knee, extending a leg to sweep him off his feet only to receive a wicked slash in the thigh that parts trousers and flesh like butter. I can see bone through the sturdy leather.

Whoever this man may be, he moves with consummate skill, the tip of the rapier catching Vicious below the eye, opening a two-inch slice that bleeds down his cheek and I wonder what the fight would be like if faced each other in the arena. The swordsman ripples forward with a thrust that slides under the skin of the man's wrist all the way to his elbow, the sword lying along the bones of the arm before he rips it free through his shirt. Vicious shrieks in dismay as bright red spurts from the wound in a fountain, his eyes wide and disbelieving as he stares at the great rent in his flesh and this hesitation allows the swordsman to slip his rapier quick as a snake's tongue against his palm, sending the assassin's sword flying.

Vicious shakes his head in disbelief as the tip of the rapier hovers a hair's breadth from his throat. Slowly, he bends his knees until they thump onto grass. Within moments he is put in manacles provided by the other man.

I blink to break the trance from my eyes, so hypnotized I was by the display of consummate skill. My eyes wandered the campsite to see Seth crouching over his mother, dagger at her throat, a snarl of pure hatred on his lovely features. No wonder she did not interfere.

Seth binds Blood's hands, working quickly, professionally while Vicious tries to stem the flow of blood from his various wounds. In the light of the campfire his blood looks very black and his skin shockingly white. I knew it would be but a matter of time before his bleeds out.

The swordsman grunts as Seth stands over Blood, who stares at her son in dismay and resignation. "Sorry, mom, but you know how this works."

"I never thought it would be you," she gasps, struggling for breath. "Your sister, maybe, but not you."

"Pretending to be a momma's boy was easy," he replies, checking the pistol load. "You and dad lapped it up. Sis isn't the type to join in the family business, you know this and secretly you hate her for it, ignoring the ancient traditions and such. What a load of dung, mom. The family, excepting sis, is and always has been, a bunch of cold-blooded killers, no matter how noble the origins."

"At least . . ." she pants, "you'll carry on our legacy."

Harsh laughter hits the air. "Are you crazy? Is that your problem? I'm going to take what I can get and retire to southern Nerrinnia where the weather's warm and I'm far away from this miserable kingdom and all its overblown history and traditions. First kingdom of Estia." He shakes his head and spits in contempt. "It's old and hidebound and not worth a copper crown."

"Our family has protected the kingdom for centuries!" she counters, blood spackling her lips.

"Old news. We *used* to protect the kingdom, but now we just murder for money." He raises the pistol and aims it at her skull. "Or just for the fun of it. What do you say, mom, are you going to try to sway me with your non-existent maternal pride?"

Blood looks down and away, obviously at a loss for words.

Sighing, Seth moves to the swordsman, "I'm impressed. You are as good as advertised. I've never seen dad defeated at . . . *well* . . . anything before."

The swordsman shakes his head. "Just doing my job."

"Not to appear materialistic, but we have what we came for, except for the final prize: gold from Ramashur." He places a hand on the man's shoulder. "Soon we all can retire and live like kings in the place of our own choosing."

Another nod. The swordsman is not one to waste words, it seems.

"As for your companion," Seth says softly. "He's a bit of a moron, letting dad get close. I hope he won't be a problem because we need to get going."

The swordsman sheathes his rapier and brushes off his trousers. "Don't worry about my companion, he'll do what's necessary."

I sigh, things have gone from bad to worse. I should have known. "You could just let us go," I say, knowing the answer.

Seth shakes his head. "You know why I can't."

"I take it your sister is not a priestess of Yrusis."

"Nah, she's a priestess all right, but of Dhiione. Honorable combat and all that tripe. Runs a gladiatorial school in West Denby and can't stand our parents any more than I can." Seth stares down at Blood who sullenly stares back. If looks could kill he'd leave in a bucket. "Money buys a lot of forgiveness, though." He scratches his head. "All right, now that it looks like my dear parents have been cowed, we can get back to business at hand."

Of course. I brace myself for the worst and am not disappointed.

"I'm feeling generous," says Seth, kneeling at my side. "So why don't you tell me how to get into Ramashur so I can get enough gold to retire in luxury."

"The answer is simple." The swordsman's voice is thick and rough with some hidden emotion. "I figured it out just a few minutes ago. Strange that I hadn't before considering how famous she is."

Tap, tap, tap. Seth's pistol rings against my manacles. "This one? Famous? Do tell."

"Famous only to Justices and then only to those who pay attention to the Far Histories."

My mouth is shut not because I do not wish to speak, but because I know this masked man and the knowledge tears a hole in my soul. He steps forward and slowly removes his scarf and lets down his hood, revealing a familiar face.

"You see, Seth, the Far Histories are required reading for those who would be a Justice, as well as a pilgrimage to the Catacombs of Justice where there are hundreds of sarcophagi, each one bearing the likeness of the interred painted on the lid. I finally recognized this one."

"Hello, Antonius," I say woodenly, staring at the man and feeling an ember of hate burn in my breast.

The Justice nods. "Hello, Niendra Goisien."

Ten

THEN

Go back to the Summer House or continue the investigation? Those two choices lay hard before me and they ate at me all the way back to the little quarry community where I had hitched my horse. The geas that I took to pursue justice for the kingdom doesn't seem to react to either choice because both involve what is best for Gylleth. Had the cave been a naturally occurring phenomenon, then the geas would have tugged at my mind with ropes of discomfort until I vomited from extreme pain that would force my muscles to contract so hard bone broke. It seemed that both instances were equally worthy of my effort as a Justice. This went to prove that while effective, the geas was not a perfect solution to hold a Justice to a course.

Bat flew around and around, still excited to have me back after my two-day ward busting endeavor that left me so hungry that even hard tack tasted good. Thankfully Taalis had tended to the horses so they didn't starve or lack for water.

There was no crafter spell or ritual to look into the future or past to catch a glimpse of the murder of Soro Divver and Taalis wouldn't divulge much about the sylvan ability to manipulate time except to say she disclosed far too much as it was. Only the importance of the event allowed her to take such extraordinary measures such as the preservation of Soro Divver's corpse.

Taalis went to scrounge up Grotek the quarry overseer while I readied my horse, a course of action finally decided upon; the bejeweled rod could wait, my duty to find Soro Divver's murderer came first. Besides, I could send a messenger to the queen on the road to Caenwylln to alert her to the situation.

Mother Moon, what in the names of the gods was that geomancer up to? I shrugged and decided further rumination needed a full belly.

After my meal of hard tack, venison jerky and small beer, I was introduced to a short man, almost as short as my dwarven companions, with massive forearms and a body made of rawhide and bone. He had a battered face, a mashed nose with far too much hair growing like lichen from each nostril, and a wild thatch of black hair that hadn't seen a comb in years.

"Grotek here found the body," said the sylvan, standing a goodly distance from the man. As I shook his hand, I realized the reason why she chose to absent herself Grotek's side. The man smelled of old sweat, even more old sweat, and a kind of funk that reminded me of aged cheese. It made my nose wish for safer climes.

"Yrusis's peace be upon you, Grotek," I said after approaching, then taking a long step back. Haddeg and Skakhir wisely found other things to occupy their attention a couple dozen feet away.

"And you, Lady Justice," replied the overseer. "I reckoned a Justice would wanna talk with me seein' how important Master Divver is, ah, was."

I queried the man about finding the body, any suspicious activity among the laborers, or even a hint as to who could have performed the deed. His answer startled me.

"Mebbe it was Rol-Venber, Lady Justice."

My eyes went wide. "The Rol-Venber Bank in Caenwylln?" I asked, more than a little curious at this strange statement. "Why would they do such a thing? Murder seems a bit far-fetched for bankers."

He shrugged and scratched at his wild hair. "Was no surprise Master Divver borrowed from the bank to purchase supplies and labor for the upcoming aqueduct and road contract for Orthengar. Everyone knows that the place will be a big thing in a few years once those two projects is done. His bid is expected to be approved by the crown any day now and most of his money is tied up into land and other ventures."

"My question remains unanswered."

"If he don't pay, Lady Justice, then the business reverts to the bank, not his son, Master Coventio, who has not time for the business, let me tell you. The bank gets a whole construction concern, the quarries and a good plot of land in Caenwylln. I imagines that they get a smart fella to run the business and they make out nice and tidy like, a good return on an investment, if you don't mind my saying so." He knuckled his forehead.

"What about Fel Rosso, his business rival?"

Grotek shrugged. "Fel Rosso don't have means to handle a job as big as that, but they're Wom's own wizards at buildings and such."

I turned to Taalis. "Is this true?"

It was her turn to shrug. "It could be true. Fel Rosso couldn't contend with the Divver family, but Soro's death allows them to borrow against their assets and better compete for the contracts. It's also true that Soro borrowed heavily from the bank, but I don't see the logic of killing him. Who would take over for the bank?"

A thought came to mind. "Fel Rosso."

That shut both the sylvan and Grotek up. They looked at each other for a moment before turning back to me. "I don't think so," they chorused.

"You have solid reasoning behind that conclusion?"

"Fel Rosso is too small," said Grotek firmly. "Not rich enough and Master Divver often said he don't have the infra-infrasuture, no, infra-"

"Infrastructure," provided Taalis.

Grotek smiled. "Yeah that. He didn't have enough of that to take over a business the size of Master Divver's. I don't think theys be up to it, even though they's rich and such. At least, richer than they was a few years ago."

The sylvan nodded her assent.

That would make sense, assuming the Fel Rosso weren't rich enough. Assets could be hidden or held in other form than gold crowns, but I didn't see the need to share my concern about that. I'd chew on it later. "With Soro dead, why couldn't Coventio Divver take over?"

Taalis answered, "Coventio is Soro's only child and heir and has made it plain he wishes no part in the family business. He's made a name for himself in the textile trade, a savvy businessman in that regard and has no need of his father's money or concerns. He would have to leverage his own businesses to pay back his father's loans to Rol-Venber and that's not going to happen. He would either sell it to pay back the loan or let the bank seize the assets." She paused a moment. "Although he has gold enough to keep the family estates from forfeiture."

"Why did he come here with his father to the quarry if he has no interest in his business?"

Taalis smiled. "Despite their views on Master Soro's business, they're still father and son. Coventio had business in Wylclow to take care of and the pair decided to travel together." Her face darkened. "After the murder Coventio returned to Caenwylln to see to the estate and make sure the business doesn't collapse so Rol-Venber *doesn't* foreclose on the note." This last was directed at Grotek, who shrugged.

It was my turn to pause. "So, Coventio Divver has no motive to kill his father, then."

Taalis nodded emphatically, although Grotek didn't look convinced.

I looked at my dwarven companions who were still doing their best to stay upwind of Grotek. Skakhir shrugged, the gesture repeated by his cousin. My eyes traveled to the sky and the gray clouds scudding along at a good pace, full of rain and ready to pop.

"Well, Mother Moon, it looks like I'm headed to Caenwylln."

THANKS TO THE WORST OF THE MALOSIAN SHIFTS, the Six Kingdoms often regressed to barbaric times, only to pull themselves out of anarchy and build anew on the bones of the previous civilization. The Long Road of Gylleth was one of the biggest bones, a well-crafted thoroughfare that stretched two-hundred miles north from Ramashur and three-hundred southwest to Drayport. It split at Ramashur to head west to Orthangar before angling north along the mountains to Eddinshrew, the city closest to Postia. It existed long before there was a Gylleth as we knew it and the tight-fitted oddly colored stones that comprised the road resisted the weather handsomely and still radiated a slight aura that indicated the power of enchantment that allowed it to last so long. Even the Arch Mages of the Hidden Academy couldn't reproduce such magic on that scale.

Each gray/green stone measured a perfect twelve by twelve inches and were fitted so well that only a thin, dark line marked their boundaries, most of which were obscured by dirt and other debris. Although the surface of the road felt smooth, there was plenty of traction so as not to be slippery, even when wet. It was this road crossing the entirety of Gylleth that helped it to recover from the worst of the shifts so well. Each kingdom contained various remnants of bygone ages: the Great Temple of Nine and Three in Biavia or the Cantilever Walls that surround Korotalum in Emment, but only Gylleth had the Long Road.

As cities and towns rose and fell in the centuries between shifts, those great works of bygone days abided. In Gylleth, each monarch tried their best to create their own roads that connected to the grand thoroughfare that crossed the kingdom. Many of those efforts failed to stand to the test of time, although there were a few that had seen a shift or two.

The first few days on the ride to Caenwylln where it lay near the Beryl Bay, we faced no great duress, only the seemingly endless tedium that occurs with such a long journey, which gave me plenty of time to ponder the bejeweled rod and the dead geomancer.

That the mage lay moldering on his decaying cot was the only reason I didn't ride to the Summer House to report the find to queen Bet. At Hodengarth-by-the-Ridge, a smallish town surrounded by rich farmland at the juncture between the Long Road and one created by Soro Divver, I paid a visit to the local shire reeve to jot down a letter with the salient details. In those details I surmised that the geomancer had his lair so near the quarry for easy access to supplies. It would be a simple task to throw a ward or two to keep the quarry workers away from the entrance to the lair. Perhaps the wizard used a Keep Away ward on the cave's exit and because such simple wards need recasting, they probably dissipated when he died. Whether that was true or not really didn't matter in the grand scheme of things.

The shire reeve, man for whom the word 'medium' was invented, he nevertheless carried himself with great dignity and an air of competence.

"I will send this missive with my son," he said as I sealed the letter with green wax and imprinted it with the signet ring on my right index finger. The crossed sword and branch symbol of the Justices stared back up at me from its waxy nest. "It will arrive at the Summer House by next Phezday."

I nodded, satisfied that my duty lay fulfilled and thanked him for his service. I then continued my travels north listening to the filthiest jokes imaginable, so ribald were they that even the infamous sylvan stoicism displayed by Taalis wore thin enough to see through.

"By me clenched butt cheeks," roared Haddeg as Skakhir finished a particularly raunchy joke involving a one-eyed wizard and a scrofulous knobblegrott. "I moost remember that one, I do!"

Taalis looked a little green around the edges and I was about to admonish my companions for the fifth time about such ribaldry when a brace of horsemen caught my eye.

We were three hours north of Hodengarth-by-the-Ridge and the road lay straight as an arrow before us, but the land rippled like a bedsheet and the thoroughfare did the same, so when we crested a rise, the riders came quickly into view; two men in motley chain-and-plate mounted on lean, well-bred horses that looked lively enough to outpace ours in the long run. They sat there fifty yards away looking as if they would contest our passage. Swords lay sheathed at their belts and a brace of small crossbows were gripped in their hands not quite pointed our way.

"Hold," I said sharply, hand straying to the long knife at my belt.

The sylvan slid off her piebald mare as if it were greased, drawing a wicked falchion from her saddle sheath before her feet touched the ground. As for my dwarven companions, Haddeg held his double-bitted axe in one hand while Skakir lifted his shining hammer that gleamed like the promise of lightning and before I could say anything, the two dwarves moved their horses in front of mine. Gone were all the mentions of clenched butt cheeks and dirty jokes, these two now bristled with impending violence, showing the two riders why dwarves were considered the most dangerous fighters in Estia.

If the two men were worried about fierce snow dwarves looking for a good bit of mayhem in the afternoon, it didn't register on their battered faces.

Mother Moon!

"Taalis," I said softly. "How fast can you remount your horse?"

She didn't hesitate. One moment she stood on the road with falchion in hand, the other she sat in the saddle, face still as a mountain pond, falchion still clenched in her hand. That was answer enough.

It was a measure of my companions' faith in me as a Justice that they immediately followed as I whipped my horse into a gallop off the road to the right, toward a stand of alder that lay a distressingly far ways off.

Behind me Haddeg grunted and let loose a string of swearing so inventive that even Father Sun must have been impressed while Taalis's horse drew even with mine. "Bandits?" she shouted over the din of hooves.

I shook my head as Bat unfolded from his hiding place in my cloak and flapped free, gaining height with every wingbeat. Through his eyes I could see the two horsemen giving chase and three more following close behind. Highwaymen weren't unknown in Gylleth, but the Long Road was well-traveled enough to make daylight robbery unlikely. Besides, their horses were far too nice for ruffians, too well fed, well-tended and of a quality not found in such company.

"Ambush! Assassins!" I roared in anger. A perfect spot, on a hilltop exposed to missile fire. While the two in front distracted, the three coming from behind would have picked us off and it was only my natural paranoia that allowed me to see the plot.

A small bolt flew past my head and Bat let me see one of the pursuers reload his small hand crossbow on the run, the move practiced and efficient. I also saw that their horses were gaining. It would be only a matter of moments before we were overtaken.

The small grove, alder mixed with some hemlock, approached quickly and our horses thudded into the copse, offering us some protection from projectiles. "Dismount!" I yelled, jumping from the saddle and landing hard, rebounding from a sturdy woody specimen. A deep, sharp pain lit my arm on fire and I cursed, borrowing some of Haddeg's interesting phraseology as I drew a long knife. My arm was bruised from hitting the tree, but nothing felt broken, thank Father Sun. Beside me, Taalis landed lightly, feet barely disturbing the grass while the dwarves fell gracelessly off their horses, miraculously touching down without breaking a bone. All of us used the alders as cover as we readied ourselves for combat. The trees helped even the odds, but they still outnumbered us by one and, although I could sling a spell or three, doing so while fighting was sure way to find what lay beyond the veil.

I saw a short bolt sticking out of Haddeg's back, a small runnel of blood coloring his mail and I hoped the missile hadn't penetrated too deeply. Skakhir shook his head, reaching out and yanking the bolt free causing his cousin to let loose with a roar involving clenched butt cheeks and Skakhir's ancestors. No, the wound didn't run deep at all.

The five would-be assassins had the brains to dismount and draw their weapons, more's the pity, and ready round shields, drawing an array of gleaming swords. I stared at my long knife and briefly wished I had studied pyromancy. Had I time and the correct reagents I could whip up a good spell to dampen their day, but I seriously doubted they were willing to offer me the chance.

"Lay down your weapons and you'll live," shouted one of our assailants, a woman. She sported a nasty looking Irramerian khopesh with a blackened blade. "You need not die."

I highly doubted they'd let any of us walk away from this. These were no bandits, despite their ragged clothing. Their armor looked too well-cared for, not like the brigands I'd encountered before. Looking through Bat's eyes, I could see that there were no more ambushers around, a fact that told me our assailants were confident in their ability to kill two women and a brace of dwarves.

"Yer kin take yer shiny swords and stuff them up yer—"

"Skakir!"

"Sorry, lass."

"What my dwarven companion meant to say," I called back. "As much as we appreciate your fair offer, he's going to bury his hammer so deep down your throat you'll be able to pound nails by sitting down!"

"Good one, lass!"

"Thanks, Skakhir." Taking a breath, steeling myself against what was to come, I gave out a bellow that shook the leaves, "Are you here to dance, or are you here to fight?"

Highwaymen would have charged, but these people were made of sterner stuff and continued to advance slowly, still optimistic of their chances, but not stupid. Each one of them looked like they were well acquainted with slaughter. They knew who I was and probably what I could and couldn't do, magic wise.

The dwarves swayed from foot to foot, eager to fight, weapons at the ready and Taalis held her falchion with grim determination and casual competence. No more talking, it was all down to wet work, the labor of blood and bone and pain, things I'd come used to in my training to be a Justice and even though my body knew what to do, fear gathered in a small, hard ball in the pit of my stomach, causing rank sweat to break out on my forehead. The attackers drew within twenty feet.

Suddenly, Skakhir and Haddeg roared dwarvish battle cries and leapt to the attack with a sudden ferocity that took my breath away. All I could do for a moment was watch as the two dwarves swung into action, Haddeg swung his double bitted axe with blinding speed and skill few could match. The lead warrior took the blow on his shield and was driven back a few feet.

Skakhir, roaring with almost berserker fury, slammed his shining war hammer into his opponent's shield, staving it in and breaking the arm behind, driving the man screaming to his knees, but before he could finish him off, two more ambushers engaged, forcing the enraged Skakhir back toward the alders and giving their companion a much-needed respite.

The woman, skirting the swirling melee, came at me where I stood amongst the trees momentarily stunned by the ferocity of the fight. I'd never seen a dwarf in action and the transition from calm to combat took my breath away so I hesitated for a brief moment and in that moment two things happened.

One: the woman charged with that wicked khopesh raised to cut me to the bone and then some.

Two: Taalis intervened, falchion flashing, moving with the grace typical of the sylvan people.

One and two met in a blurring display of swordplay as the dwarves kept the other four combatants in check with their savagery.

Taalis slid to the side as the khopesh whistled past a pointed ear, a few stray strands of ebon hair neatly severed. She answered with a slash the woman took to her shield, showering sparks. The two ferociously traded blows, their blades humming as they cleaved the air, but the warrior woman wore armor while all that protected the sylvan was thick layer of linen.

I leapt into the fight, hoping to distract Taalis's assailant and my blade was met with a khopesh, the knife flying from stunned fingers and I quickly backpedaled, shaking my hand, trying to ease some sensation back into the numbed flesh.

The sylvan took advantage of the distraction to whip her blade at the woman's knee, only to have her opponent dance back at the last instant so the falchion sliced only air. With blinding speed, the woman kicked the falchion out of Taalis's hand, then spun her shield around bashing the sylvan in the face. Taalis fell to the grass bleeding from nose and mouth, unconscious.

Mother Moon!

The woman, thin lips marred by a red scar that perverted them into a leer, looked to me and advanced.

Eleven

NOW

Ramashur looks like it did when I left it last, a sad, quiet tomb for the unquiet dead. To the uninitiated, the air looks clear and clean, but through the Father Sun tattoos I could see the dome of magic that keeps the dead from wandering free across the countryside to snack on the living in an effort to slake a hunger that, like themselves, refuses to die. I feel amazement once again that Hengeth could have cast such a thing, even during a Malosian Shift.

The land all about the city has become a wilderness, no one wishes to live near the necropolis, so nature as reclaimed what was once verdant farmland. Sugar maple, ash and sumac sprout on the graves of houses, the foundations long since torn apart by the green. It is a wild land now and until there is a mage strong enough undo Hengeth's magic augmented by the shift, it always will be.

Behind me Antonius dismounts, face still long and drawn into a mixture of what I assume is sorrow and shame. The third man, the one so easily disarmed by Vicious is none other than his cousin Artelious DiChenzi, my erstwhile dueling opponent, his face a study in massive, purple bruising. He looks at me with so much hate I can feel it like fire upon my skin.

As for Antonius's shame and sorrow, I could not give a damn. His is a forsworn Justice and that is all I need to know about the man.

"Stop," I intone before Seth can ride further. His horse halts a few inches from the dome. His mother and father ride behind in the carriage, bound in the manacles that once graced both Tennic and I, "or you will be next on the menu." There is no line of demarcation, only the invisible barrier. Tennic rides pillion behind Blood's son and I do not want the boy to come to harm. For whatever reason he is becoming dearer to me and I do not know why I suffer from this strange affliction.

"I'm surprised there aren't any boundary markers," Seth says, sliding off his mare followed by Tennic, who takes the reins. I dismount Artoch, glad that Blood and Vicious took my horse instead of leaving him behind at the camp. One becomes used to things.

Our captors know that muskets and swords will keep us in check and I am glad for the small courtesy, even if it is at my own insistence. "Treasure hunters remove the markers," I reply. "At least the obvious ones, and the more successful scavengers learn to place more . . . subtle signs." Months of stealthily observing various those doomed adventurers allowed me to note their precautions.

Seth raises one eyebrow and strolls to the carriage, letting the near naked Blood and Vicious (clad only in smallclothes) out. I ignore Antonius, still full of an icy rage that he managed to slip the bonds of his oath and has joined the ranks of the unjust. "See that holly bush there?" I point to the unassuming shrubbery.

"Yes?"

"Holly isn't native to this part of Gylleth. Someone planted that there."

While he considers the vegetation, I check on Tennic, who offers me a small smile and hug. I return his embrace, knowing that my flesh is the same temperature as the air around, but he does not seem to mind. Not for the first time I wonder what my life would have been like had Mirallelle and I had children. No doubt I would not have been a Justice and we would have lived long enough to fall prey to Hengeth's spell. The thought of my wife as one of the restless dead makes me glad that she did not live long enough for that to happen.

"Niendra," says Antonius, drawing close.

"I have nothing to say to you."

Seth laughs at my snub, ignoring the dark look the Justice offers.

"You want gold," I say to Seth. "For the past day you have made that abundantly clear while not clarifying what I will receive in turn for investing in you, young man. Avoiding my questions like a dove avoids the hawk, but this hawk is tired of your flitting about and wants you to get to the point. As an old friend of mine would say, by my clenched butt cheeks you will talk to me *now*." My face comes to mere inches from his and I sniff, smelling the fear sweat on him. From the corner of my eye I see Antonius draw his rapier with a smooth *shhiiing*. Artelious fingers his pistol

"Do not become nervy," I say, not bothering to look at the Antonius "You lot are less than a mile from becoming so rich you can buy solid gold chamber pots, so if you want to proceed to that outcome, start talking."

Seth realized his mouth is open and he shuts it with a snap of pearly teeth and both his parents chuckle. He gives them a rueful look. "What? You want assurances or something?"

"Of course she wants assurances, Seth, she's Niendra godsloving Goisien, a witch and a Justice in her own right and she needs to know that the boy isn't going to die." Antonius pauses. "And she wants to be shut of us after this is done."

Truer words have never been spoken, even if they did originate from a man I actively detest, proving one needs not be alive to hate.

They all crowd in a bit, trying to intimidate by their numbers, but men have tried this many times before and I do not back down because that would give them power and that will not do. While women hold an equal measure of status in Gylleth, those of the opposite gender often try to bully them, flexing overwrought muscles in an Irramerian peacock display. This is laughable because the strongest muscle is between the ears, not the ones coating the skeleton.

"What assurance, Lady Niendra Goisien?" asks Seth with a small grin. He thinks he has me over a barrel. Blood shakes her head slowly.

"A spell," I reply. "A simple geas that if I fulfill my half of the bargain, you will honor yours."

His smile grows. "I can do that."

I shake my head. "You do not understand; the spell is for all of you." I know that the spell will not work on Antonius, but Seth and Corris do not know that.

And that gets their attention sharpish. Before they can bluster or object, I raise my hands and silence reigns. I command the scene here and I see it makes them uncomfortable. Good. "Look at me, you five and understand this: I do not trust criminals." I point to Antonius. "Or oathbreakers." Then to Artelious. "Or petulant man babies who pick fights and are surprised and ashamed when they lose." I take a deep breath. "And I especially do not trust the foremost assassins in the land. Call it my need for compliance."

"Let us discuss this," says Antonius, gently steering his companions out of earshot while offering a curious glance as I amble toward Artoch to pet his velvety nose. His rubbery lips flick about my fingers searching for something to eat and I continue to walk around my horse. He is a fine beast, not fast, not you, but steady as the tides and I will miss him.

From a few feet away the voices of my captors rise in argument while Blood and Vicious squat on their haunches, leaning against each other in misery. Listening to the three, Antonius is resigned to the spell while the other two argue, however the Justice is the most skilled and deadliest member of that miserable little troupe and their arguments soon begin to crumble against the force of his personality. Only Artelious holds some heat in his veins and he shouts and waves his hands about in a fine display of childish pique.

This is my moment.

I take a few steps from Artoch, then a few more. A familiar tingle teases my mind, pushing at me but I persevere and continue my ambling. Within a few seconds I leave the tingle behind and begin to run.

There is a shout and footfalls thud behind me. I smile.

My feet are wings. I cannot tire, so I run full out, each stride eating great chunks of space between me and Ramashur. The once bright walls of the jeweled city come closer. More shouting from behind and a hard, flat crack. A pistol ball passes next to my ear, whirring through the air.

My clothes take the brunt of thorny bushes and clutching tree limbs, but I feel no pain, instead I rush deeper into the thicket, not minding that I mortify my unfeeling flesh. The man running behind must be feeling put upon, though.

I stop and turn.

It is Artelious who chases, Antonius and Seth shouting from the distance, but the headstrong young man ignores them, he is too focused on catching me to hear the din of his companions. He skids to a halt, skin showing through rent clothing and panting like an overheated hound.

Blood flows freely from a deep cut on his cheek and fury adds to the red on his face. He raises his sword, ready to strike me deep.

"You should not have unshackled us," I say, my voice slicing through the air like a razor.

He stops in mid swing. "What?"

"Tennic and I, you should not have unshackled us. While I distracted you three with talk of a geas, he snuck off into the bushes. He is long gone and I cannot believe the plan worked." I smile. "Fortunately, Justice Antonius is too far gone in his shame at my disdain. I dare say it would not have worked had his wits been about him."

"Dead or undead you maybe," Artelious snarls. "We'll see how you handle being sliced into steaks!"

I hold up a finger. "You forget one thing, young man."

His eyes narrow. "What's that?"

"Where you are."

By the time understanding hits, it is far too late.

THE WALLS OF RAMASHUR USED TO SHINE WHITELY in the sun, a glowing display of might, but now they are streaked with centuries of grime, the merlons crumbling, some barely nubs sticking up like blackened teeth over ragged gums. The walls still stand, however, tall and strong despite the siege of centuries and I feel a familiar stab of pride as I walk through the Gate of the Gods, and the only remnants of those proud wooden structures are streaks of rust. Nature's ivy has pulled down what enemies in shifts past could not.

Once again, I see the ruins of buildings, the broad thoroughfares overgrown with weeds, trees shattering cobble as they thrust toward the sky. Most of the buildings in the Lowers, the homes of those who stank after a hard day's work, are merely humps of greenery and broken masonry. Only the Uppers, where people had money, still boasted structures that defy the elements and that is where my feet take me. My purse lacks gold so I needed to scavenge more, then I will rendezvous with Tennic. I trust the former street rat to hide from the Seth and Antonius for at least a day.

I close my eyes for a second as I try to forget the sound Artelious made when the dead arrived, lured outside the wall by whatever sense they possess to track the living. They fell upon him quickly, but unfortunately for the young man, they began to feed while his heart still beat and I did not have the courage to watch his demise. However, his screams still linger hotly in my mind.

Passage to the Uppers takes longer than in Ramashur's heyday because of the abundance of vegetation, but I have plenty of time as well as faith in Tennic's ability to hide, so while I walk I think about the past day-and-a-half.

"Do you think it will work?" Tennic had whispered as we huddled together in the dark. Seth did not wish to light a fire so as not to attract attention and his two companions concurred. While I did not suffer from variations in temperature, Tennic shivered under the thin blanket provided by Antonius and, while I could not warm him, my embrace provided comfort.

"I very much doubt it," was my reply. "But what else can we do? I say we count ourselves blessed by Father Sun and Mother Moon that they do not feel the need to keep us in chains."

Tennic rubbed his wrists where they had chafed under the manacles. "Yeah."

"Niendra," said Antonius, emerging from the dark like a shadow given light. By Mother Moon, that man could *sneak*. "I'd like to speak with you."

I turned my head away, not wanting to look at him. "My feelings run opposite."

"I'm not asking. Come." He strode away, sure that I would follow.

Giving Tennic's hand a pat, I did so, galled that the corrupted Justice was correct. I knew that if the boy tried to run, Seth would shoot him in the back. In fact, the leader of the little group informed me that any infraction would cause the young man considerable discomfort. And a loss of flesh. I noted each and every threat for future reckonings.

We did not go far into the trees. Twigs and leaves crunched underfoot as I approached the man. "What do you need?" I asked curtly.

Antonius licked his lips and I realized he was *nervous*.

"I'm sorry," he said finally. "Know that this is not what I wanted to do."

"Imagine my ability to care has reached zero," was my reply. "Somehow you broke the oath that binds and now we are captive to whimsy with the chances of escape plummeting."

His reply surprised me. "For one in a hundred Justices the oath has no effect, the magic seems to slip away like mist in the wind." He shrugged, but would not look me in the eye. "Everyone knows this, but no one talks about it. The worst kept secret in the palace."

Now that was news that shocked me to my core. I had crafted the spell carefully and thought it to be perfect in every way, an inescapable (and voluntary) geas to prevent corruption. A thought hit me with the force of a blow. "Are you immune, or resistant, to all magics, or is it the spell?"

"Your mind is as quick as the Far Histories tell." His smile showed more sadness than mirth. "It's been discussed before and it seems that some people are less, ah, affected by spells than others. Whether it's to an effect of ancestry, diet or a fluke of nature hasn't been determined, but the thought of one percent of the population being almost immune to spells has mages losing sleep at night, I can tell you." Antonius shrugged. "One theory is that the presence of so much magic in the world has provided some people with a resistance to it."

I put the thought to simmer at the back of my mind and turned away. "You have given me much to think about, Justice Antonius Valerius. Good night to you."

"Wait!"

"What?"

A heavy sigh drifted from behind as he realized that I had no desire for further conversation. "I wanted to let you know the reason."

"The reason?

"The reason we're out here. Artelious got in deep with the Man Behind's people, racking up a debt he couldn't pay and they were going to hurt him." Another pause. "Permanently hurt him, if you catch my meaning."

"I do." Permanently. The dead kind of permanently.

"He knew I wasn't affected by the Justice Oath and in the evening after you humiliated him at Mateous's boarding house, Seth came to him with a plan to erase his debt entirely. All he had to do was find out how you got a hold of a fortune in ancient Gylleth crowns that had to have come from Ramashur. This meant I could rid the kingdom of Blood and Vicious and the Man Behind, do some good in an unlawful act."

"Evil."

"What?"

"Evil," I repeated. "You committed crimes for money. Just because you did not profit personally from it does not mean that it was anything less than a criminal enterprise. There was no pronunciation of a sentence, no witness statements, blatantly kidnapped me from my captors. My situation has not changed for the better, so you ignore justice. Things not in keeping with the Rules of Conduct in the Books of the Justices."

That set him on his heels for a moment. "Maybe," he admitted. "Perhaps. But I have captured the two most powerful killers in all the Six Kingdoms, there is justice in that. Besides, things have changed in the last five hundred years. Justices rarely rely on the Rules of Conduct. The Books have been reduced to half-adhered to guidelines."

Despite my immunity to temperature, I felt a cold chill run up my spine. The Books of Justices were established centuries before I developed the geas, rules for the Justices to live by while in service to crown so laws could be enforced fairly. Conduct to instill faith in the masses for a system that benefitted all. To hear that they were merely guidelines hurt me in a way I did not think possible.

"I see I've upset you further, Niendra. I'm sorry, but that's the way things are now. I thought you knew."

"No." I shook my head, thoughts spinning madly. "I did not. It is not like I can walk into the palace and declare myself to the king." Truth be told, technically I am a Justice no more, the geas fled along with my life. Only my personal sense of right and wrong remains and my need to pursue my own brand of justice.

For a second I ponder if it is justice or revenge that motivates me, but I throw the idea into my mind's closet. I have bigger things to worry about now.

"Well, be at ease on one thing, your service is temporary. Once you retrieve enough treasure from Ramashur, we will part ways. You can take the boy to wherever you wish and we will go live our lives."

"Until Blood and Vicious free themselves and kill you all. Slowly."

Antonius's face darkened. "They won't. Seth has already procured promises of non-reprisal, assuring me that his parents never break their word. It's bad for business. Besides, Seth really doesn't want to kill them. Parenticide is something even our stand-offish gods detest and could earn a curse or three."

While I have not observed Blood and Vicious break their words, it is not enough to comfort me. As for Seth, I have no doubts he will eventually bury me and Tennic in a deep hole somewhere and cover it with boulders. "Enough of this." I turned and took a step toward him. "If you want my understanding, then you have it, although I withhold approval. All I ask in return is that you keep absent the chains that Blood and Vicious used to bind us. We will lead you to Ramashur and I will retrieve gold from its depths. But do not rest easy, Antonius, because if you harm that boy, I will kill you. You have my word on that, which I can tell you is still iron."

Eyes devoid of hope and honor met mine. "All right."

THE PRESENT ABRUPTLY INTRUDES AS I TURN A CORNER around an immense pile of rubble that used to be a warehouse and nearly collide with a herd of the dead.

The hundred or so creatures stand listlessly, swaying gently like stalks of grain in a breeze, most nude because their clothes had rotted from their bodies long ago. Children, teenagers, adults, male and female, all here, proving that death does not recognize gender, race or age . . . all enter Tilla's Hold eventually. Their skin is flaccid and flappy, as if it belongs to bigger people and their eyes stare at me whitely. Among them are a few animals as well.

The group does not react to my presence, instead they merely wait beneath the clouds for the living to cross into their domain. A few burly looking men still in ratty leather armor attest to the fact that when treasure hunters are killed, they join their killer's ranks.

I move past and realize more and more dead are lining the street, content to emerge now that clouds obscure the sky. When the sun shines, however, the dead tend to wander to the comfort of shade, protecting their bodies from Father Sun. Perhaps the heat allows them to rot quicker, rendering them incapable of consuming the living, even the rats and birds that sometimes brave the city, although their favorite food walks on two legs. I briefly wonder if one of the dead, placed in the full light of Father Sun, would finally gravitate to Tilla's Hold and how much time would it take. Enough of fancies, experimenting on these corpses reaches beyond the macabre and is not worthy of such consideration, so I shoo the thoughts from my mind.

After many detours around collapsed buildings that clutter the streets, I come into sight of the palace, the grand, ugly structure still relatively whole, although a couple of the towers have become only so much rubble. What I look for is not in a tower.

Deep in the bowels of a palace that started as a fortress many millennia and shifts ago is a room . . . spare, square and thrust into the guts of bedrock, is a room surrounded by other rooms like worker ants surrounding their queen. These rooms, in Ramashur's glory days, once served the purpose of housing the defenders of that spare, square room that lay in center of all the others. Those defenders, having taken similar oaths to the one that created the Justices, guarded this room because it was once the Royal Treasury.

Before I started looking for the bones of Hengeth Isobold, I raided the treasury, which proved a difficult task considering the sheer volume of defensive wards and magical traps that protected that spare, square room. To one such as myself, time is something I possess an abundance of and, since I lack the need to eat or sleep, I found myself in the unique situation of being able to untangle the fell magics that protected the treasury without interruption. I knew, upon my awakening this un-life and the dawning of the situation in which I found myself, that money would be a necessity.

It took weeks to cut through those protections, weeks a living mage would not have because those defenders, while dead, still roam those dark rooms like clockwork toys slowly winding down to a standstill.

Now I can come and go as I please, although if the current ruler, King Nolistro Cra-Amre IV, finds himself in desperate need of funds, I would feel beholden to aid him, once I finished my current mission. It is his money, after all.

TWELVE

THEN

M Y ASSAILANT SHOULD'VE WORN A PROPER HELM instead of a steel cap. Bat flashed down from the sky, a lightning streak of shrieking black that covered my assailant's face like a living shawl, one that clawed and bit with such savage ferocity that by the time she threw him from her face, he had torn her left eye completely out of its socket. Blood spurted from the mortified hole as well as from half a dozen deep gouges on her cheeks and neck.

My familiar squeaked indignantly as he flew away, flapping his great, sail-like wings for all he was worth, steadily climbing as the woman screamed, falling to the grass, covering her face. I stood on shaky legs and kicked her khopesh away. Haddesh stood a few feet away panting, leaning on his axe while Skakhir swung his silver hammer and stove in his remaining opponent's skull with a mighty clangor, sending blood and brains out the man's ears. He fell to the ground in a boneless heap. I swallowed my gorge at the sight and knelt at the woman's side, placing my recovered knife at her throat.

"Who sent you?" I snarled, patience long since frayed.

Her reply offered no new information.

Anger roiled deep within, but I kept my calm as I pressed the knife harder, parting skin to the point where she just started to bleed. "I said, who sent you?"

Skakhir looked up, wiping blood and brains from his hammer with a dirty rag. "Was a gud fight, lass, gud fight indeed."

Heddeg nodded, slowly shedding his mail and gambeson, revealing a heavily muscled and almost obscenely hairy torso. By Mother Moon he had to be part hedgehog. There was the beginning of an enormous bruise under his left arm stretching from armpit to navel and his panting half-breaths attested to his deep pain. Skakhir hurried over to give what aid he could and I made note to do what I could. Healing is part of the repertoire of a crafter who has Father Sun as a patron.

The woman continued her moaning, covering her mangled face and I marveled at the damage one fruit bat could inflict. "Tell me!" I urged.

"It's useless."

I looked up to see Taalis examining the woman's khopesh. Already a large purple bruise covered half her face from the shield blow she'd received, her features distorted grotesquely by swelling. By the way she stood there unconcerned, one would never know she felt pain or that a minute ago she'd lain unconscious. "What? What do you mean?"

The sylvan pointed to a small engraving on the pommel of the khopesh, three parallel wavy lines. "Here, see this? This is the mark of the Deep Water Mercenary Guild out of Postia. You're not going to get any information out of her because she literally *can't* tell you what you need to know. Deep Water mages use a geas that compels silence on these matters on their members." Taalis gave me a deep look. "Like the geas every Gyllethian Justice takes, except instead of sworn to the law, they are sworn to secrecy."

I cursed silently at the news. I should have known that what I created for something positive could be corrupted for something perverse. Rocking back on my heels, I considered the situation for a long moment before motioning my companions to gather round and stood, holding my signet ring so they could see the crossed sword and branch engraving up close. The geas was crafted in such a way that only a certain few could break the spell. In my case it would be the ruling monarch of Gylleth or the Master of Justice.

"As a member of the Queen's Justices, I call upon you all to attend. Will you bear witness?"

All three of my companions assented.

To the writhing, moaning woman. "Mercenary, you are guilty of attempting to murder a Justice in the pursuit of her duty. I offer you a chance to testify to mitigate the sentence I am prepared to pass. Any words?" I knew the geas would seal her lips, but the question had to be asked, the forms followed. It really wasn't her fault she couldn't talk, but, then again, she did try to have us killed and just because she labored under a geas to hold her tongue didn't mean she wasn't guilty of attempted murder.

She offered me plenty of words, none that I would transcribe later. "By the power bestowed upon me by Her Majesty, Queen Betelial Til-Amre, I pass judgment upon you." A pause for a deep breath. "The sentence is death to be carried out immediately." My knife flashed faster than eyes could follow, opening up a second mouth. The woman gasped as blood spurted to the beat of her heart, spraying against my clothes and face. I took the liquid steadily, not blinking. It was my burden to bear. The others backed away.

The unnamed mercenary expired quickly, leaving me drenched in her sticky, hot blood as my companions stared in horror at what I'd wrought. The job of a Justice is well known and many have levied the ultimate sentence, but it was obvious that the sylvan and the dwarves had never seen it done.

I turned to Skakhir. "Gather our horses and theirs and see to their needs." The dwarf nodded. "I need to clean myself, but first, Haddeg and Taalis, let's take a look at your wounds."

Caenwylln came into view, a sprawling city lacking walls, but not defenders. Situated within spitting distance from Beryl Bay, the city boasted three large, outer fortresses and one in the middle (called Karilgard) surrounded by a wide seawater moat. A trading port for goods from around the known world, Caenwylln was second only to Ramashur in size and riches and first in a population that believed their city should be the seat of power in Gylleth. It was the hurt arrogance of a second child who believed their older sibling got all the favoritism and attention. Just envy, everyone knew that Ramashur sat as the jewel in the crown that is Gylleth.

First things first, we entered and made straight for the central fortress, the home of Duke Jorasio Til-Amre, nephew of Her Majesty Queen Bet and a fine person in his own right. Now a bit elderly, he was a tall, spare man with stooped shoulders and a wide, welcoming face filled to the brim with a graying beard that could make a dwarf proud. I'd met the man twice since becoming a Justice and both times I'd left with a good impression of both his intelligence and competency.

Karilgard looked every inch the impregnable citadel in the center of the ring created by the fifty-foot moat. It was accessed by a stout stone bridge that terminated fifty feet from the drawbridge that completed the span. As was polite, we walked our horses across the way, their hooves thudding hollowly against wood as we drew close to the quartet of heavily armed and armored guards standing in front of a raised portcullis.

Presenting my bona fides, I asked to see Xeristo Quell, the Justice for the region. Stable hands took our horses and a steward was summoned to escort my companions to their rooms and arrange a meal.

Xeristo Quell was sitting behind a desk when a guardsman ushered me in, standing to offer a hand, which I took.

"You look like the Long Road ate you up and spat you out," said the Justice with his habitual bluntness. Xeristo and I were the first Justices to take the oath after Queen Bet purged the previous men and woman who refused the geas. He was one of the many who were not mages, but formidable fighters and ardent supporters of the crown. Stout, tending slightly toward fat, he stood taller than most and looked strong enough to wrestle a troll barehanded and had a reputation as a wizard with his two-handed flanged mace he'd named Thumper. A slight bit of gray salted his beard since the last I'd seen him, making him look older than a man just starting his third decade.

As a Justice he was of a station to command a bigger office, but the small space he occupied suited him well enough thanks to a wide window made with real glass panes. He was never one to stand on ceremony or desire the trappings of power.

"Mercenaries on the Long Road tried to shorten me by a head."

Bushy eyebrows flying high, he gestured toward a seat. Thankfully it had a thick cushion to soften a backside made sore by riding. "Mercenaries who dare attack one of the Queen's Justices? Do tell."

I told, starting with the unorthodox audience with Her Majesty, from the quarry, the geomancer's tunnels to the Long Road. As my tale wound on, his normally stoic face became a grim mask of anger. "Deep Water? I'd heard those scum branched out of Postia, but didn't expect them in

Gylleth. This makes for muddy diplomatic waters, no pun intended." He shook his head. "I'll send a pigeon to Her Majesty immediately, along with a messenger. This can't be tolerated."

"What I would like to know is who set them on me and how so quickly. I would also like to know what would've happened if I *had* disappeared. My guess it was an effort to slow down my investigation, but whoever did this must know that if their little plot failed, it would draw more attention to the matter."

Xeristo snorted. "You're missing a step, Niendra. You spent two days unraveling the magic around that geomancer's chest, two days for someone to send pigeons, to put a price on your head. If I were to guess, this mysterious murderer has been waiting to see if the queen would put a Justice on the case, which means he or she has been preparing for such an occasion. You know how the capital is, Niendra, as soon as you were put on the case tongues wagged and word reached the murderer. I bet there are several of these small mercenary bands gallivanting around the countryside keeping an eye out for a certain female Irramerian Justice."

"But why me? Her Majesty could have assigned you to investigate the murder."

He let loose a laugh that almost blew my hair back. Beneath my light cloak Bat stirred uneasily. "Really? Everyone knows you enjoy not only the favor of Lord Petre, but the queen as well. It was *your* spell that purged the ranks of the venal and corrupt. Of course, her nibs would send you on a matter of this sensitivity." He laughed again at my discomfiture and settled back, placing his large hands on his pot belly. "You've found yourself in the middle of a spider's web, I'd say."

"You want the job?"

"Dhiione's teeth, no!" he yelped, still grinning. "I'm no good at skullduggery. I'm more of a hunt and smash kind of man."

I sighed and dug into my pack, removing a trio of letters, handing them over. "Witness statements from my judgement of the mercenary. I place myself under the mandated one-week leave for death-related sentences for review."

Ignoring the statements held in one meaty fist, Xeristo leaned forward. "As Justice of the Province of Sylth, Duchy of Coverland, Kingdom of Gylleth, I, Xeristo Quell state that with these letters, written by members of two different races what have no liking for one another, that Justice Niendra Goisien needs no leave and is found to have acted appropriately. So it is noted, this day, blah, blah, blah and etcetera." He drew forth a drawer a large book with vellum sheets bound between wooden covers. With a quill and ink he noted the time, date and particulars of the incident. A drip of wax to which he affixed the seal of the Justices on his own signet ring finalized the situation.

"Hardly within the normal parameters there, Xeristo."

"That's just tough chunks, isn't it, Niendra?"

Such a way with words had Xeristo Quell. I struggled to hide a smile as he quickly finished writing in the Justice Book for the province of Sylth. I knew later he'd transcribe my tale later, near word for word and send a report to the queen since Lord Petre was indisposed. I wondered who would fill Petre's boots should he succumb to his illness and filed that thought away for later for a time when I wasn't working on the Divver case.

"You should have the watch be on the lookout for Deep Water mercenaries," I said, trying not to yawn. "Like roaches, where you see one, there's a dozen more to be found."

Green eyes flashed. "I know my job."

I held up my hands. "Sorry. Habit. Tired."

The big Justice stood and poured two real glass goblets of fortified wine, handing me one. "Drink, then go to bed. One of the guards will lead the way. Divver won't get any deader while you rest."

The wine hit my stomach with a fiery punch, one that I welcomed and it took only a few moments for the sturdy drink to make my head swim and my eyes start to shutter, the office spinning slightly.

"Go, Niendra. You're too far gone already, practically dead on your feet." He inhaled sharply and bellowed, "Siegenthaller!"

A guard opened the door. "Yes, Justice?"

"Escort Justice Goisien to her quarters, the Beryl room in the East Wing near her friends."

"Yes, Justice."

I let the burly guardsmen lead the way to my room. The bed looked soft and inviting, but I didn't feel it when I sat on the edge, the only thing I could see was the spurt of blood and that Deep Water woman's face as she realized she lay seconds away from Tilla's Hold.

My hands began to shake. Just a little at first, but soon they were as palsied and I couldn't control them. Within moments the tears came and great, wet sobs shuddered up from my chest as the repressed humors flooded through me, bringing regret and shame. A life taken by my hand, blood spilled onto grass and a woman died as I calmy watched, my face painted in crimson.

Face down over a chamber pot, I dry heaved for what seemed like hours, my stomach an aching knot that mirrored the pain in my heart. After Mother Moon knows how long, I managed to compose myself, cleaning up tears, snot and bile before laying down.

I didn't remember my head hitting the pillow.

SLEEP CLAIMED ME UNTIL PAST NOON THE NEXT DAY and not even a full lunch of cold meats and cheeses could dispel the lethargy consuming me, but I powered through and filled my belly, sending for my companions.

I never liked being waited on, but I needed a servant to help me re-braid my hair, which had taken a beating the last few days. Usually, Mirallelle's gentle hands made the ritual a sensual one, a languorous exercise which often led to more pleasant pursuits, but the ham-fisted woman who assisted me that morning turned it into a torturous time. Mother Moon, I missed my wife. I bit my lip and let her continue, though, because my devotion to the goddess required an outward symbol of my belief.

Since my first call that day was to the Divver estate I allowed Taalis to join us as she wanted to speak to Master Coventio, to personally address the concerns of the sylvan nation now that the fate of the Frost Quarry was in flux. I think she felt guilty that Soro was killed right under her nose, or perhaps Dorendiriar felt it necessary for her to continue as my companion for their own reasons. For now, I would give her the benefit of the doubt, but if she wished to accompany me on my investigation, we would have a conversation about how things got done.

The Divver estate lay a few miles north outside Caenwylln on the shores of Beryl Bay near a stretch of shoreline dominated not by sand, but by smooth, multi-colored pebbles, each one no larger than my pinky nail. Hard, gray waves pummeled the cliff walls that thrust up from the ocean like ragged menhirs just before we came into sight of that pebbly shore where a thin track no wider than a goat trail wound up to a large two-story brick house with wooden shingles and glass-paned windows on the second floor. I expected more, perhaps a mansion or castle for one of the richest men in Gylleth, but perhaps his tastes were more spartan than opulent.

No wall or gate surrounded the house, no guards or obvious defenses one would expect so I closed my eyes and stared through my tattoos and saw simple wards. Not lethal, but enough to incapacitate intruders and there were so many of them covering the house and the immediate surrounds that it would take me weeks to parse through them all. The area around the house was bordered by a low hedge, the house surrounded by well-tended, and lush, grass.

Beyond the house stood a modest barn surrounded by a large split-rail fence. My gelding nickered at the brace of horses eating hay out of a trough who whinnied in return. A young girl with seven long braids (seven being the number for Wom in her aspect of the Goddess of Animals) wearing tough leather pants raced up as we dismounted next to a hitching post where the hedge split, revealing a paved path to the double front doors.

"Hi!" the girl shouted, her face full of smiles and freckles. She took in my companions with eyes gone round in awe. "I've never seen dwarves before, but I did see a sylvan last year. Are you real dwarves and everything? Or are you just short warriors? And an Irramerian! That is so nice! We don't get much Irramerians here, although the housekeeper and gardener are Coadians, and real nice, too."

Before she could continue, a soft male voice said "Ponnia, please, they've just arrived. Perhaps you should let them rest before you pepper them to death with questions."

The girl's mouth snapped shut and she moved to my gelding, petting its velvety nose, grinning up at me with a mouthful of bright teeth.

A tall, square man with large, work roughened hands wearing a simple brown tunic and breeches walked up from the house, a large smile on his plain, honest face. Taalis's face softened a little. "Hello, Coventio," she said.

Coventio Divver, sole heir to the Divver fortune, said, "Hello *Verr-atton* Taalis," he replied with a grin, flawlessly pronouncing the sylvan honorific. "It is good to see you again. Father's remains arrived two days ago. Thank you for your efforts."

She nodded.

"*Vlochnir* dwarves," he continued using the Khulasch term for 'honorable' to my shorter companions. It was obvious his education was not lacking. "Welcome to my home, may you find warmth and happiness."

For the first time since we started this journey my dwarven friends bowed with gravity, faces full of respect for the man. "We hope yer home is ever blessed, Coventio Divver," Skakhir replied. Haddeg nodded.

"And you must be the famous Justice Niendra Goisien."

I smiled. "I must be. Although famous might be too strong a word."

Coventio shrugged. "The only Irramerian Justice in the history of the kingdom and the one whose spell forever altered the composition of the service. When you were sworn in by Her Majesty a few years ago, there were those in the know who cursed you to Tilla's Hold and back again." He grinned. "My father and I were not among those, however. No, those who hold power in Gylleth know of you, Justice."

Meaning he was one of those who held power, of course. Needless to say, I wasn't flattered by the news of my fame. The role of Justice was my obligation to repay the crown for my tuition at the Hidden Academy, but I took it with the resolve to do the best I could. Once I cleared my debt to the queen, I planned on running my little shop and growing old with my wife, which entailed becoming fat and jolly and adopting a few orphans who needed a stable, healthy home. Considering the muckup this whole case was shaping up to be, that looked like the best thing in the world.

Truth be told, though, I was good at the job and in most cases very happy with my labors as Justice, so when my debit finally found an end, perhaps I wouldn't retire at all, just take on lesser duties that would afford more time with Mirallelle. Those who ride herd on desks serve justice for the Crown as well as those out in the field. Perhaps my humors were more in balance when striving for the greater good. Or at least some good.

"Thank you, Master Divver," I said with a short bow. "May we enter."

The smile that graced his plain face quickly disappeared. "Yes, of course. I received the pigeon from Her Majesty informing me that she was assigning a Justice to investigate my father's death. Your presence tells me that it wasn't natural." He turned to the house and made a few complex gestures. "Come, it's safe for you to enter now. Ponnia, please stable the horses."

Coventio had the Coadian housekeeper, a portly Biavian woman named Richenne who smiled a lot, led the dwarves to the kitchen where they could grab a bite. As for Taalis, she insisted on joining us at the dining table for wine served in real glass goblets. I decided not to make an issue of it, but to keep my eye on the sylvan. It was clear the two were friends, which meant that the sylvan was in danger of losing her objectivity, an uncommon occurrence for a member of that race.

"You have to excuse my niece Ponnia, she doesn't meet a lot of new people since I took her in." Coventio's smile warmed his plain face into something almost beautiful. "My brother and his wife died, killed by Coadian pirates a year ago leaving me the only child." He sat with the reckless grace of a young man. I reckoned his age to be the same as mine, or thereabouts. "I do what I can with tutors and such, but she prefers to play in the stables and take care of the horses."

The wine (a Nerrinnian red) tasted sweet with a sharp note of cardamom, a product of far off Cherensitia-tsa across the Eastern Ocean, whose mysterious people would only trade with Coad, which made that island nation a naval powerhouse. That meant this vintage cost more than an entire tun of the cheap Surmaean white I drank at home. I savored the flavor before saying, "To business, Master Divver. I believe your father met with foul play and I need to know what you know."

The heir to the Divver fortune raised an eyebrow. "Am I suspect?"

"I haven't ruled it out." Taalis's mouth opened to object, but I silenced her with a raised hand and said to her, "As an observer for the Caliate to the Frost Quarry, your job is make sure the Divver concern does not overlap or infringe upon the sylvan nation." My eyes were cold and hard. I didn't need any more players interfering in my investigation, no matter that we fought side by side. "You may observe here, but don't participate."

"It's all right, *Verr-atton*," said Coventio with a smile. "I *should* be suspect, as should everyone with an interest in father's construction empire." To me, "Taalis has been a friend to the family since father was a young man starting out with a small business laying cobbles in Caenwylln, and that friendship is the reason the Caliate sent her. The sylvan have a long memory when it comes to humans nearing the borders of their lands, and rightfully so. As for your suspicion, all I can say is that I'm not interested in father's empire or his money. I have plenty of my own. I own a successful textile business, several warehouses up and down the seaboard and own eight ships, five of them outright, with enough soldiers on each to give the Coadian pirates good pause." He raised his arms, gesturing at the house. "Look around, this is no mansion, we don't have roomfuls of servants and mother used to do all the cooking. I was raised to be self-sufficient and never took a bronze crown from father when I struck out on my own."

"He must have been disappointed that you didn't want to take over the business."

Laughter greeted that remark. "Father was *delighted*. Of course he would've loved for me to continue in the family business, but what was more important was me finding my passion and making it work. He found his in construction, I found mine the textile business and I built it from scratch, without trading on my father's name to secure financing. He was proud of me, happy as could be. Father Sun's beard, Justice, he planned on selling the whole thing in a few years and living out the rest of his life peaceably."

He said the words like he believed them, but there lay under his smiling, pleasant façade an almost palpable tension, as if he felt the need to bury an ugly emotion.

We were interrupted by Richenne, who brought out a silver platter heaped with different fruits and cheeses. I chose a sharp, white coastal that I knew would complement the wine and a small slice of watermelon which I slid beneath my cloak. Bat snatched the tidbit from my fingers and ate greedily.

"All right, Master Divver, although you seem a man of good character, I still hold you in suspicion for engineering your father's death."

That tore the smile from his face and he took a large draught of wine before answering. "Damn you, Justice, your tongue cuts deeper than a sword."

Once again, Taalis looked like she would say something, but I held up a hand and she closed her mouth with a hard *snap*.

THIRTEEN

NOW

Q UEEN BEELIAL TIL-AMRE HAD ALWAYS BEEN a highly organized
woman and the Royal Treasury reflected her tidy, brilliant mind.

It was by her royal decree that the system of currency for Gylleth,
the gold crown, received an upgrade that changed the face of commerce
throughout the Six Kingdoms. Where before currency had been represented by single units of quarter, half, three-quarter and full gold crowns,
there came in to existence coins that reflected multiple values from copper to silver to units of gold up to twenty gold crown pieces called a Royal
Round, mostly used in large monetary transactions between merchants,
legal advocates, and banks. Whereas before the other five kingdoms dealt
in their own weights and measures of coin, they quickly adopted and stan-
dardized Gylleth's Royal Round, along with the Royal Writ of Value, which
was, and still is, promissory notes as legal tender. Rag paper money repre-
senting various denominations of treasury gold. Within two decades coins
everywhere in the Six Kingdoms were of the same size and weight, only
the faces thereon showed difference.

The Royal Treasury holds its gold and gems in neat stacks and racks
filed away by size and, in the case of gemstones, monetary value. The entire
room is jam-packed front to back with stout oaken shelves full of rectangular boxes filled to the brim with coin, separated by denomination and
year. At each corner sits a crate taller than I could reach up with my fingers

while standing tip-toe and inside lay bar after bar of gold ingots, more gold one location than in any other three kingdoms combined. This used to be the beating heart of Ramashur, money earned through countless centuries of trade and the Frostback gold mines, which exceeded even the panning fields of Nerrinnia.

I pass several dead guardsmen staring blankly with white eyes, their mail armor hanging from their stick-like bodies, the gambesons underneath long since succumbed to rot. These guards are the same as I found them shortly after I woke and I often wonder how they lasted this long without decaying further. I do not wonder anymore because when it comes to magic, near anything is possible and the Malosian Shift that powered Hengeth's spell seems to provide near endless efficacy.

Everything is as I left it a short while ago except for the tinkling, rushing sound of gold coins being empting into a cloth sack. *Shhhinnnggg, tink, tink, shhhiiiinggg . . .* I slow, easing my footsteps so my boots do not clop, turning into one of the many aisles dividing the Treasury to see a man hunching over, emptying one of the treasure boxes into a sturdy cloth bag, proving that my ears still retain their acuity.

"I caution you to take only as much as you can easily carry."

The man jumps, scattering coins along the aisle and snatching up a pistol, aiming it my way, the barrel shaking.

"Who are you?" he blurts, voice husky so as not to carry. His face is pale and sweaty.

The damage done from the crossbow bolt is healed, as is all damage done to my flesh given time. The wound on my neck beneath the yellow scarf does not, but perhaps it is because it is my death wound, so it will never close. The pistol does not worry me much, there is more danger to this man if any of the undead are alerted to the sound.

I hold a finger to my lips. "Shhhh. The dead are curious about loud noises." The air seems rank, foul, as if a corpse had been sliced open to release death gasses into the air. I notice that the man is filthy with some dark matter smeared across his clothes and I wrinkle my nose. "Is that you?"

He gestures with the pistol. "Come here."

"No, I do not think so."

"I'll shoot you."

I shrug. "Go ahead. There are enough dead around here to fill the room if they come looking for the source of the gunshot. Besides, you reek."

"It-it's corpse sludge," he says self-consciously. "I smeared myself with it and the dead ignore me."

My smile feels alien, but I am enjoying myself. "Let us be civil. I will not hinder you from your task, there is enough here for thousands of people. Riches for lifetimes beyond lifetimes and I am not greedy, so allow me to introduce myself. I am Niendra. You are?"

He straightens to his full height, which is not impressive. "Gerosio." Under all the corpse sludge he looks like a sad little puppy, long face and droopy eyes. For some reason I feel sorry for him.

"Well, Gerosio," I say, leaning over to scoop some of the fallen coins into my palms. Twenty Royal Rounds, enough to buy a mansion in the posh side of Orthengar and keep it fully staffed for a long time. "This is all I need."

That seems to confuse the treasure hunter, who stares at me as if my body is absent my mind and it took several seconds for him to finally say, "Good?"

"Is that a question?"

"I-I-ah . . . no. Not really, I guess." He tucks the pistol in his belt and stands there looking lost. It seems he was not expecting to hold a conversation in the heart of haunted Ramashur.

"Listen, Gerosio, for some reason I like you. Do not ask my why, but in the last few days things have become very odd for me, so I will clue you in on a few things."

Gerosio cocks his head and licks his lips, which are dry and chapped. "Yes?"

"One: do you think you are the first one to come up with the idea of using rotted flesh to disguise themselves?"

"Oh." He considers that for a moment. "I take it . . . no?"

Again with the question. It is obvious he lacks confidence. "Correct. Two: of those who discovered the way in without being attacked, what do you think happened to them?"

"They lived happily ever after?"

"Think again."

Silence. Then, "They died?"

"Gerosio, what do you think happens to those treasure hunters who die in Ramashur?"

"They join the dead."

Of course he knows that, everyone does. "They are still here, Gerosio. Your method of camouflage only works for about an hour, then the dead come. They will find you and they will start to eat you while you scream, sucking the life from you until your heart beats its last, then they stop, rejuvenated, closer to a living state, a little bit more whole. Then you will rise, hungering for the living so you can rejuvenate."

As I talk, his puppy face becomes longer and longer and his hands begin to shake. "You're trying to scare me!" he accuses.

"Absolutely correct. Is it working?" He should be scared.

I have to give the man credit, for a treasure hunter, he is honest. "Yes?"

"Most of the treasure hunters I have met are scum, willing to cut a throat or stab a back to successfully enter the city and I would not deign to spit on them if they were on fire, so take my willingness to warn you to heart. I have met hunters who have had the same idea in the area of camouflage and that is how I know it's efficacy, so believe me when I tell you probably have very little time left. Get out while you can." I grab a small iron box from a shelf and hold it out to the treasure hunter. "Leave the gold crowns, they are too heavy." I open the lid so Gerosio can see the dozens of large sapphires within. "Take these, they are much lighter and if the dead start chasing you, you will be happy for it."

The cloth sack hits the ground with a metallic thud and muffled chinking. "Thank you?" says/asks the smelly treasure hunter and I try to stifle a laugh, but I cannot quite manage the task, letting loose a staccato snigger.

"Best we be off." I heft the Royal Rounds and slip them into a pouch.

Through long corridors and great halls we walk, the palace an oft remodeled mess of masonry, wood and marble that seems to be designed to addle the senses, although the rich trappings have been reduced to dust.

We exit the palace through the great doors to find the Monarch's Plain, courtyard between the bailey and palace proper, filled almost to the brim with the dead. All turn with whitened eyes to my companion. Hundreds of walking corpses, most naked, some in armor, some the remains of other treasure hunters whose luck ran out long ago.

"Uh-oh," whispers Gerosio in horror.

"Gerosio," I say.

"Yes?"

"Run. A lot."

I do not have to tell him twice and before the last word leaves my mouth his feet are flying faster than I thought possible. For a man who looks more puppy than person he can run with surprising speed. We are surrounded, but the dead are slow to react. That does not mean they cannot run or are not fast, quite the contrary, it means that it takes them a few moments to find motivation as he speeds through their ranks, the ones he passes spinning and giving chase while I stand watching the man run, nothing for me to do because there is nothing I can do. He will either live or die, all I can do is watch. Or not. I do not feel the desire to see such a grim outcome.

The entire herd exits the immense courtyard in pursuit, the sloppy slapping of their feet the only sound they make and I am left alone, not even the most decrepit of the dead left behind. I bother to take a deep breath for a sigh, feeling an emotional, if not physical, fatigue.

The shortest way out from the palace . . . well, there is no shortest way considering that the palace rests near the east wall and directly beyond that is the Donovaria River, which one crosses only in boats considering the strength of the current. King Oslic Til-Amre, called The Clever, had set piles rocks and trees deep into the river mud all along the length of the city wall where they lay just below the surface of the water ready to impale a boat's hull. In that way he ensured that no one would land on the coast to invest the city from the east. This was a few centuries before Queen Bet, before the formalizing of the alliance between Gylleth, Gaor and Dorendiriar when tensions between the Six Kingdoms ran high as they rose from the chaos brought forth by Malosian shifts.

Thanks to Gerosio, I do not see a single dead, which eases my way through the west gate and into the thicket grown harsh outside the walls in an area that used to be a clear killing field. The emptiness out here shows me that Gerosio exited elsewhere, if he did exit at all. The odds are against his survival, but I have faith in human perseverance. There is something about the little treasure hunter, perhaps the way he holds himself that tells me he is unusual for the breed, not the kind with the morals of a snake, but someone desperate. Yes, that is it, Gerosio carries with him a sense of desperation, desperation and sadness as if he bears crushing burdens.

Centuries of treasure hunters have cut thin trails through bracken and tall grass, past thorns and grasping limbs, trails so slight one must look hard to find them, but I have the kind of time necessary, so I manage slip through the vegetation quite well.

The barrier approaches, the shimmering dome gleams at me through the trees and I hesitate, looking around in case Antonius somehow manages to find me, but the area is Antonius-free and I force myself through the treacle-thick magic wall.

Through and free, sad that I must now leave Artoch behind. Good, obedient horses who can tolerate the stench of the dead (or in this case, the undead) are hard to find. I look around and head out, ready to make my way to the rendezvous to meet Tennic. I have work to do and sylvans to meet with. Only they can help me dispense true justice.

FOURTEEN

THEN

The Estate of the Fel Rosso family, a couple miles south and west of Caenwylln, appeared in the distance, a grand manse of pink and gray granite blocks that ascended to the heights, dominating its surroundings like a battleship among rowboats. It drew the eyes from laurel and birch, hemlock and pine to its ponderous magnificence and I estimated that at least ten Royal Rounds went into its construction. A twenty-foot basalt wall encircled the estate, looking ready to repel any attack as if the owners feared marauders more than anything else and wanted to be sure their great hall served as a fortress as well.

Beside me Haddeg whistled in appreciation while Skakhir grunted, "By my clenched butt cheeks this human has pride."

Taalis merely nodded.

I let the woman accompany us, but not without some ground rules. "You can come only as a courtesy to the sylvan nation," I had stated flatly. "No more, no less. If you interfere in any way, fail to follow my orders in any manner, and I will have you jailed for obstructing the duty of a Justice."

She wanted to object, her mouth opened a few times before snapping shut and nodding tersely. There was no argument she could possibly give to change my mind, her role at the quarry was as an observer only and not a diplomatic one, so she was subject to the full force of Gyllethian law. That didn't mean she was without connections, possibly as high as the royal court, but Queen Bet was a stickler for the law and the law was on my side.

Shaking Bat out of my cloak, he fluttered free to fly high above to get a lay of the land while we rode toward the gate. The wall that circled the mansion would have done a fortress proud and the six guards at the oak and iron gate bracketed by a pair of brooding guard towers looked competent, very competent, at their jobs which included bearing halberds, crossbows and wicked looking maces. We stopped and dismounted as three of the guards held their crossbows not quite pointing at us while one lifted a hand, palm out. "Stop and state your business," he commanded from within his open-faced helm. The steely look on his bearded face and his quiet confidence told me he wasn't one to be rattled.

"Please inform Kaarik Fel Rosso that Justice Niendra Goisien and her companions are here on crown business." I held out the sigil of my office for him to examine before stowing it away.

The guard did not seem impressed, but he did send one of the others to the mansion. "Well met, Justice Goisien. I'm afraid Master Kaarik is indisposed. His wife and daughter, Lady Winnith and Korinnia are administering to the business and the estate."

News indeed. "Is it serious?"

He nodded. "Serious enough, Justice. Master Kaarik has been struck by some strange illness that has violently altered his humors and has been abed for months. I am Dojirio, head of Fel Rosso household guard."

I nodded. "Well met, Dojirio. That's something, to be part of a guard detail out in the middle of nowhere Gylleth. Must be boring."

The smile he turned my way chilled my bones. "Not so boring as one would expect. Master Kaarik is a rich man and rich men have enemies." Before I could reply, the guard he'd sent returned and whispered. They conversed for a moment, then had his companions open the gate. He offered a short bow. "Lady Justice, master dwarves and lady sylvan, I welcome you to Ul-Torin, the home of the Fel Rosso family. The ladies will see you now." To my companions, "You'll have to surrender your weapons."

Haddeg's face reddened. "Yer ever tryd to separate a dwarf from his weapon, laddie?" He placed a meaty hand on the haft of the axe and the guards shifted angrily.

"Easy there, boys," I soothed, raising my hands. "These dwarves are my guards as is customary for a traveling Justice and cannot legally be separated from their weapons. They have my guarantee for their behavior, as well." I pointed to Taalis. "You can have hers, though."

That earned me a sullen look, but the sylvan surrendered her falchion without a word. As for the dwarves, Dojirio seemed satisfied with my guarantee and called for the gate to be opened.

Stable hands were summoned to care for our horses and we were led into the mansion by Dojirio himself, who kept up polite small talk about the history of the estate. Apparently the Fel Rosso was an old money family whose fortunes rose and fell regular intervals related to the competency of each succeeding generation. Kaarik Fel Rosso marked the current rise of the family, proving to be a man with an almost prescient ability to anticipate business trends. The mansion was constructed two centuries ago when the family was at its richest, passed down from father to son ever since. Dojirio informed us that when Kaarik's father, Ilvine Fel Rosso, died thirty years ago, the place had been near a total wreck and the majority of the current fortune had been used for its restoration.

If I thought the pinkish monstrosity of the mansion was gaudy, the statues arranged out in the carefully cultivated flower garden in front just inside the walls had my jaw dropping. Fortunately, I knew what was coming thanks to a Bat's eye-view of the surroundings.

There were nine big ones. Nine enormous statues almost as tall as the wall, towering representations in red-veined marble that hit my eyes with in an assault on good taste, lording over red and yellow roses, purple hyacinths, toad lilies and wisteria. Shorter trees and bushes, such as crepe myrtles, looked liked children at the feet of colossi, their bright red and pink flowers waving slightly in the breeze.

The statue of Wom as the Earth Mother stood closest to the path, her basket of grain and fruit in one hand, a pitcher of water in the other. There was Father Sun, his beard arranged in seven spikes to indicate the rays of the sun and Dhiione, God of War and Valor in chain and plate, great two-handed sword in hand. They were all there in gaudy glory.

"By my clenched butt cheeks," I murmured in near horrified awe. Seeing it from above was bad enough, but up close and personal hit me like a punch in the gut.

Skakhir nudged Haddeg. "Told yer it would catch on."

I closed my eyes to look through the tattoos and had to open them once again before the glare of magic could overwhelm me and I paused to regain some equilibrium.

"Are you all right, Lady Justice?" asked Dojirio with some concern.

"So much magic here," I replied, blinking. "Wards everywhere. And more than that, as well. Something woven through the entire fabric of the garden."

"Master Kaarik paid the crown for the services of the wizard Tolvio Vel-Odre, a runemaster who created the defenses here," said Dojirio proudly. "You don't get to where Master Kaarik is without needing a certain amount of protection. He lifted this family out of near poverty by dint of hard work and his formidable intelligence."

Tolvio Vel-Odre. I barely remembered the name considering he was before my time, but if I wasn't mistaken I'd heard he'd returned to Hidden Academy or somesuch.

A thought occurred to me. "Dojirio, why does the head of security sound as if he is a proud member of the family?"

The man's craggy face split into a grin and for a moment I saw the younger, comelier version of the man walking next to me. "I see you are quick as your reputation claims, Lady Justice. You got me, I am Kaarik's cousin on the distaff side. I was originally a Von-Andor, but he made me a Fel Rosso, bringing me into the fold, paid for my education and gave me this job. I owe him all that I am and more."

"You definitely sound more educated than the average soldier."

"Hey!" Haddeg protested.

"Dwarves excluded, of course."

"Thanks, lass."

We continued the walk to the giant, iron banded front doors that looked like they could withstand a battering ram propelled by cragg trolls. "Who would you trust with security, Lady Justice?" asked Dojirio. "Family or a stranger?"

"I'll have to get back to you on that."

Once inside we were met with opulence, thick patterned rugs, paintings of Fel Rossos past and present adorning the walls and more statuary, including smaller representations of the nine gods in the same red-veined marble quarried in northern Gylleth. Only Himir, God of Sleep and Knowledge, was missing. Perhaps he had nodded off in a corner somewhere.

In a formal dining room dominated by a table large enough that walking from one end to the other might take most of the day, we were urged to pick a chair and sit. Servants dressed in the latest fashion, burgundy hose and long tunics for men and women in simple dresses, also in burgundy, brought wine, fruit, cheese and cold meats to snack on while we waited. Taalis munched on an apple while I made do with a slice of sharp white cheddar and strawberries. The dwarves ate anything that came within reach and quite a few things that weren't. Dojirio bid us goodbye and made himself scarce, his chain mail softly chinking as he left.

It didn't take long before a tall woman in a dark blue formal dress with white wimple and thin veil affixed to a gold, ruby-studded circlet, glided into the room. She moved with smooth grace, almost floating, her gait that of a stalking cat. "Hello, all," she practically purred, her smile demure. "I am Winnith Fel Rosso, you are all well come here."

My mouth tried not to fall open, but it was hard keeping it closed. Winnith was perhaps the most beautiful woman I'd ever seen. An hourglass figure, large bosom and a heart shaped face possessing lips that begged to be kissed and nibbled upon, I felt such a wash of desire that shame followed quickly. There I was, a married woman lusting after another married woman while my wife waited patiently at home. Mother Moon! I felt my cheeks heating up and I stood abruptly, my chair nearly falling over.

"Lady Winnith," I said quickly to cover my reaction. "I am—"

"I know who you are and why you're here," she said, cutting me off with a charming smile and gentle voice so as not to give offense. "You want to know if the Fel Rosso family had anything to do with the death of Soro Divver."

I nodded. "Word travels fast."

"When it comes to the Divver family, word always travels fast." Her full lips pursed into a sad smile. "I half-expected a Justice to arrive earlier. Well, not you, but Justice Quell considering the Divver family is part of the Duchy of Coverland."

"And the murder occurred in the Jaantertrean province, Duchy of Iver-Taal, which is Justice Canlo's jurisdiction, so he by rights should be investigating, however Her Majesty chose me and I serve at the will of the Crown." I took a few beats to regain my composure, to put aside the shameful lust that burned through my belly. "Now, may I please see Master Kaarik Fel Rosso?"

Winnith gave me a terse nod, the smile disappearing from her perfect mouth. "Come," she said. "Just you, if you would. His condition is delicate and we must be quiet."

I signaled for the other three to stay and enjoy the repast while I followed the lady of the house and the musky/fruity smell of her perfume. It made me wonder at the color of her hair beneath the wimple and veil.

Mother Moon! I shook myself and put all thoughts to Mirallelle.

"My husband's room is on the first floor. We used to live on the fourth, but since he took ill it is easier to care for him without climbing the stairs all day." We passed several doors and over carpets so lush they tried to hold my feet fast as we walked. Eventually we came to a plain oaken door so brown as to appear black and we entered the room beyond.

I half expected place bigger than my home, but it turned out to be fairly small, big enough only for a bed fit for one and that one lay under heavy coverlets among a bevy of multi-colored cushy pillows that looked soft as mist.

The man lying there was pale, drawn, with the severe features of one who worked hard all his life, the look I'd seen on the farmers coming to market, tired men and women who bore the brunt of a difficult life well. Unlike those people, this man didn't have the flesh to spare for a long illness, he was far too thin for that. Not gaunt, just thin. Graying black hair lay splayed over his pillow around a face that might be called handsome if it wasn't for the patchy beard covering his cheeks and chin. Calloused feet stuck out from beneath the cover, the skin thin and veiny and the lady of the house moved quickly to cover them from the slight chill in the air.

"He often kicks off the blankets and I do this several times a day," whispered Winnith. As she leaned in her perfume almost made me dizzy with its sweet/musky odor and I felt another rush of desire. "We must be quiet; he gets such little sleep these days that these naps are ever precious."

"I need to speak to him about his businesses and his rivalry with the Divver family," I whispered in return after taking a step back, nervously clutching at my braids. A slight sheen of sweat made my skin shine.

As if she knew the effect of her perfume on me, Winnith took my hand and gently led me from the room. "Both my daughter and I can help you, Lady Justice," she said once the door was closed. "We have been taking care of the Fel Rosso business since Kaarik became ill. He took great pains to educate us both on business matters so the mistakes of past Fel Rossos would not plague our descendants."

"Meaning foolish investments and squandering money?"

"Precisely." We stood face to face in the hallway amid gleaming wood paneling and portraits by artists with some considerable talent and I desperately wanted to step back. We stood inches apart and I could smell sweet melon on her breath mixing with that heady perfume, the heat of her body reaching out to mine, beckoning. Her beauty and raw sensuality had me on the defensive and I hated it with a passion, but I couldn't let her see, let her know how she affected me.

By the look on her face, she knew quite well and a ball of anger started to burn in my belly, focusing my thoughts. "Tell me about your relationship with Rol-Venber," I stated flatly.

Winnith blinked a few times, nonplussed by my abrupt change in manner. "Please, Lady Justice, can you be more specific?" she asked.

Forcing numb legs, I took a step back, desperate for perfume-free air. "Do you have dealings with them and what kind? Since you've been so well educated by your husband, I think you ought to know."

She nodded sagely and took her hand from mine. I felt a sudden relief. "Of course. We have very few dealings with Rol-Venber, save for a loan or two as business dictates. At this moment they hold the lien on a property out of Drayport, but that's it. Currently we are very liquid and plan to stay that way."

"Liquid enough to purchase the note the bank holds on the Divvers? Perhaps liquid enough to assume the totality of their business assets?" I asked.

Holding a hand to her mouth to stifle her laughter, Winnith Fel Rosso let her mirth out while I waited. After a minute, cheeks flushed, she replied. "Oh, I see what you're implying . . . that somehow we engineered the Soro Divver's murder to take over his business."

I shrugged. No reason to hide my suspicions. "Of course."

"Lady Justice, I have no interest in absorbing the Divver empire. By Yrusis's golden chalice! Trying to run the Fel Rosso concerns and the

Divver's as well would turn me gray before my time and, as you saw, my husband is in no shape to handle even his own affairs." Winnith tone became grave. "He was a robust man in his prime, but now I fear he is traveling to Tilla's Hold and I have no desire to enmesh myself in such things. Yes, we have gold enough, but only for our concerns, the Divver businesses are far to large for us to handle and would drain our accounts before we see profit. Taking over Divver holdings is just not good business."

"Can you thing of anyone else who could have done it? Any enemies, any rivals who would like to see him dead?"

"People like my husband and Soro Divver always make enemies, Justice, but I no of no one else. Surely you've considered his son, Coventio?"

Her tone was sincere, but her eyes still held a glint of amusement, as if she had I secret I desperately needed. Nodding, I informed Winnith that I might need talk to her again and excused myself. Both dwarves and Taalis saw the storm clouds on my brow and even Dojirio, who was waiting by the front doors to escort us from the property, kept his mouth shut.

"What now?" asked Taalis as we exited the manse.

I grimaced. "There's trouble afoot and I need to prepare."

"Prepare for what?"

"The worst." I didn't bother to explain further.

As we left the garden, Skakhir's head whipped around. "Did yer see that?"

We stopped. "What?"

"Somethin' moved, lass. Something big, I think."

"There are several large cats on the estate," said Dojirio with a shrug. "You have good eyes, master dwarf."

"By my clenched butt cheeks, but I think it was no cat."

FIFTEEN

NOW

IT PLEASES ME TO NO END TO SEE THE SUMMER HOUSE AGAIN. From my vantage point upon a large river bluff a half-mile away it looks almost toylike, a child's plaything ready to be filled with dolls and little wooden horses.

The beech tree I lean against keeps the sun from my eyes as I wait for Tennic while watching the barely seen guards walk about the perimeter of the mansion just inside the wall. It is good to see that the rulers of Gylleth have not abandoned the site after the fall of Ramashur and that the Forever Tree still flourishes whitely a quarter mile from the building. From what I can see, the only changes from my time to now are the arms and armor of the guardsmen and women who are on patrol. Instead of heavy plate and chain they wear loose-fitting shirts under tabards bearing the Sea Eagle crest of House of Cra-Amre. Rapiers and muskets have replaced broadswords and crossbows, although it is good that science has not figured a way to replace horses. That would be one change too many.

Five hundred years has increased the Forever Tree's girth and its height, where once it merely dominated the scene, now it screams for attention from its two-hundred-foot-tall mass of silver-green leaves.

The king is not in residence, a fact bolstered by the skeleton crew of guards. His presence would require a small army of royal protectors that would fill the brace of long barracks to the south of the mansion.

Behind me, raspberry bushes rustle slightly and I smile. "Took you long enough," I say. "I have been waiting forever."

Tennic emerges from the green, indignant and fuming, brushing dry leaves from his hair with his fingers. "How did you know?" he asks, taking a seat next to me and crossing his arms on his knees.

I still watch the Summer House and the Forever Tree, remembering happier times and I my smile fades. "Craftwork, boy. You were discreet enough, but the bushes all around rustle when someone draws near, a simple enough spell to cast."

"What's discreet?"

"Subtle, unobtrusive."

"Discreet. Good word. What if I was a bad guy, like that Seth character?"

"Then I would have heard a meadowlark sing."

"That makes sense except I don't know anything about no meadowlarks." He leans back against the tree. "I could see that tree for miles. Guess that's why you gave me directions to this place. Nice house."

He says that as if the mansion in the valley below is merely a cozy cabin. I laugh and force myself not to give him a hug. "I knew you would find the place. Anyone can if they know to look for the Forever Tree. Do you know where Seth and Antonius might be?" I refuse to give the man his title of Justice. He has lost claim to that honorific.

"Gave them the slip. Ran, then hid. Those two aren't trackers at all, that's for sure." He pauses a moment looking nervous. "I heard the cracking of wood and panicked horses. Think that Blood and Vicious freed themselves."

I nod. "Not surprised. The man is a wizard after all and the fact that Seth did not gag him tells me Vicious kept that fact from his son."

"Yeah. Heard me a lot of yelling from Antonius and his idiot relative what you beat on the other day."

Good. That is what I counted on. "We will have to hope that those that try to chase us are confounded by my ability to mask our trail." The fact that another wizard follows is unsettling, but Body Mages, a rare enough specialty, tend not to study nature craft.

No more delays. No more stops for this, that and the other thing. I have sylvans to see and have been thwarted enough.

He thinks on that for a moment staring at the arboreal giant then says, "What now?"

I looked to the fading sun as it neared the tip of the Frostbacks and then to the guards, insect-like in purpose and determination. "Now we head to Dorendiriar. I have sylvans to see."

RENDERING THE ROYAL ROUNDS INTO BATTERED BITS of gold does not lessen their value as goldsmiths provide an easy way to exchange the nuggets into the current coin of the realm, losing only a silver crown or two of in the trade off. Wylclow is large enough that finding a goldsmith is no problem and soon the pair of us are freshly bathed, clothed and riding in a carriage on the Long Road toward Orthengar. I prefer to ride horseback, but there are very few horses like Artoch who tolerate my condition, so I it is either walk or have someone drive.

Tennic smiles at me, an insolent grin. The little rat knows my thoughts too well and takes delight in my discomfiture while he thoroughly enjoys the kidney jarring trip inside the carriage. I do not have the heart to cuff him about the ears for his cheek. We are children only once and I care for the boy and his dimply, cheeky smile.

An old man dressed in a fine, long, yellow tunic with tan breeches named Joovis Her-Heverfor is the only other passenger. A kindly gent, he takes a shine to Tennic and spends most of the trip regaling the lad with his youthful exploits, most of which, I am sure, are full-cloth fancy. The boy does not seem to mind. He peppers Joovis with pertinent questions and flatters the old man unashamedly, which is well received. The old man shares a flask of brandy with the boy and soon Tennic wears apple cheeks and is laughing like cat coughing up a hairball.

The carriage stops at Heddenshire where I find a perfumer who supplies me with a small bottle of lavender scent to hide my deadsmell, which, if Joovis's wrinkling nose is any indication, I need desperately. The perfumer also provides me with the location of an apothecary to assist me with my crafting needs.

On the outskirts of town, we find a horse trader with several different mounts to choose from and there I encounter a good dapple rouncey, an older mare with a sad look in her eyes, that did not mind my condition and a chestnut jennet, almost a pony, for Tennic.

The trader, a big man with shoulders like a blacksmith and a beard to his belt, hems and haws as if we ask for his finest destriers before declaring that he could not part for the pair for less than three gold crowns. As my hand dips into my pouch and the trader's eyes begin to gleam, Tennic explodes.

"Are you insane?" screams my companion in outrage, face mottling red. "Three? For these nags? They're almost ready to be chopped up for stew!"

And then the haggling begins. With my easy access to money, I feel no need to negotiate, but Tennic, on the other hand, considers what the trader demands to be no less than outright theft and it will not stand for it if he has breath in his small body.

In the end, the trader accepts a single gold crown for the pair and gives me a gimlet glare. "Next time," he says. "Leave the boy at home."

I grin. "Never."

Orthangar is out of the question, but I feel the need to make haste now that no obstacles bar my path to Dorendiriar save time and distance so the next course of action is to skirt the city and make for the Callic Pass. We travel the Long Road for a day before it terminates, transforming into a more mundane thoroughfare.

One moment our horses' hooves clop on the magical road, the next not. It is not as well fitted or even. No one knows why the builders decided to end the Long Road so abruptly a day from the pass, but it ends as smoothly as it begins . . . with an even line as if the gods had erased the remainder from existence. The new road, non-magical and ill-laid in comparison with blocks of varying size and color, vegetation poking through the seams, still offers a better passage than no road at all.

We garner many odd looks: an Irramerian woman dressed as a man in leather trousers and a tunic of blue linen on an old service horse and a young man mounted on a jennet normally ridden by ladies, but we are not accosted. Farm hands and ranchers look, some wave, but no one attempts to make conversation or approach to exchange news of the realm. Evening finds us in the mountains at a large, respectable-looking inn called Borderlands at the foot of the pass, three stories of quarried stone and beams of ash and oak, an establishment that caters to sylvans and humans alike and all the traders in-between and, as such, is busy on any given day. I feel it is a good thing to stay in the public's eye this time. Unfortunately, business seems slow, but there are people enough.

The proprietor of inn, an older man with a shiny dome lacking even a whisper of hair, welcomes us and we sit among the half-dozen patrons eating supper in the common room filled with the smell of a coal fire burning in a stove in one corner and the odor of several washed and unwashed bodies. I order a dinner of squab for Tennic and a small beer for myself, which I pretend to drink while the boy takes the occasional sip.

It dawns on me that he is not so much a boy but a young man and this is reinforced as he stares at the servers, a pair of somewhat comely girls who bear a resemblance to the bald owner. When my heart still beat, boys that age would already have a brace of children of their own and be working their father's fields. This seems to be a kinder age to children, although with Tennic's amorous humors on full display, not so much a child anymore.

"Do you fancy the girls?" I whisper.

He turns beet red and one of the serving girls flips her hair back from her face and tosses him a smile and I look at Tennic as if for the first time, realizing he is a comely lad. His hair, which had been soot stained and grimy when we first met is now a dark blond with reddish highlights thanks to the prodigious use of soap and his eyes flash a bright green like jewels cushioned in velvet. "Of course I do," he whispers fiercely, not taking his eyes off the girl. His cheeks are so flush with blood that he might bleed out of his pores.

I let myself sigh, wishing for more time and notice the owner keenly staring at the boy. He notices my inquiring look and shakes his head slightly and it is understood that his daughters are not on the menu. I return his nod and he relaxes somewhat.

As Tennic stares at the serving girls and I pretend to drink my small beer, I look around at the others sharing the common room: a sylvan trader with hair so pale the word white does it faint justice, two heavyset men with the look of caravan guards with short maces at their belts, a large woman whose curly red hair is restrained in a tight braid that travels down her back and a two men who are too busy staring lovingly at each other to notice that the world outside their view even exists.

The two caravan guards greedily shovel what could only be called beef stew into their mouths, wooden spoons traveling from bowl to mouth and back again with dizzying speed. The bigger one suddenly grunts, eyes crossing slightly and drops his spoon. His companion does not notice as the man continues to sit and stare at nothing while his eyes begin to cross.

Slowly, as if whatever mechanism keeps him upright suddenly fails, his face falls into his bowl . . . separate from his skull. The rest of him slumps to the floor trailing blood.

With a startled curse the other caravan guard begins to rise, but he manages no more than to barely move his fundament from his chair before he, too, grunts and falls, blood spewing from his mouth. The large woman shouts and is on her feet, twin long daggers in her meaty fists, eyes searching for a threat. The sylvan is already on his feet, eyes wide and staring at a point near the two fallen guards before leaping with inhuman grace to slice at thin air with a basket hilt rapier. The sound of metal striking metal rings loud in the common room.

I curse and shove Tennic unceremoniously under the table, almost certainly bruising him in the process, closing my eyes, concentrating *through* the Father Sun tattoos. The common room comes into a focus so sharp it almost hurts to look at, each wooden whorl, each flicker of flame a clearly etched vision so pure that it tears at my mind, but I push my sight to see what cannot be seen by normal eyes.

What I observe is the figure, no detail, but a blurry outline of what I think is a man due to the height and apparent bulk, a man sporting a powerful invisibility spell, one so difficult to cast that even Arch-Mages would be taxed. He moves with fluid grace as if he knows what the sylvan will do before he does. He spins and the blurred outline of a rapier parries the sylvan's thrust and executes a perfect *riposte* that opens a long cut on its opponent's side that begins to bleed freely. The sylvan stumbles back, face a rictus of pain.

The outline's arm suddenly flings to the side and the large woman sprouts a dagger from her throat, blood spurting onto her tabletop for a moment before her body falls to the floor. The two lovers yell and draw wicked long knives, standing back-to-back ready to take on anything that might come their way.

I pull a small vial I purchased at the apothecary's in Wylclow and begin to chant in Dendrich, hoping the sylvan can last against the thing that is attacking us. I have a sneaking suspicion . . .

Whirling like a Irramerian dervish, the figure kicks the sylvan in the stomach, sending him crashing into a table which is becomes so much kindling. He lays there groaning, doubled over in agony.

The innkeeper takes wild swings with a wooden club the size of a table leg, swiping at where he thinks the attacker should be and comes close, the club missing the figure's skull by inches. Almost contemptuously the outline runs his rapier through the innkeeper's heart and the man falls to the screams of his daughters.

At that moment I finish my incantation with a flourish and open the vial and fling the contents in the air. Instead of liquid, a thin mist bursts forth like steam, a vaporous spell that ripples through the air like a heat shimmer, washing over all. The outline blurs even more, flickering and sparking against my spell and I call feel its magic war with mine. It loses and what is hidden is revealed.

Standing there is a familiar figure in black with a shining rapier and brace of pistols in a holster at the small of his back. Vicious stares at me balefully, then smiles. Gone is the albino makeup and the false teeth, but his smile is all the more horrifying for it. "I knew you were good," he remarks offhandedly, stabbing the floor with his rapier and drawing the pistols. Two reports sound and the young lovers drop beneath a cloud of smoke, holes in their skulls leaking brains.

"Come with me," Vicious says, pulling the rapier from the floor and holding it loosely as if he has not a care in the world.

My humors are all a-roil as I realize that anyone who could have come to our aid is now dead, only the screaming, crying daughters of the innkeeper are left. "No."

"There is no one now to help you, witch. You realize you cannot win against me."

I smile. "Care to test that theory?"

He says three words in Dendrich and makes a complex gesture with is left hand.

The spell slams against my skin and it would have flung me against the far wall like a temperamental child throwing a rag doll, but instead I stand there while white sparks erupt all around me, showering the room.

I smile and say, "This time I am prepared."

Vicious offers me a tight smile and gestures once again, the words of magic slipping from between his lips and more sparks appear as his spell shatters against my defenses. His smile does not diminish, however. In fact, he looks positively delighted. He vaults over a table, rapier flashing in a wicked slash toward my left shoulder to render my arm useless.

The blade falls . . . and stops as if it encounters a brick wall, vibrating in place for a moment before the vibration rises in tone and volume, a metallic whining that fills the room in an instant before the blade shatters like glass. Pieces of metal fly everywhere, one six-inch spar *thunking* into the floor between my boots.

The assassin stares for a moment at the hilt in his hands, dumbfounded, and at the shining aura that flashes on my dark skin, which gives me all the time I need.

My fist flies out and catches Vicious on the point of his chin with hard *thwack*, spinning him around. I attempt a kick but even in his dazed condition he dodges, stumbling away from my attack without his usual grace.

I keep after him, but even hurt and reeling, he is beyond me, a fighter of consummate skill and cunning and for a moment I feel fear that he will escape to bedevil me again and again until he gets what he wants.

Both of us have forgotten Tennic. The boy flashes into existence behind the assassin and plunges his misericord into the meaty flesh of one buttock to the hilt. Viscous screams in pain and tries to strike the lad, but Tennic dodges the blow and strikes again, this time at the other cheek with the same effect.

Vicious falls, teeth clenching and eyes squinting almost shut. Tennic stands over him, ready to plunge the slim blade into the assassin's throat.

"Hold!" my voice whips across the common room.

Tennic is unable to stop the thrust, but he manages to pull the blade to one side so the needle point strikes floor, not flesh. He yanks the blade free and takes a step back. "Do you know what kinda man this is?" he blurts, tears at the corners of his eyes. "Do you?"

"All too well, my friend." I keep my voice steady, although I want to reach out to the lad and hug him hard. "Stand back, please."

Reluctantly he complies.

"You stabbed me in butt, boy!" yells Vicious. He is bleeding copiously, red hands over his wounded bits.

My voice has no mercy in it. "Feel lucky that I stopped him." I consider for a moment. "The first time I was not paranoid enough, I did not prepare for an attack. My only failing here was thinking you would not attack us in public." And I will be cursed if he would delay my quest further. I almost gnash my teeth at the thought of it and count to nine slowly so my undead humors will settle.

He says things I do not wish to repeat or have Tennic hear, but I see the lad shrug as if he has heard such language before. After a while the tide of invective begins to subside and the two serving girls reach behind the bar for a pair of spiked clubs and begin advancing toward Vicious with murderous looks on their comely faces.

"Hold," I say and they stop cold, although not without some grumbling. I approach Vicious with my long knife and cut his purse from his belt and check the contents. Three Royal Rounds and several silver crowns. Tossing it to the girls, I say, "Enough to pay for the inn several times over."

The girls stare in amazement at their fortune and retreat behind the bar, no doubt planning their futures.

"You win this round," says Vicious.

My eyes narrow. "I am surprised you did not see to your son."

It is his turn to narrow his eyes, but in amusement. "Who says I didn't?"

"Let's kill him and go," says Tennic. There is no forgiveness in his voice and I feel sad for it.

"Do not be in such a hurry to take a life," I say softly. "It is not worth the cost to your soul."

Vicious's laughter fills the common room for a minute or two as we stare at him.

A voice cuts through the room like a knife. "By my clenched butt cheeks, that looks like it hurts!"

My heart leaps at the familiar voice. For a moment I think I might cry. "Skakhir!"

SIXTEEN

THEN

NIGHT IN CAENWYLLN BROUGHT A LANGUID PEACE to the city and only the guard, bearing copper lanterns, provided illumination while they patrolled the streets. Overhead the stars shone down in their multitudes while hundreds of torches in Karilgard tried to compete with the heavenly display but couldn't.

My mind couldn't help but wander to the Divvers and the Fel Rossos. Two families who seemed cooperative, but I believed were not forthcoming in their conversation with a certain witchy Justice. If they planned to deceive, then I would catch them out. Both pointed fingers, both gave good motives for murder, but the truth lay hidden, although I made plans to winkle it out soon enough and had time to put a plan into play. While I waited for that plan to bear fruit, I hatched another that would bring other, more directly ruthless people to justice, people with power enough to be a clear and present danger to the Crown.

I walked down the Street of Smells where the perfumers and apothecaries held sway, passing a brace of guards who lifted their heavy lanterns to shine them into my face. Noting my clothing and bearing, they tipped me a nod and continued down the street, hobnailed boots clacking against cobbles. There was enough protection to allow those who wanted to walk at night a bit of ease to do so.

Far above Bat flew in lazy circles, almost invisible from the ground but

I knew where he soared. Through his eyes I could see myself walking as I had for the past couple of hours and I could also see the two men who followed at a casual, but steady, pace. They moved from shadow to shadow, darkened doorway to darkened doorway, but Bat could pierce the darkest of nights with his high-pitched squeaks that allowed his ears to map the world all around.

I half expected the two. Actually, I hoped for it.

Making sure that I didn't do anything that would betray my knowledge of the stalkers, I moved as if I didn't have a care in the world, a woman on the way to a specific destination, but in no hurry to get there. After a few blocks, my feet took me to an alley off to my left, one that didn't stink too bad of urine and feces and strolled in as if I owned the buildings on either side.

My boots echoed hollowly as I slowly tensed. This would be it. This *should* be it. I'd been gallivanting across the city from shop to shop for the past two days, perusing goods until my eyes were ready to cross before finally catching the two that followed thanks to Bat. I also had plenty of time to prepare for this encounter and time for a crafter is the greatest ally.

The interviews with the Fel Rosso and Divver families left me unsatisfied and the Rol-Venber bank hadn't provided even the hint of a clue, at least according to Xeristo, who conducted interviews with Torrio Sil-Atre, the woman oversaw their day-to-day operations in Caenwylln. Two of Xeristo's most trusted men had been pouring over any and all documents regarding the families and would give their findings soon.

The big Justice could have let me handle the investigation by myself, but I had sneaking suspicion that things were so quiet in the duchy of Coverland that he was chomping at the bit to *actually* do something. Since I didn't want to spend a minute more away from Mirallelle, I enthusiastically accepted his help, so I felt it necessary to take a risk, one I hoped didn't lead me to returning to Ramashur in a casket.

Bat flew just over the alley and let loose a series of squeaks and I let the information from those noises flood my mind, ignoring the tall buildings to either side. The two figures turned the corner behind me, leached of color by Bat's sound/images, a pattern of every shade of gray imaginable and rendered in exquisite detail from their misshapen hats to the sinister sneers on their faces. However, just before Bat careened wildly and our connection was abruptly severed in a painful twist that I felt deep in my mind and gut, my familiar caught sight of a person on the rooftop above. A yawning emptiness suddenly threatened to swallow me whole and it took the realization of imminent danger to pull me from the brink of an agonizing emotional freefall.

Tears started to roll down my cheeks as I turned to those following me and, in a moment, a cage made of shining bars of light sprang into existence, imprisoning me. I knew this spell and although grief threatened to close my throat and dull my mind, a worm of fury rose to the surface of my heart.

Coarse laughter bled through the alleyway as the two figures drew closer to glowing blue-white bars that surrounded me, bringing them into sharp detail.

"Relax," said one, a big man with incredibly broad shoulders. I noted he was missing an ear as he drew a short sword from the inside of his long cloak. "I'll make this quick."

The other, another large man with a face like the back end a mule, chuckled. "How about a bit o' sport first?"

An iron voice drifted down from above, "Get on with it."

"Aye, sir," said One Ear, edging closer with his short sword.

I looked up and saw through my tears a man in a long billowing cloak with hair like a pennant blowing in the wind standing at the edge of the roof overlooking the alley. "You idiots made a mistake," I growled in fury.

"What's that?" said One Ear, ready to strike.

"Kill her," screamed the man on the roof.

"I'm not alone."

There came the sound like an axe hitting rotten wood and the ugly man suddenly flew to the side to strike the building to my right, skull splitting and brains splashing against stone. One Ear turned in time to take Xeristo's shoulder to the gut and was lifted bodily off the ground to slam into the building on the left. The big Justice booted One Ear in the face as he fell and the man hit the ground and lay still. The ugly man continued to leak his brains all over the ground.

"Nice," sneered the man on the roof. "But we weren't quite so alone ourselves." Three more large men entered from the opposite end of the alley, all sporting heavy leather armor under long cloaks and flanged maces in their hands.

Xeristo looked back at my glowing cage that blocked the alley to the three advancing men, hefting Thumper in both hands. The giant mace would be hindered by the buildings to either side, limiting his movement. He looked to figure staring down from a three-story height. "Not bad . . . we saw your two thugs and you raised us three more, but tell you what, wizard."

The wizard, smart enough to stay out of physical combat, cocked his head. "What?"

"I raise you *two* dwarves."

My hands performed a complex gesture and I said a hard word in Dendrich. The cage glimmered for a moment then evaporated in a shower of sparks that quickly faded. "Time to play, guys," I yelled as the three men attacked Xeristo.

From behind the trio Skakhir and Haddedg came howling around the corner in as if demons nipped their heels, shrieking Khulaschian war cries and waving their weapons over their heads. Instead of clattery, chinking chain they wore studded leather armor.

Xeristo attacked a split second before the two dwarves collided with the three, shining war hammer striking one man so hard he fell to the ground instantly, head crushed while Haddeg spun his axe as if were a wooden switch, chopping off one attacker's arm before removing his head. That left the third who was made of sterner stuff. Whirling away from Skakhir's shining hammer, he kicked Xeristo in the gut and parried Haddeg's axe in one fluid motion, a short mace in each hand. The big Justice took a blow to chest that would have felled a lesser man, but thanks to a breastplate of reinforced leather under his tunic, he merely stumbled back with a grunt and a curse.

I was aware of all this peripherally as I had already locked eyes with the wizard and magic meshed our minds together painfully like two ill-fitting puzzle pieces that began a mage battle.

Most people think mage combat involve fireballs and serpents of ice, but the reality is that it all happens on the battlefield of the mind as will clashes against will until only one survives. Every mage battle, with no exception, ends with only one survivor, no other outcome is possible because for a caster's mind to untangle with its opponent safely, one must die, which makes wizard battles rare considering the mortality rate. Of course, no one wants to die and a single mistake, one momentary lapse of concentration, means no more Yrusisday festivals for the loser.

We stood on the broken ground of the wizard's mind, the earth a shattered mass of volcanic rock that tore at my feet, the wizard in his robes of midnight fabric billowing cloudlike around his spare form as he stared at me with eyes that shone a pestilent yellow. Now that I saw him with some clarity, I noticed that he was tall and lean, yet muscular, a man used to physical as well as magical forms of combat. A soft smile graced a hawkish face decorated with a black goatee and mustache.

"You're in my world now," he said as blue lightning raced across a purple sky with a sound like a million shields being struck by a million swords. In the terrain of his mind he had the home ground advantage as it were, which put me in the vulnerable position. "I cannot be beaten here."

I forced a smile and with a flick of my mind I floated above the rock that wanted to tear at my boots, feeling the raw edge of Bat's absence. Anger began to build in me and I knew my eyes blazed with green bale light. "You killed my familiar," I growled, heat in my cheeks. "Not a smart move."

Fire bloomed from his fingertips, racing toward me and it hit the invisible shield I erected around my body, roaring, seeking my flesh, wanting to eat me, devour me, sear my nerves and cause the fat inside to run like tallow as my eyes burst from the heat. With a nudge of my will I expanded the shield until it nearly touched his body, forcing him to dismiss the fire before it could curl back on him.

Snarling, ebon darts sprung into existence around me and raced to the wizard only to be soaked up by the midnight cloak that served has his defense. He flicked a thumb and glassine swords fell from the sky to shatter on my shield, the broken shards bobbing around, probing for a hole in my defenses.

Suddenly my shield crackled with lightning every bit as actinic blue as the lightning overhead, near blinding and with a deafening report. The wizard's glowing yellow eyes widened in alarm. His billowing cloak, so black it drank the surrounding light, tried to absorb the lighting, but it was too bright, too strong and a jagged blue shard made it through, striking his chest and sending him end over end across the broken plain.

I followed with bolts of ice and fire, fast and furious and unrelenting, peppering the wizard, pushing him screaming over the plain. From all around me the shattered stones erupted, exploding outward and sending shards into my shield with such intensity that it buckled under the force.

Ribbons of pain erupted on my flesh and the deafening laughter of a mad god blasted across the purple sky to drown out the clash of thunder.

"You think that's enough to kill me? *Me*?" The wizard was once again floating in front of me as I reeled from the onslaught. "We are in *my* mind, witch, and I am one of the greatest wizards of this generation." He floated closer as I cowered, hurt and bleeding. "There is no hope of defeating me, so surrender and I will make your death a painless one." His voice underwent the transition from contemptuous to comforting, the rich timbre soothing now, as if he had my best interests at heart.

I remained cowering on the shattered landscape of the wizard's imagination, the sharp shards of stone tearing at my knees and palms. "Truly?"

He floated closer, eager. "Of course. I have no animosity toward you. This is a job, nothing more, nothing less."

"Then why me? Who wants me dead?"

The wizard shrugged. "I don't know, it's not my job to question the orders, payment was sent by a factor in Ramashur, some agent of the Widow. They paid and Deep Water adheres to its contracts. It really isn't personal."

"Hmm." I stood slowly while the wizard regarded me with what he probably thought was a kindly expression. "You don't know many crafters, do you"

He shrugged. "No, why tether yourself to one of the Nine? Better to serve yourself then a higher power whose motives are not your own."

A common misconception by the wizard class. The Nine offered magic for devotion and crafting rituals tended to long and tedious, but it definitely had benefits. "Because when we're prepared, we're *unbeatable*." My skin suddenly glowed green and blue, the colors coming from deep within as if I was a lamp shining in the dark. The wizard recoiled in shock as the light grew brighter and brighter, becoming hard-edged daggers that flew everywhere, shearing rock as easily as flesh. Nothing escaped my dagger light, it went everywhere, penetrated everything.

As the wizard howled in agony, I said, "And you killed my familiar, so this is personal to me."

I OPENED MY EYES. THE ALLEY WAS QUIET AROUND ME, my companions staring. The place smelled of blood as well as feces and urine now and my stomach made a slow roll as nausea gripped me. My companions stood nearby staring as if I'd turned green or something.

"What?" I shook myself like a dog, a strange tingly feeling racing across my skin.

"Yer went away there, lass," said Haddeg, wiping blood of the blade of his axe.

"Mage battle," I replied with a sigh, feeling a near overwhelming fatigue. I read all about this form of magical combat and the instructors at the Hidden Academy cautioned that even the victors could suffer aftereffects. "It was my first. Hopefully the last as well."

Xeristo moved in close. "Are you all right?" he whispered.

"Fine."

A grin split his beard. "Good. We saved one for you to question." He pointed to where Skakhir stood, one foot on neck of now terrified One Ear. "You said you could remove a geas, so let's question this Deep Water mercenary piece of filth and get out of here now that your harebrained plan seems to have paid off."

Harebrained, maybe, but sometimes long shots paid off big. I figured that if there were merc gangs after me, then walking around the city at all hours was bound to attract a few. The hard part was convincing Xeristo to go along with the plan, but since the odds of finding them when they didn't want to be found were slim, he decided to give it a shot. Having the dwarves keep a low profile while subtly shadowing me proved to be the hardest bit since dwarves were few and far between, even in a cosmopolitan city like Caenwylln.

What I didn't count on was the wizard . . . and the loss of Bat. I almost cried right then and there, the raw emotional wound of my familiar's loss still bloody, but I pulled myself together and shook my head. "I don't need him; the wizard gave me a clue." I shrugged. "Besides, removing that geas would take days we don't have to spare."

Xeristo's face went hard. "Then it's time to pass judgement." He turned to go.

I grabbed his arm. "I can do it."

My friend shook his head. "My city, my judgement." He turned to the man who began to howl and beg for mercy. "You are charged with the attempted murder of a duly appointed representative of the crown in front of witnesses, including a Justice. Do you have anything to say to possibly mitigate the sentence I am about to impose?"

The pleadings became gabbled and garbled, near incoherent as Xeristo approached, Thumper in his large hands.

I turned away and walked out of the alley just as those pleadings were silenced forever.

SEVENTEEN

NOW

"IT STRAINS CREDULITY THAT YOU ARE still alive, my friend, although I am overjoyed to see you."

Skakhir sits on a padded cushion which rests on a dark oaken chair that could be mistaken for a throne. It is so ornate with intricately carved mining scenes, wooden dwarves rendered in elaborate detail as they dug with picks and shovels across the arms and backrest. Ostentatious and artful at the same time, I could spend hours just admiring the craftsmanship.

The old dwarf's face bears the deep wrinkles of a life lived far longer than average for the race, but his muscles still bulge under his green shirt and his hands remain rock steady as he drinks beer from a ceramic tankard. Bold brown eyes stare at me with amusement.

"Lass, yer looks haven't suffered any since we last talked." He belches loudly and smiles, placing his booted feet on the table.

We sit in his modest house which is located only a few miles from the Borderlands Inn in a glen, ash and poplar obscuring the structure from the road. The largest room is for dining and seems to comprise most of the structure to the point I wonder where the anyone would lay their heads at night. It has been his home for many a year, he tells me, a retirement spot for him and his immediate family.

That immediate family turns out to be an entire village in of itself, a brood of dwarves that keeps their mouths shut, but sits or stands with us in the great dining room we occupy. A dwarf woman named Gikka, apple-cheeked and as formidable as any dwarf male in her coat of shining mail, offers tea which I politely decline. Tennic accepts her offer of apple cider and sips contentedly, eyes wandering everywhere, keenly interested in the couple dozen members of Skakhir's family that stare at us in awe. The dining room strains at the seams to hold the mob while lamplight is reflected off the mirror surface of the cherry wood table that almost accommodates the them all. The rest stand against walls covered in rich tapestries depicting scenes from Gaoric legend such as the defeat of the dragon Hrrathsss by the hero Votric Hardaxe.

"I have told them of yer," says my host with a twinkle in his eyes. "They grew up on stories of Niendra Goisien, the Witch Justice of Ramashur."

I look to the throng of relatives who, as one, smile at me with shining teeth. Their faces are lit with a sort of reverential wonder and it unnerves me. "I am surprised that a modest house can hold such a large family."

Slap! Skakhir's hand hits the table with a sound like a musket shot. "By my clenched butt cheeks, Niendra, we're dwarves," he roars, laughing. "Most of this house is underground!" The rest of the dwarven clan erupts in laughter as well.

Tennic also laughs, the cheeky rat, pointing at my face which I am sure bears a look of stunned realization. Of course dwarves would tunnel deep, it is part and parcel of their nature. I shake my head in wonderment and smile, patting my friend's hand. "Oh, how I have missed you."

Skakhir's laughter abruptly ceases and he looks at me fondly, sparing a kindly glance for Tennic. "And I yer." He pauses and a small smile splits his deeply creased face. "Been far too long."

I notice that most of his Gaorish brogue has departed from his language and remark upon this.

"Ah, well lass, yer noticin' a natural evolution in me language style the lykes of which only yer would ken, that's for sure," he drawls. "I've adapted over the long years. Besides, no one will play cards with me anymore."

Tennic pipes up. "I like cards, I'll play."

That earns the lad a roar of laughter. "Of course yer do, lad, yer a natural born card player, yer are. However, I don't think yer going to take it easy on an old dwarf."

"Where's the fun in that?" Tennic shrugs.

We share a laugh while Tennic drinks more cider provided by Gikka.

"What happens with Vicious?" I ask.

After Skakhir and his brood of well-armed kin hustled us out of the Borderlands Inn, the assassin disappeared, hauled off a trio burly dwarves with no-nonsense looks on their bearded faces. As for his wife, Blood, there was no sign. Skakhir did not seem to worry much that a mean-spirited, high trained assassin might come calling. Considering the amount of dwarf muscle surrounding him at the time and all their shiny steel, I can say his confidence is justified.

"Ah, that slimy bugger," Skakhir pauses to take a large draught of thick, black dwarven ale. "Nasty bit of work, that. Well, seeing how he did so much dirty to my favorite public house, I sent the lad on a little trip to Gaor where he'll face dwarven justice at my behest."

"He's a Gyllethian criminal, Skakhir, not Gaorian. He should face Gyllethian justice."

"Begging yer pardon, lass, but yer aren't a Justice any longer and things have gotten right sloppy and criminal since yer time. I'm thinking that with his money he might not see a Gyllethian noose."

I think back to Antonius and the revelations learned and I cannot argue the point, although it sticks hard in the throat. Who am I to say otherwise considering I seek justice outside the normal bounds of Gyllethian law? The similarities disturb my humors. "What will happen to him, then?"

"Nothing good. He's a right mean mage, that one and we dwarves know how to deal with mean mages." His look becomes so dark that for a moment I feel sorry for the assassin.

A very brief moment.

"Go ahead," says Skakhir. "Ask me."

There is no ambiguity between us, despite the centuries he can still read me well. "How?" I ask, giving in to curiosity. "All these years and you still live. I thought the average dwarven lifespan is three-hundred years."

He smiles. "It is." Reaching under his enormous chair he produces a very familiar item. It is the silvery war hammer we found all those years ago in the geomancer's lair. He laid it on the dining table with a hollow *thunk*.

"The hammer?"

"I told yer it wasn't cursed." Skakhir shakes his head, eyes traveling to far off places, memories of a life too long lived haunts the castle of his mind. "I have had a lot of time to research this hammer," he says. "Do yer remember King Rikard of Nerrinnia?"

"Yes, of course."

"Seems the Wizard King got himself disappeared some time after yer death, leaving no heirs. With Nerrinnia in flux looking for someone to lead and on the brink of civil war, it was easy to bribe my way into the royal library and convince some scholars to help me out considering they have the most extensive collection of folios on magical artifacts outside the Hidden Academy." He smiles. "Seems that this hammer was known quite well a few shifts ago."

"And?" I urged, wishing he would get to the point.

A loving hand caresses the hammers haft. "I found several references to the shining hammer of Father Sun."

My mind goes spinning off into different directions, not the least is why would Father Sun, the God of Healing and Truth would need such a weapon of violence. "Sounds like it should belong to the God of War," I muse.

Tennic surprises both of us. "Hey, Father Sun is the God of Protection, too! Perhaps it's a weapon to protect his priests or something!"

My friend and I stare at the lad in amazement just before Skakhir bursts out laughing. "Oh, yer got a good lad here, Niendra, his eyes are clear. That's *exactly* what the weapon was designed for, the protection of Father Sun's temple in Suurmae. Who or how it was made I don't know, but in an old scroll some two weeks into my research I read that its purpose was to protect the warrior who devotes himself to the defense of the temple."

"And?" I urge again.

"And it has no magical ability to harm. It won't bash through walls to destroy enemies with a single blow, as yer well know. Its function is to maintain the health of the bearer and to help heal damage taken in combat." Skakhir takes a long draught of his beer. "I'm still alive because it keeps me healthy. Not immortal. I age as yer can well see, but healthy as a horse. It's merely pushing me to the very edge of dwarven life expectancy."

"But should it not be in back in Suurmae?"

"Lass, if Father Sun wants the hammer back in the temple, he can come and get it. He knows where it is."

My mouth opens and closes, somewhat shocked at the almost blasphemy, but ultimately not completely surprised. From what I understand, dwarves and the religion of the Nine do not get along much. I sit back and consider my old friend before saying, "How did you know we would be at the Borderlands Inn."

"I can't tell yer."

My eyes narrow. "What can you tell me, Skakhir?"

"Not much." He shakes his head. "Do yer trust me, lass?"

That is a silly question. "Of course I do." I place my hand on his and he does not flinch at the cold touch of my flesh. "Always have, always will." I smile. "Except when it comes to cards, of course."

The room erupts in laughter, the loudest is Skakhir's. "Oh, lass, how I've missed yer." As his laughter subsides, tears form at the corners of his eyes. "What I'm about to ask yer is a trying thing, yer gonna be put upon by it, but it's for the best, so I need all the trust in yer body."

"She trusts you, sir dwarf," pipes in Tennic with a small smile. He takes a drink of his cider and belches softly before continuing, "She told me stories about you and Haddeg and Taalis and a Justice named Quentin Bill and even Queen Bet of olden times and she knows she can rely on you." He ducks his head back into his flagon of cider, not quite meeting my eyes. "She says you're a fine friend and a consummate warrior." He cocks his head. "Consummate. Good word, learned that one all by myself."

"Yer a good lad. Reminds me of . . . me, actually, which brings me to another favor I gotta ask."

"You have not asked the first yet."

Skakhir sighs and I feel . . . apprehensive? "Yer plan on talking to the sylvans, right?"

"How—?"

"I can't tell yer, that's part of the trust thing, but what I can ask is for yer to take a wee detour from yer route and . . . do a little treasure hunting." He could not quite meet my eyes.

Anger began its slow burn as I realize I have practically promised my friend that I would do this by assuring him of my trust and it was a measure of his trust in me that he never once asked how I could still be alive or made comment about the signs of my undeath. Talk about being expertly maneuvered into a corner. The thought of another delay unbalanced my humors somewhat, but Skakhir is such a good friend, one that I fought beside and who had saved my life more than once. How can I say no to the last person from my past? Can I say no to the last tie to a better time?

I wish I could cry.

"Yes. I will do what you want."

Tears may be absent from my face, but Skakhir possesses enough for the both of us, dripping down his lined cheeks to wet his beard while Tennic pivots his head from me to the dwarf and back again, looking alarmed.

"Yer breaking my heart, lass." Suddenly the old dwarf is surrounded by his family, each laying a hand in comfort, murmuring their support and the love that suffuses the room near overwhelms me. "Breaking it right in two." He shakes himself like a wet dog. "Off of me, yer over-bearing spawn!" he barks, but not without some affection. The dwarves retreat to their seats around the edges of the big room. No dwarf has spoken except for Skakhir, so it is with some surprise that I hear a high, musical voice.

"Yer must drink, dear."

It is Gikka, who holds out a flagon of cider, a slightly worried look on her face. "Going without is not good for yer," she says kindly.

For the thousandth time I dearly miss being able to drink and eat. The desire to feel my body respond to the smell of fresh bread, to taste the sharp tang of good cheese, it all rises inside with a startling intensity and at that moment Tennic grabs onto my hand and squeezes.

"Gikka, yer a fine granddaughter, but she needs nothing at this moment," says Skakhir.

Anger replaces desire. "I need justice, Skakhir!" The words emerge louder than they should.

"Of course yer do, lass, and revenge as well. Knowing yer, I have no doubt yer will get both, but they *must* be delayed." He pauses. "For a bit."

I look down to see my hands clenched, my dark skin white around the knuckles and for a moment it is as if the violent humors of a living being course through me. Delayed. Delayed. Delayed. A mantra floating through my head like an ill humor, stealing my time, my patience, but I do not know how to say no, that is Mother Moon's own curse because he is my friend and *will* do what he asks, no matter what. I trust him.

He is my friend.

A hand grown gnarly and hard, yet still strong, grabs mine as I look down at the table and my eyes travel from the wrinkly fingers to the bulging forearm all the way to that lovely and sad dwarven face and I want to scream at him, but I do not. Because he is my friend.

"I know it hurts yer something terrible, lass." Skakhir pats my hand, tears continuing to run down his long face and even Tennic looks sad. The other dwarves will not meet my eyes. "I wouldn't do this to yer if it wasn't important."

My voice emerges as it always does, although I think it should be thick with sorrow. "What do I have to do?"

"It's not far, this place I need yer to go to, not too far at all. Remember the geomancer tunnels near the Frost Quarry all those years ago?"

I nod.

"Well, I've been telling that story to the family for years, stressing that such things should be let be unless you have a mighty wizard at yer back. All this time I warned my fold to leave the lair alone, but it seems that one of my many-times great granddaughters, a fine lass by the name of Nokrini, took into her fool head to go to find the Ninesdamned thing."

Every dwarf in the room let out a sigh, a wind almost strong enough to whip my braids around and I know that the young woman never returned from her exploits. I leaned back in my chair, Tennic unconsciously mimicking my movements while still drinking his apple cider.

"What happened?"

"I don't know. It's been three weeks since she left and I was about to go out myself to see what's what, then yer came along."

"Not quite that simple. You said you could not discuss things with me, could not tell me how you know what you know, but it is not so simple is it?"

"No it isn't."

"So you want me to find your granddaughter and what? Bring her back?"

"Among other things."

"Such as?"

"Such as I believe yer will find more like what we found last time we went treasure hunting."

"How is that?" I ask. "We searched . . ." I suddenly pause, realization striking and I want to hit myself for being so stupid. "The third tunnel."

Almost I smacked my forehead in self-disgust. How could I forget the third tunnel? Oh yes, I was slightly rushed to finish up the Divver murder mystery.

"Aye, lass," says Skakhir softly. "The third tunnel. Right before yer died old Queen Bet had Hengeth Isobold go and seal up the tunnel for later inspection. Wasn't long after that that things went bad for Ramashur. The quarry and everything within a quarter mile was seized by the crown and that was that. It pains me deep in my water ta tell yer that in all the commotion with me finding my hammer and all, I also completely forgot about that blasted tunnel."

"Until your granddaughter."

The dwarf nods. "Until her. Maybe there was nothing to find there, maybe Isobold found nothing but moldering bones and a lot dust, we'll never know because he died casting that spell what laid Ramashur to ruins." He leans forward. "Maybe he wasn't *meant* to find anything."

"You lost me."

"Hengeth was a powerful wizard, yes?"

I sigh. "Yes. Very."

"So he could find things that are magically hidden, but what if there was something there hidden by a physical barrier, not a magical one?"

Detection and divination spells are the domain of Seers, a rare branch of wizardry that few show any talent for and any other class of wizard (save a powerful crafter) would find it very difficult to not only learn, but to cast such a thing. It was not out of the realm of possibility for Hengeth to know such a spell, but odds are he did not. I said as much to Skakhir.

"Exactly. Which is why I need yer to go to the geomancer's lair and look for my granddaughter. I feel there's something there . . . no, I know it."

"And I am doing this because I trust you."

"Of course yer do."

Now was the time. Not to mention my damnable curiosity grew at an alarming rate with every passing moment. "All right, of course I will do this for you, my friend."

A wide smile split Skakhir's face. "Good, lass. I knew yer would. And I have a wee present for here, sort of the second favor I was going to ask."

"Well, I do so love gifts."

Once again my friend erupts in laughter. "Oh, yer don't get this little gift, lass." Skakhir stands abruptly and hefts Father Sun's shining hammer and looked at it lovingly for a moment before moving around the table to stand next to Tennic and I. He holds the hammer out to my companion. "Tennic, lad, yer a good lad and strong. These old eyes can see you are the one to bear this burden. I gave this wee hammer a name: Dodmatir, which means Brightforged in Khulasch."

The room explodes, every other dwarf shouting in objection as Tennic sits there stunned, eyes wide and shining. He stretches his hand out for the hammer held lovingly by the dwarf patriarch and the other dwarves crowd in, yelling and screaming in Khulasch and the din is almost unbearable.

"Shut it!" roars Skakhir at a volume greater than what all the other dwarves provide. "By my clenched butt cheeks, shut it! This is my decision and I'm making it."

As the room becomes silent, he looks at me and says, "The family knows that if I surrender the hammer the magic is surrendered as well and I will soon follow my cousin Haddeg into the Mines of *Rakuil a Glorivreas*."

My throat wanted to clench tight as I watched Tennic tentatively grasp the silvery shaft. The Mines of Rakuil a Glorivreas, like Tilla's Hold, is the home for the dwarven dead carved out for them by their god, Finamri. Skakhir has just pronounced his own death sentence.

All eyes watch as Tennic lifts the weapon from Skakhir's hands and holds it up in the lamplight. "It's beautiful," he breathes.

"That it is, lad, that it is." Skakhir smiles, suddenly wobbling and multiple hands helps him to a chair. "I can feel it accepting yer, lad. I made a good choice, that I did."

"But I don't know how to use it!" Tennic almost looks panicked.

"Yer will, lad," says Skakhir, fatigue etching his voice. "Yer will. I can tell yer the right lad. Trust me like Niendra does. Trust me." He sits there with a smile on his face and I know that I am staring at a dying dwarf and I want to cry, but I cannot. It is beyond me.

EIGHTEEN

THEN

ALL JUSTICES MUST OBEY THE LAW, but they are allowed a certain . . . latitude when enforcing them. This was true when the order was founded all the way up to and including my time on the job because the various rulers of Gylleth knew that criminals broke the rules often enough that the enforcers needed to bend them somewhat just to stem the tide. Never break, just a little bending. It didn't sit well with me, but life has a way of washing black and white into gray.

Ramashur smelled and sounded different than Caemwylln. The former lacked the salty smell of the sea, the slight stench of rotting fish and clamoring caws of seagulls that dropped their feces everywhere, which added another smell to the city by Beryl Bay. All this went through my mind as I entered Toro Rilby's shop in the Lowers.

Ostensibly a cobbler, it was common knowledge that Toro also happened to be a man who could offer a modest sum for ill-gotten gains that needed to be disposed of quickly. While no one was able to prove this fact about the man, and many a Justice tried, he managed to keep his head low enough and his illegitimate business modest enough to avoid undue scrutiny. This meant he was far too clever by half.

He was also my informant.

Back in my first year as a Justice I caught the man with silver stolen from Lord Koroston's estate in the Marbry Hills, silver stolen by one of his many housekeepers. I could have pronounced Justice upon him, sending him to a year of hard labor at the prison in Pennywell, or he could be of some value in the pursuit of larger prey. The math was easy for Toro to figure.

My dwarven companions followed me into Toro's shop like a pair of enforcers guarding a rich boss, hands on the hafts of their weapons and a grim look in their eyes, frowning at the pair of customers, a young man and an elderly woman, who were talking to Toro. At the look of alarm on the proprietor's face, they turned and spotted Haddeg and Skakhir who offered them a good dwarfy glares. They decided to take their business elsewhere.

"Aww, Justice," complained Toro as the door closed leaving the little shop empty except for us. "Why you wanna do such a thing? You're scaring away the straights."

Fortunately for Toro, my boisterous reunion with Mirallelle last evening put me in a good mood, enough so that I didn't want to fuel his sense of outrage any more than absolutely necessary. "Take it easy, Toro," I said, running my fingers along a long roll of supple brown leather. "We need to talk, that's all." My smile must have looked as insincere as it felt.

Toro, a skinny, tall man with a shaggy mop of graying black hair and a nose like long candle, squinted at me in disbelief. Both Haddeg and Skakhir stood behind me, still glowering, still fingering their weapons.

"So whatcha want, Justice? I'm clean as Father Sun's own temple I am and nobody can say otherwise." He backed up toward a rack of wooden sizing plates.

"You know, Toro, I love the smell of a cobbler's shop. All the leather and the stains and such. Comforting, you know, gives me a sense that everything's all right in the world."

The patter didn't ease him any. He kept his mouth shut.

"What I love more than the smell is the craftsmanship." I pick up a pair of cavalryman's boots, black and shiny. "I mean, look at this, look at the quality." My fingers ran across the buttery smooth leather. "Of course, you know the quality, this is for one of your customers with money, not one of the Lowers crowd at all."

"Justice . . ."

I raise my hands. "All right, Toro, all right. I'm messing with you a bit. Call it an old habit, you know?" Once again with the phony smile and Toro tensed slightly, knowing that something he wasn't going to like was about to come barreling at him. He had great survival instincts. Like a rat. "I need to talk to the Widow."

For a moment he looked stunned, as if I'd asked him for every royal he ever earned and his first born as well. "Are you out of your Ninesdamned mind, woman!" he hissed, eyes wide in fright. "No one asks to see the Widow!"

"Aren't I the first then?" My smile disappeared and my companions moved to bracket the man, leaning in, invading his personal space and Toro's head swiveled back and forth as the two dwarves gave with menacing growls. I didn't coach them on that, that was pure mean dwarfy improvisation.

"By my clenched butt cheeks, Justice, I want ta stuff thys hooman inta the nearest privy," said Haddeg in a voice like rocks thudding at the bottom of a dry well.

Toro blanched, shaking visibly.

I did my own leaning in, letting the anger and frustration lash out. "Listen you little worm, I let you do your shady business because you provide me enough to grease the wheels of justice, but listen to me carefully now: Queen Belial Til-Amre, long may she reign, has personally asked me to investigate a murder of one of our more prominent citizens. I do this not only because it's my job, but because I swore an oath and I will see it done, mind you. Now, some Ninesdamned bottom-feeder has decided to put a bounty on my head, which makes me more than a little irritable and they did it though the auspices of your boss, the Widow."

Nose to nose now, my blood up, the humors in my body definitely out of balance. "Go tell the Widow I want to meet at the Honeysuckle Gardens after sundown. Tell her to bring two minders just as I will have my minders with me. No more, no less. Tell her that if she doesn't come, I will use whatever broad authority I have as a Justice to turn this city upside down to find her, which includes conscripting the watch for my efforts." Angry, so angry. I didn't realize how much the attempts on my life affected me and I could feel the heat of blood on my cheeks. "Remember, Toro, I'm Irramerian, a member of the most aggressive people this world has ever seen, so if the Widow wants to war with me, I'm ready. Never forget that I'm a witch and I will curse you with festering boils if you don't do what I tell you to do."

I spun and stomped out of the shop in a high dudgeon, cursing inwardly at the threat I'd just made in the heat of the moment. It went against all the teachings of Father Sun to cast a curse and I would lose a good amount of my power if I were to do so, and as Father Sun is the God of Truth as well, the lie stuck in my craw. I knew my patron would call me to task for it, too.

"Slow down, lass," urged Haddeg as I strode down Bitter Street at a good clip, passing citizens without looking at them. "Yer legs are longer than ours."

I stopped and took a deep breath. "Sorry guys." The clouds above showed no inclination for rain or for letting the sun through any time soon. "I didn't know I was carrying so much . . . anger."

"Yer have every right, lass." Skakhir looked stormy himself. "We were with yer, too, yer know. They put a bullseye on you, me, Haddeg and Taalis . . . all of us."

Mother Moon. What an idiot I turned out to be, forgetting that my friends shared my danger, fought by my side and faced iron just like me. By the Nine, Haddeg took a bolt to the shoulder. Not serious, but still he could have been killed. My anger and raw-wound pain at the loss of Bat blinded me to the realities of the situation. It's not all about me . . . I had to constantly remind myself of that little tidbit.

I took a deep breath to calm down then looked at my friends. "Come on, we have preparations to make."

Haddeg gave me a squint. "What kind of preparations?"

"The sneaky kind."

That brought grins to their bearded, dwarfy faces.

SUNSET AT THE HONEYSUCKLE GARDENS. Formerly the Royal Public Gardens of Ramashur, but the designer had a weakness for honeysuckle: the common, to winter, Irramerian, Coadian, coral and the always-green variety. More variations could be found in the Royal Public Gardens among streams diverted from the Donovaria and sweet odors could be detected a mile away. It's said that the Tanner's Workshop, an area outside the walls dedicated to that business, could smell the gardens through the fetor of the tanneries if the wind was right. It wasn't surprising that the name stuck.

Tall hedges surrounded the park that stood in the middle of the Uppers and normally they would seem to add an air of menace, but oil lamps strung throughout gave a warm, yellow light that scared away the shadows. Maybe the crown wanted a romantic feel, but instead the light gave a sense of comfort. The occasional member of the city watch strolling along the crushed granite pathways added a feeling of security.

Thanks to my pull as a Justice, the watch stayed away from where I sat on a stone bench near a couple of large fox honeysuckle waiting for the Widow to make an appearance while I flattened my behind. A path lay at my feet and there was enough privacy that if there were some late night lovers strolling by, they wouldn't see me. Speaking of late night lovers, I could still feel Mirallelle's warm lips on mine, feel her hands roam across my breasts, her perfume tickling my nose . . . a hint of rose and her normal, spicy musk.

I shook my head, dispelling those memories before they took my attention from the business at hand.

Too late.

"It's not wise to be woolgathering while waiting on a sinister rendezvous. A bad habit for a Justice."

Mother Moon! I cursed myself for a Ninesdamned fool and for nearly jumping out of my skin. The woman who sat next to me was dressed entirely in black from the shapeless cap and veil that showed only her big brown eyes to the soft kidskin boots that covered her small feet. Black hose and doublet completed the outfit and all in all, she looked like someone up to no good. Talk about dressing for the part. It never ceased to amaze me that villains were so fond of black. Perhaps their tailors offered group rates.

"The Widow, I presume?" I asked nonchalantly, trying to cover for my discomfiture.

From the crinkling at the corners of her eyes I could tell that my ploy failed. "Do you think her mad, Justice Niendra Goisien? It would be quite the feather in your cap to nab the Widow, wouldn't it? I am not the Widow, but I do speak with full authority *for* her."

I expected this. In fact, I counted on it. The plan had come to me on the way back from Caemwylln (escorted by a baker's dozen guardsmen at Xeristo's insistence), leaving Taalis behind. I didn't need the sylvan tagging along to seek her own brand of justice or revenge.

The silence grew between us and I flicked my eyes around, spotting the pair of minders she brought along like I'd specified skulking about in the lee of a large Coadian honeysuckle. Skakhir nodded, letting me know that the two were the only ones present while Haddeg made a show of glaring and gripping the haft of his double-bitted axe.

Directly to business. "The Widow set up a bounty on my life, a bounty that the Deep Water mercenary group decided to cash in on, which angers me and I want to find out who wants me dead. I want you, or the Widow, to tell me who."

Laughter filled the little area as the Widow surrogate rocked back and forth. "What makes you think the Widow would do such a thing?" she chuckled. "What's in it for her to betray someone with such deep pockets."

"Because before, as a Justice, I had only hearsay and no witnesses brave enough to risk her wrath. Even the Queen doesn't want to risk the blood-shed that would happen should the crown actively pursue her, too many innocent lives lost, but *now* the Widow has crossed the line. She's made herself the factor for a bounty on a Queen's Justice, which the crown will not stand for." In fact, the look on Queen Bet's face when I presented my report before my reunion with Mirallelle would have cracked the heart of a knobblegrott clean in two. If I couldn't pry the information from the Widow's surrogate, I possessed Her Majesty's authority to do whatever I deemed necessary to resolve the matter, no matter the cost. I know that if I couldn't, Queen Bet would find someone more bloody-minded who could and that thought chilled me.

I leaned in and gripped her elbow, not tightly, but firmly enough to let the woman know how I angry I felt. "The Widow counted on the Queen's mercy and tolerance, thinking them weaknesses, which is stupid on an entirely new level because now Her Majesty will see this as a declaration of war and if it's a war she wants, she will get one." I let go before the woman could snatch her elbow away. "I will make it my life's work to find the Widow, capture her and pronounce justice upon her on the spot. You tell her that. You tell her that if she doesn't give me the name of the person who set the bounty on me, I will come for her, I will find her and she definitely does not want *that*."

The woman stood, quick and with the slinky sinuousness of a cat, so quickly that both the dwarves and the not-Widow's two minders tensed enough that impending violence crackled in the air like heat lightning. With near silent hisses, the two thugs pulled long, thin, darkened blades from their sheaths and stepped onto the granite path while Haddeg and Skakhir stepped up to stand behind me with their weapons drawn and ready.

"No, no, no," purred the not-Widow. "Look at all the men with their passionate intentions of mayhem." She made downward motions with her hands and the men, also dressed in black complete with scarves hiding their faces, sheathed their knives. "This is not how people of quality conduct business." To me, "Don't try to start something you can't finish, Justice. The Widow is not someone to cross. Not even Dhiione himself can save if you if she wants you to answer the greatest mystery of all."

"What's that?" I keep my voice calm, but let a trace of anger show on my face.

"What's on the other side of life."

It was my turn to stand and I drew close enough to the woman that her two minders tensed. "Let me tell you a couple of things: one, never blaspheme like that again. Two: life's greatest mystery isn't what happens after you die."

"What is?"

"Tell you later."

I KNEW THERE WOULD BE TAILS, counted on that fact so I took a circuitous route back to the palace where I met Justice Remee in my office. At six-foot two inches tall, Remee Occass was a lot of Justice to look at, a lean jungle cat of a man with ropey muscles and mustaches that showed his devotion to Phezdes. Skin a cross between Irramerain black and Coadian bronze, he oozed sexuality and lithe danger. If I were the kind of woman who went in for men, I would have bedded him years ago. When I had finished my report to the queen, I told him about the bounty and could feel the outrage shimmering off his body like heat waves.

Once again he let his anger be known, slamming a fist down on my desk. "So how do you want to handle this?" he asked upon my return from my meeting with the not-Widow.

"I'm giving the Widow's frontwoman a chance to go back to her headquarters, wherever that may be," I said, checking my weapons and trying to keep my nerves under wraps. Haddeg and Skakhir were there itching to get back out and cause some damage. "When I gripped the woman's arm, my fingers had honey on them. Lavender honey to be precise, mixed with a tincture of sage and adder's tongue and I have the same honey mixture in a vial in my pouch. Because the two are from the same batch, I can use Principle of Sympathy to find her location, but we have to move fast."

"Why?"

"Because she might not stay there and the Widow might just have a pet mage or crafter sniffing about for just such a thing. I only came back here so any tails she put on me will tell her that I went back to my office, safe as houses from big bad Deep Water mercs."

"If you're going out, I'm coming with," he said, fingering the hand-and-a-half sword he called Clear Conscience. As he often joked, he dispensed justice with a clear conscience.

Men.

"No," I replied, making sure I had the last of what I needed in my belt pouches. I slipped Haddeg and Skakhir a couple of steel vials, potions I'd brewed a long time ago for extreme circumstances. This seemed to qualify. "I need you here. If I don't come back at three bells past midnight, then you gather every watch commander you can and use this to find me." I held out necklace, the pendant made of a lock of my hair. "It will lead you to me. If I'm dead, then feel free to tell Her Majesty, or Lord Petre if he's well enough, that the Widow killed me. I'm pretty sure they'll let drop the reins and let you have your way on the matter."

For a moment silence fell in my office as the tall man ran the necklace through his long fingers. Although junior to me in rank, he had what it took to make a full Justice Commander one day, possibly even Master of Justice. That is, if he didn't lose his head. "If you're dead because of the Widow, she'll follow you to Tilla's Hold shortly after," he said slowly. "I promise you that."

"Don't avenge me, dispense justice."

"They can be the same thing, you know."

NINETEEN

NOW

TIME HAS NOT BEEN KIND TO THE DIVVER FROST QUARRY. Now a rectangular, algae clotted pond, it stank of rotting vegetation and animal droppings, a haven for flies and mosquitos to bother the living. Vegetation has grown up all around, the area reverting to the wild much like Ramashur.

"Looks nasty," says Tennic, slapping his cheek at an offending insect. "Gross."

I chuckle. "Back in the day it was an ugly scar on the land, so now it's not so bad."

"If this is your idea of not so bad, I really don't want to see bad." The young man points. "Is that it?"

My eyes slide down his arm to the hole in the side of an ivy shrouded cliff just above the waterline. I can barely see the void through the tangled ropes of vegetation, much of which were cut away to allow access. "How did she find it?" I marvel Nokrini's skill at locating what was hidden.

"She's dwarf, right?" Tennic shrugs. "From what Master Skakhir says, stone and soil is in their blood."

I should not be surprised, but I am. There are enough wrist-thick vines and ivy to obscure the cliff and the water below is so scum laden that I cannot gauge the depth. Perhaps she searched for days trying to locate the entrance that Hengeth closed. Perhaps she got lucky.

Later, after climbing down ivy and vines strong enough to hold a troll, we find ourselves in front of the small cave opening hacked out of the rock with which Hengeth used to plug the tunnel. As far as I can tell the transition from the original rock and the plug is seamless, meaning Isobold's limited geomancy was darn near perfect. I told Tennic so as he ran his hand around lip of the opening.

"Is this the geomancy thingie you were talking about?"

"Earth magic. A subset of the Elementalist discipline of magic."

"You've lost me."

I sigh, time for a much-needed lesson. "Okay, you know I'm a crafter, right? A witch."

"Yeah, sure, but still lost, though."

"Well, there's a place where mages are taught called the Hidden Academy which is run by a group of Arch Mages called Council of Guides, whose job it is to preserve knowledge and teach the next generation of mages as well as trying to decipher ancient grimoires and scrolls. A long time ago, many shifts, an Arch Mage called Malos formed the Wizard Postulate, which states that not all mages are equal in talent, that some find certain magics easier to perform than others, thus you have generalist mages called wizards, who are fluent in multiple disciplines, and mages of single disciples such as elementalists, crafters, runemasters, seers, illusionists and naturalists, for example. With me so far?"

Tennic nods. Bright lad.

"So there are subclasses of mages from those disciplines, specialist categories if you will. For example, an elementalist, one who can manipulate fire, air, earth and water, can specialize in manipulating one element over all others, able to achieve greater feats with that single element that they could with all of them. Geomancer, or earth master, is an example of a specialist elementalist."

"What's a naturalist? Sounds . . . odd."

"Naturalists have power over living systems such as animals, plants, and people. Specialist naturalists like Body Mages, for example, like Vicious, can heal people even to the extent of regrowing limbs if they are strong enough, but the one thing they cannot do is cure disease. Do not ask why, that is a question Arch Mages have been trying to answer for many shifts. They can also increase physical attributes such as strength and speed." It certainly explains his success as an assassin.

The lad ponders this for a moment and says, "So your discipline is crafting, which is sub *category* of wizardry, right?"

"Exactly!"

"So is there a specialist crafter, then?"

My face falls. "There are two: ritual healers and dark crafters, or black witches. Ritual healers are like Body Mages, they can bring a person back from the brink of Tilla's Hold, but not regrow limbs, that is a function of Body Mages. However, they *can* cure disease and they can apply their healing magic to animals as well, which Body Mages cannot do."

"And the black witches?"

"Black witchcraft is something not taught at the Hidden Academy." I pause, unsure if I should tell him more, but decide to do so anyway. I trust the lad. "Crafters draw power from the gods. I draw from Mother Moon in her aspect of Goddess of Magic and Father Sun in his aspect of God of Protection and Healing. Dark crafters draw power from the negative forces arrayed against the gods."

Tennic blanches. "The Demon Master!"

"Shhh . . ." I hold my finger to my lips. "We don't refer to it ever. But understand that a dark crafter's specialty is causing harm, cursing people, places and even animals, even causing plagues. It's because they worship . . . who they worship that to be caught out as a dark crafter calls for execution, but only in the holy circle of Phezdes and Mother Moon. Phezdes because in his aspect as a God of Blessings, he can counteract the cursed nature of a dark crafter and Mother Moon in her aspect of the Goddess of Magic."

I lower my voice and say softly, "Remember Tennic, there is a black mirror for every discipline, a negative to a positive just as there is a negative force to the power of the Nine." Sighing, I peer into the cave. "Enough of lessons, lad, I have no desire to discuss religion and it is time we see to business and absent ourselves from grim thoughts."

Tennic caresses the hammer like I had seen Skakhir do in the past, which makes me smile and I wiggle into the hole, the lad hard on my heels.

Like centuries before, I use a gem to shed light, having prepared in advance for the darkness beyond. Quartz glitters all around, shattering the yellow light from my gem into a million pieces. The is a smell of dust mixed with algae.

"Wow," breathes Tennic. "You told me about this, but this is *beautiful*."

"That it is, lad. That it is." I remark that there is no dust, nothing to show the passage of time. It is as if I had left the place yesterday, the only thing missing is my dwarf companions and Taalis.

We headed down the tunnel and although, to the greater world, it has been five centuries since last my feet walked this tunnel, for me less than handful of years flew by. I stride down the tunnel with the confidence of recent memory, certain of my path.

"What's that smell?"

I stop at Tennic's words and inhale. Yes, I know that odor that starts to come to the fore. "Corruption."

"You mean—?"

"Something dead." Other than myself.

We pass the branching of the tunnels, ignoring the right and left passages for the one I ignored all those years ago and it is here I start to slow. I notice the smell becoming stronger. Much stronger. Beside me Tennic makes gulping sounds as he holds back his gorge.

Our pace slows and I hold the gem with its captured fire at arm's length, worried about what we would find. Nokrini's mangled body? Some tunneling creature like a knobblegrott that found its untimely end? Beside me Tennic swallows and grips Dodmatir so hard his knuckles are white and sweat drips from his face despite the cool air. We proceed slowly and I look through my Father Sun tattoos seeing no magic traps.

"Wait!" he says suddenly, blocking my advance with an arm.

"What?"

He points. "Something wrong with the tunnel floor right there."

I follow his finger but see nothing. It looks like the rest of the tunnel, dark stone filled with a multitude of quartz fragments and I ask what he sees.

Dipping a hand into his belt pouch, he pulls out a ball of lead about two inches in diameter.

"Where did you get that?" I ask.

"Always had it. Part of a thief's trade." He winks.

I resist to urge what else he has stowed about his person and watch in fascination as he rolls the ball across the center of the tunnel. When it reaches six feet from our toes, a section of tunnel floor about four feet long abruptly splits down the center and falls away, taking the lead ball with it. After a few moments the two halves of the floor swing back up.

Mother Moon!

"By my clenched butt cheeks," whispers Tennic. "I knew it!"

"You are picking up some bad habits," I observe.

He shrugs.

"But good call, lad." I tousle his mop of hair and his green eyes crinkle in delight. "How did you spot that?" A nervous, anticipatory excitement begins in my breast, a pure feeling that near warms the cold, dead muscle of my heart. That old curiosity that forced me to seek answers, to find my justice (revenge?) gripped me with fiery talons. Once again the lure of mystery pulled me forward.

"I'm a *good* thief," is his reply as rare smile blossomed on my face. "Some sorta small pressure plate in the middle there. If your Hengeth friend came down here, he didn't step on it. My guess that this geofella you talked about has more tricks for us to find."

Not a good thought. We take care to avoid the pressure plate and he marks the spot with a copper crown. I keep looking through the tattoos for magical traps but find none.

After a few dozen more feet the tunnel abruptly terminates. No door, no room, just a section of quartz filled wall as smooth as the rest of the tunnel.

"Well, this is peculiar," I remark.

"What does that mean?"

"Odd."

"Oh. Peculiar. Good word. Can you hold the light over your head near the ceiling?" asks Tennic.

I comply as he begins to examine the ceiling, then the floor, nose an inch from the smooth stone, every square in scrutinized. After ten minutes of patient waiting, I am rewarded by Tennic's soft cry of "Gotcha!"

The young former-thief (hopefully I have rehabilitated him somewhat) points to the corner where the tunnel wall meets the terminus, about four feet up. "Here," he says. "You can barely see it, but it's there." He points.

My eyes must lack some essential element because I see nothing and I tell Tennic so.

Rolling his own emerald orbs, he reaches into another pouch and pulls out a flat strip of steel roughly five inches long slides it into the spot indicated and to my amazement the strip vanishes into the corner.

"A really narrow gap right here," breathes my companion, manipulating the strip up and down. "Usually a catch is inside and you haveta trip it with something like this metal shim here. And really well hidden, you wouldn't find it unless you were looking for it. A-ha!"

I should not be surprised, but I am as the wall before us recedes and slides to the left, almost completely disappearing. More excitement builds within my breast. "A hidden door," I say in wonder, once again impressed by the late geomancer and Tennic's ill-gotten talents.

It is then that we are assailed by the stench roiling from the space beyond. Corruption so thick that Tennic drops to his knees and vomits breakfast onto the tunnel floor and even I wrinkle my nose. Sometimes being undead has its advantages.

"Easy lad," I say, removing a cloth from my pack as he wipes his mouth. I wet the cloth from Tennic's canteen then wrap it around his nose and mouth, tying it behind his head, then I apply a few drops of lavender scent to the wet cloth. "This might help a little."

"Not much," he gags.

To take his mind off the smell, I say, "Good eye there, lad, finding that door. I am impressed by your skill. I would have never found it and I am sure Hengeth did not."

"Yeah. It's a good one, but Lord Montabrio's had a better one in his bedroom. That took an hour to find and half that to trip the catch." A pause. "Gross . . . lavender vomit dead smell. This is gonna haunt me."

"Montabrio," I say slowly, recognizing the name. "Montebrio? Is he not the baron who found his home robbed a year ago?" I raise an eyebrow. I may be dead, but I try to keep up on current events.

Tennic has the grace to blush and he slips the metal shim inside his pouch without another word.

"You know, lad, we are going to talk about your criminal proclivities one day."

"Not a criminal anymore," he mumbles. He mutters softly to himself, "Proclivities. Good word."

"Still, I have my eye on you." With that, I hold the gem forward to dispel the darkness, wishing I could dispel the odor.

What we find is a room, irregular, long, unfinished. Instead of the black, almost glassine black rock riddled with quartz, plain gray stone comprises this area, a rough and unsmooth, ugly compared the magnificence of the geomancer's hallway. Longer than wide, it seems a natural cave, the floor a hazard of deep depressions and tumorous humps. It seems a forgotten antechamber instead of a room full of treasure or secrets. However, there is something in here that is neither a treasure, nor a secret. It is a corpse.

Dressed in dwarven mail, the body lies sprawled minus its head, which rests a few feet away and decomposition is too advanced for me to determine gender by facial features, but I surmise by the lack of a beard it must Skakhir's many times great granddaughter, Nokrini. A puddle of noxious fluid surrounds both the head and body, liquefied flesh and I decide breathing will not be necessary for next few minutes. I begin to enter.

A muscle-y hand grabs my elbow. "Wait!" hisses Tennic. "Don't you even listen to your own stories?" He tosses a handful of copper crowns into the room.

Bright yellow light flashes and there is an impression of movement, too quick to be seen, and then silence save for the *tinking* of coppers as they roll across the floor.

"Trap," says my companion flatly, giving me a level stare.

"What is it?" I ask, blinking. The flash . . . so bright, so fast, faster than a hummingbird's wing.

Tennic shakes his head. "Got me. I didn't see anything but a bright light and maybe something moving, but that's it. Seems kinda witchy to me."

Kind of witchy? Wait. Maybe it is kind of witchy. I close my eyes and concentrate on seeing through the Father Sun tattoos and scan the space, looking, looking, looking.

And finding. There. Above the floor, almost thin as a hair and floating in . . . midair?

"Mother Moon," I whisper.

"What?"

"Stay here." I enter the room slowly and oh so carefully, keeping my vision on the floating line of script so small that one would need a magnifying glass to see the runes properly. Easing my way, each step a light touch that barely makes a sound, I work my way until I am two feet from the line of script.

"Someone cast runes on *air!*" I marvel almost forgetting to breath so I can form the words audibly.

"Is that good or bad?" inquires Tennic from the safety of the entrance.

"It is . . . wonderful." I squint and see the runes shift and shimmer as if they are made of fire, tiny motes invisible to the naked eye, but my tattoos render them plain to me. I see runes of air and of fire, a rune to detect . . . motion? I study the full length of the script that runs from wall to wall over the corpse of the dead dwarven girl before realizing that the rune trap kills those that touch it. I do not know how, I need more time to study the fascinating construct, all I know that should any being cross the room they die. "It seems the geomancer was not just a geomancer, but conversant with the other three elements as well. Not only that, but he had a deft command of runes and the skill to build physical traps using magic. I do not know who the mystery wizard was, but he was *masterful* enough to make Arch-Mages look like street corner hucksters. I have never seen anyone cast fire runes upon air and the fact that they are still efficacious after all these years shows a level of power I cannot hope to achieve, and I am a first-rate crafter."

"Uh . . . I'm not sure what that means, but can you like, I dunno, get rid of the blasted thing?"

"Good question." I tilt my head and continue to stare. "Seems a pity to destroy such a unique casting."

"So, destroy now, cry later. This place is making me nervous."

"Pushy lad. All right." Every rune, every ward, has a weak spot which is usually the point of origin, where the wizard began the casting and if I can find that spot, I can unravel this glowing thread of invisible fire that keeps us from continuing our exploration.

"Tennic, if I fail I will trip the spell and most likely become decapitated."

"Oh. Well, then maybe we can grab the dwarf girl and go. I can snag it with a rope. Maybe that will work."

My smile shows no humor. "What I mean to say is if it happens, I will need you to sew my head back on."

"Ugh. Gross."

"Very."

"That can't work, though. Can it?"

"Do not forget I am already dead. The wounds I died with are the only ones that will not heal. I believe if my head is reattached to my body it will eventually heal." Hopefully, but I do not say that.

"All right. Gross again."

This makes me smile and I get to work.

Having one's eyelids tattooed is both an act of magic and courage. Magic because it is a physical link to my devotion to Father Sun, who is one half of the power I draw upon to craft. Courage because one needs to sit perfectly still while a body mage plunges a needle dipped in gold ink into your eyelids, hopefully without striking the eyeball beneath. For hours. There have been accidents and pain and screaming, but the trade-off is worth the risk. My eyelids are, in fact, artifacts that pose no impediment to vision while allowing me to see magic in all its various forms.

With a flick of my will I magnify the floating thread of magic, growing it large in my sight until I see every single rune as if it were writ upon paper for me to peruse. Fiery symbols, concepts of magic given form are there for me to examine and while I am no rune master, I do know enough to recognize seven runes in ten.

Back and forth I meticulously examine each inch of the thread as I search for the point of origin, the weak spot in the spell. Many would think to read from left to right like a book, but this geomancer was a gifted wizard and clever as well. He would not start at the most obvious point. Nor would he begin on the left, the second most obvious point . . . or would he?

I shake my head, bear down and set my mind more firmly to task. Every inch if need be, every bloody inch of this fabulous rune thread. Tennic tries to speak, but I raise a hand to forestall any words because I do not want to lose my place and start over.

Ah-ha . . . there. The rune of air, of coaxing that element to lift what is asked. That must be it, ten inches from the left wall, the blazing glyph fluttering gently. I reach out with the blade of my will and, praying to Mother Moon that I am correct, sever the thread through the rune.

The metallic snapping sound is inaudible to the uninitiated, but I hear it loud as a bell and I almost flinch, waiting for a flash and the disorienting sensation of my head falling one way and my body another.

"Am I still whole?" I ask.

"Uh," replies the lad. "Yes? I think so."

I concentrate and see the thread slowly fray from the severing point, fading quickly into nothing until the entirety of the magic is undone.

"Oh, good," I say, opening my eyes.

To all sides the walls slide away with a soft grinding noise.

TWENTY

THEN

WELL, WELL, WELL . . . THE MOST wanted person in all of Ramashur lived two blocks from the palace.

I didn't recognize the large house, five stories and spanning almost an entire block in the Uppers, very impressive. Red brick black in the moonlight and the windows of the top two stories made entirely of stained glass depicting the Nine in various regalia. It oozed wealth and a willingness to use it for aggrandizement. Not quite as ostentatious as the Fel Rosso estate, but it gave its northern cousin a good run for the Royal Round.

"Drink your potions."

Both Haddeg and Skakhir complied, downing the contents of the steel vials I gave them earlier.

"By my clenched butt cheeks," grumbled Haddeg in disgust, face twisting. "Tastes like a midden stewed with beets."

"And how would yer know what a midden tastes like, yer big idiot," replied Shakhir, with a raised eyebrow. His mouth was puckered in distaste as he pocketed the vial.

"Don't be daft, yer moron, anyone who's smelled one can tell."

"Well, yer fancypants, maybe—"

"Shut it boys," I whisper.

"Yes, mom."

I rolled my eyes. If they weren't such good fighters, I would've left them at home.

It was just the three of us across the street looking at the manor with more Justices and trusted members of the watch only a couple blocks away to come running if needed. I'd given Remee a spelled coin that would turn ice cold if I found myself in dire straits.

Do whatever is needed, said Queen Bet after the debrief. *You have Our Authority and Trust.*

That was a whole lot of responsibility right there and I had vowed not to abuse it. The queen was not one to mess around, it seemed, and I breathed a sigh of relief knowing that political concerns wouldn't get in my way.

"Time to go, boys," I said, striding across the street to the front door. The plan was to boldly enter the house and cause mayhem if opposed. Sometimes the simple, direct methods are the best.

I figured that someone like the Widow would have lookouts, children and adults who would sound an alarm, but once again preparation is the key to crafting. All three of us bore charms, a sort of 'Don't Notice Me' spell that allows the wearer to go where others didn't want them to. That is as long as the wearer didn't do anything violent. I had a feeling the charm wasn't going to last for too much longer.

Giving the go-ahead to Haddeg, he pounded on the stout front door with the butt of his axe. *Boom! Boom! Boom!* When dwarves knock, they don't muck about.

After a minute it swung open to reveal a tall, blond man carrying a lantern in one hand and a stout, spiked oaken club in the other. Broad as a barn door, with a face that must've been used as a battering ram a time or three, he looked every inch an underworld bruiser. His massive chest strained his linen tunic to the breaking point.

"What you want?" he growled, frowning mightily.

"Excuse me sir, but whose estate is this?"

He looked me up and down in a most insulting way, as if he were evaluating a horse. "Ain't none of your business, sweet britches."

Mother Moon, I hate it when they do that. "Go ahead, Skakhir."

Before the man could react, the shining silver war hammer descended, smashing into a booted foot. The man screamed like struck rabbit, dropping the lantern which shattered on the granite tiles, splashing burning oil everywhere. Shakhir followed up with a blow to gut the folded the bruiser up while I whispered a cantrip to douse the flames.

"Let's go," I urged, jumping over the groaning doorman. Inside I had a choice between searching the ground floor or taking the stairway to the next. I opted for up. It seemed to me that those filled with a sense of self-importance would want to look down on people, both figuratively and literally.

Second floor we found ourselves in a hallway confronted by a pair of roughs with crossbows, which they fired before we could react. They dropped their weapons in surprise as both bolts flew wide to strike off the walls, tearing off sheets of plaster. The armor potions would work for little while and while the reagents were hideously expensive, this bit of protection I'd whipped up for the three of us after our adventure with the mercenaries up north seemed like a sensible precaution.

Haddeg and Skakhir roared and charged the two roughs, who did the most sensible thing I'd seen in days . . . ran like their lives depended on it. The dwarves halted their mad rush.

"Where to, lass?" they asked.

"Up. Rich people like up." We went for the stairs.

On the third floor landing we ran into a trio of black-clad women who came at us with short knives flashing, moving like the wind through the trees, fluid and fast. One blade sliced at my abdomen, but was turned aside by the armor charm. My return thrust missed, but I followed with a kick that connected to the chest of my opponent, sending her back over the railing. She flipped in midair, trying to grab at anything, but disappeared with a wail followed by an abrupt thud.

Meanwhile, my dwarven companions attacked with abandon, not bothering to defend against blades that were turned aside at the last instant. Haddeg swung wild, axe barely missing his opponent while Skakhir fought with more skill, the silver hammer a blur of motion that suddenly put his adversary on the defensive, her knife a steely net. Skakhir swung and there came a metallic *ping* as hammer met knife and knife lost big, snapping in half. The woman barely had time to widen her eyes in shock before Skakhir dashed her brains against the wall. As for Haddeg, he rushed his opponent who stabbed for an eye, but the knife was forced wide by my magic. The dwarf dropped his axe and took the woman in a bear hug, squeezing for all his worth, face turning beet red as arms as thick as my leg slowly crushed the woman. Bones snapped and she howled in agony before going limp. The dwarf unceremoniously dropped her and retrieved his weapon.

Fourth floor landing: Nothing. I was starting to get a little winded. I expected villains, not staircases. If the Widow had been thinking it out, she would've lived in ten-story mansion so we'd be too tired to put up a fight by the time we reached the top.

Fifth and final floor and more crossbow bolts . . . all flung wide as stained glass windows shattered, becoming the recipients of damage meant for us and we rushed our opponents, nine men and women also dressed in black like the women of the third floor. There were no words, no battle cries, just the wet work of death as weapons flashed in the bright lamplight.

One of the men opened his mouth impossibly wide, wide enough that I could see his uvula twitch like a worm from twenty feet away, jaws unhinging with a *crack*, and shouted, a noise so loud and stunning that the walls shattered, showering the area with plaster and what remained of the stained-glass windows on the landing were reduced to dust. The force of the sound blast was enough to tear flesh from bone and shatter teeth. I'd heard of such spells, but this was the first time I'd encountered one. The air around the dwarves and I suddenly flickered with golden light, repelling the hideous cacophony that emanated from the open jaws of the wizard, a long note of pulverizing noise negated by three small charms I'd made earlier. I could feel the charm (a small silver pendant) around my neck heat up and knew it wouldn't last for much longer.

With a leap, Haddeg spun in the air and, in a welter of blood, removed the startled wizard's head from his shoulders, the protective magic still flashing around the dwarven warrior like sparks from a bonfire. Shakhir killed two men in the space of one heartbeat, his hammer destroying a throat, the backswing driving a spike through a temple.

Grunting and panting, I laid about with long knives, slashing arms, kicking and cutting wildly, forcing three black-clad opponents back with the ferocity of my attack. Anger pulsed like blood through my veins, giving me the energy to slice open a second mouth on a woman to my right while kicking the man to my left. The man in front went for my skull with a club, but it was driven aside by my magic. I took him in the heart with the knife in one hand, leaving it there when I found it stuck fast in bone.

Haddeg removed arms and legs with single blows of his axe while Skakhir's hammer made a less showy demonstration of his prowess, smashing shoulders and skulls, breaking bones with each swing.

Within a minute we were left alone on the landing with the dead, all nine foes vanquished. I panted, my heart racing from the aftereffects of a pitched battle, blood taste in my mouth, offal smell in my nose. Haddeg and Skakhir leaned on their weapons and took great gulps of air, covered head to foot in blood. We dripped gore with every motion and sheets of crimson matted my braids.

"You . . . all right?" I asked when I had the breath.

"Aye, lass," they replied. I thought Haddeg whispered something about butt cheeks, but my heartbeat was too loud in my ears to hear.

I stretched, taking a great gulp of air and pulled forth a bronze crown. I breathed on the coin and whispered a word in Dendrich. I knew that somewhere Remee would feel it turn icy and have his men surround the mansion in a matter of moments. Normally I would've charged in with a small army, but with someone like the Widow, that meant I could've been leading that small army to the grave and I didn't have the time to mix that many potions or craft enough charms. "Let's finish this already."

"Aye lass, what a good idea."

We began a room by room search of the top floor, not knowing what the Widow, or her surrogate, had in store for us and not wanting to find out the hard way. In a couple of minutes we searched most of the floor before we finally came to what I could only describe as a library, a large space where every other wall was a bookshelf crammed full, with chairs and couches arranged decoratively upon rugs so expensive I doubted I could afford them even if I lived a couple more centuries.

A woman stood near the far wall drinking from a crystal goblet, was staring out a large window. Long and lithe, she had honey hair and fair skin, almost beautiful except for the scar across her brow which she unsuccessfully tried to conceal with bangs. I immediately recognized her black, skin tight clothing.

"So, you found me," she said, quite unconcerned, not bothering to look our way.

She was too cool, too collected. I began to worry a bit as we stepped inside, the dwarves flanking me. "You *are* the Widow," I said, gripping my knives tightly.

"Of course. Every now and then I like to . . . stretch the legs, so to speak." A sip from the goblet. "How did you do it?"

"When I gripped your arm. My fingers were sticky with a honey potion I transferred to your shirt." The vial of honey in my pouch led us unerringly to the mansion.

My mouth felt dry, my tongue a strip of leather, and I didn't know why I bothered carrying on a conversation, I just felt the need to take things slow. Standing not more than forty feet away was one of the most dangerous people in the kingdom and my sense of peril was screaming at me.

The Widow grinned around her goblet. "Cute. It seems I underestimated you, Justice Goisien. Good show."

"The house is surrounded by the watch and every available Justice along with a mage or two, you have nowhere to run, so why don't you just cooperate and I will take that into consideration before pronouncing judgement." This wasn't going to work, but the law said I must try sweet reason.

Apparently it wasn't sweet enough. "I think I will take a different tack, thank you." The goblet fell from her hand and I dove across the floor toward her, feeling the hairs on the back of my neck starting to rise. Behind me Haddeg and Skakhir cursed, lifting their weapons.

A harsh Denrich word lashed out and the ceiling exploded downward burying the dwarves in a rumbling mass of timber and plaster, spewing dust everywhere in think, grayish clouds.

I kept rolling until my back cracked against the leg of a large, overstuffed chair. Pain rendered me speechless as the Widow said, "I underestimated you once. Never again." Lightning erupted from her fingertips, crackling against my spellbreaker charm in a shower of yellow motes before disappearing. I felt the charms efficacy wane as, for an instant, she looked nonplussed.

That gave me time enough. Springing to my feet, I flicked a Coadian fetish at the woman and she tried to bat it away, but the eagle feather tied to a virgin's finger bone exploded on contact, tearing a pinky clean off. The Widow screamed in agony, clutching her bleeding hand to her chest and staring daggers at me as tears coursed down her cheeks.

Ugly words dropped from her lips and the chair next to me sprung into motion, growing wooden claws at the ends of its legs and oaken teeth in its cushion. It spat and growled deep, a grinding, tearing sound and I felt my insides turn to water.

"Kill her," she ordered.

The chair sprang, cushion mouth growing large and I flung a piece of parchment down its throat, a one-use spellbreaker charm and I prayed to gods that it would work. Its mouth snapped shut with a crunch and it stopped, trembling before it literally fell apart into a pile of feathers and splinters.

I guess it worked.

Before the Widow could speak, I opened a small leather bag and flung a grayish dust into the air between us, the dust I threw mixing with the pulverized plaster from the detonated ceiling. Instead of settling, the powder hung there unmoving. Not even our panting breaths affected the billowy cloud.

Once again the Widow, now barely seen through the gray haze, let loose with a string of Dendrich, a spell I had heard before, one designed to literally freeze the blood and I charged, desperate to stick a knife in her before she could complete it, a shout of denial ringing in the air. Time slowed as my boots clomped upon hideously expensive rugs and I saw a slow smile of satisfaction bloom across the woman's features as she realized I wasn't going to reach her in time.

The last syllable fled her mouth.

Nothing happened, the freeze spell was absorbed by the gray dust hanging in the air. I grinned and kept coming, covering the last few feet between us in a leap.

Eyes growing wide in shock, the Widow barely had enough time to shriek before I tackled her, forgoing the blade for fists. I scrambled on top and pinned her shoulders down with my knees while raining blows down on her, not caring if I killed her, all I could see was that great big pile of scrap that buried my friends and she was responsible. Her nose broke with an ugly *crack* and blood flew to spatter against priceless books, but that didn't bother me, she was near unmoving, letting loose little mewing sounds like a drowning kitten and I broke her jaw, sending teeth scattering across the rug.

Strong hands grabbed my fists, stopping me cold. "That's enough, lass. Yer don't wanna kill her." Skakhir's wise brown eyes stared at me from a face powdered white with plaster. Haddeg nodded, looking both sad and grim.

My arms found my friends as my knees near gave way, hugging them close. "I thought I lost you two idiots," I sobbed in joy and relief into their arms as a host of other emotions I couldn't name flooded me. Remorse coursed through me as I stared at my hands, bloodied and raw from striking the Widow so many times.

"Nah, yer not going to lose us, lass," Skakhirr replied, adding a little spice to his return hug.

"By my clenched butt cheeks, woman," Haddeg put in, eliciting a bark of laughter from me. "It's going to take more than a mere wizard to put a dwarf down."

"Mother Moon and Father Sun, don't ever get caught flat footed again."

"Not in the cards, lass, not in the cards."

"Well, I certainly don't want to play cards with you two."

We shared a laugh over the battered and bloody body of the Widow, her face near unrecognizable. After taking a few deep breaths to still my racing heart and balance my humors, I brought forth another coin, a silver crown, and slid my breath over its shiny surface and spoke a few words, letting my fellow Justices know my location. In less than a minute Justices Orliss Auresio, Remee Occass and Quentin Bill entered the library.

Orliss was dressed in strong canvas trousers and a leather vest over a soft tan tunic that complimented his gray curls. Still strong in body and mind despite seeing over seventy summers, he looked a decade younger and stood straight as an arrow. He frowned at the scene inside the library as he picked his way across the debris. Quentin Bill, a young man with brown hair cut short and a ready smile that transformed his usually homely face into something wonderful, studied the room with a keen eye. As for Remee, he charged in like a bull chasing a cow in heat, eyes wide, searching for trouble, Clear Conscience in both hands ready to slice and dice.

"By the Nine," Remee gasped upon seeing the bloodied Widow. "What happened here?"

"Looks like this woman might have angered Justice Niendra a bit," said Orliss drily, crossing his arms. "Something no sane person would want to do."

"She looks like one of the criminals after Samtell gets done with them in the arena." Quentin's husband Samtell was a gladiator in the Royal Arena where violent criminals were given the choice between trial by combat or execution, assuming they weren't caught in the act by a Justice, then there was no choice. The man never lost a bout and had only ever been wounded a couple of times.

"No," said Remee in awe. Clear Conscience found its way back into its sheath. "She looks worse. Niendra, you beat her like it was your soul purpose in life."

I stood. "Orliss, if you would do me the honor of interrogating the prisoner."

"Of course, Niendra, but do you know who this is?"

Skakhir replied, "As yer can see, yon lady ys the bloody Widow, a wee criminal broot ta joostice by our gud lass here." He laid the brogue on thick, perhaps hoping to play cards with the older Justice. I could have told him Orliss was not so easily fooled.

"Niendra," Orliss continued with a nod to the dwarf, "This is Lady Hildrep Ul-Ofre, Viscountess of Riverend shire.

That set me back on my heels, but I didn't let it show. "What is the Viscountess from a backwater place like Riverend doing in Ramashur? And how in the name of the Nine does the Countess Immielda not know what her deputy is up to?"

"All good questions, Niendra." Orliss rubbed his stubbled chin and nodded to the broken and bloody Viscountess. "Why don't I ask her?"

Twenty-One

NOW

I STAND IN THE MIDDLE OF A PLACE THAT HAS NO WALLS because darkness sucks the light from the gem I hold without revealing its secrets and I resist the urge to fling the stone into that void to pierce its secret heart.

When I cut the magical thread, the walls sank slowly, with great ponderousness, into the floor and the ceiling retreated, leaving me in a small puddle of yellow light and Tennic at my back, framed in the archway to the tunnel beyond.

My companion's nostrils flare. "You smell that?"

A faint, musky odor, similar to that of a wet dog. "Yes."

"What is it?"

"My tattoos allow me to see much, but I cannot see in this particular darkness, which I suspect must be augmented by runes."

"What does that mean?"

"Your guess is as good as mine."

"Wonderful. Now what?"

Good question. I ponder it for a moment before saying, "Come here, look for traps as we go. I have a . . . feeling about this."

"I thought you said you can't feel anything?"

"If I wanted cheek I would ask for it." I cannot help but grin at his insolence, although I can practically feel the fear streaming from him that puts a lie to his sarcastic façade. I reach for a hand and he takes mine and we walk slowly into the dark straight ahead, holding the gem up and out.

The darkness gives way to more uneven gray rock beneath our feet and although it looks natural, I cannot help but think about the stone walls disappearing into the floor. The geomancer was obviously a master, perhaps even an arch-mage, which only served to heighten my curiosity as to his identity. Our footsteps should echo, but the sound is muffled, as if the black eats it all and hungers for more, which provides no comfort. Perhaps that, too, is a product of magic. If so, the geomancer certainly worked hard to create a forbidding atmosphere.

Within a few minutes we come to a wall, rough and uneven like the floor. At the pace we walk and the time it took to reach this spot, I estimate that the room is no less than two-hundred feet long, give or take. Tennic shivers beside me as he comes to the same realization.

"Let's go back," he whines, sounding more a child than young man.

Far behind us is the archway, a section of dark a little less so than the cavern, a product of the dim light spilling in from the hole to the outside world, perhaps. "A few minutes longer, my good lad, then we'll go back for Nokrini's body. Sound good? Which direction should we go? Left or right?"

"This is the kinda place what means to get us eaten by monsters," is his reply. I cannot fault his fear. "Left."

Left it is. The floor passes beneath us, the wall on our right within reach and before long it begins to curve to the left. I feel Tennic's fear rising and I am just about to turn toward the lesser patch of dark where the archway lies when we come upon a small box made of rough black stone set against the wall. For a moment I mistake it for a piece of darkness that refuses to yield to my light, but its shape is unmistakable.

"Hold, lad," I whisper, not sure why I do so. I look through my eyelids and I see nothing. No magic, no aura to indicate runes on the exterior. "Tennic," I say. "Please check it for traps."

Tennic complies, now absorbed by the task suited to his skills to feel much fear. He takes several long minutes before he pronounces the box clear of traps. Stepping back, he looks to me as if to say, 'Your turn.'

I cock my head to the side and consider the box, once again utilizing my tattoos. Still nothing, and that gives me pause. The geomancer was an obviously a careful, brilliant mage who thought all this through judiciously and each trap and ward proved more dangerous than the last, so caution is called for.

Who was this man and why did he come here to a fairly remote part of Gylleth? This level of power could only come from an arch-mage, yet I am sure I would have heard of one gone missing. And how did he acquire the jeweled rod, which is an artifact of incalculable power that brought me back from Tilla's Hold?

Taking my courage in hand, I give the light gem to Tennic and raise the stone lid and set it aside. The inside of the stone box is lined in green velvet and on that velvet is a mask of gold. Smooth as butter and shining in the gemlight, it is the face of a beautiful, yet somehow cold, woman with high cheekbones with an imperious aspect. In the middle of the forehead there is a raised half-moon the size of a copper crown.

"I know this," I say in whispered wonder. If I had vital humors, my stomach would flutter and my hands shake. Instead, I can only look in shock at a legend.

"What is it?" breathes Tennic. His hands do shake, causing our little puddle of light to shimmy.

"It is the mask of Mother Moon," I reply, the words barely disturbing the still air.

"And?"

"And it is an artifact thought lost for three-thousand years. Legend has it that Mother Moon, in her aspect as Goddess of Secrets, created this mask herself based on her own features and bestowed it upon the High Priestess Uweldia of Biavia during a time of the Six Kingdom War."

"Uh, all right. Then, what's it for?"

I shake my head. "I am not sure. All I know is that it offers some sort of protection to the wearer, the details are lost to history. I am certain were I to travel to the temple of Mother Moon in Biavia, I could find out."

"Grab it and let's go do just that. I want to get out of here."

That sentiment I can understand quite well, so I lift the mask from the velvet and that is when everything goes wrong.

Light suddenly floods the cavern from blazing runes high upon the distant ceiling and we see exactly how large it is. Turns out my estimate is pretty much spot on at two-hundred feet and a few feet away lies something at sends real fear through me.

"Aw, no," squeaks Tennic in terror and urine drips from his trousers as his bladder lets go. "Wrath troll."

Far too close for comfort lies another legend, this one far more sinister, one that every person in the Six Kingdoms knows; it is a monster without equal upon Estia save a dragon.

Unlike its hairless, scaled cousins the rock and cragg trolls, wrath trolls are furred like bears and have vaguely bear-like features which include a muzzle filled with triangular, shark-like teeth. Twelve-feet tall, wrath trolls are notoriously resistant (but not impervious) to magic and attack anything with berserker fury, even other wrath trolls, hence the name. One of the reasons they are so dangerous is that they can hibernate, sometimes for centuries, and upon awakening, ravage the countryside consuming everything in their path. I do not know if it is hibernating or simply asleep, but I do not want to find out. The specimen lying there is a prime example of the species, with finger-length black hair and tree trunk thick arms and legs that allow it run on all fours with equal ease as upright. Four fingered hands sport three-inch gray talons that look like they can shred steel as well as stone.

This one is wearing a leather collar studded with silver spikes.

"Tennic," I barely whisper.

"Yes, Niendra?"

"Run."

He needs no more urging, but we barely take ten steps when the collar around the troll's thick, hairy neck flashes bright blue and the monster's pale white eyes open.

Mother Moon!

Tennic's feet fly, blurring into incredible speed as terror spurs him on and I can *feel* his fear as if it is my own, as if living, vital humors are coursing through my undead veins and the sensation causes me to stumble a bit, but I keep my feet as I hear the giant creature stir.

Suddenly the entire cavern shakes as a roar that is more a physical force than sound washes over us and I risk a look back to see the wrath troll standing, face to the ceiling and muzzle open wide as it peals its anger and ferocious hunger. Then it looks at me.

I sense its malevolent, all-consuming appetite and its single-minded, furious intelligence blazing from that all-white gaze, those eyes raging with its need to consume and consume and consume and it drops to all fours and charges the two little morsels trying to run away.

"Tennic!"

"Yeah?"

"Run faster!"

No more roaring, the monster is a frighteningly fast blur of motion as it chases us and my legs pump, not quite as fast as Tennic's, but I can do it all day. Unfortunately, I do not have all day. I have seconds left before I find myself in the belly of the beast and I am confronted by real fear, not just for the lad, but for *me*. I can face down assassins, mages, mercenaries, and the undead, but this wrath troll can actually *destroy* me.

The doorway to the tunnel approaches and I know that the troll will have a little trouble squeezing through, but not so much that it will hinder him much and although I am immune to panic, at that moment I come close.

"Niendra," comes the lad's cry. He is far ahead of me, already in the hallway. "When I say jump, you jump!"

There is no time for questions, only action and I run, imagining the stinking hot breath of the monster on my neck. I can hear its iron hard claws rake the stone behind me, so close and I find that little bit of extra *oomph* to propel myself ever faster and I know it will not last, that not even my undead legs can work forever at these speeds and suddenly, as I barrel through the archway bypassing the vomitus the boy spewed earlier, I hear Tennic shriek.

"Jump!"

Without looking where I leap, I do so and I have a vague impression of darkness beneath me and the sound of claws skittering on smooth stone. A high-pitched wail comes from behind as my feet find stone once again and I slip, the floor underneath too smooth and I slide several feet before coming to a stop as my hands produce a pair of long knives. I leap to my feet and spin around ready to meet furry death.

Nothing. Instead, I see a hole in the tunnel, the trap sprung and two sets of long talons gripping the edge as the wrath troll desperately tries to claw its way back to the top. The shrieking sound of talons tearing at stone reaches my ears a moment before Tennic howls and brushes past me, swinging Dodmatir with all his might. The silver hammer smashes down on a troll finger and the monster screams, a sound that near forces me back with its intensity. A three-inch gray talon flies off spinning across the tunnel. Tennic continues to smash at the troll, breaking a finger with each hit and Father Sun's hammer takes chips out of the floor when he misses. Finally, with one mighty swing, my companion crushes a finger and the troll drops into darkness.

Tennic stands there panting, sweat running down his face in streams as he stares into the abyss. "The trap door isn't closing," he observes. His hands shake on the haft of his weapon and I marvel on the depths of his intelligence and bravery.

"The troll probably broke it," I reply, realizing I am still holding the gold mask. "Well done, lad. Well done."

Beaming and never taking his eyes from the void, he says, "I figured that those claws of his wouldn't do him no good on this slick floor, so I sprung the trap before you got here and told you to jump, which you did real good, cleared the hole by more than five feet and that great big whol-loping troll come running in all fours and tries to stop because the ceil-ing is too low for it to jump and you shoulda seen those claws trying to scrabble on the floor, but he slips in my puke and he slides right on in as pretty as you please."

As winded as he is, I am surprised that he can rattle off all that without taking a breath. I am about to remark on this when a great claw rises from hole and grasps the edge, one talon snagging the hem of my trousers.

"Get it off! Get it off!" I slash at my trousers, not worrying about the flesh underneath.

Glowing white eyes slowly rise out of the darkness in front of us fol-lowed by a muzzle full of far too many teeth. A second hand tries to grab the lip of the hole but three fingers are broken and cannot grip, it keeps sliding off, but the one hand that is holding on has talons sunk deep into stone and I know that the monster will be out in a second to rend and tear and devour. I stab at the beast.

At the same time the point of my blade pierces an eye, the spiked end of Dodmatir plunges deep through the top of the troll's skull and the resul-tant scream slams into us. Tennic is blown back but keeps hold of the ham-mer, trailing brains and blood, landing on his behind with a loud thud while I am flattened against the wall, trousers slashed and torn where the talon pierced it while the troll's shriek follows it down into the void. The scream lasts a long time before silence swallows it whole. The trap door slowly closes and the only thing to mark the existence of the wrath troll is the little trail of vomitus that runs from the archway to terminate in the middle of the hallway.

I scramble to the lad, hands slipping on smooth stone and grasp him as he lays there, ears bleeding and mouth open, emitting little panting breaths. My hands roam, seeking wounds and worry clogs my throat for a moment because Tennic has become dear to me, dearer than I thought, and if he is hurt I will not forgive myself for allowing him to follow me into danger.

"Are you all right?" I ask, searching his wide green eyes. "Are you hurt?"

He stares at me. "What?"

I speak louder. "Are you hurt?"

"No." he tries to stand, but is wobbly so I assist. When he reaches his feet, he brushes me off. "I'm all right." A shake of the head as if he is trying to remove water from his ears. "I think so. Let's get the dwarf and get outta here."

In full agreement, I sidestep the pressure plate and grab a handful of dwarven mail and the skull, hauling the noxious dripping body behind as we exit. When our faces meet the outside world the sight of the sun is a welcome relief, almost as welcome as mounting our horses and leaving the Ninesdamned place in the distance.

TWENTY-TWO

THEN

MY HEART HURT AND MY LIMBS SHOOK, but I survived the encounter with the Widow and now it was Justice Orliss's turn to take over. As for me, I wanted nothing more than to take a large swig of ale and curl up next to Mirallelle for the next century.

Fate, it seemed, had other plans.

We were standing outside of Hildrep's mansion directing the watch on clean up when Hengeth showed up as if by . . . well, magic. Before I could open my mouth the big lug had me in a bear hug and was squeezing me hard enough that I saw spots. My boots hit the ground before the dwarves could take offense.

"Let me look at you," said the big wizard, concern writ large on his bearded face. "I heard all the foofaraw and came right on over." He checked my face and limbs and I didn't have the heart to shake my friend off. "Good to see you're in one piece, Niendra." He turned to the dwarves. "Haddeg, Skakhir, good to see you're well."

"No lyttle wizard wooman gets the better o' a dwarf," said Skakhir, laying it on thick.

"Aye," agreed Haddeg. "Was a gud row, it was. Stirs the bloood."

I bit my lip to keep from laughing and said to Hengeth, "So you heard all the foofaraw, did you?"

He stood up straight and smiled. "Have friends in the watch."

"People have big mouths."

"Aww, girl, they're worried, that's all. You're right popular, you are." Another hug. "I was worried a bit, too."

"Lay off, you big oaf." My smile belied my words. "Everything is all right. Was a good day for everyone, all things considering." I looked back at the mansion. "But the fallout from this is going to be *huge*."

"But worth it. You've already stirred the hornet's nest with that wizard cave at the Frost Quarry. Queen Bet herself wants me to give it a look."

"Be careful, that's all I can say." I certainly didn't want to return to that place.

Hengeth leaned in and said in a voice pitched so only I could hear, "Care to give me the details? Anything you might have left out, maybe? Even dead wizards are dangerous."

I shook my head. "No, nothing, but definitely be careful. I don't know who that geomancer was, but he was *talented*."

"How so?"

"It was obvious by the books there that he was researching geomancy, but wasn't a master, yet he was able to create a beautiful tunnel system complete with a clever little water trap. Not only that, the wards I encountered were some of the most sophisticated I'd ever seen."

As I spoke, Hengeths' face grew longer and longer. "If there's nothing else . . .?"

"No, nothing."

Once again, I found myself in a bear hug which I returned with interest. "You ought to come home with me. Mirallelle is probably awake worrying about me and we can have a drink and swap stories. She'd love to meet you."

A rubbery sigh passes his lips. "Ah, not tonight." He looks up to the night sky at its multitude of stars and the red crescent moon hanging low just above the walls. "It will be morning in a couple of hours and I need to prepare for the trip to the quarry." He fished into a pouch and brought out a tiny wooden carving of a bird. "If you think of anything else, or you need me, just tell the little birdie here and let it go. It will find me." His grin lights his face as he presses the carving into my palm and closes my hand over it. "Good luck to you, Niendra, I'll see you soon." With that he strode purposefully toward the palace.

I noticed the dwarves staring at me. "What?"

"Oh, nothing lass," says Haddeg with a shrug. "Just wondering how far you trust the man, being that he's a wizard an all."

"I'm a wizard."

"Nah, you're a Justice. Different animal altogether." Haddeg hooked his thumbs behind his belt and gave me a look that dared me to object. All I could do was smile and head over to Quentin Bill where he was talking to the Watch Commander.

"Yes, Niendra?" He looked as exhausted as I felt, with bags below his puppy eyes and deep lines bracketing his mouth.

"I'm to bed, Bill," I replied. "It's been a long couple of weeks and I need some sleep. You help Orliss out if he needs it."

He nodded toward the mansion. "This is Countess Immielda's mansion, not the Viscountess Hildrep's. I don't know if she knew her deputy is the Widow or not, but it does raise some interesting questions. What do you want to do with the place?"

"It's Orliss's call, but I say we should lock it down, set a guard. Set *ten* guards and tell the Countess that if she wants her home in Ramashur back, she must submit to formal questioning to Lord Petre. If Lord Petre is still indisposed, then I'll do it once I've had some sleep. If she objects, she can take it up with Her Majesty, I'm too tired to care at this point."

Quentin's grin erased some of the fatigue from his face and he wished me a good night.

Before I left, I said, "And keep a watch on people paying too much attention. I'm pretty godsdamned sure that the Widow has agents all throughout the city. There's going to be a power vacuum soon and we need to be on top of things."

Haddeg and Skakhir had been staying at my place ever since we returned because they felt sure that bad things would happen should we part ways and, truthfully, I was happy for the company. The house I shared with Mirallelle comfortably fits two, but four stretched it a bit thin, but safety trumped comfort.

Our boots echoed off cobbles as we walked, too tired to banter, too tired to even try. The house, located between the Uppers and Lowers in the area called Merchant's Row, was nestled between two taller buildings, one a home to a tinsmith, the other a widowed seamstress who made quite the living for herself as one of the best in the city. I got along well with my neighbors, even though wizards tended make non-magic folk uneasy but because we kept to ourselves and treated them with genteel respect, we earned the same in return.

When I laid eyes on Sandry the smith's place I felt the tension start to drain away, my shoulders dropping, the headache from unbalanced humors easing, fading like mist in the sun. For a moment I was happy, looking forward to seeing my wife, holding her in my arms and planting a kiss that might last forever.

My stomach froze, iced over in horror, the scream threatening to burst forth stopped at my throat while my companions swore vile oaths in Khulasch.

The door to my house lay in splinters, a broken heap almost hidden in the clinging shadows and in that brief instant in time I knew my whole world was broken, shattered like door and that nothing would ever be right again. It was information so deeply ingrained in my flesh as to be divine knowledge from the Nine.

I didn't remember running, only the wood bits skittering under my boots as I burst into the house with the dwarves at my heels. I didn't remember screaming my wife's name, only that my throat hurt so bad it felt like it should bleed. All I remembered was terror and the feeling of my heart beating so fast, so hard, that it would burst forth from my chest and explode in a rain of gore.

Something hard gripped my shoulder, a vise that lifted me up and threw me across the main room to crash into my small dining table. Pain lanced my back as the table collapsed beneath me, the muscles where the vise grabbed me protesting almost as loudly. Air left my lungs and for a moment consciousness left my head.

Loud, crashing sounds, deep, growling cursing and metallic clanging brought me back from Johlyavt, Himir's House of Dreams. My eyes snapped open to see sparks accompanying that strange metallic clanging, sparks that illuminated a scene from a nightmare.

In brief flashes I saw Haddeg and Skakhir whirling around the house, weapons flying, teeth bared in furious hatred for a large, whitish, man-shaped being that swung its arms with massive *whooshing* sounds.

I didn't know what it was, but with every strike it put an arm clean through a wall or destroyed a piece of furniture, which indicated a hideous strength, and the sparks that flew from the dwarves' weapons as they connected with it told me its skin was rock hard. My mind shifted through the possibilities as training took over. Gargoyle, rock troll, stone galt . . . could it be one of these? I dismissed the stone galt because of the lack of a third arm.

Cursing, I rose and drew a piece of parchment from a pouch, one of the spells I'd prepared in advance for the assault on the Widow's home. I tore the parchment in half and felt the exhilarating rush of spell release as a bolt of lightning erupted from the two halves and struck the creature in the head. I had a glimpse of a white, battered face with no nose and chipped features just before the bolt was swallowed up and disappeared as the thunder that followed near deafened me.

That got its attention. With swiftness belying its size, it rushed me and I barely dodged one of its arms, which punched right through the wall at my back. Plaster and wood erupted as it drug its limb free and both dwarves coordinated an attack, striking the arm at the same time. Hammer and axe met shoulder and it exploded, sending rock chips flying. I felt one graze my cheek and then the warmth of blood drooling from a cut.

A wall hit me in the face and I fell to the floor, stunned and gasping for breath, yellow spots dancing in my eyes and the smell of blood in my nose. An intense pressure inside my left arm eclipsed everything, as if it was an overfilled bladder ready to burst and all I could do was stare at the thing that loomed over me, sparks ringing from its hide as the dwarves struck and struck again and it lifted what I thought was a foot to smash my skull into red/gray paste and I consigned my soul to Mother Moon and Father Sun, sure in the knowledge I was looking at my death.

It was Haddeg. That brave, mad, wonderful dwarf flung himself at the creature with such strength that they both fell to the floor with such a resounding crash that the force of it flung me into the air and when I landed, it was on my left arm.

Pain became everything for me as I felt the ends of the broken bone in my upper arm ground together and my sight went white. For a short time the world went away as I tried to cope with the agony consuming me. Nothing pierced the fog of pain and horror that cocooned my senses.

When reality returned, I found myself on the floor clutching my arm with tears in my eyes and blood in my mouth. Buttery lamp light met me and I could see the devastation my house suffered . . . holes in the wall, smashed furniture and plaster dust everywhere. Sobbing floated on the air, a keening that tore at my heart and I gathered myself to rise.

Oh . . . Mother Moon! My arm hammered me with pain as the house spun about me, more spots clouded my vision and I took deep breaths to steady myself as the sobbing continued. After a few moments everything steadied and I was able to see what's what.

Haddeg. Skakhir held his body gently as he keened, tears flooding into his beard, his face a rictus of grief and loss. His cousin looked peaceful in death, his face unlined, serene, but the shard of stone piercing his chest gave lie the illusion of sleep. Shattered red-flecked white stone lay all around, a hard bed for the sturdy dwarf.

"Oh, Skakhir," I moaned, tottering over, trying not to fall over in a heap. "Oh . . ." Words failed to come, my throat had closed up tight, the lump inside a hard denial of what met my eyes. Haddeg, my friend. Tears blurred my vision.

"He tackled the great beast," sobbed Skakhir. "He was something to look at, lass. A wonder to behold. It lifted its foot to smash yer and he tackled it. They both fell and that's when I hit it square with the hammer right in the head and it exploded, just exploded into a thousand bits and it killed him." His hand hovered over the shard that penetrated dwarven chain to pierce his cousin's mighty heart.

"Mirallelle!" My panicked scream shook the house as sudden, terror-filled realization struck and I fled, stumbling and crying to our little bedroom in the back where we celebrated our lives, our joys and triumphs. The only thing left of the door were splinters and iron hinges and my heart dead in my chest as what I dreaded, what I prayed so hard against, lay within the room.

Mirallelle, like Haddeg, lay as if asleep, but it wasn't sleep because of the angle of her neck, the sick cant of her head that told me it was broken clean, as if with a savage twist and I knew that's exactly what happened and my arm didn't hurt as I tottered over to the bed, the image of my wife swimming through the tears. I sat and took her to my lap and let the grief flood out in a torrent of despair.

My wife, whom I loved the instant I met her a few years ago when I first assumed the mantle of Justice. That beautiful Coadian woman whose eyes sparkled when she baked, when she made a joke, when we made love. All of her passions, foibles, jests and japes were gone, gone forever to Tilla's Hold and I would never get her back, never make love to her, never hear her laugh or cry or moan. All of it was gone and so was I.

I didn't know how long I sat there with Mirallelle on my lap, fingers brushing her straight, black hair over and over again. Time was an elusive construct. All I knew was the void in my chest and unceasing despair.

Strong hands lifted her from my arms and unintelligible voices bleated in my ears, but I wasn't there, I wasn't able to react because everything was gone. Being a Justice, crafting, it was all meaningless. Eventually I slipped into darkness.

Twenty-Three

NOW

S KAKHIR, OF COURSE, IS TRUE TO HIS WORD. No more delays in my quest, no more side jaunts to Ramashur or dead wizard's lair, it is time to do what is necessary.

The dwarf looks even older now, the skin hanging loosely from his frame, the wattles around his neck deeper, more pronounced and his beard, once snow-white, is now gray as morning mist. But his eyes still sparkle with humor, vitality and wit as he bids us good bye after solemnly receiving the remains of his granddaughter. He does not ask if her death was a good one, does not remark on the haunted look in Tennic's eyes, instead he bows to the lad before embracing me and I feel the thinness of his arms. It won't be long now and that knowledge hurts. He is last tether to my former life and I do not want to be there when he dies.

"Good travels, lass," he says hoarsely. "Yer still got a long way to go."

"I know." The dapple rouncey shuffles beneath me, eager to be off while Tennic's chestnut jennet whinnies. "Phezdes blessings to you, my friend."

His smile is pure dwarven humor. "And may Father Sun protect you, lass."

We part without another word. None suffice to express how we feel.

MY MIND IS SUCH A WHIRL OF THOUGHTS AND ANTICIPATION that I hardly notice the Borderlands Inn or the sheer granite walls of the Callic Pass rising to either side until the sky is a wide, blue strip overhead. I do not pay attention to the thin tower that rises on the north side of the pass at the midpoint or the sylvan guards in white chain who look at us with impassive, almond eyes under finely arched brows. Tennic notices, but keeps his mouth shut because he possesses some extrasensory ability to divine my mood and knows that I have no thought to converse.

Good lad.

Past the tower and we are officially in sylvan territory, a protectorate of Gylleth and ally should any or all of the other kingdoms decide it is a good idea to begin an armed conflict. Although the delicate balance of the Great Peace has stood for many centuries, there was a time when war crawled across Estia on feet of fire and blood. It is this peace that staves off the depredations of the Coadian pirates and the militaristic city-states of Irrammeria far to the south.

Still, Postia lies directly beyond Dorendiriar and has contested the land for generations, stating that all Dorindiriar originally belonged to their kingdom, but does not wish to risk Gylleth's ire. Not yet, anyway.

The horses' hooves ring across stone and I do not care. I only wait to see the sylvan trees and speak to someone of import. I pray they will listen and consider my plea. I fear that they will not, considering my nature.

After a night of watching Tennic sleep by firelight, we finally exit the Frostbacks into the gentle, rolling foothills, descending slowly to the flatland forest beyond. I am almost giddy with anticipation and at the same time apprehensive. This is a big risk, the sylvan could decide I am too unnatural to continue to exist and render me fully dead, sending my spirit shrieking back to Tilla's Hold. The risk is worth the reward.

It is not long before we reach the edge of the forest where spruce holds sway, the road before winding through old and hoary trunks. Soon the spruce makes way for oak, chestnut and sugar maple. In this rich clime there are over a hundred species of trees, more than I recognize, the glory of the Nine made manifest in nature. Their beauty briefly takes my mind from the quest at hand and Tennic cranes his head in delight, laughing and pointing at squirrels and woodchucks as the horses walk along the thin forest road.

"Hold." The voice is smooth as butter and crystalline, piercing the ears cleanly. The forest becomes silent, even insects seem realize that noise is not wanted now.

We hold. I raise my hands and say to the trees all around, "We have business."

A sylvan male with long copper-red hair and clothed in a dapple green and brown tunic with matching trousers emerges from the trees to stand in front of us, bow strung and nocked. The arrow is not quite pointed in my direction. Those clothes have given him almost perfect camouflage in the forest and I understand now that there could be an army at his back and I would never know. "What business does the dead have in Dorindiriar?" he asks. There is an edge to his voice I do not like.

"I wish to speak to *Vel-ho* Ilmatten, if you please."

The sylvan narrows his beautiful, gray eyes. "For a dead thing, your pronunciation is quite good."

"And for a sylvan, you are quite polite."

We stare at each other until Tennic says, "You got a jakes? I haveta go something fierce I don't know if these bushes will give me a rash or what."

A few seconds go by as the sylvan stares at the boy until suddenly, like the sun finally spearing through a part in the clouds, he smiles and begins to laugh. "I don't know if you are wise or innocent, young human," he says, teeth shining whitely. "But if this one has a traveling companion like you, then she might not be so terrible."

Tennic grins. "Oh, she's terrible all right, but someone has to keep her out of trouble."

This earns more laughter and I turn to the lad and say, "Finished?"

"You think I'll ever be?"

Now the sylvan is *roaring*. I shake my head in exasperation.

"This is the one," cries the sylvan when he catches his breath.

Without fanfare a dozen sylvan appear from the trees dressed in the same manner as the red-haired male, proving my earlier point about camouflage. One at a time they take turns staring at me intently, as if each needs to take my measure before we can proceed, then they give Tennic a once-over. Most smile at the lad and a couple shake his hand.

"I knew you would be here," says the last sylvan to approach. "I knew it the moment I rose this morning. I knew it before I had breakfast. I've been waiting."

My feet hit the forest floor in a crunch of leaves. "Taalis?"

IT SHOULD NOT SURPRISE ME, BUT IT DOES. The former representative of the sylvan nation of Dorendiriar to the Divver Frost quarry is here and leading me into the depths of her homeland. Two sylvan lead the rouncey and jennet through the trees while the lad and I walk with Taalis and that is all I see of the over dozen sylvans we encounter. The rest shadow us, but their clothing and effortless moment through the forest renders them invisible and virtually inaudible.

Before too long we come across the first of the Forever Trees, the goliaths dominating the sky above and I cannot help but feel like a midge upon the skin of the world approaching the true masters of Estia. Surely the Nine themselves created such magnificent specimens. The white bark when seen up close is actually subtly gnarled so as to offer easy purchase for those who might want to climb and the limbs that stretch so wide and far overhead are large enough to build houses upon.

Tennic stares up, his neck surely creaking as he walks along and I have to guide him so he does not run into one of the smaller trees that cluster around the massive trunk like supplicants.

Beyond the first Forever Tree lies a stretch of hundreds, perhaps thousands, and the sun soon becomes a memory as we are clothed shadows thrown by those massive branches and leaves the size of houses. At that point I notice a strange whitish glow and realize that it emanates from the trunks of the mighty trees, as if they soak up the sunlight and channel it through their bark so the small creatures that gambol around can see. Everything seems to have a hard, argent edge as if the light has been painted everywhere.

"This is amazing," Tennic exclaims in wonder, holding up his hands. The glow makes his skin look pale.

"We call it, *Puilois*. Treeshine." Taalis gives the lad a smile. It is the first time she has spoken since we met, having said that more would be explained when we reached Koskaankirkas, the sylvan everbright city closest to Gylleth.

Now I see that we are here. The buildings cluster around the trunks of the Forever Trees as if they have grown there, an organic molding of wood that, to me, resembles bee hives and wasp nests. There are no ninety-degree angles, no squares or triangular formations, all structures have rounded edges and many are dome-like, including the largest which are as tall as any tower in Ramashur.

"I thought you would live in the trees," Tennic laughs, clapping his hands. The sylvans we see are dressed in light tunics of some pale shimmery fabric with matching trousers of some thicker material. Here and there are humans, traders from the various kingdoms taking their ease in the treeshine with their sylvan hosts, but the people of this nation know my status simply by staring at me, I can see the subtle distain in their almond eyes and in the arch of their delicate brows. Here I am known and alone, my undeath a sign for all the sylvans to see.

"We utilize only what the trees give us," replies Taalis, her eyes on me as if divining my discomfort. "When a limb breaks off, there is enough there for our *puunpuujai*, woodtalkers, to shape an entire city."

"Woodtalkers?"

Here is something I do know. "Think of them as a specialist naturalist mage, lad. They use magic to shape the wood into whatever form is needed."

Taalis smiles. "A simple explanation, but fairly accurate." As we pass a hemispherical building she reaches out and caresses the shining surface. "This wood is still alive, and will continue to live as long as those inside care for it. If a building is abandoned, it will slowly die. Our people and the trees have a symbiotic relationship."

Tennic cocks his head. "Symbiotic?"

"When two different organisms live and grow together for mutual benefit."

"Huh." The boy strokes his chin. "Not sure about that word."

I run my fingers across the building and am surprised at how smooth it is, as if it had been polished. The wood has a light cherry finish to it, as do most of the structures here. It glows bright enough for me to read by.

We walk for a short time later until we come to another building, this one a slender tower with circular windows, the wood dark and rich like mahogany. Taalis bids us to enter and we step into a room that looks like any main floor of any tower in Ramashur except the walls and floor are wood instead of stone. A Suurmaen carpet lies on the floor under a round table with six chairs. Our host sits and we follow suit.

Descending the staircase that spirals up to the floors above is a sylvan man dressed in dark blue trousers and crimson tunic. His steps are careful and measured, the soft, blue shoes easily traverse the smooth wood as he carries a tray with wooden bowls and cups, which he sets on the table.

"Anything else, Vel-ho?" he asks, sparing a smile for Tennic.

"No, Ilvartian, that will be all." The sylvan leaves, ascending the stair.

My eyes fly wide. "*You* are the high mage of Dorendiriar?"

Gold eyes twinkling, she says, "Of course. I've had five hundred years to become Vel-ho, have I not? Vel-ho Ilmatten has chosen to travel beyond the bounds of this world and I'm his successor." To Tennic, "Eat, drink. It is hart stew and the beverage is *kuu-vini*, or moon wine. We export it to the Six Kingdoms and it's considered a very fine vintage indeed."

Tennic grabs a spoon and tucks in with a will, all stomach with hollow legs.

I do not know what to say, I am completely at a loss so I stare at nothing for such a long time that Tennic shifts uncomfortably. My thoughts travel to conversations five hundred years in the past with the sylvan woman, sifting through all the relevant data, then slides back to our meeting when we arrived.

"You have already done it, have you not?" I ask, clasping my hands in delight, my mood rising on wings of hope. "That is why you knew I would be here. That is how Skakhir knew we would be in the Borderlands Inn, how you both anticipated me. It has already happened. Will happen."

"Uh, Niendra?"

"Yes Tennic?"

"What in the Nine are you *talking* about?" he asks around a mouthful of stew.

I point to Taalis. "She knows."

His bright green eyes spear the sylvan. She smiles and says, "Ask your question, young man."

"Can I have more stew?"

It is so unexpected, so ridiculous, so *Tennic*, that we both cannot help but laugh, the room echoing our mirth for many minutes until tears fall from the sylvan's face.

"I've forgotten how *immediate* young humans are," she chuckles, wiping her face. As if summoned, Ilvartian descends once again, this time with a much larger bowl, and sets it down. Tennic attends to the task of filling himself to the brim with a will. This Taalis, unlike the Taalis of Queen Bet's time, seems more carefree, with smiles that come easier to her face. She looks happy.

"Young man," says Taalis. "Has Niendra told you about me?"

He nods.

"Did she tell you the story about the Frost Quarry and the death of Soro Divver?"

"Some," he mumbles through his food. "Never finished, although she did mention that she thinks you and Coventio Divver were, ah, *romantically* involved."

True, I did mention it offhandedly, but I did not think the lad would blurt my assumption out to like that. I would blush if I could.

Taalis cocks an eyebrow. "Really?"

Nothing to do but plow ahead. "I felt it obvious. He called you Verratton, which means he knew enough about sylvan culture and ways to apply that honorific." I shrug. "And the way you smiled at him. It was the smile of real affection. I also believe that when he accompanied his father to the Frost Quarry, it was to see you, not for business."

The sylvan Vel-ho shakes her head. "You are apparently more perceptive than I gave you credit for. Yes, Coventio and I were romantically engaged, but that was a long time ago." Her voice is filled with longing and loss and I realized she loved the human every bit as much as I loved Mirallelle, which makes her situation a little more bittersweet. How it must have hurt to love someone you would outlive by centuries if not millennia.

Before we could be stuck in the morass of memories, Taalis turns back to Tennic. "Did she mention that we sylvans can manipulate time to a degree?"

A nod.

"What do you know about time?"

Tennic considers that for a moment. "It is. Like the weather. Not much we can do about it, why?"

"Everything that has happened in this world in the past, is happening now, will happen in the future . . . it is always happening. It will always happen. Time is merely the construct that keeps it from happening all at once." At his blank look Taalis raised her hands. "Think of it like this . . . everything that has, is and will happen are words on a page. If you write the contents of an entire book onto one page, then the page will be black with words and no can read it. Now, time is a book with thousands of pages each with just enough words to be read easily."

"By who?"

Taalis shrugs. "The gods, perhaps? Who knows. All that is known is that time simply is. Every decision we will make in the future has already been made, you just haven't caught up to the moment yet."

"Uh . . . wow." Tennic scratches his head. "So, what does that have to do . . ." he stops and thinks for a moment, then looks to me. "You want to go back in time?"

"And she has already sent me," I say. "Or is going to."

"Bright lad you got there, Niendra. I can see why he's your familiar."

The world comes crashing to a halt. "Say what now?" My mind spins almost out of control. Familiar? I had almost completely forgotten about the ritual I had completed in Mateous's little basement and had often wondered why Mother Moon and Father Sun denied me a familiar. I stare the lad and realize that if I concentrate hard enough I can *feel* his confusion, taste the chunks of venison he chews and see myself stare at him with my mouth agape. It explains so much, not the least of which I was so willing to take him under my wing after he tried to pick my pocket.

"Mother Moon!" I whisper. "I am a Ninesdamned fool."

Taalis looks puzzled. "You didn't know?"

"No one has ever had a human familiar before," I say, still staring at the lad.

"I don't think there's ever been a revenant crafter before, so there are a couple of firsts here, aren't there?"

"I'm her familiar?" Tennic asks disbelievingly.

"It surprises me that you two didn't know."

Me, too. I sit there for a minute while Tennic slowly shovels food into mouth. How he still has an appetite, I do not know. "What is the price?" I say changing the subject.

"You know the price," Taalis says reprovingly. "You've always known, Niendra."

I breathe in just so I can sigh. Without a word I reach into my pack and flick open the secret compartment and draw forth the jeweled rod. "This."

Dorindiriar's high mage took the wand and smiled softly. "I've been waiting five hundred years for this." She frowned. "What's this? Where's the last gem? Tilla's diamond?"

"I do not know. It was like that when I returned from Tilla's Hold."

She thinks on this for a few moments, then nods. "It'll do. It still has the power needed."

"What power? For what?"

"To send you five hundred years into the past, of course. Only a mighty artifact such as this can help power the spell. I certainly can't do it by myself."

"Do you think it will work?"

"It already has, remember?"

TWENTY-FOUR

THEN

I WOKE TO LIGHT AND THE SOUND OF BIRDS. The light came from large windows that stretched floor to ceiling and the birds flitted outside, singing and cawing to their hearts content. My eyes felt scratchy, so I rubbed them, giving my body a good stretch because my muscles felt all knotted up, stiff and a little sore. Soft coverlets caressed me, much softer than I had at home.

Home?

Home.

Home!

The events of the past few days rushed in like floodwaters down a ravine, implacable and irresistible and for a moment I felt my sanity crack like window glass. Mirallelle!

Oh, *Mirallelle.*

My throat closed as the tears came with the flood and all I could do was dig my face deep into a pillow softer than cat fur and weep as if my soul was being torn from my body. Where I was and how I got to be there took a distant second place to the aching loss, the great and terrible void in my chest that used to be my heart. I wanted to crawl into that hole and pull it in after so the terrible ache would go away.

Minutes, hours, later I managed to sit up, my braids in disarray around my head, and took stock of my surroundings. Rich woods, blue and gold wallpaper and a set of three enormous windows with real glass panes. The bed in which I found myself looked big enough to house a community of dwarves and the sheets were coral-colored silk. Real Irramerian silk. If the ruby nightgown I wore wasn't silk, it came close enough not to matter.

Obviously someone had crowns to spare.

"We see you are aware."

My head ratcheted around to see Her Majesty Queen Betelial Tol-Amre stroll across the expensive Coadian rugs toward the bed. She was dressed in black from neck to toes with white lace at the collar and cuffs. A fine gold mesh covered her gray hair and a simple circlet of silver rested upon her head holding a thumbnail-sized blue opal in the center of her forehead.

As I began to scramble out of bed, she said, "Stay, Niendra. It is a time for rest and We cannot let such a valuable citizen of Gylleth strain herself during recovery." The queen produced a scroll, handing it to me and then moved with slow, measured steps and settled herself into a heavy, cushioned chair of Postian craftsmanship. "There now. We are comfortable, you are comfortable. Let us chat a bit, yes?"

I nodded, then opened the scroll, reading eh contents. "By the Nine," I breathed.

"That scroll came this morning by post rider from Our Justice Xeristo. We felt it sufficiently urgent enough to present it to you upon awakening. What news from Caenwylln?"

"Coventio Divvier is near flat broke," I replied numbly. "Xeristo's men found evidence that he took out extensive loans from Rol-Venber to cover losses from Coadian pirates. Apparently he lost two ships, along with their crew, and is in debt for the cargo and death-price to the crewmembers' families." Coventio, with all his seeming honesty and grief over his father, *lied* to me. But why? The answer hit a moment later . . . he needed time to send ships to Irrameria to trade his goods to cover his losses.

"We wonder what your next move shall be, Justice."

My laughter felt brittle and carried no humor. "Arrest Coventio Divver for lying to a Justice and the possible murder of his father, Soro Divver." I laid back on the softer than soft pillows and realized we were in the Summer House. The palace never looked this good.

"It shall be done. We shall send a pigeon to Justice Quell to have the young man put in chains. Well done, Justice Goisien."

"Begging your pardon, Your Majesty, but I should have investigated his finances sooner. Now I have to interrogate Coventio to get to the bottom of the matter."

"Rest first, Justice. Know that We are still well pleased with you, even though the news of Viscountess Hidrep Ul-Ofre's traitorous actions displeases Us immensely as it embarrasses the Crown immensely. Having a noble, even a minor one like Hidrep, conducting criminal activities in the capital is insulting to Us beyond measure. We will be talking to Countess Immielda quite soon and she will explain her blindness to her deputy's transgressions. We wonder how this 'Widow' kept out of sight for so long."

"Your Majesty, the Widow is a wizard, a fairly powerful one at that. It isn't hard to believe that magic came to play regarding secrecy."

For a moment the queen sat lost in thought before answering. "We consider that while conversing with the Countess." She sighed, seeming sad and a bit lost, which alarmed me.

"Your Majesty, is everything well?"

There came another long pause, then, "Lord Petre Ul-Mavre has succumbed to his illness and will be laid to rest in the Catacombs of Justice in a week. We trust you will attend?"

Another loss of a fine person. It was almost too much. "Of course, Your Majesty. Lord Petre was a fair and honest man and deserves such respect," I said through a tight throat.

"Yes he does, child. Yes he does." She stared at me with eyes that had broken lesser people before saying, "Have you a thought as to who should replace Lord Petre?"

"Justice Orliss Auresio, Your Majesty." The answer came without thought.

"And why do you say that?"

I shrug. "He is brilliant, decisive and kind, but he is getting on and should be given a role that is less physically taxing. One where he can put that keen mind of his to good use."

"Your reasoning mirrors Ours, Niendra. Yes, it shall be so." Queen Bet continued to stare and it was unnerving, but one holds their tongue and temper around a monarch. "You have Our sympathy and condolences for your loss, Niendra. We are told your wife was a fine woman. The crown shall take care of all expenses, including the repair of your house."

"Thank you, Your Majesty," I said hollowly. Mirallelle!

"When you were brought here your injuries were severe, but not life threatening."

"How long have I been here, Your Majesty?"

"Sixteen hours. You were very tired, child. Our personal healer, body mage Anders Wil-Calle, tended to you and brought you to full health."

Mirallelle! Grief clouded my eyes once again, but I was in the presence of royalty and didn't want to show weakness, so I cast my mind to . . . "Haddeg?"

The queen made a grumbly sort of noise and her deeply creased face grew sadder. "Yes, Our loyal ally Haddeg Whitgut has passed to Rakuil a Glorivreas, no doubt. His cousin Skakhir was granted leave to exit Our service, but has insisted on remaining, stating that he believes you will find justice for his loss."

Justice. For both Mirallelle and Haddeg. I felt like declaring 'by my clenched butt cheeks, I will, Your Majesty,' but I knew that would not be well received. But I could do justice, justice and a severe reckoning to those who hurt me, hurt us, so. The image of Haddeg lying there with that red shard of red-flecked white stone in his heart . . .

White stone? Marble? Red flakes? Or veins, perhaps?

Logical deduction is fine and well, but inspiration and epiphanies help, too. Perhaps I needed to sleep on it (sixteen-hours at least), but my realization had me cursing myself. "By the Nine! I am a fool to end all fools!" I sat up, angry at myself. The clues were there all this time and I failed to see them for what they were. If only I had, maybe Mirallelle would still be alive and that thought, I knew, would haunt me forever. My hands clenched so hard that my nails bit into the skin deep enough to leave marks.

"Child? We would like to know why you think of yourself as a fool." This was not a request.

My head swiveled to Her Majesty the Queen and I felt fresh tears at the corners of my eyes. "I know what happened, Your Majesty. The murder of Soro Divver, the mercenaries, my wife . . . everything."

"We give you leave to inform Us."

And I did. Every piece of the puzzle fit neatly into place. I told the tale slowly, with great detail only omitting the geomancer's lair as that was not germane to the case. When I was done the queen stood slowly, bright red spots on her pale, wrinkled cheeks.

"You are sure, Justice Niendra?"

I nodded. "Very, Your Majesty."

"You have given much for Us to consider, Justice. Stay abed until the new morning and We shall inform you of Our decision." With that the queen moved slowly, ponderously, toward the exit, each measured step thudding with royal gravity upon the lush rug until she reached the door. Queen Bet turned and regarded me with a mixture of sorrow and resignation. "Well done, Justice."

THE NEXT MORNING SAW ME EXAMINED MOST THOROUGHLY by the queen's body mage, Anders Wil-Calle, a portly, middle-aged man in a wine-stained red doublet. Unlike most men, he wore his long, chestnut brown hair freely, showing off his lustrous curls which set off his rather plain face quite well. He had apple cheeks and a ready smile.

"Fit as horse, you are!" he exclaimed happily upon completion. "Of course, you know that. I am so Ninesdamned good, if I do say so myself."

His grin was so infectious I found myself smiling back despite my melancholy and even waved when he left the great bedroom. Before I could rise a chambermaid arrived with a fresh set of clothes perfectly tailored to my size. Leather trousers so soft they almost felt like silk and a workman-like green tunic that draped to mid-thigh and belted with a leather girdle. Calf-high riding boots with laces completed the ensemble and I marveled at the quality and speed with which they were made. I guessed it must been good to be the queen.

The chambermaid then began to assist me with my braids, many of which were snarled and undone by the fight. As soon as my hair was done, Justice Orliss arrived and shoo-ed the woman out.

"My condolences," he said, thumbs hooked into his belt. Dark circles shadowed his eyes and for the first time his normally upright frame was stooped.

I nodded, not wanting to speak about my loss.

"It has come to my attention that I have you to thank for my sudden promotion."

"The queen asked who should succeed Lord Petre, I merely made a suggestion."

His offered me a wry smile. "I don't know whether to thank you or kill you. Her Majesty went and made me a Lord of the realm, which doesn't please me much but it's part and parcel of the position." The now-Lord Orliss Auresio rolled his eyes and I gave a little bark of laughter.

"She also told me of your deductions, putting it squarely in my lap to decide what to do next. Really, Niendra, you know how to ruin a perfectly good day."

"Yeah, perfectly good. You look like you haven't sleep in a week." I paused. "My lord."

"By the Nine," he swore and sat on the corner of the bed. "I'm never going to get used to that." He took my hands in his. "If I give the matter to Justice Remee or Xeristo, will you stand down?"

Anger quickly flared and just as quickly faded, leaving me cold and hard inside. "Probably not."

"You understand that personal matters affect judgement and because of that, revenge replaces justice."

"Sometimes, Lord Orliss, they are the same thing."

His sad and tired eyes stared into mine for a long moment. "I will not ask you to stand down, then. I've known you for a few years now and have come to believe that you will do what's right, but let me warn you, Niendra, that you *are* a Justice of Gylleth. If you fail in your duty, if you let your personal feelings interfere with true Justice, then it is up to me to judge you. As your superior, it is my role to evaluate your performance and give accolade or punishment as in accordance with the Rules of Justice."

"I understand." The words proved harder to say than I thought.

"Good." My new boss stood and said, "What do you need?"

After a few moments thought, I told him.

THE HIDDEN ACADEMY HAD GIVEN EACH KINGDOM a way to contact the school called a Far Scryer and Lord Orliss allowed me access to the one in the palace.

In a small stone antechamber located near the throne room, the Far Scryer stood on a small oak table next to the wall with one chair placed next to it. An inch-thick hoop of red stone a foot in diameter, the scryer balanced on edge and never moved, in fact was incapable of being moved since it was placed there four centuries ago. It would take an Arch Mage to intone the counterspell in person for the scryer to be moved should the queen desire it to relocated to, say, her bedroom and, since the Hidden Academy was a city state unto itself, that wasn't going to happen anytime soon.

I sat on the uncomfortable wooden chair, placed both hands on either side of the scryer and said a word in Dendrich.

After a few minutes a swirling gray mist formed within the hoop and a loud, sonorous voice uttered, "Who calls the Hidden Academy?"

I knew that voice. "Mage Nosso, is that you?"

The mist swirled and sworled, forming a cherubic face I recognized. "Niendra Goisien? Oi! As I live and breathe . . . you look terrible."

Mage Nosso Mar-Efrin taught runes at the Hidden Academy and was one of my favorites. Small and puckish, he had a mind as sharp as a razor with a tongue to match. He also lacked any sense of tact. He was the kind of mage the arch-mages who ran the Academy kept from speaking to rulers lest he cause a diplomatic kerfuffle, which begged the question . . .

"What are you doing manning the scryer?" I asked.

"Oi! Lost a card game to Adept Perrelio. Ninesdamned inconvenient. She said she'd wipe the debt clean if I took her week of manning the scryer. So inconvenient."

"Adept Perrelio? Never heard of her." An adept was second only to an arch-mage in power, which meant this Perrelio was fearsome indeed.

"Ach!" spat the mage. "Sarky wench. Reminds me of a certain Irramerian sprat who drove me crazy with questions about runes and wards."

I smiled, remembering the long hours in the common room discussing runes with the irreverent mage. He was so sure that would be my calling. I almost hated disappointing him. Almost. "I already like her."

"Oi! She's strong, but your mind is sharper, that's the truth. We still talk about your geas. Having someone *choose* to surrender their free will to a geas, magic forbidden by this school because it steals free will. Nice little loophole that."

And a *good* loophole because mages in the Hidden Academy were all about the rules considering the vast forces they employed and taught. I'd gambled my future as a crafter to the Arch Mages' adherence to those rules. Geas were absolutely forbidden, being capable of enslaving others and they were only taught so a mage could counter them. The fact that my graduate spell required a willing subject meant that it could not steal what was freely given. I still remember like it was yesterday the arguments at my review hearing that could have led to my expulsion and magical neutering, as it were.

"Mage Nosso, I have a few questions I need to ask you. Important questions as a Justice of Gylleth."

"Oohh! All hoity toity now, are we? A Justice of Gylleth! I swoon with the importance of your title." His misty face assumed a faux-awestruck expression.

Mother Moon he must be bored. I ignored the sarcasm and asked my question.

Nosso soon forgot all about sark and listened intently.

TWENTY-FIVE

NOW

I SIT ON THE FLOOR IN THE ROOM ATOP THE WOODEN TOWER. It is plain, not a sick of furniture for decoration nor rug for comfort. Beside me sits Tennic, who seems at ease anywhere. Sitting across from me is Taalis, who is wearing a diadem of gold and silver, studded with small rubies. It is symbol of her status as Vel-ho. Between us lies the jeweled rod, glittering in the flickering light of an oil lamp, which is our only illumination.

"Tell me what you know of this rod," says Taalis.

That one is easy. "Nothing, save it is what I believe brought me back from Tilla's Hold."

She snorts in amusement. "It seems I will have to start at the beginning." Taking a deep breath, she continues, "A little over three-thousand years ago the wizard Malos began investigating the series of anomalies humans call shifts, a subject that he knew would take several lifetimes to complete, so he came up with a plan that would give him time to complete his research: immortality."

"There was a reason he's referred to as Malos the Mad," I say drily.

"Indeed. Everyone thought him mad, but in truth he was simply brilliant, more so than any other human wizard since. There is a fine line between genius and insanity. Malos actually *achieved* immortality thanks to the help of Vel-ho Ilmatten. We sylvans cannot die except by accident or violence and Malos came to the Vel-ho to see if he could mimic our longevity. Long story short, he couldn't, but Ilmatten postulated that what the sylvans couldn't do, the gods could."

"*One for Phezdes for he is kind,*" I murmur.

That earns me a smile. "Yes, you remember. Nine stones, nine high priests and priestesses performing a blessing upon each to impart a portion of divine power in the name of the gods they worshipped. One rod, part of a Forever Tree infused with the magic of possibly the greatest Vel-ho Dorendiriar has ever seen."

"Ilmatten."

Taalis pauses for a moment before saying, "Think of it, Niendra, Malos and Ilmatten convinced the high priest of every major religion in Estia to entreat their gods to bestow a measure divinity upon a flawless gem, then these to Arch Mages used them to create a device to bestow immortality. Even greater, to bestow life on the lifeless. It is the single greatest magical achievement in the history of the Six Kingdoms. This artifact, if properly harnessed, could rival a major Malosian Shift for changing the fundamental laws of the universe."

"Or harnessed for ill, could create mayhem not ever seen on this world." The words slip out before I can stop them.

My statement earns me a smile. "Good. I want you to understand the nature of what you are carrying and why it is needed to power a time spell of such a magnitude. Nothing else I know of could help me achieve what you desire."

We sit there for a few moments before the sylvan mage shakes her head. "Enough of that, back to my story . . . as long as the rod stayed with Malos, he could not die, so he passed from history, choosing to isolate himself in Dorindiriar and continue his research. To the Six Kingdoms, this was his infamous disappearance, although to Dorinderiar, he didn't disappear at all. Oh, he often left for Gylleth or one of the other six to seek human companionship, even taking a human wife, but the pull of his research, his obsession, always brought him back. Eventually he ventured to Nerrinnia to access their impressive trove of magical literature a few decades ago and that is when he truly disappeared, leaving Dorendiriar and Vel-ho Imatten behind."

She picked up the rod and pointed to the empty setting. "See this, the diamond that represented Tilla's blessing is gone, which is why I think you still have one foot in her Hold. If the rod was whole, you would have been brought back fully."

"It is a good thing it is missing," I say with a smile. "I would probably be dead several times over if I was not undead."

"Quite."

I steeple my fingers under my chin. "So the . . . geomancer, he was Malos?" The thought made my head spin. Malos was a wizard of near incalculable power, despite his reputation for insanity. Perhaps he was not insane, as Taalis stated, only thought so by those who could not comprehend his genius. Or perhaps to be a genius of that caliber is to invite madness.

"I believe so. I also believe he tired of living so long. Humans can't tolerate the centuries bearing down on them, outliving everything and everyone they love, so he created that lair, the wards and the water trap and placed the *kuolema-tomus* inside to hide it forever. Once separated, I believe he simply began to age swiftly until he died abed. How swiftly is unknown."

"What did you call it?"

"It's the sylvan name for the jeweled rod. Now, if you were to find the diamond, I think it would bring you back fully to life, but I don't know what would happen to you if you were separated from the *kuolema-tomus* for a length of time. Would you die swiftly, or would you decay slowly?"

Did I want to come back fully? I always expected that once I finished my quest for justice that I would simply will myself back to Tilla's Hold, or step into a bonfire let the flames take me there. The thought of breathing once again, of eating good food and drinking fine wine has great appeal, but do not know if I want to live in a world without Mirallelle. I have had my time, my life is over, is it right to take it back while others more deserving cannot? No simple answer comes to mind.

"But why would Malos hide himself like that? Why not simply give the rod to Ilmatten and walk away?"

"No one knows. Perhaps he was, in the end, mad as the stories made him out to be."

Another thought hits me. "Or perhaps he was hiding from someone he feared and he did not want to leave the rod with the Vel-ho in order to spare him harm from that person." I proceed to tell her about Nokrini and the wrath troll and Mother Moon's mask. Someone Malos feared would be a dire opponent, not one I care to encounter.

She strokes her chin. "Perhaps. It would certainly explain the level of paranoia."

A sideways glance at Tennic shows me he is bored out of his mind, but politely staying quiet about it. "Tell me more about Malos, please."

Taalis nodded. "For nearly three-thousand years he labored at his research until he determined, if not the true nature of the shifts, at least their reason for being,"

That grabs my attention. "You know!"

"As successor to Ilmatten, of course." She grins an un-sylvan grin and I resist the urge to slap her. Taalis eventually relents and says, "When the gods were young and in the first bloom of their power, before humans ever set foot upon Estia, a blight came to this world, a force of uncreation."

"The Demon Master!" blurted Tennic. Finally, he pays attention.

"Yes. There was a war between the gods and this powerful being *whom we will not name.*" Tallis looks reprovingly at the lad, who does not seem fazed at all. "The two forces, creation and uncreastion warred and tore the fabric of the universe part. Stars exploded and whole worlds were destroyed, millions upon millions of souls across the firmament were obliterated before the gods claimed final victory, but the price was a heavy one. All over creation there are patches of unreality, an uncounted number, like holes in a bedsheet and as our sun and our world moves through the vault of the heavens, they encounter these holes, these patches of unreality. These holes cause the very laws of the universe to bend, they cause reality to warp. These are the shifts. The Malosian Shifts, named for that powerful, lonely wizard. We encounter shifts, these patches, all the time, most are too small to make an impression, but the larger ones alter our reality. Five hundred years ago the last big shift augmented and warped magic, not for long, just long enough that the wizard Hengeth Isobold, for whatever reason, attempted a necromantic spell as the shift began, changing and augmenting the nature of the magic, rendering Ramashur a necropolis and turning its citizens into soulless monsters."

"And there is no way for me to save the city?" I knew the answer but I wanted her to say it out loud.

Taalis obliged. "You may travel in time if you have the power, but you can no more change the course of history than you fly by flapping your arms. All of time has already happened, you are just choosing the moments in which to experience."

"No matter what I do?"

"It has already been done. You have already failed."

"Did I achieve justice?"

"That I don't know. All I do know is that I have sent you into the past. Whether you succeed or not is yet to be seen, although it's already been written."

Tennic groans. "My head hurts."

"Time does that, my boy." The sylvan mage smiles. "The more you learn, the more it hurts."

My mind tries to grasp the fullness of what I have learned, from the possibility that the legendary Malos was in fact the geomancer, to the discovery of the true nature of the jeweled rod, kuolema-tomus. It turns out I succeeded (will succeed? Had succeeded? Tennic is right, it hurts) in my quest to travel to the past, a long shot base on sylvan time magic I observed at the Frost Quarry all those centuries ago. I half-expected to surrender kuolema-tomus, I half-expected to be destroyed out-of-hand for being undead. I did not expect success and the twisty, turny thoughts of the past and time travel have my head spinning, but I must keep my focus . . . there is a quest to finish.

"Send me," I say to Taalis. To Tennic, "You should go. I will miss you, lad."

"No!"

Taalis intervenes. "Easy, boy, you'll accompany her because it has already happened."

Tennic shoots me a look that I imagine the parent of every teenager is acquainted with. I roll my eyes and nod, knowing this argument is lost. Besides, he is my familiar and perhaps I will need him. I realize that spurning this gift from Father Sun and Mother Moon might not be the best idea in my career as a crafter.

"Now," says Taalis. "The kuolema-tomus will go with you because it must power the spell for your journey, but I need your promise that you will return it to me when your quest is done."

Of course she wants the rod. "How?"

She gives me a wry look. "You are a revenant, Niendra, you can easily wait five hundred years and return it to me on this date. I fully expect to see you at the border after I leave this room. Now give me your word as a crafter and swear upon Father Sun and Mother Moon you will do this."

I seem to have little choice and I do as she asks.

"Thank you. You have the Mother Moon's mask. Put it on, you'll need it."

I stare. "How did you know what it does?"

The sylvan sighs. "Still not getting the fact that I'm Vel-ho, are you?"

Feeling exceptionally stupid, I remove the mask from my pack and carefully place it on my face. It feels cool at first, then starts to warm. There is a strange sort of pressure on my skull and I *feel* a tingle centering on my forehead which slowly spreads throughout my body, which fades once it hits my fingertips and toes.

"Whoa," breathes Tennic in wonder. "That is . . . great!"

"What?"

The sylvan hands me a small hand mirror.

Staring back it me is a young woman with a pale complexion, chestnut curls to the shoulder and freckles across a pert nose under hazel eyes. My mouth opens and the girl in the glass does the same, also touching her face as I touch mine. Cool, smooth metal meets my fingertips, but in the mirror I see only flesh. "What is this?"

"Mother Moon in her aspect as the Goddess of Secrets," says Taalis, "protects your identity, keeping it a secret from the outside world. You are still wearing the mask, but to the outside world you look like a young woman of Estian descent, perhaps Biavian or Nerrinnian. When you want the illusion to end, simply remove the mask."

It is strange. I do not feel like I am wearing a mask, my mouth moves without hindrance and there is no stuffy feeling. However, the smooth touch of metal is still there if I place my hand to my face. I stare at my reflection for a few moments more, the woman there quite pretty in a non-Irramerian sort of way, and nod slowly. I guess it is time.

"Send me back, then, please."

Taalis' grin is pure mischief. "Look around."

I oblige and am startled to see that we no longer sit inside a small tower room, that it has faded away to be replaced by . . . nothing. There is simply a pool of lamplight we sit in with no floor (although I can feel one under me), no walls or ceiling. Blue-ish streaks mark the darkness, faint pastel streamers that swirl gently all around in the middle distance beyond the lamp light. Beside me Tennic yelps in surprise.

"What is this?" I turn to Taalis and she is not there. "What *is* this?" I repeat. On the floor at my feet is the kuolema-tomus, each jewel now a blazing star.

"Don't be afraid, Niendra." The sylvan's voice comes from all around. "You're in the passageway to the past powered by the rod. You need do nothing but wait. I will warn you, however, the trip might become a little . . . odd."

Odd? I look to Tennic and see that is features are blurring and by the circle of his mouth and his exclamation of surprise, I must look the same. Holding up my hands, I see my fingers begin to elongate, stretching to impossible lengths, my arms becoming rubbery as if the bones have disappeared.

"This is strange." Tennic's voice is oddly calm and with a flicker of concentration I feel what he does, which is a sense of wonder and excitement. Not a trace of fear or worry, he is absolutely sure of our safety and, if Taalis is to be believed, we have already been to the past, that our arrival is certain, so this trip must be safe.

Unknotting the complexities of time travel would give me a headache if I still suffered them.

The blue streaks swirl faster now, revolving in the void at impossible speeds and we watch the display in fascination as our bodies contort to strange formations, although we feel no different. As Tennic's neck elongates and knots and my legs become rubbery stilts, the blue streaks begin to merge, eclipsing the dark of the void until all that remains is the pastel blue which becomes the whole world, The lamp is gone, we are gone, only the blue remains and I hear my companion laugh and laugh and I, too, feel laughter begin to bubble up and I take a breath to let it burst forth as we are both consumed with absurdity of our situation.

Soon even the laughter fades and all is gone. We are gone.

ALTHOUGH I HAVE NO NEED OF SLEEP, APPARENTLY I AM SUBJECT to some sort of magically induced unconsciousness because the next thing I know is that my eyes open to more blue, but instead of the glowing pastel blue of the time passage, this blue contains clouds.

I sit up. Tennic is lying next to me on verdant grass as sweet birdsong flutters in the air and a slight breeze brushes the leaves of a hemlock a few feet away. The kuolema-tomus is gripped tightly in my hand and my transition from unconsciousness to awake is seamless, one second I am not, the next I am, aware and awake as if I am a clock to be wound into motion.

"Tennic, wake." I push the lad's shoulder and his brilliant green eyes open wide. He bounds to his feet with the vigor of youth, but he is a living person, so he reels a second later from rising too quickly.

"Whoa," he says. "Dizzy."

I stand and grab his shoulder. "Steady, lad."

When he gets his bearings, he slowly turns around. "Where are we?"

That is a good question. My eyes wander over the land. We stand on gently rolling hills of green that have been terraced, leafy vines growing thickly upon the slopes, a copse of trees at our back. Far to the east is the ocean, a gray smear on the horizon, while to the west is another smear, but this one of the far distant Frostbacks and to the north, well . . . the north is easy.

"That is Caenwylln," I say, pointing. The city is not a smear, but a hive of activity only a couple of miles away. We are among the vineyards and farms that supply the food and drink for the metropolis. "By the Nine . . . she did it."

PART TWO

Justice and Thief

TWENTY-SIX

JUSTICE

T HE LONG ROAD FLEES UNDER OUR HOOVES AS WE RODE, Skakhir on a
stout courser, me on a coal-black Biavian destrier with near unending
endurance. Behind us rode four solid soldiers in chain and plate, veteran
fighters whose job was to ensure my safety in case any Deep Water mercenaries tried to be feisty. I didn't know their names, nor did I care to learn
. . . my only concern was with their ability to do what I say and how well
they performed. Everything else was minutiae.

One pigeon sent from Ramashur to Xeristo when I began the ride on
the Long Road and one from Hodengarth-by-the-Ridge to tell him we
were drawing near and to be ready. I carried with me a writ from the queen
allowing me what resources I deemed necessary to accomplish the task
at hand, essentially giving me the key to the Royal Treasury, as it were.
Although I could bring a battalion hard-bitten, stone-cold killers to the
endeavor, my hope that a speedy and energetic mission would carry the
day instead of sheer numbers.

For Skakhir and I, the ride was a quiet one. We kept our lips shut and
our minds to task, both of us bearing the scars of loss and pain that left
skin unmarred. Only our souls bore these marks and would for the rest of
our lives. We were companions in misery, which made us family of a sort
and that was fine by me if the mission was accomplished.

When Caenwylln came within sight I felt an incredible tightness in my chest, as if my ribs were encircled with iron bands drawing ever tighter. It was anticipation, anticipation and anger and all the feelings that bear no name but plagued me so since the death of my wife.

Call it justice. Call revenge. All I wanted was to call it *done* because I knew in my heart that now my sense of justice was forever altered by the death of my wife and that I really didn't want to carry on in her absence. My heart no longer felt up to the job.

Somehow I didn't think Queen Bet would let me off that easy, though.

Farmers and vintners watched us pass, some waving some not, while travelers on the road moved aside to let us by. One young man and woman stared at me as if I was a sight new under the sun. Not many people could say they had seen an Irramerian woman at the head of a rough-and-tumble group of warriors moving at speed down the Long Road.

Before we reached the city a small contingent of six horsemen rode out to meet us, Xeriosto at its head, Thumper slung from a loop on his saddle. The big Justice pulled back on the reins as we rode up.

"Been looking for you," he said solemnly. He was dressed head to toe in heavily battered but mostly serviceable field plate. A good third of the armor on the limbs had been replaced with chain, but Xeristo still looked like a man-mountain atop a sorrel that overtopped my destrier by at least a hand. "You have my condolences, Niendra."

"I think you for that, Xeristo." The white-hot anger that fueled my ride had faded to a cold hard knot in my gut. The pain still lingered, but the cold surpassed it. "You ready?"

"Of course. Are we doing this now?"

"Yes. Did you take Coventio into custody?"

He nodded. "The man broke down and began to sob." Xeristo spat off to the side. "I hate it when they cry. Let's do this, assuming you're prepared."

My jaw clenched. "I've had enough time and I'm prepared for whatever they have in store." I handed the Justice a large pouch of steel vials. "Take this. Have you and your men drink them when we come within sight of the estate." Skakhir and our soldiers had similar vials and similar orders.

Xeristo Quell snorted as he took it. "I almost feel sorry for them."

"Don't."

He shrugged. "I said almost."

The Fel Rosso estate wasn't that far away and I felt speed was necessary so they couldn't prepare for our arrival, but some little birdie must
have sung a song because the manor gates were locked tighter than a
miser's purse. As we drew closer a crossbow bolt thudded to the earth a
few feet away. Considering there weren't more guardsmen or a troop of
mercenaries at their beck and call, they couldn't have received much of
a heads up. We reined in our horses as a voice shouted, "Go back. You're
not welcome here!"

Dojirio Fel Rosso. I could see the man in one of the gate towers. He
held a wicked looking arbalest leveled at us, most probably straight at my
heart.

"This is a delaying action," I said to Xeristo. "Have four men ride around
the wall, someone's trying to scarper off."

Xeristo nodded. "Havers, Rook, No-thumbs and Draug, you heard her."

I made a mental note to inquire about the No-thumbs nickname and
watched as the horsemen split into groups of two and barrel off to the left
and right around the estate.

"That is a great, big, heaping pile of ugly," said the large Justice, spitting
off to the side.

"Yer got that right," said Skakhir, the first words he said the entire trip.
I looked back to see bloody murder in his red-rimmed eyes.

Putting my best no-nonsense face on, I turned back to the gate. "Open
up, Dojirio. We're on the queen's business. You know that."

"I don't care if you have warrant or if the queen herself on the way her
in a little pink wagon drawn by fairies," he shouted back with some heat.
"You're not coming in."

Twenty-foot walls, at least seven heavily armored and armed guards
with crossbows and who knows what on the inside. Easy. "Tell you what,
Dojirio," I hollered, drawing my long knives as I slid out of the saddle.
"You think you can take on a Justice? Man-to-man, so to speak?"

"What's in it for me?" The crossbow was no longer pointed at my heart.
I felt a stab of hope.

"If you win, you get a day's reprieve. If you lose your men open the
gates and surrender. And you can use whatever melee weapon you wish." I
performed a series of stretches and mock lunges with my knives, loosening
up, making sure that he saw that I was no slouch when it came to blades.

From the smile on Dojirio's face I knew he would go for it. "Agreed."

"Your oath. And your men's oaths as well." Not that I trusted him farther than I could toss a cragg troll.

"Done!" After all the guardsmen swore to Dhiione in his aspect of God of Honorable Combat, the gate ponderously opened wide enough to allow Dojirio to walk out with broadsword already drawn. Another guard, his second, accompanied him. This one had a serviceable hand axe in a loop on his belt.

"Xeristo, come with me."

We walked until we were twenty feet from the pair.

"Your second?" asked Dojirio. Like Xeristo, he wore field plate, although in much better repair, not a dent or scratch in sight.

I shrugged.

"Now I want your oath."

Easy enough. "I swear by Mother Moon and Father Sun, my patron gods, that if you win we will leave and not come back this day."

He nodded and swung his sword around in impressive arcs. "Come get some, woman!" he taunted.

"Xeristo?"

"Yeah, Niendra?"

"Go git him."

As if shot from a catapult, Xeristo sprang forward, so fast for such a big man, Thumper coming up with blurring speed. Dojirio took a step back raising his weapon, but he might as well have tried to parry a flood. The two-handed mace took Dojirio at the elbow and there came a sickening crack as the arm suddenly bent the wrong way. The guardsman had a moment for a scream before the mace swung back down and smashed his head down into his chest cavity. He didn't fall as much as was near driven like a tent peg into the ground. Dojirio's second swung his hand axe, but he was hopelessly outclassed and in a second joined his boss on the ground, muddying up the dirt with his blood and brains.

"I didn't say the Justice you'd fight was me." There was no pity in my voice.

Arbalests *twanged* and bolts rained down only to be deflected by my potion. Knowing they'd never voluntarily open the gate, I pulled out a scroll and said a few words in Dendrich and slapped the parchment against the wood. It stuck there as if glued. We calmly walked back to my horse as the guardsmen got busy to cranking their arbalests.

"What's going to happen, Niendra?" asked Xeristo as he cleaned Thumper with a rag.

"Wait for it."

"Hope it's good."

The gate detonated, exploding in a fireball that rose thirty feet into the air, consuming both gate towers in a conflagration that killed all within in an instant. A hot wind accompanied by a near deafening thunderclap smacked our faces and spooked most of the horses except my destrier who stood calmly as if fireballs happened every day. Most of the blast force was directed up and back toward the house, leaving us riders untouched although it took a few moments to calm the mounts who wanted to bolt.

"By the Nine, Niendra," shouted Xeristo through the ringing in my ears. "That was worth it."

"Wizard are good for casting quick spells," I shouted back. "But crafters, if we have time to prepare, are darn near unbeatable. Let's just hope they don't throw too much at us or I'll run out of potions and such."

He stared at the conflagration that used to be the main gate. "What about that?"

I shrugged and pulled out vial, this one of green glass, and walked toward the fire until the heat became almost unbearable then threw it at the ground where the gate used to be. When the glass shattered, blue/gray smoke erupted and billowed out and up, growing and growing until it eclipsed both towers and, for a moment, I could see the bright orange flames glow through the smoke. Only for a moment. I said another word in Dendrich and the smoke suddenly disappeared, taking the fire with it. All that was left were charred timbers, shattered stone, and puddles of melted iron, all covered in a thick rime of frost. My breath steamed in the chilled air.

"Like I told you, Xeristo, I came prepared."

Beyond the gate was the ruined garden with the broken remains of the statues of the Nine. They had taken the brunt of the explosion that destroyed the gate and even the front doors were blown off their hinges. Anything that resembled a flower or other plant were now only ash and dust floating lazily in the late summer sun. I stopped the group before we could fully enter the grounds along with wisp of acrid smoke.

"Hold a second." I pulled out another piece of paper and read the words written there aloud, more Dendrich, then scanned the area through my Father Sun tattoos. "All clear."

They were all there in the dining room, the Fel Rosso family from Kaarick (who looked far spryer than when last I saw him) to his daughter Korinnia, a somewhat chubby young woman with strawberry hair and a petulant face. Winnith Fel Rosso seemed less attractive somehow, almost mousy and I felt none of the instantaneous lust I had before, which cemented a conclusion I'd reached a few days ago.

There was no sign of the servants. I hoped they took what they could and fled.

Kaarick was dressed for travel in serviceable trousers, a mail shirt with a mace at his belt and the other family members carried luggage, including what I could only assume was a small sack of Royal Rounds.

"Going somewhere?"

That earned me a sneer from the head of the family. "Think you're pretty smart, do ya?" he grated. His hand strayed to his mace, but one look from Xeristo quelled any violent thoughts. He was far too calm considering the situation.

"I do all right when my mind's put to good use."

More sneers. He didn't bother to bluster or bribe, he went straight to the word I knew he'd use. A word in Dendrich.

The small statues of the gods that I noted on my previous visit, those within earshot, turned their heads to the Fel Rosso patriarch. "Kill them," ordered Kaarik.

No, I couldn't have that. With a smile that was certainly not very nice, I countered with another word, one given to me by master Nosso. Instead of leaping off their short pedestals to attack, they slowly began to crumble into a piles of whitish dust flecked with red. In a matter of moments all that remained were the pedestals and the mounds of fine debris.

Kaarik's eyes grew round and his skin white as the last one, a statue of Aris in her aspect of the Goddess of Voyages, became a silty pile at his feet. "How? How?" he gabbled.

"It was Dojirio who gave me the final piece of the puzzle," I said. "He

bragged about the wizard Tolivio Vel-Odre, the runemaster who created the wards that protected your property." I took a step inside the dining room and the family retreated, shuffling and trembling in fear. "You
shouldn't have tried to kill me, Fel Rosso, the attempt gave me the last
clues I needed to figure things out." A gesture toward the statues' remains.
"And I have connections at the Hidden Academy. I learned that in addi-
tion to runes, Tolvio is pretty good at animation spells, like the ones he
cast upon your little works of art here and in the garden. Once the mages
at the Hidden Academy learned you tried to take the life of an agent of the
Crown, they were more than happy to supply me with the countercharms
to your wards and the deactivation words for your statutes."

My eyes tracked to Winnith. "Let me guess, a glamour perfume, right?
Must've bought it from a crafter in Caenwylln." That was why I practically
panted when she came close. I felt kind of sheepish I didn't figure it out
while I was here last, but that what happens when one thinks with their
loins instead of their brains. Must be how men operate most of the time.

Winnith's mouth compressed into a thin line, confirming my suspicion.

I turned to her husband, my heart an icy lump of iron in my chest.
"Kaarick Fel Rosso, you are accused of the murder by proxy of Soro Divver,
the attempted murder of a Queen's Justice, the murders of Haddeg Whitgut
and Mirallelle of Chozi'Vielle. I also charge you with placing a bounty on
the head of a Justice. Do you have anything to say in your defense? Do you
deny your guilt?"

For a minute Kaarik Fel Rosso stared at me with smoldering hate in his
eyes, his hands trembling not in fear, but a fury so intense I half-thought he
might burst into flames. "Even if I proclaimed my innocence, you wouldn't
believe me," he finally ground out through clenched teeth. "So yes, I admit
it. Now what."

I sighed.

"I'll do it, Niendra," whispered Xeristo, hefting Thumper.

"No," I replied, the word slicing the air like a razor. "My case, my jus-
tice." To the man who caused so much misery I intoned, "Kaarik Fel Rosso,
I find you guilty of the charges presented and fine your family ten Royal
Rounds to be distributed to the family members of those you had killed.
Additionally, I will allow one hour for you to settle your estate before you
are put to death. You may commit suicide if you prefer."

With every word their faces grew whiter and whiter until Korinnia fainted dead away into her mother's arms. Winnith glared daggers at me, full of rage. Not for the sentence of death, but for the Royal Rounds, which was an enormous sum of money and most likely the bulk of their liquid assets in the pouch at Kaarik's side. As for her husband, he simply nodded and suddenly a knife was airborne, flying straight for my heart.

It hit my deflection spell and *thunked* into a wall ruining some nice oak wainscoting. "I had to try," he said with a shrug and a sneer.

I nodded. "I understand." Reaching into my own pouch I pulled out a small ball of twine, duck feathers sticking out here and there. I hefted it for a moment before tossing it gently to Fel Rosso, who caught it deftly. "What?" he said, puzzled.

"Wait for it."

He died with that same puzzled look on his face, falling face first on the table and bouncing off to thud on the floor. Winnith screamed, dropping her daughter.

"There it is."

Xeristo stroked his beard. "I thought you would've stabbed him or something."

"I didn't want to go near him." I nodded at the corpse. "Coadian Death Fetish, only kills you if you willingly touch it. He willingly touched it, all right."

"By my clenched butt cheeks, that was anticlimactic." Skakhir heaved a long sigh that fluttered his mustaches. "There's satisfaction, but not much I can tell yer that."

Moving across the room and around the table, I gave the dead man a wide berth, the ball of twine Kaarik's hand now mundane, the magic drained having been used. I came nose to nose with Winnith Fel Rosso. She recoiled. "Don't you dare run or try to faint on me," I snarled, feeling a vein throb at my temple. "I'm going to tell you what I think and you're going to verify if I have the facts straight, understand."

She glared hateful death at me, but nodded,

"Good. Here's how I figure it: Your pig husband wanted to buy the note on the Divver loan held by the Rol-Venber bank and had the crowns to do so because he's been far more successful at increasing his fortunes than most realize. The only way he reckoned he could do it, however, was to kill Soro Divver because Soro wasn't selling and Coventio didn't want his father's business, he had his own to take care of and would be willing to let it go considering that paying the note would bankrupt him considering his already large debt. Kaarik would get the business for one-third the price. He sends one of the statues to the Frost Quarry where it throws Divver off the stairs and then it jumps after, crumbling and rendering itself into such small pieces as to leave very little evidence. Only problem was that the queen didn't buy it and assigned the case to the only mage Justice in the kingdom, one with the best chance to piece things together. Kaarik sends a pigeon to his factor who puts a bounty on my head. Fortunately for Kaarik, the mercs were already in Gylleth and amenable to cashing in on the contract, but they failed and he knew I would come to see him, so he concocted the phony illness and you put on a glamour perfume to turn my head and muddle my mind. This might have worked except he rightly figured that I would unravel the plot because I'm a mage and damn good at my job, so he activated another statue and sent it to kill me." Here I lost my voice for a moment and Sakakhir growled. I didn't bother to ask how the statue tracked me down or how wound up in Ramashur without being detected, but I guessed it wouldn't have been too hard for a rich, intelligent man like Kaarik Fel Rosso to sort out those details and I didn't care, I had my man and justice was served. "How did I do?"

Winnith Fel Rosso finally found some backbone. I had no evidence on her and glamour perfumes were not illegal. "May the Nine damn you," she hissed.

"They already have."

TWENTY-SEVEN

THE THIEF

W E WALK ON THE LONG ROAD WITH OTHERS going to the city to sell goods and such and the sun is out and it's warm, so I'm enjoying myself pretty well because why not? I'm five hundred years in the past and there's no Man Behind to tell me what to do and I'm having an adventure just like in stories! Turns out having an adventure is a splendid thing.

Splendid. Good word, learned it all by myself.

Next to me Niendra is now a pretty young girl with kinda brown red hair and a bunch of freckles thanks to that odd Mother Moon mask, but she still smells the same, lavender almost covering the faint scent of rot. I don't mind, I've smelled worse. Spend some time in the slums of Orthengar and one gets a nose what's used to anything.

Before too long a band of riders comes thundering past and guess who's riding out front as pretty as you please? Yep, Niendra. Then-Niendra, not now-Niendra who stares at herself in wonder. Then-Niendra looks really pissed about something so I think this is when she is going to get that Fel Rosso guy. A really young Skakhir rides behind her, no wrinkles or anything even though his hair is summer-cloud white, and he's got Dodmatir on his belt. I think about that same war hammer which is now in hidden in my pack and my head starts hurting again what with all the time travel business. Two Dodmatirs here, how strange. They thunder off into the distance to meet with some other riders headed by a real big guy in beat up armor like they wore in the old days and it takes me a second to realize I *am* in the old days and they ride off the road to that Fel Rosso place, I guess. At least, that's what now-Niendra told me earlier. We continue on to the city with now-Niendra teaching me this old way of talking that the people here have. There are a buncha new words I've never heard and that's good because words are a kind of magic in themselves. It's power and a street rat like myself needs to gather as much power as possible to rise out of the gutter, although I'm not a street rat anymore thanks to now-Niendra.

Some of the expressions I learn are different and now-Niendra has to explain them to me so I don't make a fool outta myself. Most I can figure out if I listen to the context.

Context. Good word, that. Now-Niendra taught me that one.

A good thief knows how to blend in so as not to attract attention when it's not wanted and I'm so good I'm practically *invisible*, so learning all these things is easy. Still raw about now-Niendra catching me pick her pocket that one time, though, but I guess it was the familiar thing what linked us together so what it came down to is she cheated.

Streets in the past are dirtier than in my time. The future, or whatever. Smells worse, too. I guess they dump more chamber pots in the alleys here 'cause they don't have no sewers or such. It got so bad that it almost put me off food, which shows that being practically gentrified by now-Niendra done spoilt me for the streets, which gave me a pang of shame because there's nothing wrong with the streets except for the cold.

But now I'm clean and dressed real nice thanks to now-Niendra and I'm her familiar, too, which is kinda weird, but also neat, so I'm not complaining. I get to eat when I'm hungry and drink good watered wine or ale and don't have to sleep with a dozen other kids all over each other like puppies in a smelly warehouse in Orthengar, so I say my situation is pretty much improved in spite of being in the past and all, which still makes my head hurt when I think about it.

Since Taalis told us that the past is the past and one can't do anything about it now matter what, I wonder if it is true now that I'm here. I mean, what if I find Blood and Vicious's ancestors and do them wrong, won't that make them go poof in the future? I guess not because I'm not the kinda guy what goes around murdering people I don't know, which is why I think the sylvan sent me back in the first place. My head hurts even more now.

People are dressed funny, a lot of them in hose instead of trousers and tunics instead of shirts, but other than that they pretty much look the same and smell the same. I guess people are people whatever the century.

My tummy grumbles loud enough for now-Niendra to hear and we stop at a street vendor for a meat pie and I order two and they are really *good* and gravy dribbles down my chin as I gobble them down even though they're hot as blazes. Sure beats stewed rat any day of the week. Now-Niendra stares like she's never seen a kid eat before.

She takes a breath like it's new to her and says, "Feel better?"

I give her a thumbs up and order another pie. The lady at the stall smiles at me and hands over another and its even hotter. I eat that one quick, too. Always appreciate the food because it might not be there tomorrow. First lesson I learned as a street rat. Second is don't get caught.

Now-Niendra leads me to the docks and we stare at the great big ships being unloaded, cargo from places what I've never been to like Irrameria and Coad and such and since Niendra is Irramerian I ask her if she's ever been as a soft breeze that smells like salt blows in our faces.

"No," she replies with a smile. "I was born in Gylleth. My parents emigrated from Irrameria, the city-state of Tolagio."

"Do you know about Irrameria?"

"You have questions?"

"About a thousand."

She laughs. "Give me one."

Only one? But there are so many. Not fair! I think a bit and say, "I heard that the Six Kingdoms are at peace because of Irrameria. How come?"

"I guess you are lacking in education, something not afforded by life as a thief," she muses. "Irrameria is separated from Estia by the Mandervy Strait, a stretch of ocean about two days ride across and Irrameria, while a large continent, is not ruled by one single government like a kingdom but of a collection of fractious city states."

"Say what now?"

"Each major city is a kingdom in and of itself."

"Sounds confusing."

"I have not even begun to confuse you, lad, safe to say that these city states war among themselves as much as with outside governments, but when they come together to face an external threat, the result is terrifying.

Irramerian heavy infantry is the best fighting force in the world, the greatest warriors you will ever see if you have that misfortune."

"Then why hasn't Irrameria conquered Estia?"

"Good question and the answer is absurdly simple: sea travel."

"All right, now you're just messing with me."

Now-Niendra laughs. I like it when she laughs, it makes her sound more . . . alive. "Irramerians believe that Aris, (who they call Coro'lovvis) Goddess of the Sea, is their mortal enemy and is actively trying to kill them and they are mortally afraid of her. So much so that there have been open rebellions by armies who were ordered to board Coadian transports."

"Coadian transports?" I ask.

"There are no Irramerian ship or sailors. All sea trade is handled by outside entities like the island nation of Coad."

"Don't take this the wrong way, Niendra," I say, staring out at the ocean. In this light it is gray and foreboding, like it wants to eat a Tennic-sized person. "But your people are weird."

"You think the people of the Six Kingdoms are not?"

I consider that, remembering everyone what I've encountered since meeting now-Niendra and leaving Orthengar. "Good point."

"Remember, lad, the Six Kingdoms remain stable because of outside threats such as Irrameria and the Coadian pirates. Fear goes a long way to help maintain stability."

"That and the shifts."

For a moment now-Niendra doesn't say anything. "The shifts are a bane to all civilizations. Every few hundred years the fabric of our world changes for a time and we descend into chaos. Five thousand years ago legend has it the Frostbacks were created by a shift. One moment there stood a great forest, part of the sylvan nation, the next, mountains stretching from the Mandervy Strait all the way to Gaor. No one knows exactly what happens, save perhaps the sylvans, but the Six Kingdoms suffered such a decline due to the other effects of the shift that they barely clawed their way back. All we know of that legendary time are the remnants, such as the Long Road."

She talks a lot when she's on a roll, maybe because she thinks I need a better education, but I have my letters and I can do sums, plus I can pick a lock quicker than winking, so I don't think I need that much educating.

I'm still alive and a lot of the other street rats aren't, so I'm ahead of the game by a good length. Plus, I know a lot of good words I learned all by myself, so that's neat, too.

I even know about the balance of powers and such because being part of the Man Behind's gang was all about that. Every lieutenant had a gaggle of kids under their wing and each one had a section of the city and the Man Behind made sure that one wasn't stronger than the other. He also made Ninesdamned sure the lieutenants hated each other for some reason or another so they wouldn't gang up and try to rebel or something. All the kids knew this, we had more brains than our bosses for sure because they never seemed to twig onto what the Man Behind was doing, but we sure saw it and kept our mouths shut. I guess the Man Behind (or Blood and Vicious because it was them that what were the real bosses) were just politicians after all. They just dealt in crime. Maybe exactly like politicians, I guess.

"Hey, I have one last question," I say. "But it doesn't have to do with geography or governments and such."

"This should be interesting." She gives me the old raised eyebrow treatment.

"Funny. Wait, what's the opposite of funny?" Before she could open her mouth I barrel ahead. "Let's say you get your justice and do what needs doing and all that . . . what then? How do we get back to our time, or do I have to live here in the past?"

"Do not worry, I have a plan."

"You're not going to tell me, are you?"

Now-Niendra reaches out and gives me a hug, which I don't mind even if she smells a little dead under that lavender perfume. "You are learning. Let us get through the next few days, shall we?"

I nod. "What now?"

"In a couple of hours we have to be at the Anchor and Pipe tavern near here. I need you to pick a pocket. Or try to, anyway."

At last! Something I'm good at. I can hardly wait.

THE SUN IS HITTING THE FROSTBACKS AS I LOUNGE with Niendra near the Anchor and Pipe, a nice looking place, even though the whitewash is fading fast in the salt air. This part of the dockside doesn't look as mean as the south end, which kind of scared me when we walked through a little while ago, with hard looking, mean-eyed men and women staring at us like we're meat pies ready for the table. I stuck close to now-Niendra the whole way and kept my hand on the wooden headknocker I keep on my belt because having a big old silver war hammer visible is likely to draw a few eyes. Street rats learn how to hide their valuables.

No one tried anything, which is good because now-Niendra probably would've turned them into frogs or something and we don't need that kind of attention, although that would've been neat.

Just as the sun is halfway behind the Frostbacks and the shadows are starting to grow dark and long, we enter the tavern and have a sit near the wall near a couple of sailor types who are drinking hard and fast.

A serving woman who must've been pretty about twenty years ago comes over and I can't but help but stare at her bosom. I mean, it's practically hanging out all over the place! Now-Niendra takes the opportunity of clapping her hand over my eyes and ordering two jacks of ale.

"I can't drink before a job!" I whisper fiercely as the serving woman leaves after giving me a grin that shows everyone she used to have a lot more teeth.

"Pretend," is all the answer I get.

"Can I have some food, though?"

That earns me a look what people call incredulous. I like that word, learned it all by myself.

"Hey, what can I say, I'm hungry."

When the jacks arrive, Niendra orders food.

"We have fish stew or lamb stew," says the lady with way too much chest.

"Lamb," I pipe up, excited by the prospect. I love lamb. "Two bowls if you please, madam."

This earns me another grin and I manage not to shudder. I should've kept my eyes on her bosom. A little while later while I pretend drink, the bowls are set down and I begin to eat.

After the first one, I feel now-Niendra stir beside me, tightening up. Strange how this familiar thing works, I can feel her like an itch at the back of my brain, just like she says she can feel me and I'm still not entirely sure I like that thought.

I look at what's got her all tense and see her walk into the tavern with Skakhir and the big guy I saw earlier, except this is then-Niendra, the Niendra as she ought to look, not like the cutie pie with the Mother Moon mask sitting next to me, what gives me the willies. I stare hard enough that Skakhir somehow feels it and looks my way and instead of frowning thunder at me like an adult usually would he smiles and nods. I liked old Skakhir a lot and I think I'll like young Skakhir, too.

Then-Niendra looks like she should, but there is a lot of sadness around her eyes and I know this is the time after her wife died and she killed that Fell Rosso guy (who totally deserved it) and is getting ready to head back south to Ramashur.

Now-Niendra places a hand on my forearm, interrupting my meal. The lamb stew is really good and spicy and hot; this place makes good food and I don't want to stop eating yet. "You remember what to do?" she asks.

Rolling my eyes, I say, "Yes, mom." Really, how stupid does she think I am? We only went over the plan for about a million times.

"Repeat it to me, then."

It's almost like having a big sister, except I never had a big sister, but it feels like this should qualify. I take a bite of lamb and say to now-Niendra, "The then-Niendra has a secret pocket on the outside of her left thigh where she keeps the Rod of Immortality."

"The *kuolema-tomus*."

"Really, you want me to call it that? Sounds stupid and it's hard to pronounce. I'll stick to Estian words, thank you. Anyway, when she's not paying attention, you want me to pick that pocket and we scarper off fast. Only problem I can see is she might check that pocket or feel that it's gone."

"I can assure you she has forgotten all about it."

"Why?"

Now-Niendra looks troubled. "I may have an idea on that, but thrust me when I say this past me has forgotten the k . . . . rod exists. If we can get it now we can avoid all sorts of issues."

"But why would you-she-forget. Kind of an important thing to forget, you know."

It takes a while, but now-Niendra finally says, "My idea is that I think the rod clouds the mind, forces the wielder to forget its existence. A by-product of its creation, perhaps. Magic is a tricky thing, after all and this is the only explanation I can think of as to why I did not inform the queen of an artifact of such importance."

"I'm surprised Malos didn't forget about it, then."

"He had a hand in its creation, perhaps that allowed him a measure of immunity." She pauses, going so still she's like a temple statue. I wish she wouldn't do that, it's *creepy*. "Or perhaps it is because he was an Arch-Mage and his natural power fended off the mind-altering capabilities of the rod. I do not know."

Shrugging, I finish my stew as the big guy, Skakhir and then-Niendra start to drink ale from leather jacks. I'm not a big fan of leather jacks because the insides are coated in pitch or tar and it makes the ale taste like it was brewed in smallclothes, so I guess being in the past has its drawbacks.

Then-Niendra is starting to explain something to the big guy, the Justice Xeristo Quell, with lots of hand waving and stuff. She definitely looks more *alive* than now-Niendra because she blinks and breathes normal and she has this habit of smoothing her braids from her forehead, and I stand to casually make my way toward the trio.

I'm a good thief, a Ninesdamned good thief, one of the best in Orthengar and I've never been caught by the watch or a Justice (Antonius doesn't count because it was now-Niendra what caught me first and he wasn't a *real* Justice, anyway), so I'm pretty sure I can do this because she's in animated conversation with the big guy.

Only a few feet away now and I'm all casual and, what's the word? *Nonchalant.* Yeah, Good word, learned that one all by myself. I'm all nonchalant and everything is going to go my way now.

A hand the size of a dinner plate lands on my shoulder. "Yer a fyne loookin' laddie, now. What are yer so interested in?"

It's Skakhir, about four feet wide and sturdy as a wall and he looks a little cross and a little sad and I realize that this is the time after his cousin, Haddeg, died. I completely forgot about him. Stupid Tennic! Forcing a smile on my face I turn to the dwarf and I see we are eye-to-eye, he's right *there*, and I put Tennic's Plan B into motion. Always have a Plan B because Plan A usually goes pear-shaped somewhere along the way. "Is that the Justice Niendra? The witch?"

Plan B is a winner. The dwarf blinks, grins and the sadness seems to melt from his face. He takes his paw off my shoulder. "Yer heard o' her, then?"

"Of course! She's *famous*!" I lay it on nice and thick.

"Well, laddie, yer gonna have ta loook elsewhere for a moment because she's a myte busy ryte noow," says the dwarf, laying his own dwarfy accent on heavy and I know the game is a bust. I'm not sure what to do. Leave? Try to bluff my way out.

Skakhir might be a little silly, but he's sharp, I can see it in his eyes. He thinks I'm harmless, but he's not going to let me close to then-Niendra and I can see the now-Niendra give me a slight shake of her head. No go, so it's time for Plan C. I always have a Plan C.

"All right." I keep the fake smile on my face, the one that shows all my dimples and makes me look as innocent as a priestess of Yrusis on a high holy day. Time to have a bit of fun, which I haven't had in *ages*. "I better get back to my sister there." I wave my hand to now-Niendra. "I'm fixing to find a good game of cards tonight, anyway."

A big old smile splits the dwarf's beard. "Why, laddie, why didn't yer say so?"

Twenty-Eight

JUSTICE

THE TAVERN WAS XERISTO'S IDEA, A PLACE WHERE we could have a few drinks and settle back and relax while I tell the tale. Skakhir was all in as well, declaring that he could use a jack of ale or three and that didn't sound so bad to me. Both of us were hurting from the loss of our loved ones, but we had each other for now and that would have to be enough.

Still, the cold lump in my chest hadn't gone away. Even the memory of Fel Rosso's sightless eyes couldn't melt the iron of my heart. Not yet.

As it turned out, the place wasn't half-bad, much nicer than I was used to and since Xeristo was buying, I ordered a bowl of lamb stew and an ale from an aging bar maid who showed off far too much cleavage. My companions leaned back and listened as I filled in the gaps.

"It was the white stone, you see," I began. "Red flecked. Turns out it was red-veined white marble. There were tiny bits near Divver's body at the quarry and I thought the red flecks were blood, so I dismissed it but blood turns black over time, a big oversight by me. I should've examined those leavings closer because they stood out as different than all the other rocks in the quarry. I wasn't paying enough attention, I guess."

Xeristo shrugged. "Most everyone would've failed to note that, Niendra. Not your fault. Even Shakhir here didn't notice and he's a dwarf."

Shakhir nodded. "And me and Haddeg were distracted by the cave opening, so yer have to forgive me a little for that."

Right now I'd forgive Shakhir if he stole Queen Bet's own jewels. There was enough blame to go around. We paused for a moment to drink and I took a bite of the lamb stew. Pretty good. I could see why Xeristo liked this place. Looking at his growing middle, he visited often. "Yeah, but the last clue was the big one. I should've seen it clear and I didn't."

Shakhir stood and wandered off. He knew this bit and I figured he was going to look for a sheep to fleece at cards. Xeristo motioned for me to continue.

"So, Dojirio Fel Rosso supplied me with the first half of the next clue, which was that Kaarik Fel Rosso had been struck ill and had been abed for quite some time, but when I saw Kaarik in his bed, his feet were sticking out and they were *calloused*." I paused to take a drink. "Calloused like he'd been in riding boots for quite some time, not the soft, pasty feet of a man who hadn't got out of bed for weeks, but that Ninesdamned perfume his wife wore had my head spinning back and forth so quickly my neck nearly broke. A glamour perfume, a simple crafter concoction although making them is frowned upon."

"Why is that?"

More lamb stew went into my gut before I answered. I'd been neglecting myself since Mirallelle died and it felt like my stomach was eyeing my liver for lunch. "Because it comes dangerously close to tampering with free will. We mages are strictly forbidden to subvert the natural choices the gods gave the people of Estia and are told in no uncertain terms what will happen to a mage who does. You should have seen the debate concerning that geas we Justices voluntarily take, that stirred a knobblegrott's warren, I'll tell you. Almost didn't graduate."

"Well, for me, Niendra, I'm sure glad you did." Xeristo stretched and gave me a lazy smile. "We did some good today and it's all because you're part of the Queen's Justices, believe that. Gylleth is better off now."

"Kind of you to say, you're probably right." I grinned, although it still was a sickly thing. "It's nice that most of my teachers like me and were willing to help with the counterspell for those animated statues. If we didn't have that, well . . . I'm afraid more people would've died because I would've had to bring at least a hundred more men." My head swiveled around as I again I wondered where I'd misplaced my dwarven companion. I spotted him across the tavern playing cards with a broad-shouldered boy whose face I couldn't quite see and I hoped he wouldn't take the lad for too many silver crowns.

"I wanted to ask you, Niendra, whatever came of that cave you found down at the Frost Quarry? You mentioned it once, but I hadn't the chance to follow up until now."

"Ah, the geomancer's lair? I sent a missive and a messenger to the queen about the," my mind stumbled for a moment and the words stopped. What? My head felt heavy and my sight dimmed for a split second. What about that cave? Something . . . something.

It hit me like a war hammer to the skull and my hand flew to the pocket I'd sewed on the outside thigh of trousers. A familiar bulge that I should have noticed long before met my hand and I drew forth the bejeweled rod.

"What in the name of the Nine, Niendra?" hissed Xeristo. "What is that?"

I felt as if the world suffered another Malosian Shift and my insides felt watery. "My oath to Father Sun and Mother Moon, Xeristo, I had completely forgotten about this thing. It's a magical artifact of some sort. I don't know what it does. Yet." I quickly placed the rod back in its pocket, but not before noticing a pretty girl sitting by herself staring at me. Something about her unsettled me and I learned a long time ago to trust my instincts. "Really, I forgot!" Forgot to the point I know I didn't include its existence to the queen when I sent the message.

"I believe you, Niendra, but by Phezdes hairy armpits you can't ride around with something like that. You know any valuables found by a Justice has to be turned in as evidence." The big Justice shook his head and took a drink. "If you hadn't taken the same geas I had, I'd be pretty Ninesdamned suspicious."

He was being kind because of our friendship, but certainly correct. I should have turned it in days ago. Why did I forget? Was there an outside agency at work here, or did my grief get the better of me? Doubtful it was grief; I was in Ramashur long enough to visit the Summer House before I tackled the Widow.

"You are correct, my friend," I murmured. There was only one way this could get sorted. "Come with me, please. To Ramashur. Help me bring this back to the Queen. Maybe Hengeth Isobold can figure it out as well."

"That is if you could drag his nose from Countess Bethora's skirts, you mean."

I raised an eyebrow.

"Oh-ho," he chortled. "You haven't heard? Word is the queen's favorite wizard has been seen sniffing about the fine lady from the Duchy of Jaantertrean." He held up his hands. "At least that what the word's been. I'm not one for gossip now."

Sure.

He continued. "But I can and will come with you, Niendra. If that thing is a magic artifact, it belongs locked away until someone can figure out what it does. I just have to square things with the Duke. I think he'll mind more than bit if I head to Ramashur without a by-your-leave."

"You lost how much?"

Skakhir had the grace to look embarrassed. "A gold crown," he paused. "And four silver crowns. And maybe handful of copper."

He didn't appreciate my roaring laughter or the finger I pointed at his face, but Mother Moon! The dwarf had been hangdog all day muttering to himself and looking like a knobblegrott was eating at his guts.

We left Caenwylln at first light, Xeristo with a head grown large from too much ale and Skakhir in foul mood that lasted through lunch at a village whose name I couldn't remember. Finally, as the Long Road lay beneath our horses' hooves, I couldn't take the dwarf's obvious self-pity any longer. It was with a great deal of hemming and hawing that he finally came clean.

It was *hilarious*!

"A sprat beat you at cards?" The words could hardly emerge through the laughter. "Really? A kid?"

"Not so much a lad, mind yer," huffed Skakhir, pointedly not looking at me. "Almost a man grown with a good frame on him. Probably a blacksmith's apprentice." He sighed. "I couldn't trick him, couldn't fool him, couldn't do anything of fancy shuffling or sleights, he knew 'em all, I tell yer. Downright indecent, if yer ask me."

Chuckling almost the entire trip to our next stop, Hedengarth-by-the-Ridge, we decided stay there instead of making camp in the wide open. I had no problems sleeping out-of-doors, but I like a good bed under my back more and the one in the inn we found was relatively clean and flea-free, so I felt content.

The night brought ill dreams and I tossed and turned, moaning and sweating. Himir, in his aspect of God of Sleep, decided that I deserved a poor one and unbalanced my humors to the point where I woke suddenly still fully clothed in the wee hours before dawn with skin damp and hands shaking.

That little danger sense that served me so well kicked my behind out of bed and saved me from the knife that opened a furrow along my ribs and I faced a dire choice: do I concentrate through the Father Sun tattoos to see the peril that faced me, slowing me down, or do I let training take over and fight virtually blind?

No time for thought, a glimmer of moonlight through the open window flashed off the edge of a blade and I ducked back, drawing my own and crouching, skin prickling with fear. I cursed my laxity for not even placing rudimentary wards and closed my eyes for a moment, trying to catch a glimpse of my opponent.

There! A tall man in dark clothes, face painted black so I couldn't see his features clearly. All I had time for was a glimpse, seeing him and the Ninesdamned long knife he held in one hand and then I had to open my eyes because he was coming for me again.

I dove and slashed, feeling my own long knife slice through cloth and flesh and I heard him grunt as a smile leapt to my face. He would find that killing a Justice was no easy task.

"Help!" I screamed, coming up from my roll and spinning about with the knife. Another hit and another grunt. "Help!"

A foot caught me in the knee and I folded hard, hitting the ground, the joint singing in agony. A weight slammed onto me, pinning me down and I squirmed hard, knowing full well the price of failure at this point, my muscles reacting without thought. The taste of metal in my mouth, my breath coming in wheezes as I tried to shimmy and shake my opponent off and finally! I got my feet under me for a second right before a fist doubled me over, forcing the breath from my lungs.

The cold bite of steel along my neck. I saw Mirallelle as if she's at the end of a long, dark tunnel . . . she beckoned to me and for a moment I felt hope and love and everything seemed all right.

Then the blade sliced against my neck and a rush of red exploded outward from my skin. It was a mortal wound, I knew. My hand clapped to the injury and I fell to floor, tears of anger in my eyes, blurring the darkness that suddenly fled from light as the door exploded inward.

Xeristo stood in the doorway with Thumper in his hand. He was only half-dressed, but by the wild light in his eyes he didn't care. He took in the scene in an instant and howled in fury, charging the assassin who leaped away toward the window in an effort to avoid the avenging hulk of a man with righteous anger in his eyes.

Thumper took the assassin square in the back with the sound of an of a hammer hitting a side of beef and the man was splatted against the floorboards so hard that they splintered. Thumper rose again and again, over and over, rendering the killer into paste because Xeristo lost all reason, anything resembling sanity was far gone and he kept striking and striking.

"Lass!" Skakhir ran in, shining war hammer in hand and knelt next to me, tears sprouting from his kind eyes. "Look at what he did to yer," he cried.

My hand was tight on my neck, stemming the tide, but like a river I couldn't keep it back forever, it would break through the dam of my fingers and I knew this was it. My death. Strangely, I felt all right about it, at peace.

"Don't worry," I said, grateful that the assassin was professional enough to know how to slit a neck. Too many try for the throat itself and wind up cutting deep into the windpipe instead, making the death a painful and messy one. At least his knife was razor ship, it didn't hurt at all. "I'll see you again, my friend."

Skakhir lowered his face. "Ah, lass," he sobbed. "Too soon, too soon."

Xeristo came into my field of vision and he was bloody from navel to crown and Thumper looked like it had been dipped into a bucket of chum. "Niendra," he began.

"Tell the queen everything, my friend. Tell her that the Deep Water mercenaries finally succeeded." They would never collect the bounty. With the crown holding the Widow and the Kaarik Fel Rosso dead, there was nothing to collect. No doubt the factors involved would have been rounded up and in custody already.

"I will, Niendra," the big Justice intoned somberly as Skakhir wept.

And there stood Mirallelle. She looked so beautiful in her burgundy dress and coal black hair pinned back, with that secretive smile I loved so much playing at the corners of her mouth. I raised a hand and felt her fingers against my palm.

"Come," she said. "It's time to go. Tilla's Hold has many halls, plenty of room for us."

That sounded so nice. I smiled and somehow the light started to fade in time with the slow beating of my heart and the wetness against my hand.

I stood in a field of yellow poppies, a tall gray manse in the distance. Mirallelle held my hand and I felt pretty good. No wounds, no blood. Just the two of us, the flowers all around and the sun bright in a field of blue.

It looked like it was going to be a good day.

TWENTY-NINE

THE THIEF

"**W**HAT DO YOU MEAN YOU THOUGHT it wasn't going to work?" It's morning and we are riding far behind then-Niendra, Skakhir and the big Justice. The horses in the past don't shy from now-Niendra like they did five hundred years ahead and I think it's because of the Mother Moon mask what makes her look all different, although she sure smells the same to me. I don't know, magic is too strange and I try to avoid it at all costs. Fat lot of good that does me. I managed to haggle a good price for the horses real quick so we wouldn't lose then-Niendra in the distance and not be able to do what now-Niendra has planned.

"I wanted to see if you could pick the rod from her pocket," says now-Niendra slowly as we ride. Her chestnut mare whickered at my gelding who doesn't seem interested in horsey conversation. "Just to prove to myself that the past is not mutable."

"Say what now?"

"Changeable."

Mutable. Good word. I'll have to remember it. "Well, I don't mind. I cleaned out Skakhir but good last night. I mean, he's a fine cheat, but I learned cards from the best and I could see all his moves before he made them. It was almost too easy, not that I'm complaining."

She smiles and there are dimples. "I remember."

By my clenched butt-cheeks, this time travel nonsense is really start-ing to wear on my skin. I sigh and we keep riding. At least the food and drink for the next few days are already paid for thanks to my friend the dwarf.

We ride and we keep well back from the trio ahead so it doesn't look like we're following them, keeping everything casual and mixed in with the other travelers on the Long Road. Eventually we come to a small village where the only tavern is a wide stall selling ale in wooden bowls and some sort of fishy soup. There are maybe a dozen huts and two real houses and that's it and it's here that now-Niendra says then-Niendra stopped for lunch. I look at her like she's crazy, I mean, the woman selling the ale and soup looks dirtier than the average street rat, which means that I don't want get within ten feet of her or her food. I make do with some cheese and dried meat along with some water from the local well that looks clean and I pray to Father Sun that I don't start soiling myself after drinking it.

As the sun is hitting the horizon we come to a fairly decent sized town, Hodengarth-by-the-Ridge. Stupid name, I don't see a ridge anywhere which makes the name insincere. "Isn't this supposed to be Hodden?" I ask now-Niendra.

She nods. "Hodengarth-by-the-Ridge is its name now, but in our time it is simply Hodden."

I don't like that much. Cities shouldn't go up and change their names, no matter how many years have passed, it seems dishonest. Oh well. I shrug and we continue to a little inn near a blacksmith shop and get a room for the night. No separate quarters, now-Niendra doesn't want us parted and I think that's a little paranoid, but one thing I've learned is a little paranoia is a good thing.

In the privacy of our room, now-Niendra asks, "You remember what I told you and what to do?"

Like I'll forget. "Climb up and enter then-Niendra's room through the window, grab the rod from her pocket and leave without a trace. Got it. Then-Niendra won't have put up any wards or such, so I don't have to worry about magic." Almost too easy. "How do you remember where she'll be and what window and such? I know it's only been a few years to you, but how?"

She becomes absolutely still like she does when she is trying to think of the right answer, not even breathing or anything, which is sure strange to see. "Since my . . . awakening into what I am now my mind is clearer. There are no unbalanced humors to cloud my thinking. I do not know how else to explain it."

Unbalanced humors. Please. Everyone knows that it's evil spirits, small demons what cause sickness and cloud the mind, but I don't have the heart to correct her. She's just a product of her time, I guess.

When night falls I leave the little inn and stick to the shadows, making my way to the Wild Boar Inn where now-Niendra says then-Niendra is staying on the second floor with a south-facing window. This town is large enough to have a night watchman, but small enough that it's an elderly soldier with an ale-gut in a bad-fitting chain hauberk and an old wooden club at his belt. I could pick his pocket and truss him up like a pig before he'd notice if I feel like it, but he's just doing his job, soft as he may be. He'd be eaten alive in Orthengar in my day. Five hundred years from now, that is.

Ninesdamned time travel . . .

At ease with the dark, I make my way slowly so my eyes have plenty of time to adjust. One of the reasons the Man Behind likes using kids is that we have great night vision. After a while when one becomes an adult the sharpness fades. Darkness is still my friend and I can slither through the entire city without anyone the wiser.

There it is. The Wild Boar with its sign showing, well, a wild boar. Pretty simple, I guess, although I do miss signs with actual writing on them. I slink around to the south side of the inn and look up and lo and behold there's the second story window with oiled parchment panes. The wall is made of field stone, which practically begs me to climb it, so I indulge the nice wall and scamper up quick as striking snake. There are plenty of handholds and toeholds and even though the moon is nearly full and shining on me, the stone facing is a dark gray, which combined with my darkish clothes leaves me almost invisible. It's like the Nine are practically begging me to rob then-Niendra. One must never thwart the will of the Nine. Thwart. Good word, learned it all by myself.

Once at the window I consider slicing the parchment, but that'd leave evidence and I'm too good of a thief to do that, so I pull out a thin, steel shim and slip the latch so easily it might as well not be there. The hinges are on the inside, so I open one panel real slow, just wide enough slip an arm in and hear a soft creak. I freeze.

Apparently then-Niendra is a good sleeper and I can hear her snore. It's adorable. Now's the time where things get a little tricky. Holding on with one hand and my feet, I pull a small bladder of rendered fat from my pouch (I always have one with me in case I want to do just this sort of thing and thanks to now-Niendra I can buy all sorts of thiefly items) and reach in, squeezing the bladder gently onto each hinge, greasing them nicely. It works beautifully and the panel opens wide without a single creak. I am so good they should make a statue of me some day.

Inside quick and quiet and I crouch there, not making a sound and listening carefully. It's at this point where most burglars make a mistake that usually ends up with them behind bars or in a hard-labor gang. Then-Niendra still snores. There's enough moonlight coming in that I can see great and I tiptoe my way to the bed.

There she is, her braids splayed around her head, mouth open, still snoring, but it looks like she's having bad dreams because she's moving a little, not too much, but she's starting to sweat and her face is all scrunched up. The cover is tangled at her feet, which makes my job even easier, thank the Nine. I guess they really like me today.

I see the pocket and I have to admit it's really well hidden, right in the fold of her loose trousers and I examine it carefully in the dim light as she begins to thrash about a bit and it looks easy enough. Now-Niendra said no wards, so I'll trust her and I tease pocket open and slowly remove the Rod of Immortality (really, I can't put my mouth around that long sylvan name) and slip it into my shirt and slink away like . . . like . . . a thief in the night, I guess.

Just as I make the window I hear the scrape of well-oiled iron hinges and the hair on the back of my neck stands straight up and fear jolts me into action. I leap through the window, catching the ledge with one hand and slam my soft shoes into the outside wall, stopping the swing cold and scrabble for good purchase so I don't fall and break something vital. I guess everything is vital, actually.

I barely breathe, my senses are screaming at me to run, but I can't because I have to know, so I chin myself up so my eyes clear the window ledge to see a tall drink of water standing over then-Niendra with an enormous knife in hand so I do the only thing I can think of which is to slap the window ledge hard, the sound cracking through the room and she sits bolts upright.

The tall guy doesn't look at me, he is busy trying to give then-Nindra another mouth to breathe from but he misses because she moves so quick and slices her side instead.

I know now-Niendra is a good fighter, but not terribly fast, I can take her if it comes down to that, but this then-Niendra is *lightning*. She's out of bed so fast I hardly see her go from bed to window and I duck outta sight before she can spot me. Then I hear some ruckus going on and look.

"Help!" screams then-Niendra at the top of her lungs, which carries something awful and she yells again while giving the guy a couple good slices with her own knife. I pull myself up because I have to help her, need to help her because even though she's fast, this guy is big *and* fast and they wrestle for a moment before she slips free, but his clobbers her with a punch to the gut that doubles her up.

This is it. This is when she dies, I know it and I'm frozen, I can't scream, I can barely breathe and the guy puts his Ninesdamned big knife to her neck and slices.

My stomach does a slow roll as nausea grips me and my tongue is a lead weight in my mouth and things blur because I'm crying and crying like a little baby and I almost let go, almost fall fifteen feet to the ground, but I don't, I hold on to that ledge and watch.

The door to then-Niendra's room bursts inward, turning in an instant into kindling thanks to Xeristo's boot and he stands there, a little fat, but with a serious amount of muscle holding the biggest mace I've ever seen. The head is cold iron and has to weigh at least ten pounds and he sees his friend on the ground with her hand to her neck and hot blood pumping through her fingers. Xeristo Quell screams like a demon from stories, like that wrath troll in the tunnels, and charges in after the assassin who knows he's outclassed by the Justice.

The assassin makes it halfway to the window when that mace falls and there's an ugly cracking sound and the assassin is *hurled* at the floor and it splinters under him. I can't quite see the look on his face, he's wearing too much paint, but I know he can't feel good and the mace comes down on his head making Ninesdamned sure that he's not gonna feel anything ever again and I want to scream, to go in and strike that dead meat with my own knife, but I don't because I'm still frozen.

Skakhir is there and takes then-Niendra into his arms while Xeristo pounds the assassin into a red goo, literally smashing a hole in the floor to force the remains down into the first floor in a wet rush.

Tears stream down my cheeks and Skakhir's crying, too, as he talks to his friend and I can't say anything, I'm still a useless lump and right now I hate myself so much.

I could've done something, anything. I'm good enough with a blade that the both of us coulda beat the guy if I had joined the fight, but I didn't and now I'm watching my friend, who's not my friend *yet*, die in the arms of another friend who's not my friend yet.

This time travel stuff can go pound for all I care. It leads to nothing but misery and I curse the day I met now-Niendra, then immediately wing a prayer recanting (good word recant, learned it all by myself) that curse because she's my friend and she got me away from my life in Orthengar and that's worth more than I can say.

Don't know why I'm so emotional. I seen others die before in a lot of horrible ways. Like when Big Teo kicked the insides out of Gloober, or when Smiler cut Walker's eyes out before cutting his throat so deep the bone showed. I seen worse, but this is the worstest and I feel even more useless.

I climb down and slip into the night before Xeristo looks up because he doesn't look sane anymore and I don't want him to clobber me with that big mace of his because all it'll take to send me to Tilla's Hold is one hit.

The shadows comfort me. I'm used to them, they're my friends and I make it to my little inn and slip up that wall, too, and climb through the window like I promised now-Niendra I would do when I'm done.

There she is, standing so still, looking at me and she begins to blur as I hold out the rod and there's something tight in my chest, like it's filled with too much air and I stutter out a sob which busts the dam free and I begin to cry like a big baby.

When her arms go around me I throw myself at her and weep like I'm never gonna stop and I can't help it because I just saw her *die*. This Niendra, my now-Niendra, still smells kinda dead, but it's comforting because she's always smelled this way.

A million years later I pull my face from her chest and say, "You knew, didn't you? You knew what I was gonna see up there."

She doesn't say anything, which is answer enough. I want to scream but I settle for some more bawling. What is wrong with me?

"Yes, I knew," she says as she continues to hold me. "I remember quite well what happened."

"Why didn't you tell me?"

"Would you have gone if I did?"

No. Probably not, but I'm not gonna say that out loud because there's a fist-sized lump in my throat, so I keep up with the crying.

After a while she takes the rod, staring at it. There's a diamond on the end of this rod, the then-rod, while the now-rod we brought with us has a setting where the diamond should be. "Hmm," she says.

"What?" I wipe my eyes with my sleeves.

Now-Niendra hands me the then-rod, diamond and all. "Hold on to this."

"Why?"

She shakes her head. "A feeling."

I untie my trousers and pull out a roll of silver and copper crowns from my stash in a pocket in the small of my back, a trick learned early while on the streets. The pocket at the was just big enough for the then-rod. I snug it away and retie my trousers and drape my tunic over so it hides the lump, but it's snug, not uncomfortable at all.

"Won't Skakhir and Xeristo notice that it's missing?" I ask.

That gets me a smile and I find myself smiling back. "I do not think so," she says. "I think that whatever magic the courses through the artifact causes the people to forget it exists, remember?"

Well . . . that sounds stupid and I'm about to say so except I forgot she told me this already.

By the smile what hits her face, she knows my thoughts, which isn't right at all. "I like to think that Malos crafted it into the kuolema-tomus. It is my hypothesis that only he could remember that it exists. I believe that come morning, both Shakhir and Xeristo will have forgotten all about it."

"They how come Taalis remembered it?"

"She is the Vel-ho of Dorendiriar, an incredibly powerful mage in her own right and heir to the sylvan that helped Malos craft the rod. And the fact that I exist in a state between life and death means that I remember it as well. Crafted into the rod or not, it seems only the extremely powerful or the undead remember the rod. To be fair, I really do not know for sure. Despite the thousands of years of study, even the Hidden Academy knows less than you would expect about magic."

Great. That doesn't work for me at all. I close my eyes and vow to myself that I'll remember the then-rod at the small of my back, that no hunk of jewelry is gonna get the better of Tennic the Light Fingered.

Yeah, that made me feel better. Positively capital. Good word, capital. Learned it all by myself.

THIRTY

THE THIEF

THEN-RAMASHUR DOESN'T LOOK LIKE NOW-RAMASHUR. It looks *clean*. And the land all around is given to farming and such businesses that a big city needs to keep itself going, although tanneries are way out of town because of the smell. We can see the city from miles away down the Long Road and there a dozens of small villages that don't exist in the future because all around is wilderness.

We don't enter through the gates. In fact, we don't enter at all because we're going somewhere else.

It's been a week since then-Niendra died. We stayed away from the city in one of the little villiages waiting for a real big procession of people in carriages and such taking then-Niendra to the Catacombs of Justice almost a day's ride to the south of the city along with the old Master of Justices, Lord Petre Ul-Mavre. Now-Niendra says this is what is needed because she has some plans she refuses to speak of, but I understand secrets, so I go along with it.

We made sure to hang back from Xeristo and Skakhir, following a lot more leisurely (good word) because now-Niendra says we should so the majority of muckety-mucks will be occupied with the interment while she does her sneaky. I can get behind sneaky any day.

There are soldiers and watchmen, Justices and all sorts of people who traveled to pay their respects and we easily sidle into the line of people heading down the Long Road, including Queen Bet in a humongous black carriage and an entourage consisting of more knights in full plate and soldiers in chain than I am really comfortable with. It looks like an invading army.

In the middle of all this are a pair big wagons with black bunting and lanterns on poles at each corner, the things what takes the bodies to their final resting place and I feel a lump in my throat, but I swallow it down. It's time for business and I haveta have a clear head about me.

The sun is shining bright and clear and there aren't any clouds or anything, which is kinda sad because when someone like then-Niendra dies there should be rain and mud, like the gods are washing the world with their tears. Seems only fair.

At the back of this long line of people, driving an open-topped carriage is the wizard Hengeth Isobold, a large man, but not fat, with a jolly face and a bushy brown beard. He holds the reins to the quartet of white horses like he's done it before and I can see by the way he moves and carries himself he's not only a man of magic, but one of action as well. Sitting next to him is another man in a long dark cloak with a hood pulled up around his face and the only thing I can see of him are his gloved hands and end of a pointy, blond beard.

I can't get a read on now-Niendra's false face, it's all closed to me, but the link that we share what makes me her familiar is a cold knot that almost takes my breath away. I imagine winters in Gaor are warmer than what's in her heart right now and every time I try to get her to talk she shuts me down. Not mean like a cuff to the head, but soft and frosty and it's scary. Her eyes never leave the guy next to Hengeth.

We ride for hours and my backside is sore, but I'm used to pain because life on the street has lots of it, so I suck it up and keep riding, wondering what now-Niendra has in mind. Eventually we come to a decent-sized town name Gollia where the Long Road curves southwest and it's there that the procession stops to water the horses and people leave their carriages and dismount so they can work the rust out their legs. It's there we run into Skakhir again.

Actually, now-Niendra arranges for us to be within sight of the dwarf and when he dismounts his eyes light on me and spark with recognition. Now-Niendra takes me by the arm and leads me a little way down the street and of course Skakhir follows because he's curious.

"Lad!" he calls out in his deep voice. "You there! Stop."

Every time someone yells stop I get the urge to run like Coadian monkey down the road because someone saw me nick a pouch or steal an apple or something. This time I have now-Niedra's hand on my arm and she holds on tight enough that I might have a bruise in the morning.

"Ah, I thought it was yer, lad," Skakhir puffs as he catches up. "Whatcha doing here? Come to take me for more crowns?" His words are light, but his tone is all business and I know he's ready to pull Dodmatir from his belt because the thinks that seeing me his is no coincidence, which shows how smart he really is.

"Hello, Skakhir Shadowmail," says now-Niendra smoothly, so smooth you could spread her words on bread with honey and butter. "The person you should be interested in is me."

This gets her a squint or two. "And you are?"

"A messenger," she replies all mysterious like. "From Niendra Goisien."

And that pisses him off, but before he can start hollering, she holds up a hand and says, "I can prove what I say."

I can hear Skakhir's teeth grind. "Prove away."

Good, he's giving her the benefit of the doubt, which a Ninesdamned sight more than I would have if I was him. I can't wait to hear this.

Now-Niendra obliges. "Niendra Goisien wants me to tell you that you and your cousin, the late Haddeg Whitgut, used that annoying Gaorian brogue to lull people at cards." She smiles and I can see it's genuine, as if she's remembering the good times with the dwarves. "And that by my clenched butt cheeks you tell the filthiest jokes."

During this explanation Shakhir's jaw begins to drop and does so until I can see the back of his throat. Then tears form at the corners of his eyes. "Are yer a person what can speak to the dead?" he asks, hopeful and sad at the same time.

"No, Skakhir. Well, only with the right spells, but not this time. I am simply a messenger."

More squinting and the dwarf strokes his white beard for a moment before saying, "Yer got a message, then get on with it."

"Meet us at near the Summer House at this time in one week from today at the old, lightning-struck willow right next to the creek where you used to fish. I know you and your cousin tarried there quite a bit."

Again, Skakhir looks surprised. "Why?"

"You will have this information then. I hate to say trust me, but you must. I have nothing but the best intentions. All I can say is that I will have the final piece of the puzzle to Niendra Goisien's death. If you want to know why she died and who did it, be there."

It looks like he wants to raise a fuss and get the other Justices to clap us in irons, but he keeps his mouth shut and stares at the two of us for a while until finally he nods. "Yer swear this by all yer gods, then?"

There's a sad smile what comes to now-Niendra's face and she says, "By Mother Moon, by Father Sun and the rest of the Nine I pose no threat to anyone but to those of evil intent. We will be there at the appointed time."

That seems good enough for the dwarf, although the look he gives me raises my hackles. I'm sure he doesn't mean anything by it. "Yer seem familiar, the way yer talk . . ." his mouth snaps shut and he nods once. "If yer not there, I will find yer."

"I will be there, Skakhir."

So it's there we part ways with the funeral procession and head on north to Ramashur and this time we do enter the gate just as the sun is reaching the horizon. I can't help but stare at the tall walls all white and such because the last time I saw the city it was practically buried under ivy and vines so thick you could tie up a wrath troll with them.

We stable our horses and the little kid who takes them gives me a grin. He reminds me so much of a boy named Dahveed what I knew back in the future that I flip him a couple of copper crowns. Sometimes I'm pretty sentimental. Sentimental, good word. Learned it all by myself.

Before darkness fully comes, as my friends the shadows come out to play for the evening, we reach a smallish shop in a decent part of town and wait for the watch to go strolling by. Unlike now-Orthengar, then-Ramashur doesn't have gas lights, which means that people tend to go indoors when it's dark and the only ones out and about (besides the street rats like me) are the watch. Since we're dressed real nice and look pretty clean, the watch barely gives us a second glance, which I don't mind at all.

"What is this?" I ask.

"My shop."

"What are we doing here?" I look closer and see the place seems tidy, the exterior paint is fairly fresh and the panes on the windows are real glass, which is nice, I guess. I check the door and find it locked and am about to ask if she wants me to pick it when she waves her hands, her fingers going all squiggly like a spider on a frying pan and the door opens.

"I need some things."

Inside the place is a palace of wonders with lots and lots of shelves full of glass and ceramic jars filled with all sorts of mysterious liquids and powders and herbs and such and there's even a stuffed alligator hanging by the ceiling over the counter and there's a neat, musty/sweet smell all over and I could spend hours and hours exploring. My eyes are open so wide that it feels like they'll pop right outta my skull and now-Niendra is grinning real big and I guess I'm acting like I'm in a pastry shop or something.

"What?" I say.

"All this," she replies, raising her hands. "is very nice, but not especially valuable. Good for curing croup or attending to a headache, but the valuable items are not on display."

Ah, secrets! That I can get behind.

We go back beyond a curtain and there's small room and this one is filled with . . . nothing. "All right," I say with a complete lack of awe. "Air. I guess that's valuable."

"Your cheek astounds me lad." She ruffles my hair and I let her. If anyone else tried that I'd remove their hand at the wrist, that's for sure. "You are failing to understand a woman of my talents." She waves a hand and says something in that throat-tearing language she calls Dendrich and the back wall disappears. Just sort of ripples like a heat shimmer and fades.

Wow.

I don't have the words for what I'm seeing (and I know a whole bunch of good ones) but it's another room filled with glass jars full of strange and weird substances (good word that) and what looks like copper pots of all sizes and small wooden boxes and a rack filled with colored candles and chalk and so much more that I can't describe it all, but it sure makes the main shop look hum-drum. In the middle of it all is a wooden table topped with a two-inch thick slab of polished black slate. The stone looks like it's been set on fire a time or three and there are old chalk marks on the surface.

More wow.

"This is my laboratory," she pauses to let that sink in and even though I don't know what a laboratory is, I nod like I do. Never show a grown-up how ignorant you might be. "The reagents in this room took several years to gather and quite a few crowns. This is where the real magic happens."

I scratch my head. "Witchery?"

This makes now-Niendra sigh. "Lad, do you know why my particular discipline of magic is called crafting?"

"Uh, you make stuff?"

"Ah, good to know the space between your ears is not entirely empty. Exactly, I *craft* things: spells, potions, fetishes, Coadian gris-gris, Irramerian witch bags and dream chasers, and so much more. If I have the right reagents, ingredients, then I can craft just about anything. Crafting requires hours of ritual and alchemical items brought together to form magic that few wizards can match."

"But then . . . why wouldn't everyone be a crafter instead of a wizard or elementalist or such?"

"Because it is dangerous. One mistake can kill you, or make you wish you were dead. Another is a lack discipline . . . it takes great concentration and effort to craft, more so than common wizardry. That and time.

"Wizards, elementalists and the like can cast spells quickly with the correct amount of concentration and we crafters can cast a few quick spells, true, but the majority of crafting is in the preparation of spells and items. Once I run out crafted items, I am at a disadvantage to the average wizard."

"So, if you had the time, you could load up on items and potions to take out an ordinary wizard, right?"

"Yes, but the ingredients for each item I craft are not easily found: tears of a dead virgin, the wing of an albino bat, the fur of a wrath troll, and so on."

I shudder at the mention of the wrath troll and the thought of trying to shave one. "So what now?"

"Now, lad, it is time for you to be my assistant and receive an education in the art of crafting, not that you have the talent for magic, but some education is better than none."

"What's the plan?"

Now-Niendra loses all her good humor and gets a serious look on her false face. "I have an idea why I was killed and I know who is responsible, but I lack for details and I need that."

"Why?"

"For justice."

"You mean revenge." Justice is sort of a vague concept, but revenge I understand real good.

"Revenge is inflicting punishment in return for injury while justice is the principle of moral rightness. Those two can overlap in some instances, like now, but it revenge is done out of passion, boiling humors, while justice is served with stoic resolve." She pauses and her eyes unfocus before continuing, "I need to ask an old friend some very pointed questions, then we will see which applies. Also, my young friend, I need to *know*." She does that standing still thing what always makes me nervous and I get the feeling that she's doing some soul searching. That is, if she still has her soul. I don't like to think about that.

Now-Niendra begins to gingerly open a few boxes and tins, placing them on the table. "Yes, I need to ask some very pointed questions. Come, we have at most a day. Let us not waste it."

Thirty-One

THE THIEF

At last I get to use some of my Nines-given talents once again and pick a lock. A real good lock, but it can't stand up to me worth a copper crown and I'm through in no time at all. The house what front door I just picked is a grand thing, two stories with paintings and a real chandelier in the foyer what looks to be more than I can illegitimately earn in a year.

Good thing now-Niendra is with me because this is the house of a wizard, at least the house he's using right now, given to him by Queen Bet while he does her royal bidding and such. Apparently being a wizard for hire means the sky is the limit, which puts my trade into an even more unflattering light.

"Upstairs," now-Niendra whispers. I ask her why since Hengeth doesn't have any servants or even an animated statue to wait on him or anything and she just says silence is the better part of paranoia, which I can't argue with.

Eventually we come to a big room filled with books and nice rugs, a library. There are some comfy looking chairs and I can't help but look at all the books because if I could steal them, I'd be rich. Not just a little rich, but buy-a-mansion rich and I begin to make some calculations on what I can get away with.

Now-Niendra tosses me a look what tells me she knows exactly what I'm thinking and I shrug. Can't blame a guy for trying, right?

"You remember what to do, right?" she asks after doing some of her own perusing.

"Sure. I remember."

"Good." She drags a chair with a nice leather cushion into the far corner and hands me a little brown leather sack. "Then hold this and have a seat."

I sit and cup the little sack in my palms and remember helping her craft it, a Not-Now fetish, which sounds strange but apparently it makes the bearer invisible.

"Not invisible," she'd said as she put the final ingredient into the bag, a midge retrieved from the stomach of a Biavian dosh toad. Even I knew about dosh toads what had skin that glistened with slime that causes human flesh to rot and not even knobblegrotss would stoop so low as to try to eat one. For some reason dosh toads are considered valuable magical reagents. "The bag allows the bearer to be noticed last," now-Niendra said with a satisfied air as she used needle and thread to sew the thing shut. "Essentially, a person will see you, but relegate you to the back of their mind, considering you unimportant at the moment. Basically, they forget about you even though you might be standing right in front of them."

That sounded neat at the time, but sitting there in a comfy chair with a little brown leather sack in my hand about to confront whoever we're gonna confront (she still hasn't told me because I'm pretty sure she's raw about it), I wish I held something a little more powerful. Like a cannon.

Now-Niednra walks around the room, sprinkling powders and such, making small marks with various colored chalks and chanting in Dendrich. There's a strange prickling in the air that makes it feel like ants are crawling under my skin and I realize it's magic what's so thick here from her chanting and casting that I'm just about ready to jump up and scream to relieve the tension.

I finally have enough and blurt, "What are you doing?" By the Nine, it feels good to *say* something.

Apparently my irritation has made it through the link that binds us together and now-Niendra tips me a nod. "It is a come-hither spell. One of the many spells I have prepared."

"Say what now?"

"Come-hither. I have summoned the one I need to talk to. You certainly do not think we are going to wait around all night, do you?"

"Uh, no?"

"Good lad. I am just expediting matters."

"What's that?'

"What?"

"Expediting."

"Accelerating, advancing, furthering, rushing."

"Oh. Good word." I chant that to myself five times so I remember and can use it later. That is if I survive whatever we're about to do to see a later.

I guess the expediting spell worked because a little while later I hear a door slam down below hard enough that dust falls from the ceiling and now-Niendra chooses that time to take off the Mother Moon mask.

We've been traveling together for a bit (at least five centuries) and I've seen her face in all sorts of moods from happy to sad to anger and resigned, but the look on her face now put cold water into my bowels. I realize I've never seen now-Niendra *pissed* and she has her fury on something terrible and it's barely under control. It looks like she's about to chew horse shoes and spit out nails.

The door to the library bangs open, warm lantern light spilling in and I see it's the wizard Hengeth Isobold what stands there panting and sweating like he's done run a mile or so. For a second nothing happens, then he sees now-Niendra and just about has kittens right then and there, face turning ash white.

"Wha-?" is all the emerges from his now slack mouth.

"Enjoy my funeral?" is all my friend says. She's still mad as a hornet whose nest had been dropped and staring a hole through the wizard.

"Wha-" Again. For a wizard he sure has a rotten command of Estian.

"It was the bird you gave me, the little carving. It was not to allow me to contact you, but to spy on *me*. It heard me talking to Xeristo about the rod and that is why you sent the assassin after me, ambushing me at the inn in Hodengarth-by-the-Ridge. You are the reason for my death." She takes a deep breath and I think she's about to loose a scream that will shake the walls, but all that comes out is, "Why?"

Hengeth Isobold isn't looking at me, which is good because my right now my bladder feels painfully hot and full, when he finally finds his tongue. "I had no choice, Niendra."

"We all have a choice," she gritted.

"I don't. You must believe me, I don't." Hengeth raises a hand and tries to make a gesture. I say tries because at that instant now-Niendra throws a small rock that hits him in the chest and he slowly crumples to the carpet. The lantern lands next to him but doesn't break.

It looks like now-Niendra is about to say something and instead shakes her head sadly. "You were my friend, Hengeth. I thought that meant something to you."

Suddenly she is floating in air, her arms and legs spread wide apart and a little wheeze issues from her mouth as the rest of the air remaining in her lungs is forced out.

"So, you're the one," says a voice. It is mellow and soft and so self-assured, like the speaker is used to commanding attention and being obeyed and such. Like the Man Behind. "Nice to finally meet you. I'm not just saying that."

In walks the cloaked man who sat next to Hengeth in the open-topped carriage, but this time his hood is thrown back and I see a face almost painfully handsome, so much so that the only word that comes to mind is beautiful despite the gray that's creeping around his temples. No man should look like that. He needs a scar or two to sort him out right. He's got a blond mustache and goatee and even his curly hair what falls to his shoulders is blond. One hand is raised and I know somehow that he's the one what has now-Niendra floating helplessly in air.

"Hengeth wasn't lying, you know," he says conversationally. A happy smile is plastered to his face and it sure doesn't make me happy. "He really didn't have a choice in the matter." The blond man looks down at the wizard and says, "Get up, boy." He gives him a solid kick and the wizard groans. "It's a simple sleep spell. What are you doing not wearing a ward charm? Didn't you learn anything I taught you? Were you even listening?"

More moaning from Hengeth and he starts to rise. "I'm sorry, Rikard."

Rikard rolls his eyes. "Kids." Hengeth flinches. Blondie turns to now-Niendra. "Allow me to introduce myself, I am his Royal Highness, King Rikard of Nerrinnia. Also known, infamously it seems, as the Wizard King. Perhaps you've heard of me?" His smile is dazzling, his teeth too white and even to be real. Ivory, maybe?

Now-Niendra can't do anything but blink, but I can feel her rage through our connection . . . and a caution to stay put. Easy enough to do.

"And this lump of meat," says His Royal muckety-muckness, "is my son, Prince Hengeth of Nerinnia. No need to bow, he's not worth it." A pause. "You may speak."

And now-Niendra suddenly takes a deep breath like it's her lifeline, which I know it isn't considering she's already dead. "I thought he was beholden to Emment."

Rikard gives again with the smile he must perform in a mirror every day. "Of course, that's what I wanted the world to think. He couldn't be a good little spy if the world knew him as my only son."

"You said he had no choice," now-Niendra says as if she hangs in the air at the whims of a tyrant every other Womsday.

"Of course not, he's under a geas. You of all people must be familiar with that class of spell, are you not?"

No reply. Not that I expected her to make one, but I could feel her surprise through our link.

"Your little report about the 'geomancer's lair' certainly caught my attention." Rikard's face is lined with cruelty and determination that doesn't take away from his beauty. "I traveled across the continent the second Hengeth made his report, burning a significant amount of magical capital to arrive as quickly as I did." He walks slowly, like he owns the place, which irritates because he reminds me of that dirtbag Vicious. "I could only bring one retainer and he died, but not before killing you." He shrugs. "Or so I thought. Really, Niendra, you must come work for me, you'll love it. I'll give you the kind of freedom that Bet would never dream of offering, access to magic tomes most wizards would wet themselves for." He slows and his smile becomes predatory. Predatory, good word. "Name your price, a woman with your talents is really appreciated in Nerrinnia."

Now-Niendra grimaces as if in pain, hamming it up for her audience. "Unless you can bring my wife back from Tilla's Hold, we have nothing to talk about."

"Ah, that little geas of yours altering your reason, no doubt. I could get rid of it for you, but that takes time and I'm a very busy monarch, things to do, a kingdom to rule, you understand. Too bad about the offer, though, you would've been happy." He slaps his hands together and rubs them vigorously. "Now then, where is the kuolema-tomus? And don't try protestations of ignorance, I know you have it, that little bird carving of Hengeth's brought us the news. Grandfather's immortality belongs to me, now."

"You—?"

Another smile. It's starting to get irritating. "I am the last heir to Malos the Arch-Mage and I really need my birthright, you understand, I'm sure."

"He was running from you, that's why he created the cave."

"Of course. I surpassed my many-times great grandfather in magic and tried to take the rod a few years back when he tried to sneak into the Royal Library, but he managed a clever little escape and I've been searching ever since. I had a feeling he'd try to hide in Gylleth near his precious sylvans and I was right." Smug drips off him like sweat and I almost grind my teeth in anger before realizing what I am channeling is now-Niendra's rage.

"Let me guess, with the rod you can begin the dream of empire." Each word exits now-Niendra's mouth as if they are bitten clean through.

"Empire?" Rikard looks incredulous, amazed. "Are you mad, woman? If I try for an empire, the resultant war would cause massive chaos before I could even unite three of the Six Kingdoms and you know the Coads and the Irramerians would invade in a second in such a time of weakness." He sighs. "Oh, sure an empire would be wonderful, but the reality is I will settle for being the immortal Wizard King. Empire comes a few centuries down the line as I use magic to influence politics. Of course a treaty will have to be signed with the Hidden Academy, but with the kuolema-tomus, I'll be too powerful to sanction." As he speaks his eyes are far away. I seen crazy before and this guy has it in bucketfulls.

"So this is the last piece of the puzzle." My friend sounds sad and tired and a couple of other things I can't name.

"Yes, you're very clever. Now hand over the kuolema-tomus, if you don't mind. I'm very busy, have a schedule to keep."

"Oh," she says, reaching slowly into a pocket and pulling out the jeweled rod, the one with the missing gem. "You mean *this* kuolema-tomus?"

And the king about loses his mind and his fair face does a good tomato impression. "Where is Tilla's diamond?" he shrieks in horror. Hengeth recoils, hiding his head behind his arms.

Now-Niendra tries to shrug while floating, but can't quite pull it off. "Actually, I found this rod in this condition."

Sneaky. She's not lying, the rod originally came missing the diamond and she is definitely not then-Niendra what found it whole in the geomancer's tunnels. Nice bending of the truth and I wish had a quill, ink and paper to take notes.

As for his royal blondness, he raises his hand and says quietly, "Tell me or I will pull your limbs from your trunk and keep you in misery for decades."

Her smile is so ugly that he falters a bit. "I can outlast you, you putrescent glob of dung."

Putrescent. Nice word. I'm going to have to ask her what it means if we live through this. As for Rikard, he starts to slowly clench his fist and now-Niendra arms and legs begin to fold the wrong way and I hear in my mind, '*Now!*'

Good thing I'm fast and nobody is looking my way because I'm on my feet with my misericord in hand and I do what I done to Vicious, plunge the blade deep into the wizard. Right in his clenched butt cheek.

Somehow that seems right.

Rikard screams in pain and Hengeth, blubbering and mewling, falls back into the hallway and I take that moment to slam the door shut. Now-Niendra, released from the wizard spell what held her up, lands almost perfect on the rug with a smile so evil it sets me back on my heels.

The blond king is hobbling and I stab him again, this time in the other butt cheek and it hurts so bad he can't concentrate to cast a spell, but he's still a strong man and his fist comes around and buries itself in my gut, which puts me in the position of reintroducing lunch to the outside world as darkness floods my vision and the ache spreads from tummy to toes.

While I'm retching, now-Niendra sprinkles a red dust in the air where it floats like a cloud and she's still smiling even though I feel her concern over our link and I try to send back that I've felt worse, that I'll be all right and she must've got it because she focuses on Rikard.

"I've negated your wizardry now, Rikard. Surrender to me and you will walk out of here."

Bleeding all over the place and panting like a winded horse, Rikard circles around and snarls in reply. Now-Niendra shrugs and tosses more powder, which immediately rushes toward the wizard and sticks to his exposed skin.

The man howls in dismay as large patches of flesh begin to slough off and he's starting to bleed more and more and now-Niendra says, "Surrender," as the king carries on with his caterwauling.

All I can do is try to breathe as Rikard hobbles to the middle of the room, blood on his trousers, face a red ruin and he says, "I am an Arch Mage, you nitwit. You think common wizardry is the only magic I possess?" With that he strips his gloves off, revealing that both of his hands are full of rings. There are so many that I wonder how he's able to make a fist.

Rikard says something in that Dendrich language and both hands blaze into disks of bright, pulsing, violet light. He thrusts both fists to either side and reality seems to ripple, the walls stretching and bending like taffy, waves shooting everywhere but nothing shatters and the walls don't come crashing down, which is real strange when they're acting like warm taffy. All that dust that now-Niendra flung in the air begins to fall to the carpet and the pulsing continues, but this time there's a hum, a real low drone that seems to scratch my ears before rising in volume, becoming so loud I can barely hear Hengeth shrieking from the hallway.

"I didn't want to do it this way," yells the Wizard King, face a bloody ruin, but he's got that smile on his face and it looks really gross in all that raw meat. I can seek the muscles of his cheeks stretching "You leave me no choice. I have magics you cannot comprehend!"

Now-Niendra looks on in horror. "Stop! You do not know what will happen! You will destroy the city if you continue."

With a look of pity, Rikard says, "No, Niendra, just you." He brings those pulsing, violet disks of light together over his head in a thunderous roar.

At that moment there's pressure what suddenly builds up in my ears and the bright, violet light suddenly warps, twirling around and around leaving purple streamers in the air like ink in a whirlpool. Old Rikard suddenly looks real scared, his bloody eyes going wide and so round I can see the whites clear as day. A subtle roaring happens, but it's not a sound, more of a feeling like when your friends spin your about when you're blindfolded and you try to walk. The walls and floors seem to warp and the violet light screams like a terrified girl.

Something happens what makes my ears pop and I'm dizzy, my tummy reacting violently again as some force, some sound that's louder than the screaming light purse pierces the veil of my skin and I feel all light and floaty as if the world isn't working right no more and it's just too much, too overwhelming.

The world decides to go sideways from there and I fall into a big, black hole what swallows me up.

A COLD HAND SLAPS MY FACE. Now, I've been slapped before by professionals, so this feels like a love-tap, but it does the trick and my eyes open.

Now-Niendra is looking down at me and she takes a big breath to sigh and I feel the relief coursing through our bond and for a moment I glimpse the love she has for me and everything gets blurry as the dust that she threw in the air makes my eyes water.

All of a sudden I'm in her arms and that's good and we hug it out for a long time even though her flesh is room temperature. "For a second I thought I lost you, lad," she finally says.

"I'm hard to kill," is my reply. I wipe my face.

Her hand wanders to the laces of my trousers and I feel a momentary alarm as she fiddles around, but she withdraws her hand with the complete jeweled rod in it and suddenly I curse myself for an idiot. I completely forgot I had the Ninesdamned thing. Goes to show that the gods will make fools of the wisest of us.

"This helped," she says and takes a big enough breath for laughter and helps me to stand.

In the middle of the room is Rikard's body and boy, does he ever look surprised and his skin looks waxy and stretched where it isn't eaten away. I'm so tired I can't muster up any hate and without a word we decided to leave.

Outside the door Hengeth Isobold stands, a vacant look in his eyes and his skin all pasty like the blood has been drained from his body or something. For a moment he does nothing, then his eyes track to me and he starts to lurch my way.

Before I can jump away now-Niendra puts another bag into my hands and suddenly Hengeth goes back to being an ugly living statue. "I anticipated this. As long as you hold this, you will be safe, but it only works for a very short while, so we must make haste."

"What is this?" I whisper, afraid of the big wizard who looked at me a moment ago like I was on the menu. My hands are tight around little bag. Not going to drop this.

"Rikard, that Nindesdamned idiot, was casting a necromancy spell when a major Malosian Shift occurred. He just destroyed himself and all of Ramashur. I was able to construct that bag using one of the rarest reagents, the bone of a necromancer." Now-Niendra shakes her head in dismay. "We cannot change what happened," she whispers. There's a wealth of sadness in her voice.

We stare at the now undead Hengeth Isobold and now-Niendra cocks her head to the side. "How very interesting."

"What?"

"When I finally found this place and the bones of the necromancer, I thought they belonged to Hengeth, but now I know different and a little mystery has been solved."

"Mind telling me?"

"There was a man wandering with loose skin on his bones. I could tell that when living he was large and I did not recognize him because time had not been kind, but that undead was Hengeth." She gives me a sad smile. "Funny how things turn out."

Nice story, but my skin is crawling and my danger sense is going crazy. "Oh. We better leave posthaste."

Posthaste. Good word, learned it all by myself.

Epilogue

THE THIEF

YEAH, THE WILLOW SURE LOOKS LIKE IT'S BEEN STRUCK by lightning, all split to one side and covered in old char, but it's still green and the mossy roots dig deep into the damp soil near a stream what pools nearby and if I look closely I can see fish swim among the reeds.

It's been a week since we left Ramashur and Queen Bet's army tried to enter the city but they were beaten back by the hordes of the undead and those that fell soon rose to wander the cursed city. Good thing for Her Majesticalness that she was putting then-Niendra and the Lord Petre into their tomb when that Ninesdamned Rickard destroyed the city. Good thing too that whatever spell he cast got itself warped and put boundary between the city and the rest of the Six Kingdoms or things might have gotten undead quick.

Now-Niendra says that there aren't enough wizards to go around to brave the city and they wouldn't if they could because why give up a cushy job for the chance to get eaten by the shambling dead. And it's not like they're giving away necromancer bones at the local apothecaries, are they? Only someone like her can enter the city with impunity and the nearest dead necromancer what has some spare bones is in the city filled with walking, hungry dead people and I'm pretty sure there's a lesson in there somewhere. This is what now-Niendra calls ironic.

Ironic. Good word, that.

Queen Bet has pronounced Ramashur off limits although I know treasure hunters will come by the score in the next few centuries to try their luck and right now Gylleth faces economic collapse which now-Niendra tells me will take down the other five kingdoms along with it. I'm not big on economics, but I know that when trade goes sideways in the Six Kingdoms, everyone suffers. This will lead to a time when the Coadian pirates do their Ninesdamned best to pillage every city they can get to and it will also lead to yet another Irramerian invasion headed by an alliance of the city-states of Charthis and H'irenthia. The combination of Coadian naval might and Irramerian heavies will plunge the Six Kingdoms into a war that will last over a century and see over a hundred-thousand dead. Now-Niendra says she read all this in a book soon after she came back from Tilla's Hold, all this future history stuff. Ugh, time travel..

I hear Skakhir approach before I see him. He can't tiptoe to save his life and the thought of a tip-toeing dwarf makes me giggle.

"What do yer find so funny, lad?" says Shakhir as he pushes through some bushes to stand nearby. He's got on hand on the haft of Dodmatir because it's the smart thing to do. "Where's yer sister."

"She's not my sister and she's right behind you."

Now-Niendra can tip-toe and she smiles at her friend. She's not wearing the Mother Moon mask.

Skakhir's jaw drops and the next thing I know he's got her in a crushing hug and he sobbing while she tries to comfort him.

This goes on for a little bit as I stare at the fish in the pool and enjoy the mild weather. Eventually the two get to talking in hushed voice and I really don't want to listen because this is their time and I skip some rocks. I find a really nice flat one and manage thirteen skips before it vanishes with a *ker-plunk*.

Now-Niendrah holds up the rod of immortality, the one what saved me from becoming undead, and plucks out the diamond. Now it looks like the one what brought her back and she gives it to Skakhir with the instructions to put it into her sarcophagus five hundred years from now.

"Normally, this rod would make a mortal forget it exists," she says. "But I have a theory that without Tilla's diamond, that effect disappears."

I have to admit it's a good theory and I was wondering how Skakhir remembered to put the rod into now-Niendra's sarcophagus in the future.

Grrr . . . I realize that that sentence has more mangled tenses than necessary. Time travel plays merry hob on syntax (another good word, learned it from now-Niendra).

Eventually they gets to the part where she tells him the truth and shows him the neck wound under her yellow scarf and he finally understands that this is not his Niendra, but someone quite different and I can see it hurts his heart some. She then tells him to inform the queen that it was Hengeth Isobold what cursed the city by mistake due to the Malosian Shift and spins him a tale about Hengeth practicing necromancy and such, that he should tell her nibs the queen that then-Niendra told him that Hengeth had told her he was checking into a new magical means into communicating with the dead and how the wily dwarf put two-and-two together. This is a total fib, but I reckon Father Sun will forgive a little lie since it doesn't really hurt anyone living.

Skakhir looks skeptical and I have to admit the story is thin, but considering that everyone in my time knows it, maybe it's not so thin after all. My head hurts.

Now-Niendra motions me over. "You will see this lad in the future, too, Skakhir," says now-Niendra. "Show him, Tennic."

I know what she wants and I open my pack and take out my Dodmatir and Skakhir's eyes go real round and I say, "Yeah, time travel is weird," and that seems good enough for him. He understands that he will live a long time, long enough to meet us at the Borderlands Inn and that he'll give me Dodmatir and such. He takes it real well.

"What now?" asks the dwarf, scratching his snowy beard..

"Tonight, my friend, I need the Forever Tree."

SKAKHIR IS A GOOD PERSON AND does what now-Niendra asks and we stand in front of the Forever Tree at the Summer House. We both hold small bags like the one I had in the library what made people not notice the holder and we need it because mean-looking guards patrol the Summer House grounds and they're not messing around with them big crossbows and such. One woman with a face like a closed door looks big enough to snap Xeristo in half with her bare hands.

Now-Niendra uses some chalk to draw some squiggly lines all over one small portion of the Forever Tree's white trunk and that monster of a vegetable is so big that the trunk looks almost flat up close. I can hear creakings coming from the thing as the breeze kicks up and I hope that one of the city-block size limbs don't come crashing down to squish my favorite enterprising thief/adventurer.

Unlike the Forever Trees in Dorendiriar, this one doesn't glow, so the dark and now-Niendra's magic hides us pretty good although I can't hardly see anything and that means putting my trust in my crafter friend, which is actually easy to do. I do keep a lookout for guards so we can crouch and remain still so they don't see us, but we don't want to push our luck any. A brace heads our way every fifteen minutes or so and I am getting anxious for now-Niendra to finish already.

I have question that's itching at me and I ask, "Do you think Skakhir will remember to put that rod into your tomb five hundred years from now?"

That earns me an amused glance as now-Niendra draws a whorly, loopity-loop pattern at waist height. "He has already done so, has he not?"

"Oh." This time travel thing is really getting on under my skin.

"The spell is almost complete," whispers my witchy friend. Her eyes are glued to the task at hand.

"What is it again?" Some hundred feet away a pair of guards turn our way and began another circuit of the grounds. They will be here in less than a minute. My hand is sweaty around the spell bag.

"A variant of a naturalist spell. We will use walk into the tree, hidden from the outside world while the spell uses the tree's life essence to keep you young. Considering the size, it should not damage the tree one bit. The spell can only be cast on a living organism, but we need a five-hundred year jump and I know the Forever Tree will still be here then."

Sleep for five centuries. I am not looking forward to this. I try to tell her, but the guards come and we have to keep low and quiet. It's dark enough and they're far enough away they don't notice the squiggly lines and runes on the tree. They soon pass out of sight.

Now-Niendra senses my fear. "Don't worry, lad. This will work and when we emerge it will be five hundred years later and we can return the kuolema-tomus to Taalis along with Tilla's diamond. After that I will be free to journey to Tilla's Hold." She actually smiles wide. "I want to see my wife."

I get chills, but there's nothing more I can say because I do want to see the future again and now-Niendra tells me that we will be sleeping the time away, so I won't hardly notice anything and I shut my trap because there's a cracking sound coming from the tree and the bark splits open wide like a flower and we see a pale woody tunnel leading deep into darkness.

"Sleep for five hundred years, huh?"

My friend gives me a smile. "Sleep and sweet dreams, Tennic. When we wake you will be back in our proper time." She takes my hand.

"Not really sure what I'm going to do, though," I say.

"You will have money enough and time enough to make your way. Perhaps you should visit Gaor. The dwarves were quite taken with you. You can make your home with them."

Home. What a good word. Everyone should learn that one by themselves.

ABOUT THE AUTHORS

BORN IN HELSINKI, FINLAND, MARK EVERETT STONE arrived in the U.S. at a young age and promptly dove into the world of the fantastic. Starting at age seven with the Iliad and the Odyssey, he went on to consume every scrap of Norse Mythology he could get his grubby little paws on. At age thirteen he graduated to Tolkien and Heinlein, building up a book collection that soon rivaled the local public library's. In college Mark majored in Journalism and minored in English. Mark is feverishly working on his next book while his amazingly patient wife, Brandie, keeps him and their two sons, Aeden and Gabriel, in check.

BRANDIE M. STONE, BORN IN CALIFORNIA, is an educator and a principal of a K-5 school in Red Bluff, CA. She is the wife of Mark Everett Stone and has helped him immensely in his creative works, serving as a foil for his ideas. She lives in Redding and tries to keep her husband on sons from killing each other.